THE GIRL
IN THE MOON

BY TERRY GOODKIND

THE SWORD OF THE TRUTH SERIES

Wizard's First Rule
Stone of Tears
Blood of the Fold
Temple of the Winds
Soul of the Fire
Faith of the Fallen
The Pillars of Creation
Naked Empire
Debt of Bones
Chainfire
Phantom
Confessor
The Omen Machine
The First Confessor
The Third Kingdom
Severed Souls
Warheart

THE CHILDREN OF D'HARA

The Scribbly Man
Hateful Things
Wasteland

THE NICCI CHRONICLES

Death's Mistress
Shroud of Eternity
Siege of Stone

Nest

THE ANGELA CONSTANTINE SERIES

Trouble's Child
The Girl in the Moon
Crazy Wanda

The Law of Nines

THE GIRL IN THE MOON

TERRY GOODKIND

Skyhorse Publishing
NEW YORK

Skyhorse Publishing books may be purchased in bulk at special discounts for sales promotion, corporate gifts, fund-raising, or educational purposes. Special editions can also be created to specifications. For details, contact the Special Sales Department, Skyhorse Publishing, 307 West 36th Street, 11th Floor, New York, NY 10018 or info@skyhorsepublishing.com.

Skyhorse® and Skyhorse Publishing® are registered trademarks of Skyhorse Publishing, Inc.®, a Delaware corporation.

Visit our website at www.skyhorsepublishing.com.

10 9 8 7 6 5 4 3 2 1

Library of Congress Cataloging-in-Publication Data

Names: Goodkind, Terry, author.
Title: The girl in the moon / Terry Goodkind.
Description: New York : Skyhorse Publishing, 2018.
Identifiers: LCCN 2018002635 (print) | LCCN 2018002674 (ebook) | ISBN 9781510736429 (Ebook) | ISBN 9781510736412 (hardback : alk. paper) | ISBN 978-1-5107-4782-1 (paperback)
Subjects: LCSH: Paranormal fiction. | Suspense fiction.
Classification: LCC PS3557.O5826 (ebook) | LCC PS3557.O5826 G57 2018 (print) | DDC 813/.54--dc23
LC record available at https://lccn.loc.gov/2018002635

Printed in the United States of the America

To my dear friend, Jeffrey Cheng,
who always reminds me to take some time to come out and play.

CONTENTS

TROUBLE'S CHILD

ONE

Angela slowly reached under her coat for her gun as she carefully reversed her steps to back away from the corpse of a young woman.

She forced herself not to make any sudden moves, and especially not to run. She gripped the weapon in both hands, locking her aim between the piercing eyes of the predator guarding its meal.

She stole a quick glance around at the silent, snowy woods, looking for any other threat. She saw none, but she knew that in the fading gray light the woods could easily conceal someone, or something, lurking behind expanses of brush and young fir trees.

Although the creature hunched over the corpse looked like it might be a cross between a wolf and a German shepherd, this was not someone's pet.

There was a hint of coloration beneath the mostly black fur. Its winter coat had long since come in, giving it a thick ruff. Against the white snow it was an intimidating sight.

Angela knew that wolves sometimes made their way down from Canada. She could only assume that along the way a female must have bred with a big shepherd. There was no doubt in her mind that the resulting wolf dog snarling at her was as dangerous as it was powerful.

She checked the surrounding woods for others. This animal appeared to be alone. If there were a pack, she would have seen some of them. They would have wanted in on the meal.

Pack or not, this wolf's bared fangs told her that it was more than willing to fight to keep its scavenged meal. Or make a meal of her.

There were ligature bruises and lacerations on the dead woman's neck, so Angela knew that the wolf hadn't been the one that had killed her. She had been murdered. Angry, red, human bite wounds on the breasts told her this was a killing out of hate and rage. Whoever had done this had likely killed before. Angela knew that this kind of killer would kill again if not stopped.

She was often amazed that she had never ended up like the dead woman. It could easily have happened to her more times than she cared to remember. That gave her a unique empathy with these kinds of victims—women who had not been lucky enough to survive. It also gave her a purpose in life.

The light, fluffy snow had only just begun to cover the ground and trees, gradually turning the forest white, but that snow had only started to accumulate on the hands stretched out over the dead woman's head. There was still enough warmth in the body to melt the big flakes. This woman had not been dead long.

The wolf had both front paws protectively over the naked corpse, clearly ready to defend its meal. Its muzzle dripped blood and gore. Wisps of steam from the open belly rose into the cold, still air. Wolves were predators that hunted large hoofed mammals like elk, deer, and moose, but they were not above scavenging dead animals for a meal.

It might have been nature's way, but Angela didn't like seeing an animal tearing into the body of a freshly dead human. She understood that it wasn't a malicious act, and she certainly had no desire to kill such a magnificent creature.

She wanted to fire a round to scare the wolf off, but since the woman hadn't been dead for very long it was possible the killer was still nearby. If so, she didn't want to tip him off that she was there and give him a chance to ambush her. She didn't want to be his second kill of the day.

Angela felt a hot wave of emotion igniting at the prospect that the killer might still be nearby and that she might be able to catch him. It had been quite a while since those inner needs had been sated. Now, they were again crackling to life.

Once Angela had backed far enough away, the animal went back to ripping out bloody pieces and gobbling them down. It looked to be starving.

There were a lot of bird tracks around the body from the nearby ravens waiting for their turn at the carrion. Every once in a while one of the ravens would carefully approach the carcass, put one foot forward, then spring back when the wolf snapped at it. Ravens were opportunistic and often followed wolves to have a chance at the scraps.

Angela saw that there were also human tracks, but the snow was light and fluffy, and there wasn't yet enough of it to make for good identification of the footprints. She saw those footprints and the drag marks going off to her right, toward the highway. The snow was picking up, so she knew that what footprints there were would soon vanish beneath a growing blanket of white.

The wolf guarded its meal as Angela inspected the footprints and drag marks leading off through the trees toward the highway. The woman had apparently been dragged in by her ankles and dropped. That was why her arms were stretched out above her head.

Angela reluctantly left the animal to its meal so she could follow the drag marks, hoping she might be lucky enough to catch the man who had done this. Even with the snow beginning to accumulate, the trail was still easy enough to follow.

She was acutely aware that this was a very recent event, and not wanting to inadvertently become the next victim, she moved cautiously, quietly, keeping an eye on the woods all around and her gun at the ready.

The body had obliterated most of the footprints as it had been dragged through the leaf litter and into the woods to be dumped.

There wasn't enough snow, yet, to make the footprints clearly readable, but she could see enough to tell that the killer had followed the drag marks back to where he had come from.

By the time she reached the highway, there was no sign of the killer. She saw tire marks in the gravel where he had backed off the road a short distance into the woods so his vehicle wouldn't be easily seen by passing cars.

The tread marks weren't distinct enough to be identifiable. There were smears in the snow where the body had been thrown on the ground and then dragged off into the woods like a sack of garbage.

Angela looked up and down the empty highway, then finally relaxed a little. The killer was gone. Frustration took over at missing her chance to have him. She had been so close, and now she had no idea who he was or where he had gone.

But if she ever got the chance to look into his eyes, she would know him and know what he had done.

Angela pulled out her phone. She was too far out of Milford Falls for the police, so she expected her 911 call would go instead to the sheriff's office.

TWO

Angela looked up when she heard a car coming from off around the bend of the lonely road. The snow, along with the wind, was picking up. She saw the flashing lights on the distant wall of snow-crusted trees. Not wanting a sheriff's deputy to see that she had a gun, Angela put her Glock back in the holster at the small of her back.

She usually carried a Walther P22 in her truck, but when she went hiking for the day she carried a 9 mm Glock. The .22 was like a scalpel, with virtually no worry about overpenetration. The Glock was like a hatchet. In the woods, where she might encounter a bear, she didn't care about overpenetration, so she carried the Glock. Either way, she didn't want the police to see her with a gun.

As a rule she always did her best to avoid talking to police, but this time it was necessary. Angela didn't like the thought of the woman's remains being left out in these woods all alone for animals to feed on. She should be taken back and put to rest with respect. Since the authorities would likely never find the body on their own, Angela had to show them where it was, and to do that she had to talk to law enforcement.

When the white sheriff's car with red stripes came around the curve, lights flashing, she stepped out on the edge of the road and held up an arm so the deputy would see her. The car slowed as it pulled over, tires crunching to a stop in the snowy gravel.

The deputy put on a black Stetson hat as he unfolded himself out of his car. His uniform was black, and he wore a black leather jacket. He was tall, with creased, sunken cheeks and the kind of eyes that said everyone was guilty of something. He looked to be about twenty years older than Angela, maybe in his early to middle forties.

His steely gaze locked on her as he closed the door and strode purposefully to the front of his car.

"You the one who called us?"

"Yes." Angela pointed up into the woods. "I found the body of a dead woman up there."

Not turning to look where she pointed, he instead continued to stare at her. "And what were you doing up there?"

"It's my day off. I was going for a hike."

"A hike. In the preserve." There was nothing illegal about that, but he made it sound somehow criminal. "Day off from what?"

"I have a courier service. And I tend bar."

"Uh-huh." He regarded her as if she might be the killer. "What's your name?"

"Angela Constantine."

His gold name tag, with A. Nolan in black letters, stood out against his black shirt. He looked professional. Hard-ass professional. And dangerous. She was already regretting having placed the call.

His glare took in her platinum-blond, red-tipped hair, the earrings down the back of her ear, finally settling on the tattoo across her throat.

"Let me see your ID."

She wanted to ask him why, but she had a rule never to argue with authorities. She wanted to always remain above suspicion and to never be regarded as trouble. She pulled her driver's license out of her pocket and handed it to him, trying to look friendly and cooperative.

He took it without a word and went back to his car to run her name through their system. In a few minutes he came back, she thought looking a little disappointed that she didn't turn up as being wanted for murder.

"Constantine," he said to himself as he stood before her carefully looking over her license. He looked up. "Your hair is blue on your license."

Angela shrugged. "I like to dye my hair different colors."

He nodded his dissatisfaction to himself as his eyes narrowed. "I know a Constantine residence—in the trailer park in Milford Falls."

"That's my mother's place," Angela volunteered before he could accuse her of living there, or of her mother's sins.

He was looking at her like he was beginning to suspect she must have drugs on her. "I've been there a few times. You had to still be living there when I pulled people with warrants out of there. Along with lots of drugs."

Angela wanted to say she didn't do drugs, but she knew that would make it sound like she did, so she kept her mouth shut.

"Nothing but lowlifes living there," he said, "doing drugs day and night. Drinking, fighting, fencing stolen goods."

He did indeed know the place. Angela had grown up in the midst of all that. Because of all the meth, heroin, and booze continually in her mother's system when she had been pregnant, Angela had been born different from other people. She knew she could never be normal. She was a freak.

"I'm sure I remember arresting your mother along with some scumbag drug dealers at that trailer."

"Probably," was all Angela said.

"Your mother is a tweaker. Every time I saw her she was flying on crystal meth."

"Yeah, well, that's why I moved out."

He idly tapped her license on the knuckles of his other hand. "Who's your father?"

"I don't have any idea," Angela said with a shrug.

He had undoubtedly been one of her mother's dealers or a random tweaker. She was always getting laid by one or the other.

The deputy's glare looked to have formed permanent creases in his brow. "Everyone in that trailer was trouble. You grew up there. Now you go for a hike, wandering around out in these vast woods, and you just happen to find a dead body."

"Yes, so I called 911."

He handed her license back to her. "Let me see your hands. Both of them. Hold them up."

Angela did as he asked, fingers spread, showing him the fronts and backs of both hands. She knew he was looking for defensive wounds. He wanted to satisfy himself that she hadn't been in a fight and killed the woman.

He grunted his dissatisfaction that her hands were clean and free of any wounds. "Your mother is trouble. That means you're the child of trouble."

Angela looked off down the road. She was just about to tell him to go find the fucking dead body on his own when he gestured toward the woods.

"Come on. Show me what you found." He put emphasis on the word "found" like he thought she had invented the story.

Without a word, Angela turned and headed into the woods. The fat flakes were falling faster. The drag marks were already mostly covered over, as were her own footprints, but she knew the way.

THREE

When they pushed balsam limbs out of their way and came out from the thick brush and trees, they saw the body off in a low area of the clearing.

"Jesus Christ!" Deputy Nolan shouted as he drew his sidearm.

The wolf, still guarding its prize, rose up, snarling and snapping.

Without hesitation Deputy Nolan fired off two quick shots. The second shot went high and just flicked the hackles on the animal's back. The wolf bolted away. At the sound of the shots the ravens all took to wing, squawking their surprise and displeasure. They scattered in all directions, disappearing into the trees.

The deputy took two steps forward and emptied his gun as fast as he could at the wolf as it raced away, kicking up snow in its wake.

"Why didn't you tell me about that damn animal feeding on the body!"

"It wasn't here before," she lied.

"Well," he growled as he pulled out the empty magazine and shoved in a full one, "that should keep the filthy beast away. I think I may have hit it."

Angela didn't mention that he had pulled down and to the right when he fired the first shot, a common mistake, so that first round hit the murder victim in the rib cage.

Deputy Nolan racked the slide to chamber a round and then holstered the weapon before approaching the corpse. He looked around carefully for tracks. Any that had been there were now covered with snow. His circle got smaller as he closed in on the dead woman. He finally knelt down beside the corpse and pointed at the neck.

"See here? Looks like she's been strangled."

Angela wanted to say "No shit," but she kept her mouth shut. She couldn't imagine the horror of being strangled to death like that, the terror of not being able to breathe.

Deputy Nolan looked at the many human bite wounds on the breasts but didn't mention them.

"Looks like maybe her ribs have been broken," he said as he looked more closely at the marks on her side.

Angela pointed. "Your first shot hit her in the ribs."

He cast her a sour look but didn't say anything.

He finally stood and made a call on his radio. He reported what he had found and asked for a crime scene team and the coroner.

Despite not liking having to deal with law enforcement, Angela felt better that someone would finally take proper care of the woman's body.

When the deputy finished on the radio he turned his attention back to Angela.

"Did you see anyone or anything out of the ordinary—other than this body?"

Angela shook her head. "No, nothing."

He looked down to study the woman's face for a moment. "Do you know her?"

Angela had seen the woman in the bar a few times, but not enough to know her name. "I'm afraid not."

He shook his head once. "She's a prostitute."

Angela wasn't surprised. "How do you know that?"

"Her name is Kristi something." He considered a moment. "Kristi Green, I think. She's been arrested for soliciting a number of times. I remember the face. She hung out in the area of the Riley Motel. Whores use the Riley to conduct their business."

Angela tended bar down the hill from the Riley, so she knew all about it. The prostitutes who used the motel didn't waste their time coming down to socialize with customers at Barry's Place, the bar where she worked. Occasionally, though, they would hang out there hoping to pick up a customer. Most of them used the Internet now, rather than invite trouble from police by soliciting in bars or hotels.

"I showed you where I found her. I don't know anything else," Angela said. "If it's okay with you I'd like to get home before it gets too dark. And I'm getting awfully cold just standing around," she added, trying to elicit some human sympathy from the man.

He appraised her with a look lacking human sympathy. "Where do you live?"

Angela pointed. "I have a place over that way. Next to the preserve."

"If you wait until help arrives and this business here gets taken care of, I can give you a ride."

"Well . . ." Angela drawled as if she were actually considering it. The last thing in the world she wanted to do was get in a cop car with this hard-ass and have him come to her house. "It's not that long of a walk. I'd like to get home."

Actually, it was a rather long walk, and it would be dark soon, so she would have to hurry to make it home before it was too dark to see.

"Yeah, sure," he said with a flick of his hand. "Go ahead. I need to go back to my car and start writing this up while I wait. I have your information from your license so if we need anything else we'll know how to get in touch with you." He opened his wallet. "If you think of anything else we should know, give me a call. Here's my card."

The card had "Deputy A. Nolan" printed to the left of a sheriff's badge. There was a phone number below his name. The phone number was one of those repeated numbers that stuck in her head.

Sometimes numbers did that and she couldn't get rid of them. She knew she would never have any reason to call him.

"Okay, if I think of anything else I'll call you," Angela said as she slipped the card into the pocket with her driver's license. "Do you mind me asking your first name?"

His glare was back. "Not at all. It's Deputy."

All right, then, she thought. *Asshole it is.*

FOUR

Because she had spent so much time waiting for the deputy and then with him and the dead woman, it was getting much later in the day than she would have liked. The light was seriously gloomy, to say nothing of the increasing snow.

If it got dark on her, Angela wanted to be on a road rather than in the pitch-black woods. She carried a small flashlight, but still, in the woods it would be slow slogging and dangerous.

She knew that if she went down to the road where Deputy Nolan's car was parked and walked home from there, it was quite a distance, because the road first wound around a mountain to the south before coming back up north and then past her place. By taking a shortcut over the ridge she would get to that same road, but after it went on that loop for miles out of the way. Going through the woods over the ridge saved miles of walking.

As she plodded up the hill, head down against the snow swirling around fir trees and blowing in her face, she spotted tracks. They went in the same direction as she was headed. After following them for a time, and because they were so clear in the fresh snow, she realized they had to be the tracks left by the wolf when it ran away as Deputy Nolan shot at it.

When her foot displaced some of the fresh snow, she saw blood beneath the top layer of white. The wolf had apparently been hit by at least one of the deputy's bullets.

The farther Angela went, the closer she knew she was getting to the wolf. It was becoming clear to her that the wounded animal was bleeding and slowing down. She drew her gun and kept it out as she crossed the ridge. She didn't want to come on an injured wolf and be defenseless if it attacked.

As she reached the bottom of the far side of the ridge, not far from the highway, she came upon the wounded animal. It lay on its side in the snow, panting in distress. There was a good amount of blood in the snow.

Her first thought was to put the animal out of its misery. It was clearly suffering and would not survive. She stood back and pointed her gun down at its head. One eye rolled back, watching her. She stood over it, looking into that eye. She hated to shoot the animal, but she didn't want it to die a long, painful death, either.

It occurred to her, then, that if she shot the wolf, Deputy Nolan, just back over the ridge, would hear the shot. He would come to investigate. Then she would be caught carrying a concealed weapon. Even if he let it pass, which she seriously doubted, she would have made herself noteworthy. That was something she always avoided. She didn't want that to change now, just to put this creature out of its misery.

Carefully, experimentally, she squatted down while still holding the gun pointed at the animal, and slowly reached out.

The wolf didn't move. It lay panting, watching her as she ever so slowly put a hand to its heaving chest and gently stroked the fur.

She expected a protest of some sort, even an attack, but there was nothing. It was as if the animal watching her was saying, *I'm finished. Go ahead and do what you will. I don't have it in me to stop you.*

She found herself mesmerized by stroking the warm black fur.

"I'm sorry you were hurt," she whispered to it. "I didn't mean for that to happen."

The big dark eye continued to watch her, but the wolf made no move to defend itself.

"I suppose it's my fault. I'm the one who called the police. I'm so sorry that jerk hurt you."

As she was stroking the black fur, the wolf let out a sigh, as if comforted at least a little by Angela's gentle touch and soft words.

She let out a sigh of her own. "What am I going to do now? I can't leave you here to suffer."

Listening to her voice seemed to reduce the panting.

Angela slowly stood, trying not to alarm the creature.

"I'll tell you what. I'm going to go home and get my truck. If you will let me, I'll take you to a vet and get you some help. All right? Will you let me help you?"

In answer, the wolf let out a soft whimper.

Angela knew better than to ascribe human reactions or understanding to animals, especially wild animals, but in this case she was willing to take it for a yes.

FIVE

Angela held her coat closed and the lamb's wool collar tight against her neck and ears as she hurried along just beside the shallow ditch. The road would eventually run past her place, so she knew she wouldn't get lost. Since traffic was rare on the remote road, she didn't worry too much about covering her ears and not hearing a car. There was no hunting or logging allowed in the vast preserve surrounding her place, leaving little reason for anyone to use the road or be out there unless they were taking a back way to or from the small village of Bradley.

She supposed that was one reason the killer had used the desolate area to murder Kristi Green and dump her body out here. It wasn't the first time a body had been dumped in the woods around Milford Falls and it wouldn't be the last.

Angela was a bit surprised when she saw the lights of a car coming from behind. As it drove past and its lights reflected off the snow-covered road and trees, she saw that it looked like a Lincoln that was several decades old.

The old, boxy car slowed to a stop. As it began backing up, Angela put her right hand under her coat and gripped the handle of her Glock. She could see that the car was a light tan color with a darker tan vinyl roof. The rocker panels beneath the doors, along with the lower part of the fender behind the rear wheel, had been eaten away by rust.

As the car slowly backed up it stayed toward the center of the road, rather than backing close to her. The brakes squealed as the old car rocked to a stop. Angela gripped the gun tighter, but didn't draw it. If this was a guy getting a bad idea at seeing a woman all alone on a lonely road, he would soon discover just how bad the idea really was.

The passenger door creaked and popped in protest as it opened. When it did, the interior lights came on and she could see there were two people inside.

The driver was a frumpy woman with a head of thin, frizzy hair. She had on a collarless pale blue dress with little flowers all over it. It was the kind of dress that looked like it had been found at the bottom of a box in a thrift store. Because the dome light was behind her, her face was in shadow.

The passenger was a middle-aged man in a dark suit, black shirt buttoned all the way up, and no tie. Both his hands were resting over the head of a white cane standing up between his knees. He was wearing dark glasses. It was already dark out.

Angela realized by the dark glasses, the white cane, and the way the man's head moved to hear sounds rather than look toward their source that the man was blind.

He smiled as he leaned out a little into the snowy night. When he did, she could see that in front of long sideburns he had a large cross tattooed on each cheek. His full head of straight black hair had been slicked back with a comb through styling gel.

"It's an awful night to be out in the weather," he called out into the snowy night. He was looking off at nothing, the way a blind person would, not knowing exactly where she was.

"I'm fine," Angela called back. "I'm enjoying the first snow of the season."

"It came up pretty quick. Maybe quicker than you expected? May my sister and I give you a lift to someplace warm and safe?"

Angela stood in the swirling snow, wishing this car would leave. She at least felt better knowing that she was armed.

Being the daughter of a meth addict, she knew she was a freak. She was a girl born broken. That was the reason she rarely felt anything, rarely cared about anything, but when she looked back over her shoulder she felt a pang of empathy for the wolf lying wounded in the snow.

It was an innocent victim, much like the dead woman. Now, it was suffering. The longer it took her to get back to the animal and then get it to help, the less its chances of survival would be.

"If you don't mind, I guess I could use a lift."

The man reached out with his cane and tapped the tip on the back door. "Come on, then. Get in."

Angela slammed the heavy door behind her as she climbed into the overly soft backseat. The inside of the car smelled musty, but the warmth felt good on her throbbing cold face.

"I'm Reverend Clay Baker," he said, turning his head only a little without looking back at her as the car started forward. "This is my sister Lucy."

"I'm Angela. Thanks for the lift. My house is up the road a few miles, on the right. You can drop me there."

"What are you doing on foot so far from home at night, in a snowstorm no less?" he asked.

"I have a day off, so I went for a hike through the woods. I . . . got distracted off the path and didn't realize how late it was or how far I was from home. But the road leads back home so I knew I couldn't get lost."

"Ah," he said with a nod. "A lot of young people get distracted these days and stray off the path." He chuckled at his own double entendre.

Lucy, hands at ten and two on the big, thin-rimmed steering wheel, stared ahead as she drove into the heavy snow. Lucy struck Angela as a timid, apprehensive woman. She seemed more than a little cautious about driving in the snow. Angela wished she would hurry it up.

"What is it you do for a living, Angela, if I may ask?"

"I have a courier service and I also tend bar."

"Ah," he said again. "We are couriers, too, of a sort."

Angela frowned. "What do you mean?"

"We are a traveling ministry. We were just in Bradley for the day, but we have been staying at the Riley Motel in Milford Falls for the last month or so. Milford Falls is a much bigger place with a larger need."

The Riley Motel, just up the hill from where Angela tended bar, was a dump used by the hour by hookers and by transients who stayed by the week.

"You mean you don't preach at a church?" she asked.

"We bring the word of God to those who otherwise might not have the chance to hear it. Churches are limiting. We bring God out to those places where the people are."

Angela already wanted out of the car. "You are both ministers, then?"

"I am the minister," he said. He laid a hand on his sister's shoulder as she stared ahead into the snow, wheeling the big Lincoln down the narrow, winding road. "Lucy is the sighted one. She used to work in a hospital, but after I lost my sight in an accident, she has devoted her life to helping me in our calling."

He had a Southern accent mixed with an evangelist's practiced tone. But it was the big black cross tattooed on each cheek that really made him distinctive. That was true commitment.

Angela had a large, distinctive tattoo across her throat. She knew a thing or two about true commitment.

As she watched the dark forest gliding past to each side, she cast about for something to say into the dragging silence. "Lucy, it must be interesting watching your brother in his work."

Reverend Baker lifted his left hand out, palm up. Lucy put her fist in his cupped hand and started making a series of rapid movements. Angela immediately realized that it was some kind of sign language.

She was trying to figure out their odd relationship when he said, "Lucy is a mute. She hears, but can't speak. I am her voice. She is my eyes. Lucy lost her voice to cancer of the vocal cords. Now she is able to speak to me through our hands. She says in answer to your question that it is a blessing for her to be at my side and see the chosen welcomed into God's embrace."

"That's nice that you have each other."

Reverend Baker nodded as he stared off into his blank vision. "Yes, it is a blessing. I believe that God wants us together in our calling and so He afflicted us each in ways that meant we could only accomplish His work if we work together."

Angela realized that since he couldn't see, Lucy couldn't use conventional sign language. He wouldn't be able to see her signing, so she used the odd language of letters or words signed into his hand.

"Do you know God, child?" he asked in a thin, rising tone without looking back from the front seat.

"I've met the devil on a few occasions."

Being a freak of nature from all the drugs her mother took, Angela had been born with the strange ability to recognize killers and know what they had done by looking into their eyes.

He chuckled at her answer and was apparently so taken by it that he didn't press the issue.

In the snowy light from the headlights, Angela at last spotted her driveway. She hurriedly leaned against the front seats and pointed forward between them.

"There. That's my drive up there on the right. You can let me out there, please."

Lucy rolled the big Lincoln to a stop in front of the cable stretched across Angela's drive.

"We can drive you up to your house," Reverend Baker offered.

Angela wanted out of the car and away from these two, and she certainly didn't have time to have them come up to her house and preach the gospel to her.

"Thanks, but it's not necessary." She popped open the door. "I can walk up to my place before I would get the cable unlocked."

He turned enough for her to see the big black cross tattoo on his cheek. "You watch out for the devil now, will you?"

He had no idea.

"I always do. Thanks again for the ride."

SIX

Angela slowed and parked her truck at the edge of the road. She would still have to hike quite a ways through the woods to get to the injured wolf. She felt a sense of urgency and wondered if she was being foolish going to all this trouble for a wild animal that would probably die anyway.

With the heavy cloud cover there was no moon or stars, so that once she switched off the engine and killed the headlights the world became an oppressive void of total blackness. It felt a little frightening.

Once she had locked her truck, Angela switched on the light on the headband she wore over a knit hat. The headlamp would allow her to have her hands free. If for some reason the light on the headband failed, or she fell and broke it, being all alone in the woods at night in total darkness in a snowstorm could easily be fatal, so she had a backup flashlight in her pocket as well as a small light on her key chain.

Without hesitating she plunged into the woods. She had hiked these woods since she had been a little girl, but that would be of no value in the dark. The falling snow lit by the light on the headband was disorienting, but at least the light allowed her to see well enough not to walk into a tree.

The cold air felt brittle. Every time she exhaled it made a cloud around her face. Even though her footprints from earlier had been covered over, they left depressions in the fresh snow that she was able to follow.

Slogging through the snow was tiring, but those footprints from earlier led her right back to the wolf.

She was relieved to see that the animal was still alive. She could see by the marks in the snow that it had tried to get up, but in the end it had fallen back onto its right side, the way she had left it there earlier.

Angela spotted ravens up in the tree branches, patiently waiting for their meal to expire.

Patches of snow had started to collect on the wolf's fur. If it died, the carcass would quickly freeze and drift over. She wanted to try to keep that from happening.

"Okay, here's the deal," she said as she slowly squatted down, gun in one hand. "I want to help you, and I think I can, but you're going to have to let me help you."

He followed her movements with the one eye that faced up. The other was on the underside of his head, in the snow.

"If you attack me, I will kill you." She waggled the gun where he could see it. "I mean it. You try to bite me and I will shoot you in the head."

She didn't really believe he could understand a word she was saying, but she hoped the sound of her voice would be enough to calm him. She tried to make every movement slow and deliberate, the tone of every word nonthreatening.

She carefully reached out to stroke his fur the way she had earlier. Now, she could feel him trembling. That really hurt her heart. With him unable to move, the cold was settling in on him.

She pulled the blanket down off her shoulder and held it up before the animal. "See what I brought? You're too heavy for me to carry, so what I want to do is get you onto the blanket and then drag you across the snow to my truck. I think the blanket will make it pretty easy to slide you across the snow. Plastic would slide better, but I think that might stress you too much. I think you'd rather lay on a soft blanket. Am I right?"

Angela gently stroked the animal's fur as she talked to him, hoping to get across the idea that she meant him no harm, that she was going to try to help him.

His mouth was open as he panted, and she saw that he had awfully big teeth. She was acutely aware that she was very close to a very dangerous animal. She didn't want him using those teeth on her. She would hate to have to shoot him, but if he attacked her, she would not hesitate.

"Okay, what do you say we get this show on the road?"

She laid the blanket out behind the wolf's back, then gently started pushing some of it into the snow and under him. That alarmed him enough that he suddenly started scrambling to try to get up. Angela jumped back. The wolf struggled briefly, his legs wobbling, then collapsed back down onto his side.

Amazingly enough, though, he fell mostly on the blanket.

The wolf's eyes half closed as he panted.

The effort of trying to get up seemed to have used up what little fight the animal had left. He didn't protest as Angela gathered up the corners of the blanket. When she pulled it all tight, the wolf was snugly encased inside. She thought that the darkness and being cocooned in the blanket, along with not being able to see what was happening, might help to keep him calm.

Without delay, she started dragging the wolf through the woods, weaving her way among the trees, following her own tracks back to her truck. It wasn't as easy as she had imagined it would be. The weight of the animal made him sink down in the fluffy snow, rather than glide over the top of it. Still, it was the only way she was going to get him out of the woods and to help, so she held the corners of the blanket over the front of her shoulder and leaned into the weight, dragging it behind her.

The wolf didn't make any sound of protest. She thought he must be so exhausted and cold that he had given up. She knew what it felt like to be at that point of giving up.

She panted herself with the effort of pulling the heavy load through the woods. Every so often she had to tug fallen branches out of the way from under the blanket.

Several times she fell forward into the snow. Each time she got back up as quickly as possible, brushed snow off her face, and kept going. Her nose was running, and even though she had gloves on, her fingers were freezing. Her toes hurt from the cold. She ignored the discomfort of the struggle and forged onward. She kept telling herself that it wasn't all that far and she could make better time if she quit worrying about herself and only worried about getting the wounded animal to help.

When she finally reached her truck, she dropped the tailgate and sat on it briefly to catch her breath. The metal tailgate was icy cold, so she didn't sit on it for long.

She knew the hardest part would be lifting the wolf up into the bed of the truck. It had to weigh somewhere in the neighborhood of a hundred pounds.

Urged on when she heard a pitiful sound from in the blanket, she bent down and pulled the blanket back to take a look. His eyes were closed.

Angela covered him again and scooped him up in her arms, putting one arm under the front of his chest and her other arm under his rump, folding all four legs into the middle so that his weight was in the crook of her arms.

She didn't know how she did it, but with a last, mighty effort she managed to lift him up onto the tailgate. From there the blanket slid easily into the bed of the truck.

Angela gently rubbed the wolf's side as she caught her breath.

SEVEN

The warm cab of her truck finally thawed her fingers. Her thighs burned from the effort and from the icy cold. Angela pulled her gloves off with her teeth as she raced into town. She wished she could give some of the warmth inside the cab to the injured animal. She was sure that the wind blowing over him was not helping. At least he was covered with the blanket. Since she couldn't do anything about it, she did her best to hurry.

It was quite a ways into Milford Falls, but once she reached town the streets were virtually empty. Since there was no traffic, she did four-wheel drifts around corners and through red lights, not wanting to slow any more than absolutely necessary.

Angela felt a sense of triumph to finally turn in to the twenty-four-hour emergency veterinary hospital. She spun a one-eighty through the empty parking lot, stopping with the back end of her truck facing the front door.

Angela had done courier work for the emergency animal hospital several times, but she didn't really know anyone there the way she did at the regular hospital. Inside, an older woman at a computer behind the long counter asked how she could help. Angela told her that she had an injured dog and she would need help getting it inside. The receptionist called people in the back.

In a few minutes a vet tech came out through a swinging door pulling a cart behind her. She wore blue scrubs like the nurses at the hospital. She didn't look much older than Angela.

"Hi, I'm Carol. You have a dog you need help with?"

Angela gestured toward the door. "Yes. He's in my pickup. I think he may have been shot. I can't carry him by myself."

Outside she helped Angela lift the wolf, still in the blanket, onto the cart. Blood spread through the blanket and then the paper covering the stainless-steel top of the cart.

On the way in through the doors, Angela put her hand on the wolf and felt that he was still breathing.

"I'll take it from here," Carol said, rushing for the swinging door. "You can wait out here. After the doctor evaluates your dog she'll come out and talk to you."

Angela grabbed her sleeve. "Listen, Carol, you all need be careful. This dog is part wolf. It's injured and afraid. I don't want anyone to get hurt."

The woman lifted the blanket for a look. "I understand. We deal with situations like this all the time."

Angela didn't think they really did.

"I mean it. He could really hurt you."

The vet tech smiled her understanding before she started wheeling the bloody, blanket-wrapped wolf through the swinging door into the back area. "The doctor will be out to talk to you as soon as she can," she said back over her shoulder.

Angela wondered what she had gotten herself into.

"Could you fill out the admittance form, please?" the woman behind the long counter asked.

Angela took the clipboard with a pen attached by a string and sat down in one of the orange, molded plastic chairs. The form asked for all kinds of personal information. Angela never let people know where she lived. She used a box at Mike's Mail Service for her mail and packages. She put that address on the form. She filled in what other information she could. She didn't think they would have her arrested if she left a lot of blanks, so she didn't worry about it.

She was brought to a halt by the list of questions about the "pet." They wanted to know how old it was, when it last had its shots, its ailments, injuries, and all kinds of other things Angela couldn't answer. She simply wrote "found the injured dog by the side of the road" and left everything blank.

It was an hour and a half before Carol led her into a consultation room to meet with the doctor. The doctor was a big-boned woman with a warm smile and a professional disposition. She folded her arms as she leaned back against the mauve counter.

"So, is he going to be all right?" Angela asked.

The doctor peered down at Angela. "Well, that's kind of up to you."

"What do you mean?"

She regarded Angela for a moment, apparently gauging how well she could take bad news. "What's your wolf dog's name?"

Angela drew a blank. "Well, it's not exactly my pet. I live out in the country." A story she thought would be satisfactory formed in her head. "I've seen it around a few times, but I'm pretty sure it's wild. Tonight I found it laying in the ditch at the side of the road. I think some jerk must have shot it."

The doctor nodded. "I see. Well, I think you're right. We have him sedated right now so he's comfortable. What we do next is up to you." She handed Angela two pages with a lot of boxes checked and things written in. "The wolf dog is going to die if we don't do emergency surgery. It sounds like he doesn't belong to anyone, so I guess it depends on how much he means to you."

Angela looked down at the forms. The doctor leaned in to point with her pen at several items. "This is for anesthesia, the IV drip, an MRI, the operation itself, various miscellaneous things we'll need, and the estimated stay under observation."

In the rear of the building, beyond the door at the back of the consultation room, small dogs barked nonstop. One cried continually. It was nerve-racking trying to think with all the racket.

30

"So what's the bottom line," Angela asked. "How much?"

"It's this number here, but this is just an initial estimate. We won't know for sure until we see how much damage was done to know if it will cost more or not. And you can see here with the total, it's going to be at least thirty-four hundred dollars. I'll do my best not to go over that, but if we're going to operate we'll have to do what we have to do."

Angela wasn't surprised by the estimate. She had expected at least that much. She knew surgery wasn't cheap. When she had gone home to get her truck she had brought four thousand dollars in cash with her. She let out a deep breath. That was a lot of money for a wild animal that still might not even make it.

She had started out the day just wanting to go for a hike in the woods, to have some peace and quiet, to get away from the drunks and guys in the bar always hitting on her.

She felt a pang of guilt for thinking only about herself. That woman she found, Kristi Green, had a much worse day. She had been brutally murdered.

"Can you save him?"

The doctor was ready with an answer. "I think so. The thing is, he's hurt pretty bad so I can't promise anything. Right now we have him anesthetized—he's asleep. If you prefer we can just let him go. He's not a pet so I would certainly understand that decision. He will feel no pain, I promise. It's up to you if you want to let him go and have a peaceful, pain-free end to his life. I can make that happen."

"But you can operate and save him?"

"I can't promise, but I'm pretty damn good."

To a degree Angela felt responsible for the creature being shot. She was the one who had called the police. Then that jerk deputy showed up, shooting first and asking questions later.

It was just a wild animal. But still . . .

"Angela, I can't afford the time to describe the damage and injuries right now or what I need to do. If you want to let him go, I completely understand. But if you want me to try to save his life, time is of the essence. He's losing a lot of blood. I need to get in there and operate immediately if you want me to try to save him."

Angela didn't know why, but she didn't want his life to end this way.

"I'd like you to go ahead and do the surgery. I'd like you to do everything you can to save his life. I'll pay for it."

EIGHT

The doctor was apparently as good as she'd said she was. The wolf survived the surgery. They thought everything had gone as well as they were hoping.

Angela was relieved.

She came by the animal hospital every day to check up on him. At first it was sad seeing him lying in a small enclosure, a blanket covering him, an IV in a shaved spot on his front leg. The vet techs assured her that he was getting pain medication and he was resting comfortably. His eyes were closed and he was unresponsive to all the barking and yapping of the other dogs.

He belonged in the woods, running free.

The third day she visited the animal hospital the wolf was awake. He didn't get up, but his eyes turned to look at her when she walked up to the enclosure door, which had clear plastic on the top half. She talked softly to him for a few minutes. She wanted to reach in and stroke his fur, but she suspected that would be a bad idea. The people there had equipment to handle him. They were careful with him, and about their own safety.

On the fourth day Carol told her that he had eaten and was doing remarkably well and getting stronger all the time. The doctor said that he could go home the next day. That eventuality had been continually on Angela's mind and she didn't know what in the world she was going to do when he was released.

She obviously couldn't take him home into her house. He would likely kill her. He was beautiful and had his place in the world. But he wasn't domesticated and never could be. He was a wild animal and that was what she wanted for him—to be wild.

Fortunately, the animal hospital had an old dog crate someone had donated. The vet techs told Angela that she could have it and that they would get the wolf dog into the crate for her so she could take him home.

When Angela came the next day to pick up the wolf, they had managed to get him into the crate. He cowered in the back and snarled when anyone got close.

"He's been here long enough that we've all gotten kind of fond of the big guy," Carol said. "We rarely see wolf dogs in here. He's magnificent. We named him Bardolph. 'Bardolph' means 'ferocious.' He's shy like most wolves, but he's also pretty ferocious."

Angela thought it a fitting name.

Carol and a male orderly helped lift the crate into the bed of Angela's pickup and tie it down.

Carol handed her some papers. "These are instructions on his postoperative care."

Bewildered, Angela looked through some of the instructions. "I don't know if—"

"I understand," Carol said. "Between you and me, just feed him and keep him quiet for a while. The incisions are small and most of the sutures are internal. Keep him quiet so he doesn't tear them open. They will all dissolve over time. If you think there's any problem give us a call, but I think he's going to be fine if you just let nature take its course and finish healing him. What he really needs most is rest."

"How long? How long should I keep him in there?"

Carol shrugged. "Maybe a week? Hard to know exactly. I think you'll know when it's time to release him."

Angel tied a heavy old bedspread over the crate to help keep him calm. She drove home relatively slowly, not wanting to give Bardolph a jarring ride or have him fall and rip stitches.

It was cold and clear by the time she got home. She hooked some aluminum ramps on the tailgate and then carefully slid the bedspread-covered crate down onto a bed of straw she'd laid on the ground. She had to go to work to tend bar, so she left the thick bedspread over the crate to help keep him warm. She knew wolves felt safe in dens, so she hoped he would feel that way in his temporary den. There were several big old blankets inside the crate that he could arrange to his liking for bedding.

Before she left for work, she lifted the edge of the bedspread and carefully opened the door just enough to toss in half a raw chicken. Bardolph was pressed up against the back of the crate watching her. His low growl let her know he was not pleased.

Angela talked to him in a calm voice each day when she gave him the chicken. She mostly tried to leave him alone so he wouldn't get stressed or agitated. She wanted to let him rest and heal. Every time she threw in another meal, there was not so much as a scrap left of the previous meal. He managed to do his business in one corner so at least he wasn't lying in it. She would have liked to clean out the crate, but she knew that would be far too dangerous, and besides, once she opened the door enough, he would be out.

After eight days she could tell by how active he was in his crate and the way he snarled at her that he was feeling better and he wanted out. Angela waited two more days and finally decided it was time. She put the ramps back on the tailgate, covered the crate with the old bedspread, and with great effort slid it up the ramps and into the pickup bed.

She didn't really like the idea of releasing a wild wolf by her house. She thought it best if she took him back to where he had been living—near to where the murdered woman had been dumped. He would recognize his territory.

She parked by the side of the road and dropped the tailgate. She pulled the bedspread off and peered in at him in the back of the crate. He growled and snapped at her.

Angela smiled, happy that he had not learned to be unafraid of people.

"I hope you have a good life in your woods," she cooed to him.

Angela climbed up on top of the crate. Holding her gun in one hand, she leaned over to look inside and then carefully opened the latch on the crate with the other.

"Don't you dare attack me now. It cost me a lot of money to get you fixed up. After all that, don't you make me have to shoot you. Run off back to your woods, you hear?"

The wolf remained quiet in the back of the crate. Angela reached out and with a flick of her hand sprang the crate door wide open.

When he still didn't make a move for freedom, she banged a fist on the back of the crate. That was all he needed.

The wolf dashed out of the crate, leaped off the tailgate, and raced away into the woods.

It was a bittersweet moment seeing him stop and turn to look back briefly before loping off into the woods.

Before leaving, Angela flung two raw chickens off into the woods. She hoped he would find the meal and get his belly full.

NINE

Shit," Brittany said under her breath just before she picked up the tray off the bar.

Angela had just finished putting the four beers on the tray for Brittany to deliver to a table. "What's the problem?"

Brittany gestured with a nod of her head toward the door. "That creepy blind evangelist and the mute are back."

Angela saw that, sure enough, it was the Reverend Baker and his sister Lucy coming in the door. Once she had closed the door, Lucy took her brother's arm to guide him into the room. He swept his white cane from side to side as she led him in.

"Back?" Angela asked. "They've been here before?"

"Yeah. A few weeks ago—when you were off." She stuck a finger through her tangle of teased blond hair to scratch her scalp as she tried to remember. "It was that night we had that first big snow. You remember that big snow?"

"I remember the snow," Angela said, absently, as she watched Lucy lead her brother to a table in the corner on the far side of the restrooms where they both took off their coats. "That was the night I found that woman's body. Kristi Green."

Brittany turned back as it came to her. "Yeah, that's right, the hooker from up the hill. That was the night." She laid a hand on

Angela's forearm. "That must have been horrible, finding her body in the woods like that."

"It was," Angela said.

From what she'd heard on the news, the authorities still hadn't found the woman's killer. Angela knew that it wasn't the guy's first kill. He was a serial killer. That kind of killer was smart, devious, and hard to catch. Sometimes the police never found them.

Angela smiled. Sometimes things happened to them and they simply vanished before the police could ever find them.

One thing was for sure: the killer wasn't going to stop until someone stopped him.

"So the reverend came in late that night?" Angela asked.

"That's right."

Angela guessed that it must have been after the two gave her a ride home. "God's messenger drinks?"

Angela had told Clay Baker and his sister that she tended bar, but she hadn't told them where. It seemed an odd coincidence that they would come into the bar where she worked not long after giving her a ride. Angela didn't like coincidences.

On the other hand, they said they were staying at the Riley Motel. That was just a ways up the hill. If they were looking for a bar, Barry's Place was the closest one.

"They each sucked on a beer for a couple hours," Brittany said. "I think they only bought a couple beers so they could have an excuse to sit there and talk to people."

"Talk to people?"

"You know," Brittany said, popping her gum, "talk to anyone who would listen about life's miseries without Jesus Christ as their savior and how returning to the path of the Lord could bring you eternal happiness, or some shit like that. He bent my ear about God, telling me how I needed to walk the Lord's path."

From what Angela knew about Brittany, she was already a good long way off the path.

"He wanted to talk to all the girls about God," Brittany said. "Barry went over and told him that the girls were working and he'd have to talk to them on their own time, after work or something. So then the reverend did the strangest thing."

"What's that?" Angela asked as she washed a glass in the bar sink.

"He and that woman with him left. A little while later they came back with a couple of working girls from up at the Riley." Brittany leaned in with the juicy gossip. "The reverend bought the two hookers drinks just like they were his dates or something. He talked to them for quite a while—trying to 'save' them, I imagine."

"Were they 'saved'?" Angela asked as she dried glasses.

Brittany snorted a laugh. "I don't know, but as long as he was buying drinks they seemed happy to sit there and knock them back while he evangelized. I'd bet you anything they were willing to sit there because they were on his dime."

Angela frowned as she leaned over the bar toward Brittany. "He paid for hookers just so he could preach to them?"

Brittany leaned her head in confidentially and to be heard over the pounding rock music. "From the way they were hanging on his every word, it had to be. Those two weren't going to waste their time just for a drink. They were on the clock. If they can fake an orgasm, they can fake interest in the Lord."

Angela shook her head as she put another glass in the sink. "Wouldn't be the strangest thing I've seen in here."

"That's for sure," Brittany agreed. She turned serious again. "At closing time, they all left. Together."

Angela frowned. "Together?"

"Yeah. I stuck my head out the door to sneak a peek and I saw the girls climb in this big old car with them. They all went back up to the Riley, I guess. For all I know he and the mute paid for a party and all the two girls had to do was sit on his bed and sing hallelujah to him."

Angela watched the pair across the room as she dried another glass. They were too far away and the bar was too dark for her to be able to see them very well, but she could see that Lucy was signing in Reverend Baker's palm.

The rotating ceiling light sent sparkling flecks of light slowly meandering across everything and everyone. It made it harder to see faces. Barry thought the rotating lights gave the place a dreamy, party feel. It was his idea of atmosphere so people would want to stay and buy drinks. That and serving girls in cutoff shorts or miniskirts. The rock music Barry played was so loud it was hard to talk with people without leaning close, which gave men a chance to get in close to women.

"Okay, I have to admit that is pretty weird, but he's just preaching," Angela said. "You said before that there was something creepy about him. What did you mean?"

"I don't know," Brittany finally admitted. She picked up the tray of beers when her customer waved. "For some reason those two just make my skin crawl. Maybe it's those cross tattoos on his cheeks. Maybe it's that mousy, flat-chested woman he has with him. They're a real fucked-up pair, know what I mean?"

Angela arched an eyebrow. "Maybe they're what people are talking about when they say that God works in mysterious ways."

Brittany, holding up the tray with the beers on her upturned palm, was moving her hips to a song she liked. "Could be. He actually tipped me pretty good the last time, so as long as they're buying I guess they can be as mysterious as they damn well please."

As Brittany turned to the room, one of the men sitting close by smiled at her. "You look good moving that fine tail of yours."

"Fuck off," Brittany snapped.

The guy and his buddy laughed. He gave her ass a backhanded smack as she went past. Brittany grinned as she departed with the tray. She liked the attention, and only pretended to object. The guys knew it.

"You know," the guy sitting at the bar said as he munched on a pretzel while turning to Angela, "if you cut those shorts of yours any shorter they won't be able to contain the girls."

She looked up into his eyes. They weren't evil, just bloodshot.

"Thanks for the tip, but I prefer my tips in cash."

The guy and his buddy laughed. They were regulars. They were annoying but harmless. The cutoff shorts Angela wore kept them sitting at the bar, drinking beers. Along with her courier business it helped earn her a good living. Guys like them, though, made her need an occasional hike in the woods.

Guys who were less than harmless made her need other things entirely.

Angela watched Brittany delivering the beers to two couples at a small table. When she was done, Reverend Baker summoned her to his table. She bent close, holding her hair back as she listened to him. Angela assumed they were placing an order. After a brief conversation she returned to the bar.

"What does he want?" Angela asked.

"He wants a couple of beers." She looked over her shoulder briefly and then back at Angela. "And he wanted to know about you."

The hair on the back of Angela's neck stood up.

She set the first beer on the tray. "Me? What did he want to know about me?"

"He wanted to know when you got off. He said he's already talked to all the other girls here about the Lord's path and he would like the chance to talk to you as well. I told him that I thought you knew your path better than anyone I'd ever met. He asked what your path was. I told him, 'Honey, if you ever find out would you please let the rest of us know because we ain't got a clue.' "

Angela smiled. If he gave her any trouble she could knock his cane out of his hands. He'd never be able to catch her.

Still, her inner sixth sense was stirring—the one she had acquired as trouble's child growing up around dangerous men.

TEN

Reverend Baker struck up a conversation with an older man and his wife at a nearby table. Angela could see the couple listening politely. Being so far away and with the music so loud she couldn't hear anything that was being said. It all looked friendly enough, though, with the couple nodding their agreement occasionally. Once they even chuckled at something he said. The reverend didn't look like he was pressing the couple, he looked to be having nothing more than a casual conversation with them. For all Angela knew he might not even be evangelizing.

He and his sister each had two beers and left several hours before last call. They never came over to the bar to say hello to Angela, but he did turn in her direction and wave before going out the door. She was relieved that they didn't want to stay until closing to talk to her. She was tired and just wanted to go home and get some sleep.

It being a weeknight, business slowed down considerably around midnight. By closing time all the other girls had gone home. After last call Barry shooed out the last few customers and locked the door. Angela had put the Reverend Clay Baker and his sister Lucy out of her mind as she cleaned up behind the bar. It was her turn to straighten up after closing. While she swept the floor, Barry went to his little back-room office to close out the night's tally.

After she finished cleaning up, she called out that she was leaving. Barry hurried out with a smile and handed her some folded bills for the previous week's work. As he followed her to the door, he told her to have a good night, and then he locked the door behind her. It was a surprisingly warm night, so Angela simply draped her coat over her arm.

Across the road she could see the jagged tops of the trees in the light of the nearly full moon high overhead. Most of the snow was off them. Barry's Place was at the edge of town, a last stop of sorts, an oasis, for those needing a drink before venturing into the largely uninhabited forested mountains.

Angela's pickup, its gray primer dull in the streetlight, was the only vehicle still in the parking lot. Barry always parked around back. With the above-freezing temps, most of the snow had melted, leaving the parking lot wet and clear of snow except at the edges where it had been piled up by the snowplow that had cleaned the lot.

Just as Angela put the key in to unlock her truck, a car rolled up behind her. She quickly turned the key, unlocking the door. She always carried a Walther P22 in the center console.

She was about to dive in to retrieve the gun when she saw that it was the old, tan Lincoln that Lucy and Reverend Baker drove. She let out a weary sigh, her alarm lowering but her annoyance rising. She wanted to get home and go to bed. She didn't want to have a theological discussion in a chilly parking lot in the wee hours of the morning with a traveling evangelist who had crosses tattooed on his face.

The car sat idling next to her, the cloud of its exhaust rising into the still air. Angela waited patiently for him to open his door so that she could tell him, politely, that she was tired and didn't want to talk to him. She folded her arms and leaned back against her truck. After a moment, both doors of the Lincoln opened.

Reverend Baker stepped out, without his cane, while Lucy emerged from the driver's side.

Frowning, arms still folded, still leaning back against her truck, Angela decided not to wait for his pitch.

"Reverend Baker, before you start telling me about God, I have to stop you. It's late and I'm tired. I don't want to have a discussion tonight."

Out of the corner of her eye, Angela saw Lucy coming around the front of the big, square Lincoln. Whatever expression might have been on her face Angela couldn't see because it was in shadow under the streetlight. Angela realized she had never really gotten a good look at the woman's face.

An odd kind of smile came over Reverend Baker. "I'm not here to discuss God with you, Angela."

"Good."

"You see, God has already chosen you."

Angela frowned. "Sorry, but I didn't raise my hand."

"Oh, but I'm afraid you did."

He lifted his dark glasses and for the first time, in the light from the streetlamp, Angela saw his eyes.

It was like being hit by a bolt of lightning.

They were the eyes of a killer.

In that brief instant, Angela saw the men and women he had murdered. She saw Kristi Green struggling as he wrapped a lamp cord around her neck. The cord was from the Riley Motel room where she thought she was being paid for sex. In her mind's eye, Angela saw him throwing her clothes in the trunk of their car, then dragging her by her ankles into the woods.

Angela saw the young man he had abducted only the day before and intended to torture to death. Clay Baker had an almost uncontrollable hatred of the young man, because he was a male prostitute. But as he was being castrated, the young man had an asthma attack and died. Clay Baker was furious. The man was in the trunk of their car that very moment, waiting to be disposed of.

Looking into his eyes, Angela had instantaneous visions of all the things he had done to all eight women and two men he had murdered over the course of several years. She saw his knife flashing overhead in blind rage as he slammed it down over and over into one woman. Angela saw him carefully, slowly, peeling the skin off a young man gagged and tied to a pole in a dark and grimy railroad yard. She saw him raping a woman after he had beaten her nearly to death.

During it all, his sister was there.

Angela saw that the bite wounds on Kristi Green's breasts were not his. They were Lucy's. He had not broken her ribs. Lucy had.

Angela looked over at the mousy woman standing in the headlights. Her eyes, too, held a world of evil. They were the eyes of a person who enjoyed the slaughter. She was his partner. She lived to see their terror, to be a part of it, even if she let her brother be the one to finally end their lives.

It all came into Angela's mind at once, an instantaneous otherworldly infusion of knowledge. That cascading vision of depravity came to her so fast and hard it hurt.

In that flash of comprehension from what she saw in his eyes, his memories became her memories.

It was the same as it always was when she looked into the eyes of a killer. They were the same kind of visions that always made her bones ache when they flooded into her.

They were the same kind of visions that made her lust to kill these evil men. But this time the visions had her at a distinct disadvantage.

"Ah, I can see the surprise in your eyes," he said with a wicked grin.

"You're not . . ."

"No, I'm not blind. Not at all. You see, I've happened across a few people before who could recognize in my eyes that I've killed people. As I'm sure you can imagine, that became quite awkward and in several instances nearly got me caught.

"As a result I learned that it's in my own best interest to cull that kind of threat from the world before it can harm me. I use the dark glasses of a blind man to hide in plain sight and hunt those like you who can see my secrets in my eyes.

"I have to tell you, I also find it a delightful treat to make that kind suffer. Of course, those others could never have stopped me, but you're different, Angela. I suspect, given the chance, you could.

"That day I took that whore out into the woods, before I could enjoy myself with her, I happened to look up and there, way up through a small open patch in the forest, I saw you coming over the ridge. So I had to kill the whore and leave.

"But I stayed in the area. When I saw you on the road after you found the body and called the police, I knew I had to see who had prevented me from the ecstasy of introducing another whore to Hell. I had to look into your eyes, see if you are one of those who plague me.

"When I offered you a ride I saw that you were. More than that and unlike the others of your kind, I got the feeling that you can see exactly what I've done to those I've killed. Am I right? You see it all, don't you?"

Angela couldn't stop herself from answering. "Yes. I see you for who you really are."

He smiled as he arched an eyebrow. "The devil?"

It suddenly all made sense. They had been out on that desolate road not because they were on their way back from the village of Bradley. Angela had interrupted their kill. That was why they just happened to be there in the area to give her a ride. That was why they had come to the bar.

Angela was angry with herself at how stupid she had been. She knew better than to accept coincidences at face value. But Clay Baker's blind-reverend trick had worked. She had seen what he wanted her to see.

Whatever mistakes she had made were irrelevant now. What Angela needed to do now was kill this bastard.

She turned and yanked open the door of her truck. She dove inside to reach the center console and the gun she kept there. Her fingers grabbed the lid.

As she did, his big fist snatched her by her hair and yanked her back out. Her coat fell from her arms and the keys from her hand.

Angela kicked behind at his shins. He danced away from her strikes. With a firm grip on her hair at the back of her head, he wrenched her around so that her back was to him. She frantically tried to pry his fingers off her hair.

As she did he snaked his left arm in under her arms and around her neck. He released her hair and instead gripped his left arm to put her in a headlock.

Angela struggled, trying every way she could to hit him, scratch him, or gouge out his eyes. She swung with fists and elbows, but with the way he was holding her she couldn't connect effectively. He kept his legs spread so she couldn't kick him or stomp on his feet. She knew he was toying with her.

Then he leaned back, holding her tight up against his chest, lifting her feet from the ground to put more pressure on her neck. As he tightened his arms to compress the carotid arteries in her neck she could feel the world getting fuzzy as the blood supply to her brain was being cut off.

In mere seconds she could feel herself beginning to lose consciousness. Her fingers tingled as the world dimmed.

Her arms flailed, but they flailed with all the limp power of a dream.

In her darkening vision, Angela saw a hand grab her right arm. It was Lucy. She had a syringe in her other hand. She pulled the cap off with her teeth and bent close to put the needle into Angela's arm. She felt the cold sting of something inching up the veins.

With the way Clay Baker had his arm around her neck cutting off not only her circulation, but her air, she couldn't even scream.

She had seen into this monster's mind.

She knew what she was in for.

Sounds faded away as blackness closed in over her.

ELEVEN

Angela became dimly aware of an oppressive darkness. She felt herself being jostled. She was lying on irregular, hard shapes. She had such a horrific headache it made her nauseous.

She blinked, trying to see, but there was only blackness. For a moment, she feared he might have blinded her. He had done that to several of the women before he murdered them. Then she saw a faint glow of red light that finally convinced her that she really was regaining consciousness and she could still see.

But it was an odd, dreamy state of consciousness. Her mouth was dry. Hard as she tried, her tongue couldn't work up any moisture. She was freezing cold. There was something frigid pressed up against her back. Try as she might, she couldn't understand what it was.

After a time of gently rocking back and forth and up and down, it registered that she could only be in the trunk of the big Lincoln. The faint red glow was the light from the taillights leaking out of their housing.

She reached up to push at the trunk lid and found that her wrists were tightly locked together with something hard. She held her wrists up before her face, staring at them as best she could in the faint red glow. Handcuffs. It was handcuffs.

She felt her stomach, breasts, legs, and realized that she was completely naked. She found a small pile of oily rags. She didn't know if her clothes were among them, but she collected all of them together and hugged them to herself as she curled up in a ball, trying to fight off the cold and nausea.

The icy thing behind her kept softly smacking into her back. She struggled to turn around a little, both to get away from it and to try to see what it was.

Once she was on her back, she found that the red glow wasn't enough to reveal what was in the trunk with her. She used her handcuffed hands to reach over to her left. She felt something cold, smooth, and rather firm. She groped along it, feeling for anything that would tell her what it was.

Her fingers glided over a series of bumps. With icy dread she realized it was a human spine. The skin was dead cold.

When the brakes came on, the red glow from the brake lights was considerably brighter and Angela was able to see that the wrists and ankles of the skinny young man had been tightly bound with duct tape.

She realized then that it was the male prostitute Clay Baker had abducted the day before. His body was still there in the trunk with Angela.

When she finally managed to prop herself up on an elbow, she realized that her ankles were taped together with duct tape just like the dead man's. That explained why in her drugged state she couldn't comprehend why her legs weren't following her mental orders. She was pretty sure that if she worked at it she would able to get through the tape, but it would take some time.

Whatever Lucy had injected in her arm had left her groggy and weak. It was a struggle merely to think. Simply moving her arms took great effort.

Summoning her strength, she managed to scoot a little bit away from the dead body. The irregular, hard shape of the trunk floor hurt her back.

The spongy movements of the old Lincoln, the rolling rise and fall, told her that the shocks on the car were shot. Besides her headache, the up and down movements were making her feel seasick. She knew by the dazed way she felt that the drugs were contributing to the nausea. It was taking an effort not to throw up. The last thing she wanted was to have to lie in cold, wet vomit.

Angela thought that maybe when Reverend Killer and Lunatic Lucy eventually opened the trunk she could jump out and run. She realized that was a lousy plan, because even if she could get the duct tape off her ankles, when they eventually opened the trunk it would take a slow, clumsy effort to climb out, and even if she was able to get out she didn't think she had enough strength in her legs to run. She was so dizzy she wasn't even convinced she would be able to stand.

Angela wondered what had been in that syringe. By her uncoordinated thinking and floundering attempts to move she knew it had to be something powerful. Clay Baker said that his sister had once worked in a hospital. She would have had access to drugs and syringes.

These two had done this before. They were experienced. They knew what to do to make sure their victims didn't have a chance to fight back or escape.

Angela hated drugs. Drugs had robbed her of her childhood. They had robbed her of a real mother. They had brought danger and pain into her world. After everything she'd seen, she would never take drugs. She didn't even drink.

But now these two depraved psychos had drugged her.

TWELVE

Angela didn't know how long they drove, but she guessed it must have been about an hour. In the beginning they stopped at lights or stop signs, but once they started moving at a steady pace she knew they had left Milford Falls. She had no clue where they could be taking her, but it seemed obvious they were taking her out into the countryside. When Reverend Baker was done with her, he would dump her body in the woods like he had done with the murdered woman Angela had found.

She could tell that the drugs had begun wearing off a little, because her thoughts weren't quite so fragmented. As they drove on into the night, Angela worked at the duct tape on her ankles. She had to scoot farther away from the body behind her so that she had more room to work. The effort took time, and at first she didn't know that in the dark she could do it. But bit by bit she tore through all the layers and was finally able to pull off the thick mass of duct tape. She felt a flush of triumph at the small victory.

As they drove for a while through what she knew had to be the countryside she picked through the rags trying to find her clothes. In the dark, pitching trunk, she found her panties. Putting them on was the second small victory. Before she could find any more of her clothes, the car slowed. It crept along the road briefly, and then turned abruptly and stopped. The transmission clanked and the car reversed direction, backing off the road. As they bounced through the dip of a shallow ditch, it banged Angela's head against the trunk lid.

The engine shut off. Angela listened, trying to hear what was going on. Almost immediately she heard the doors open and then slam shut.

She urgently turned herself in the shallow space and drew her knees up to her chest as best she could, getting ready for when they opened the trunk. Her heart pounded in her ears. She swallowed back against the fear rising in her throat.

This might be her only chance—her last chance. She reached up and behind with her handcuffed hands and grabbed hold of metal around the trunk's hinge. She had learned long ago, growing up at her mother's trailer, that when dealing with psychos you couldn't hesitate to take any opportunity that presented itself to escape.

The trunk lid suddenly sprang up. In the moonlight she could see a tall, dark shape, and a short one.

The taller shape bent down. With all of her strength, with her hands braced on the metal framework above her head, Angela kicked her feet out at the head of the dark shape leaning in toward her. She felt her heels connect. He cried out in surprise and pain as he stumbled back.

Angela snatched up a jack handle she had found during the long ride. Armed with the metal bar, she managed to climb out of the trunk. With all her strength she swung at him. His hands covered his face, so his arms blocked the blow she had hoped to land against his head. Even so, it was clear by the way he cried out how much it hurt when the metal bar hit bone.

"Fucking little bitch!" he screamed.

He immediately reached for her. Angela swung, this time connecting with his outstretched hand.

He flinched back, bending over holding his hand. He let out an angry howl of pain. Angela had no strength left. She was moving on sheer force of will fueled by fear. She hoped that if she could stop him for long enough she could run and hide. They might never find her if she hid in the dark woods. She just needed one more blow to stagger him back far enough so he couldn't reach out and grab her when she made her escape.

As Angela took another mighty swing, he backed away just in time to avoid her landing another blow.

As the heavy jack handle swung around in the follow-through, Lucy suddenly flew out of the darkness and slammed into Angela from the side. Angela crashed to the ground with Lucy on top of her.

Clay Baker's boot immediately came down on the back of her neck, pressing her face into the ground. Lucy twisted Angela's arm with the jack handle behind her and with a knee in the small of her back helped her brother pin Angela down. The small but surprisingly strong woman wrenched the metal bar from Angela's hand and tossed it away out of reach.

Lucy used her teeth to pull the cap off a syringe and used her free hand to jam the needle in Angela's bottom and shove the plunger home.

Angela felt the hot sting of all the liquid tearing into the muscle all at once.

With one boot already on her neck, Clay Baker stepped up and placed the other on her back. He balanced on top of her to keep her down. She had trouble drawing a breath. It had been a valiant effort. She had struck several blows to the monster, but in the end, Angela was on the ground, struggling just to breathe under the weight of both of them.

She could feel herself tingling as the drugs moved through her bloodstream. Her mind grew numb as she struggled to remain conscious. It seemed not to matter anymore. In mere moments she was incapacitated. Clay Baker stepped down off her. Lucy brushed herself off as she got back up on her feet.

Angela lay on the ground, the world slowly spinning and tipping every which way around her. She tried to stand. Her legs folded. She realized she couldn't even remember how to stand.

Clay Baker kicked her in the ribs, knocking her back down. "You stupid fucking little bitch!" His scream echoed back from the still, moonlit forest. "You goddamn whore!"

She could feel hot drops of blood from his bleeding nose falling like fat drops of rain on her back. He leaned down toward her, cursing at her in a blind rage.

Angela couldn't even feel satisfaction at having hurt him. She could hardly feel anything. She scarcely knew where she was anymore.

Clay Baker grabbed her by the hair and hauled her to her feet. He gritted his teeth as he put his bloody face close to hers.

"I don't think you can begin to imagine what we're going to do to you." He pointed at his broken nose. "You think this hurts? We're going to show you what hurt really is. This is nothing compared to what you're going to feel."

He pulled Angela from her feet and dragged her across the small opening in the forest until he reached an area of deadfalls. He hauled her limp body beyond the half dozen tangled logs on the ground and the splintered stumps to a tree that was still standing. He pushed her up against the trunk.

"Hold her," he told his sister.

Lucy put a hand under each breast and pushed against Angela's ribs to hold her back against the rough tree bark. He grabbed her handcuffed wrists and grunted with the effort as he lifted her up until he was able to hook the cuffs over a limb.

The limb of the tree had been cut recently. As Angela hung from that limb she could see out over the small opening in the forest. The spot, clear of tress, lit by the nearly full moon high overhead, looked familiar.

With dread, she remembered then, what was familiar about the spot. This was where she had found the wolf feeding on the corpse of Kristi Green.

Angela remembered the visions she'd had looking into his eyes. He had taken Kristi Green out of the trunk and dragged her to this place. This was where he had started to torture the terrified woman. But then he had spotted Angela hiking up on the ridge. In a hasty act of self-preservation, he had stabbed her in the chest at least a dozen

54

times—quick violent punches—and then left her lifeless body there on the ground while he and Lucy escaped.

After leaving, they had driven around the area, going up and down the road a few times. After the police and crime scene people had arrived, he drove down the road and found Angela walking home through the snowstorm. Angela had foolishly thought it was a lucky break to get a ride home.

"Get the bag out of the car," Baker growled at his sister.

She hesitated and then signed something. He went ballistic.

"What! How could you be that stupid! How could you leave our tools at the motel!"

Lucy withered under his screaming fit. She backed away a step, clearly afraid he would hit her. Her fear was well founded. He punched her once, then a moment later hit her again.

After a few minutes he started to calm down. She signed, apparently offering to drive back to the motel and get what she had forgotten.

"No," he finally said after glaring at Angela for a time. "No, I'll go get them. I want to bandage up my nose. I'll get the bag."

Lucy hung her head, not wanting to look up at him.

He stepped close to Angela, hate twisting the crosses tattooed on his cheeks. "We have a bag of special tools. Things we use to make whores like you suffer. I can't wait to get started in on you." He smiled. "While I'm gone, I'll let Lucy introduce you to your new world of pain. Lucy really hates cheap godless whores like you. You'll see."

Angela wanted to spit in his bloody face, but she couldn't seem to summon the strength or the spit.

He turned to Lucy. "You can get started on her while I go get cleaned up and get our tools."

As he hurried back to the car, Lucy finally looked up at Angela and smiled. Her smile was just as wicked as her brother's.

THIRTEEN

After her brother had left, Lucy foraged around on the moonlit forest floor among the deadfall for a time, picking up limbs and then discarding them as unsatisfactory. She at last found one that seemed to satisfy her. She stepped on the end and broke off the extra until she had something just a little longer than a baseball bat. She whacked it against a fallen tree trunk, then took a few test swings. She seemed satisfied.

Angela contorted herself as she hung by the handcuffs, trying to get them loose from the limb. With her arms stretched over her head and the handcuffs hooked over the stump of the limb, she couldn't get herself free. She looked up and saw branches that had been sawed off the limb, leaving stubs that kept the cuffs from sliding off.

Angela's weight was largely hanging in the handcuffs. She had to stretch up on her tiptoes to take weight off her wrists and catch her breath. She could feel warm blood running down her arms from where the cuffs cut into her flesh.

Lucy returned and without ceremony took an experimental swing, landing a blow on the side of Angela's ribs. She gasped at the shock of sudden, brutal pain.

Lucy stepped close. Leaning in, she inspected her handiwork. She ran her small fingers over the spot where she had landed the blow, feeling the torn skin, testing if she'd broken a rib.

Then she put her mouth on the side of Angela's left breast and bit down as hard as she could.

Despite being in a dazed mental fog, Angela screamed. Tears of agony ran down her cheeks as she twisted from side to side trying to get away from the viselike grip of Lucy's teeth. The pain was stunning. It felt like Lucy was taking a big bite of flesh out of her.

When she finally let go, Angela couldn't hold herself up on her toes. She hung in the handcuffs, panting from the pain, unable to comfort the bite wound. Lucy immediately swung her club, slamming it into Angela's right side. It hit just below the ribs. Before she could get her breath, Lucy bit down in a new spot on Angela's left breast.

All Angela could think of was how much she wanted the pain to stop.

Lucy straightened and showed Angela a bloody smile. Lucy was a psychopath. Along with her psycho brother they were an incredibly dangerous pair. They had tortured and murdered innocent people in the name of spreading the word of God.

Lucy swung again, landing a blow on Angela's ribs on the other side. It made a sickening sound. The eye-watering pain made Angela dance on her toes, trying to find a way to make it stop hurting.

In that instant the pain crossed over to rage.

Angela strained with her arm muscles to curl up, drew in her legs, and with all her strength suddenly slammed both feet into the center of Lucy's chest.

Angela had strong legs. The powerful blow knocked the wind from Lucy's lungs and violently threw her back.

As the small woman was flung back, her body twisted as she stumbled and fell. She landed on one of the standing spearlike splinters rising up from the stump of a deadfall.

Still angry, Angela managed to bounce herself in the handcuffs enough that they popped off the limb.

Finally free, she snatched up the club that Lucy had used on her. Fearing to lose the advantage, she ran around the stump, intending to use the heavy club on Lucy. She saw, then, that there was no urgency.

Lucy had fallen forward onto the large spike of wood. It had gone in through her soft upper belly just under the bottom of her rib cage. She was so deeply impaled she couldn't pull herself off. The shock of it had stunned her. She scraped at base of the stump with her toes, trying to lift herself off, but the wooden spike was in so deep that it was clearly hopeless.

Lucy's wide eyes stared at Angela pleading for help. Her hands clawed the air as if she was trying to find something to pull herself off the jagged spear of wood.

Her mouth opened wide, trying to scream. Only a gurgling, wet cry came forth.

And then blood started oozing up into her mouth. It ran out and poured off her chin. Her eyes blinked as she started choking, coughing, and gagging, trying to get a breath as her lungs filled with blood.

Angela, still panting with rage, stepped closer. She could have used the club to bash in Lucy's skull and end the woman's misery. But Angela didn't want the misery to end. How many people had this woman hurt? How much misery had she inflicted? How many victims had she tortured before her brother killed them?

Angela left the struggling woman drowning in her own blood and staggered away, intent on escaping. The effort had taken everything out of her. The adrenaline had overpowered the drugs briefly. Now she was sinking back into a stupor.

As she tried to take a step she collapsed onto her side.

The bleeding bite wounds throbbed so painfully that even in the drug haze Angela could hardly take it. She clawed at the ground, scooping up handfuls of snow that hadn't yet melted. With trembling fingers she pressed the snow to the bite wounds on her breasts. The freezing snow hurt, but it helped numb the greater hurt of the bites. She put snow on the painful wound on her ribs. She didn't know if they were broken or not.

As she lay in the bed of dried leaves panting, watching Lucy's struggles slow, Angela felt herself slipping away into unconsciousness.

FOURTEEN

The cold and icy snow against her flesh brought Angela awake. She didn't know how long she had lain in the snow. It might have been that the cold had to a degree overcome the effects of the drugs, but for whatever reason she was starting to be able to form coherent thoughts. Angela realized that if she lay there on the ground she was going to die. Even if she didn't die of exposure, Clay Baker was going to come back and find her there. When he did, he would kill her.

Angela forced herself to her feet. She couldn't feel her toes. Her fingers were numb, too. She needed to get away before he came back. She needed to escape, or hide, or something. She just knew that she had to move if she wanted to live, and she desperately wanted to live.

In the moonlight she could see that Lucy was dead. A little bit of blood still dripped from her chin, so Angela knew the woman couldn't have been dead for long.

Angela looked around. She remembered the place from the day she had hiked in. She remembered where the dead woman had been. She could go back the way she had come when she hiked in.

She decided that naked, in the dark, she would not make it far. The fastest way out or to get help would be the road.

She forced herself to start moving down toward the road. It was a struggle to put one foot in front of the other. She was so cold all she could think about was getting warm again. She staggered along and soon saw the moonlight on the ribbon of road off through the trees. That gave her a bit of hope and she moved more quickly. If Clay Baker came back and found her she was a dead woman.

Not quite to the road yet, she stopped in the place where the big Lincoln had pulled in off the road so she could listen for cars. She didn't want to walk out on the road and be in the open just as he came driving up. She decided that if she couldn't hear any cars, she would walk along near the ditch, and if she saw car lights or heard his car coming she would dart into the woods and hide.

As she considered that idea, she realized that if it wasn't Clay Baker coming back and it was just someone driving down the road, she would lose the chance to stop them for help. She would lose her chance to get into a warm car. She very well might lose her chance to live.

She was so tired she just wanted to lie down and rest, but she knew that if she did that she would never get up. Instead, she stood while she rested, hands on her knees, letting her head hang for a moment. As she stood panting from both terror and the effort of moving with the cold and the drugs in her system, she saw moonlight reflect off something.

Frowning, she stared for a moment, trying to figure out what it was. She realized it had square corners.

Angela finally squatted down and picked it up out of the tire track in the forest debris.

It was a phone.

The cheap phone was bent a little and the lower right corner of the glass was cracked. Clay Baker must have dropped his phone when he went back to his car. When he drove away he had run over it, breaking the glass.

Angela pressed the button and was stunned to see the screen light up. It wasn't locked. It had over half its battery life left.

Hope shot through her in a flash of hot excitement.

She could call 911 and get help. They would come. She would be safe.

She hit the button for the phone. A number pad came up.

Angela pressed the 9 to call 911. Nothing happened. She pressed all the other numbers and they all worked. But the severe crack going right across the 9 kept it from working.

Angela wanted to scream up at the sky for fate bringing her so close to salvation, yet leaving her so far away.

She reminded herself that she didn't believe in fate. She believed in herself. She racked her drug-hazed brain trying to think of something.

Deputy Nolan's number popped into her head.

She had seen that number on his card. She remembered it because of the repeating 2s. Hoping against hope, she hit the first number. The phone beeped and put the number up on the screen. Shaking with excitement, she dialed the second number and then the third. They worked. She dialed the 2s and they all worked.

Giddy with excitement she put the phone up to her ear, listening to it ring. The call rang and then went to a recording. Angela growled in frustration. She dialed it again, and again got voice mail. She left messages, telling him it was Angela Constantine and she needed help. She told him where she was.

Her moment of relief faded. She knew it could be hours before he woke up and got the messages. Some people didn't even look at their messages until later in the day.

She would be dead by then.

In frustration she dialed the number over and over. Listening to it ring, and then go to voice mail. She kept dialing, furious that he wasn't answering.

"Who the hell is this!" an irate voice suddenly said.

Angela blinked. "It's Angela."

"What? Who the hell are you and why do you keep calling me?"

He was clearly angry. She remembered his angry eyes when he looked at her.

"It's Angela Constantine."

"Who?"

"Trouble's child."

There was silence for a moment. "Trouble's child? You mean the girl who found that body? That Angela Constantine?"

"Yes!" she said, tears in her voice. "Help me! Please, I need help. He's going to kill me."

"Are you drunk? You sound drunk."

"They abducted me. They drugged me. I'm sorry I can't talk very good. They stuck me with a needle and drugged me."

"Who drugged you?"

"Reverend Baker."

"Who the hell is Reverend Baker and why in the world would a reverend drug you?"

"He's the one!" Angela cried into the phone as she sank to her knees. "He's the one who murdered that woman—Kristi Green—and dumped her in the woods! He's a psychopath. He's going to be back soon. He's going to murder me. Please, I need help."

"Why didn't you call 911?"

"I can't, goddamn it!" she screamed. "The phone's broken! The nine doesn't work! I remembered your number."

Angela froze when she heard a car. As it sailed past she saw that it was a pickup, not Reverend Baker's car.

Phone to her ear, Angela staggered back into the woods. She had to hide.

"Where are you now?" Deputy Nolan asked.

"The woods," Angela mumbled.

"That doesn't tell me anything. What woods? Where?"

Her head was spinning. The whole forest was spinning.

"The woods where he left the body. He took my clothes. I'm freezing to death. He'll be back any second. He's going to find me and kill me."

"All right, you stay on the phone. I'm going to get help."

Angela started crying with relief. Her fingers were so numb the phone fell to the ground. She staggered a few steps, knowing that she needed to run and hide. She couldn't take another step.

Her head spun. She felt sure she was going to throw up. As blackness overwhelmed her, she collapsed to the ground.

FIFTEEN

Angela was jolted awake when light and sound suddenly flooded through the woods. The engine and headlights cut off and she heard a car door open and then slam shut.

"Lucy!" he called out. "I'm back!"

Angela blinked, trying to wake up enough to think what to do. She had to get away. She had to run and hide.

She heard another car door open as he got something out of the backseat. By the metallic rattle, she assumed it could only be his bag of torture tools. When he found her, he would use those things on her. He would see his sister dead, and then he would find Angela.

Angela forced herself to her feet. If she didn't get away, she was going to die. Sheer willpower made her move. Sheer terror of him catching her made her put one foot in front of the other. He must have heard the noise she was making as she stumbled through the forest, because she could hear his footsteps rushing in her direction.

Angela's legs gave out and she fell on her face not far from Lucy's impaled body.

Clay Baker saw them both at the same time. The canvas bag he was holding hit the ground with a metallic clank.

"What have you done? What have you done!" he screamed. "What the fuck have you done!"

"I killed the bitch," Angela said. "And now I'm going to kill you."

She rose up with the metal jack handle that was on the ground where she had fallen. As he came for her she started swinging. She could hear the bar whistling through the air as she swung at his head. She connected with his forearm when he thrust it up to protect his face. By the sound, she broke the bone.

Clay Baker staggered back, howling in pain and rage.

Angela kept swinging as she advanced. She wanted more than anything in the world to kill this monster. She wanted him dead. She swung with all her might. She swung with everything she had.

He caught the metal jack handle in his fist.

The crosses tattooed on Clay Baker's cheeks distorted when he grinned at her in the moonlight. His broken left arm hung down. He held the jack handle in his fist with more power than she had any chance to overcome. The metal bar might as well have been stuck in stone.

"Now you die," he said in a terrifyingly soft voice.

He ripped the jack handle from her hands and threw it off into the woods. She heard it thunk against a tree trunk.

Angela turned and started to run, but it felt like her legs were trying to run through knee-deep mud. She knew she wouldn't be able to run fast enough to get away from him, but driven by sheer terror all she could do was run. The drugs were weighing her down, but at the same time a flood of adrenaline was lifting her up and helping her run.

Over her shoulder Angela saw him bend down and open the canvas bag. When he stood, she could see the moonlight reflect off the blade of a big knife.

Angela ran faster. At least, in her mind, she was running faster. But he wasn't running. Taking big strides, he had no difficulty closing the distance to her.

When he caught up with her, he shoved her from behind, trying to push her down. Angela staggered forward and managed to stay on her feet. She spun around to fend him off.

He was still grinning. "First, I'm going to stick you good. Then I'm going to cut you open and let your guts spill out on the ground."

He smiled as he showed her the knife in his big fist. Angela was spent. She knew she had no strength left to fight off a knife-wielding killer.

Knife high overhead, he lunged forward to stab her.

In the moonlight she saw the blade flashing down toward her.

All of a sudden, Angela saw teeth come out of nowhere. The big black wolf crashed into Clay Baker, clamping its jaws onto his arm.

As he tumbled back to the ground, the wolf madly shook the arm, ripping flesh from bone. The reverend screamed, trying to bat the wolf away with his broken arm. But the wolf had a death grip on the arm. He shook it so hard it flopped Clay Baker's body across the ground like a rag doll. He shrieked as the wolf shook violently, twisted, and yanked.

As the reverend tried to pull the mangled arm back from the jaws, Angela could see white bone down through torn flesh. Baker was still shrieking at the top of his lungs.

Angela tried to stand and couldn't, so she crawled on her hands and knees, groping around on the ground for the knife he had dropped.

Clay Baker finally managed to get his arm out of the wolf's jaws, and started kicking frantically to keep the animal off him. As the wolf circled, the reverend turned himself on his back and kicked at it.

When he kicked again, the wolf snatched the ankle in its teeth and started wildly twisting and shaking. Clay Baker screamed and kicked with his other foot. He landed a powerful kick on the animal's rib cage. The wolf yelped in pain as the blow sent it rolling through the snow.

On her knees, the knife held in both fists, Angela lifted her arms high over her head. His eyes went wide as he saw what was coming. Angela slammed the blade down through the center of Clay Baker's face, where the bones were most fragile.

His legs fell limp to the ground. She let go of the knife. Only the handle and an inch of blade stood proud of the bloody face. He had died in an instant. She wished she could have made him suffer, but she would take simply killing the monster.

In the sudden silence, with both of the killers dead, Angela's strength was exhausted. She crawled a short distance away and fell over into a thick bed of leaves.

As hard as she tried, she couldn't keep the darkness from taking her. She knew that, this time, she would never wake. This time, death would finally have her.

SIXTEEN

Angela felt hands on her shoulders. She struggled, pushing with her heels, trying to back away from the grip of the killer.

"Easy," a voice said. "You're safe now."

She didn't know how the monster was still alive, but somehow he was and now he was grabbing her.

"Easy. It's all right, Angela. Calm down. You're safe."

Angela blinked. It was the stern face of Deputy Nolan. He was down on one knee beside her.

She half laughed, half cried in relief.

He straightened and took off his black leather jacket, then swung the coat around her bare shoulders and pulled it together over the front of her.

He had driven his patrol car right up past the Lincoln and into the clearing. The lights from the car lit up the scene.

"They drugged me. They were going to kill me," she said, "like they killed that other girl in this same place. Kristi Green. They wanted to kill me here as revenge for interrupting them before."

He was nodding as he unlocked the handcuffs. "It's all right now. You're safe now."

Angela could hear sirens wailing in the distance.

"I killed the bastard," she said.

He looked back over his shoulder. "Killed him dead," he confirmed. "He looks pretty badly torn up, too."

"It was a wolf that saved me. Just as he was about to stab me to death, the wolf came out of nowhere and took him down. He dropped the knife. I grabbed it. As he was fighting off the wolf, I stabbed him with it.

"After that . . . I don't know what happened after that."

Deputy Nolan frowned down at her. "Well, without any clothes and as cold as it is you should have died of exposure out here."

Angela shook her head. "I don't understand why I didn't."

The deputy gave her an odd look. "When I ran in here I had my gun drawn. In the headlights I saw those eyes shining at me from over the top of you. It was a wolf."

"What? He was still here?"

"He sure was. He was laying down, pressed up tight against you. If I didn't know better, I'd say he was trying to keep you warm. Craziest thing I ever saw."

"Bardolph. That's his name. He was keeping me warm?"

Deputy Nolan nodded. "Damnedest thing. When I first pulled in here and saw him I almost shot at him, but I decided not to for fear I might hit you. He just looked up at me a moment, then he ran off."

"Yeah," Angela said, "you pull your first shot low and to the right."

He puzzled at her briefly. "Come on, let me help you up. I need to get you to my car where it's warm."

He finally gave up trying to help her walk and instead scooped her up in his arms. He carried her to his car and gently placed her in the front seat where the heater could blow on her. His patrol car was toasty warm inside. Even so, she couldn't stop her teeth from chattering. With shaking fingers she clutched his warm coat tight around herself.

"I think some of my clothes might be in the trunk of his Lincoln. There's another of their victims in there as well—the body of a young man."

He shook his head at the news. "Okay, let me go see if I can find you some clothes, then you're going to have to explain all this to me."

Angela nodded, not entirely sure how she could explain it all.

Deputy Nolan, hand on the window frame of the open door, paused and leaned back in. "Anthony."

Angela frowned up at him. "What?"

"You asked my first name before. It's Anthony."

Angela finally smiled. "Thank you for coming to help me, Anthony."

For the first time she saw him smile, too. It wasn't a big grin, but it was a smile. She could tell he was a man who didn't smile often. He probably thought it made him look weak.

"Sit tight. I'll see if I can find your clothes," he said before shutting the door of his patrol car.

Angela sat with her knees pulled up to her chest, huddled inside his warm leather coat.

She looked out the front window and saw eyes shining back from the woods. Bardolph was sitting on his haunches, watching her from back in the woods.

She smiled out at the wolf and lifted her hand so he would know she saw him.

He turned then and trotted off into the dark forest.

She looked over and saw Deputy Anthony Nolan coming with her clothes. Clay Baker was dead. Lucy Baker was dead. Angela was alive. Bardolph, the fierce wolf, was safe and free.

But Angela had learned a hard lesson. It was illegal to carry a gun and having it in her truck wasn't close enough to always save her. From now on she was going to carry a knife.

A serious knife.

THE GIRL
IN THE MOON

ONE

When Angela glanced up and saw him out in the parking lot beyond the neon beer sign hung in the bar's small front window, her first thought was to wonder if this was the night she was going to die.

The unexpected storm of emotion drove other thoughts from her mind. She wondered if this might be why she had just that morning changed the color of her hair from a bright violet to platinum blond that down the length gradually changed to pale pink that became darker until it was a vivid red at the tips, as if her hair had been dipped in blood. Signs sometimes came to her in such subtle ways.

Under the lone streetlight, she could see that the man was wearing a hooded, camo rain slicker. He paused momentarily to glance around in the drizzly darkness. The rain slicker gave him a hulking appearance. His gaze went from the bar's sign, BARRY's PLACE, to the neon beer sign, and then to the door.

She suspected he wanted a drink in the hopes of keeping a high from fading as the distance of days dulled the rapture.

They sometimes did that.

His indecision was brief. When he came through the doorway, his dark shape made it seem as if he were dragging the night in with him.

Seeing him standing in the dim light inside as he paused to glance around at the patrons, Angela felt a sickening mix of hot revulsion and icy fear laced with a heady rush of lust. She let the feeling wash over her, euphoric that she could feel something, even this.

It had been too long since she had felt anything.

Her hand with the towel slowed to a stop at drying a glass as she waited to see how long it would take him to notice her—her fear hoping he didn't, her inner need hoping he did.

That dark, awakening desire won out.

Out of the corner of her eye she watched as he started toward the bar. Slowly rotating flecks of colored light from the ceiling fixture played over his camouflaged form, almost making him look like part of the room. Behind him, out beyond the window, the headlights of a passing car illuminated the murky drizzle. Fog was moving in. It was going to be a nasty night to be out in the mountains.

Other than a couple of older local men down at the end of the bar arguing baseball, and four Mexicans she had never seen before at a table near the front chattering in Spanish over their beers, the bar was empty. Barry, the bar's owner, was in back checking stock and paperwork.

The man pushed his hood back as his gaze took in her platinum-blond hair tipped in red, her black fingernail polish, the row of rings piercing the back of her right ear, the glitter on her dark eye shadow, and her bare midriff. As he hoisted himself up on a stool, his gaze played over her low-rise cutoff shorts and down the length of her long legs to the laced brown suede boots that came up almost to her knees.

Barry, the owner, liked her to wear cutoff shorts because it brought in men and kept them longer to buy more drinks. It made her better tips as well. When she'd cut the legs as short as possible, she left the pockets so she would have a place to put her tips. They hung down below the frayed bottoms of the legs. But, with the late hour, there weren't many customers left or tips to be had.

And then, for a fleeting second when he lifted his face and looked up into her eyes, she stopped breathing.

In that instant, looking into his dark, wide-set eyes, she saw everything. Every horrific detail. The flood of it all was momentarily overwhelming. She thought her knees might buckle.

Angela finally leaned in on the bar to steady herself and so that she could be heard over the pounding beat of the rock music. "What can I get you?"

"A beer," he called back over the music.

He was youngish although older than her, maybe in his late twenties, with shaggy hair and scraggly stubble on his doughy face. She noted that he looked strong. When he took off his dripping wet slicker and tossed it over the next stool she saw that she had under-estimated how powerfully he was built—not bodybuilder strong, but sloppy, stocky strong, the kind of man who didn't know his own strength until it was too late.

To others his features might appear ordinary, but Angela now knew for certain that this man was anything but ordinary.

After she drew the beer, she set it on the bar in front of him. She licked foam that had run over the glass off the back of her hand and then from her red lipstick as she glanced past him to the clock on the wood-paneled wall to the right. It was less than an hour to clos-ing. Not much time. She pulled a bowl of corn chips from under the counter and set it beside his beer.

"Thanks," he said as he took a chip.

She turned back to drying glasses, but not so far as to let him think she was spurning his obvious interest in her. "If you want more just ask," she said without looking at him, giving him the opportunity to stare down the length of her body.

He took a long drink along with the long look and then made a satisfied sound. "That hits the spot."

"You live in the area?" she asked, looking back over her shoul-der.

"Not really."

She turned toward him. "What does that mean?"

He shrugged. "I've been staying just up the road at the Riley Motel." He deliberately glanced down at her legs. "But I may stay for a while longer, find some work."

The Riley Motel wasn't the kind of place tourists visiting the upper reaches of the Appalachian Mountains or the Finger Lakes region would likely stay. The Riley was used mostly by the hour by prostitutes and by the week by transients.

"Oh yeah? What kind of work? What do you do?"

He shrugged. "Whatever needs doing that pays the bills."

Angela poured a shot and set it down in front of him. "On me— for a first-time new customer who may be staying for a while."

He made an appreciative face and tossed back the shot. As he plunked the shot glass down on the bar, his gaze again drifted down the length of her.

"Kind of a dumpy place for a girl like you."

"It pays the bills." She had to deliberately slow her breathing. "What's your name?"

He held her gaze as he took another corn chip. "Owen."

She had trouble looking away from his eyes and all that they told her.

"And yours?"

"Angela. My grandparents were Italian. Angela means 'angel' in Italian." With a flick of her head, she tossed a disorderly shock of red-tipped hair back over her shoulder. "My mother named me Angela because when she was pregnant with me my grandmother said that God was sending her a little angel."

Angela's grandfather told her once that the meaning of the name Angel was "messenger from God," and that while the messenger had come, Angela's mother clearly hadn't gotten the message.

Owen's gaze moved from her eyes to the tattoo across her throat. "Is that some kind of joke?"

Angela flashed him a cryptic smile. "Maybe sometime you'll have the opportunity to answer that question yourself."

76

His expression darkened. "You fucking with me?"

She leaned in on an elbow so no one else would hear over the music and looked at him from under her brow. "Believe me, Owen, if I ever start fucking with you, you'll know it."

He didn't quite know what to make of her answer, so he drank the rest of the beer. It was obvious that he was more interested in leering at her legs than trying to figure out what she'd meant.

Rather than wait for him to order another as he set down the empty glass, she set a fresh beer in front of him. She took the empty away and put it in the bar sink.

"Attentive little thing, aren't you?"

She put on a flirty smile. "Someone needs to take care of a man like you," she said as she poured another shot and dropped it in the beer.

He returned a grin and drank it all down, almost as if showing off.

"Maybe," he said as he set the glass down and wiped his mouth with the back of his hand, "you could take even better care of me? What do you say?"

Her smile turned empty. "Sorry. You're not my type."

"What the fuck does that mean?"

She placed both hands wide on the edge of the bar as she leaned in and spoke intimately. "I like dangerous guys who take what they want and don't take no for an answer. Know what I mean?"

He frowned. "No. What do you mean?"

She paused for only an instant to invent a story. "I started going with my last boyfriend after he killed a guy."

"Killed a guy? Straight-up killed him?"

"Well," she drawled, "not like murdered him for the rush of doing it. I don't think he had the balls for that. He killed the guy in a fight." She gestured to the door. "Some drunk jumped him out in the parking lot when he left here. He broke the guy's neck." She winked as her smile returned. "Turned me on no end, know what I mean?"

"Sounds like a badass."

"He was." She shrugged as she pulled back. "That's my kind of man. You don't have what it takes."

He weighed her words as he studied her face, her wild shock of red-tipped hair, the tattoo across her throat, the piercings. "I have my rough side."

Angela huffed a laugh to dismiss his claim before turning to reach in and replace the whiskey bottle on a shelf in front of the smoked mirror on the back wall.

In the mirror she could see him looking at her ass.

She knew what he was thinking.

In a million years he would never be able to guess what she was thinking.

TWO

As Angela crossed the room with a tray of beers for the table of Hispanic men, the two older men passed her on their way out. They cast disapproving glances her way as they went by. Despite their silent scorn, they usually came in on the nights she worked and sat down at the end of the bar, nursing a beer or two as they talked sports and stared at her cutoff shorts over the tops of their beers.

They may have considered her dress and decorum improper for a young woman, but they couldn't help being drawn by her raw femininity. She noted the irony but it didn't really matter to her. Nothing much mattered to Angela.

Except men like Owen.

The four Hispanics had all fallen silent as she approached—not that she could have understood a word of what they were saying anyway. Spanish wasn't all that common around Milford Falls. It struck her that they didn't want to be overheard, even if they didn't think she could speak their language.

By their furtive glances and whispers, it was clear that for some reason they didn't approve of her any more than the two older men did. It was a different kind of disapproval, though, somehow more visceral, more vicious, but she couldn't quite put her finger on it.

Even so, it didn't matter to her any more than the scorn of the two older men.

There was something about all their eyes that bothered her. They weren't like Owen's eyes, but still, she knew that she didn't like what she saw. But she couldn't concern herself with it. She had something else on the front burner.

"This is going to have to be your last round," she told them as she set down the beers. "It's closing time."

She could just read part of a receipt sticking up from the shirt pocket of one of the men. It was for the Riley Motel. She wondered which kind of guest they were, the by-the-hour kind, or by-the-week.

One of the men closest to her, the one who'd spoken for them whenever they'd ordered drinks, had dozens of moles all over his face. Some were large black lumps, while many more were as tiny as grains of sand. The largest number were clustered around his dark eyes. They made it hard for her not to stare at him.

As she set a beer down in front of each man, Mole-face smiled up at her. It wasn't a friendly, or even polite, smile. It was a creepy, confrontational smile.

As she reached out with her free hand to take the ten- and five-dollar bills he was offering her, he ran his other hand all the way up the back of her thigh.

Before he could grab her ass, Angela stepped back, breaking the contact. At the same time, she snatched the two bills from between his extended first two fingers.

All four men laughed uproariously, as if it had been the punch line to an inside joke. She could only imagine what they must have been saying.

Mole-face grinned. "Keep the change."

"Thanks," she said. "Now I can finally buy that bar of soap I've been wanting and wash my leg."

Three of the four men laughed. Mole-face didn't. She noted that they understood English well enough. She also noted that up to that point they had acted as if they didn't. She couldn't imagine what difference it made, except that maybe it allowed them to play ignorant and eavesdrop.

Angela was rarely rude to customers, even the ones who occasionally got lewd or grabby, but there was something about the looks of these four men that she didn't like.

Mole-face said something in Spanish and they all laughed again.

"Problem?" Barry called from behind the bar.

"I was just telling them it was their last round for the night," Angela said on her way back.

"How about you," Barry said as he gestured to Owen. "Last call. You want another?"

Owen lifted a hand to turn down the offer. Apparently, he was not as eager to take a beer from Barry as he had been to take the drinks Angela had offered. He slid off the stool, unsteady on his feet, his fist pulling his camo slicker off the seat next to him.

As he turned to leave, Owen smiled at Angela. She could read the message in that big grin and deliberately didn't return it. She briefly glanced at his eyes before openly ignoring him. She walked around the bar, put the tray away, then put the ten and five in the register. She didn't take her tip from the two bills. She didn't want any money from those four.

Owen paused in the doorway to look back. She could feel his eyes on her but she didn't turn to look at him. She already knew what was in those eyes.

She wanted him to get the impression she had dismissed him and had no further interest in or use for him, that he had been no more than a customer, a source of a tip. She knew that the simple rebuff of indifference would be enough to take him from a simmer to a low boil. He finally turned and went out the door.

After the other four men left, Barry turned off the music and the rotating light, breaking the spell, leaving the barroom simply old and rather decrepit, smelling of spilled beer, sweat, cigarette butts, and the urine on the floor of the men's room. The quiet, at least, was a relief.

Angela dumped out the ashtrays and washed them along with the glasses in the bar sink while Barry counted the money from the till. After wiping down the bar, she did a quick job of sweeping the floor.

"Been pretty slow this week," Barry told her as he handed her some folded bills. "Sorry it isn't more, Angela. I know you could use the money to help your mother and all . . ."

"I know. Not your fault."

No one and nothing could help her mother. Nothing ever could. As far as the money, she usually made good money at the bar, so she couldn't complain about an occasional slow week.

"The other girls already blocked in on the schedule are enough to handle the place for the rest of this week."

"Sure," she said. "I understand."

He hesitated, thinking of how to fill the silence, before he pushed the register closed. "Why don't you come in next Friday and see if we can use you? Okay? Hopefully things will pick up soon and then we'll get you back to your usual hours."

Angela didn't count the money he'd handed her. She knew that with as few hours as Barry had her working it wouldn't be much. She nodded as she stuffed the bills in the front right pocket of her shorts along with her tips. They didn't amount to much, either, and she'd paid for the drinks she gave Owen out of them. They were usually respectable, but with business being slow her tips had slowed down as well.

On her way to the door Barry called her name. She turned back.

"Be sure to wear some of those shorts next time you come back in to work. I think they were the only thing that kept that last guy buying drinks. They may have been the only thing that kept me in the black tonight."

And kept Owen from slipping away.

Angela smiled back. "Sure thing, Barry. Can do."

THREE

In the late hour the rain and drizzle had trailed off, leaving behind a potent quality to the air saturated with the sharp smell of rain, pine trees, and dirt. It was a primal aroma, the scent worn by Mother Earth herself, absent mankind's touch. The elemental fragrance was a refreshing contrast to the unsavory collection of man-made smells in the bar.

With the rain ended, fog had crept into the valley to nap for the night. It was the thick, intimate kind of fog, the kind that reminded Angela of the feeling she got when someone stood too close, invading her personal space. She wished she could push it back away from her. The oppressive quality of it served to put her nerves further on edge.

Although she could smell the pines and balsam firs, the trees across the road were invisible beyond the soft gray wall of fog. She could barely see the silent road. This time of night there were few if any cars. Anyone out this late would be up in town either carousing, working night shifts, or going home from partying.

Her pickup stood all alone in the parking lot, like a phantom in the mist. Barry's car was always parked around in back.

Owen was standing beside her truck.

She had known he would be there.

In gray primer, the older, regular-cab Chevy pickup didn't look like much. But looks were deceiving. The lowered truck had an LS3 crate engine, Wilwood brakes, and a lot of suspension mods.

A tattoo artist she knew had all the work done by a reputable shop. His intention had been to paint it something wild to advertise his tattoo shop, but he lost interest in it when he fell for a panel truck that he thought would better serve his purpose. After doing the tattoo across her throat, he sold the pickup to Angela for a good price because, as he'd said, she was the only one he knew who was "badass enough to drive such a bitchin' truck."

He offered to have the truck painted for her, but Angela wanted to keep it in primer gray. She liked the lack of color. The flat gray matched her feelings about life. Dyeing her hair vivid colors, along with her piercings and tattoos, was her way of concealing her colorless existence within.

It was rare for her emotions to flash to life, to rise up from those inner, dark depths. But, unexpectedly, they had this night. This was one of those exceptional times when everything sizzled with meaning. Every sound was sharper, every sight more vivid, every nuance more significant, every word laced with danger. This was a night when life itself hung in the balance.

Owen unfolded his arms and with a knuckle rapped the square magnetic sign stuck on the truck's gray-primer door. " 'Angela's Messenger Service, Give your package wings.' I figure this had to be you."

"Good guess, genius."

Even as she kept her voice from sounding interested, her nerves felt electric. Everything around her seemed to crackle. She stared into his dark eyes, letting the wickedness she saw there wash over her.

It had been too long.

"What's with the messenger service?"

Since her name meant "messenger from God," Angela thought it appropriate that her courier service be called Angela's Messenger Service. She liked the play on words.

"There's not a lot of work around here. I like being a courier and it fills in the dead spots when I'm not tending bar."

"So, you're a drug dealer," he said with a knowing smirk.

Angela's brow drew down. "That's about the last thing in the world I'd ever do."

He dismissed her denial with a shrug of one shoulder. "If you say so."

"I do," she said.

He stepped aside for her to unlock the door, swaying on his feet a little.

"Good night, Owen."

"Okay, fine, so you don't deal drugs. That narrows it down. Escort service . . . suck some cock to fill in the dead spots when you're not earning a buck tending bar?"

She shot him a dark look. "I said, good night."

"I was thinking that you could give me a lift." He shrugged again but this time he added a stupid grin. "It was easier walking down the hill than it will be walking back up."

"The walk will do you good."

He wasn't about to be discouraged. "Think of me as a package to deliver. Besides, I've seen the kind of girls up at the motel. I bet you've spent enough time on your back in the rooms up there."

She let it go without taking the bait. His smile wasn't sincere, it was a calculating provocation.

She could see the contempt in his eyes. Women were all the same to Owen. They were all whores and that was all they were good for. She didn't know what had brought him to that attitude in life and she didn't really care. All that mattered to her was that his hardened convictions governed his thoughts and those thoughts resulted in deeds.

"Come on, give me a ride?"

Angela straightened after unlocking the door. "I said *no*."

She knew quite well by what flashed in his eyes that Owen didn't like the word "no." Not one bit.

He abruptly grabbed her by her upper arm, spun her around, slammed her up against the truck, and gritted his teeth. "Said I'd like a ride."

There he was. There, at last, was the real Owen showing himself.

His breath stank of corn chips soaked in alcohol. His powerful fingers felt like they might crush the bone in her arm.

With the heel of a hand to his chest she shoved him back. "I told you, I don't date normal guys."

He slammed her up against the truck again and forced a hard kiss against her mouth. She noted his preference. She let him have his way for a moment lest he get more violent right then and there, before she had found out what she wanted to know.

"I'm a lot more than you think," he said, breathlessly, as he pulled back. "I'm the kind of guy you get all wet for."

"Bullshit."

Angela watched his face as he considered yet another snub. The alcohol was confusing his thinking, but it was also loosening his inhibitions and as a result, she knew, it would loosen his tongue.

"It's true," he argued. "I'm not some average guy like you think."

"Don't flatter yourself, Owen. I don't think you're average. I think you're a pussy."

Anger flashed in his bloodshot eyes. His brow drew tight. He swayed on his feet a little as he glared at her, considering. He finally broke the gaze to glance around to see if they were alone.

"Give me a ride and I'll tell you about it."

She appraised his dark eyes for a moment, enduring what she saw in them, letting it wash through her like gasoline sloshing over glowing embers.

She had a gun, but it was in the compartment under the center armrest of her truck.

Finally, Angela let out a heavy breath.

"All right, Owen. I suppose I can at least give you a ride. It's not like you're dangerous or anything. It would be kind of exciting if you were, but you aren't."

His expression briefly turned murderous before he went around to wait on the passenger side for her to get in, reach across, and unlock the door. Finally granted entrance, he quickly climbed up into the truck.

Once settled in the driver's seat, Angela twisted the key and the engine rumbled to life. The windows glittered with trembling droplets of water. She turned on the wipers to clear the windshield.

"All you're getting out of me is a ride." She looked over at him. "Got it?"

"Sure," he said, grinning with a world of dark intent. "That's all I'm after—nothing else."

Angela didn't believe a word of it.

FOUR

Every once in a while on the half-mile ride up the winding road a streetlight appeared out of the fog, looking like a hovering alien spacecraft. The dark, featureless mass of woods glided by to either side. The yellow center line and the stripe along edge of the road seemed like the only things grounded in the real world.

As they drove by ever more houses at the edge of Milford Falls proper, Owen rested an elbow on the armrest. Her gun was under the lid of that armrest. With him leaning on it, she knew she would never be able to get to it.

When the neon sign for the Riley Motel began to materialize out of the fog, his left hand reached down to gently clasp her bare right knee. As she turned in to the motel's parking lot, the hand slid up the inside of her thigh to her crotch. When she put the truck in park, he twisted toward her and shoved his big right hand down inside the top of her low-rise shorts.

Before he could worm his fingers into her, and without making a fuss about it, she simply put her wrist under his and levered his hand back out, as if to say she considered him nothing more than a harmless oaf.

"You feel nice down there," he said, speaking from a daze of desire. "I like a natural pussy, not shaved bald like whores do today. I like the way you left a patch of hair."

"Glad you approve," she said in an icy tone. "We're here. Get out."

"Why don't you come on in and we can finish what we started."

She knew he was speaking from within the fantasy he had already begun to construct.

"We didn't start anything. Like I said, you're not my type. Ordinary guys are a turnoff."

"Come on—"

"No."

He sat back, the stern finality of the word yanking him out of his trance. He blinked.

"I'm no ordinary guy," he said, rather defiantly.

"Bullshit. You're halfway decent looking, but I already told you, I'm into bad boys and you aren't."

"You don't know that."

"I know that you haven't got what it takes to be the kind of guy I go for. You're a gutless nobody, a poser, trying to talk yourself up and playing the part of a badass to impress me. I've met a hundred guys like you. You're all the same. You're ordinary, like them."

His eyes flashed with anger. "I'm not ordinary. I've killed people."

Deliberately showing no reaction, Angela looked over at him for a long moment. She rolled her eyes as she shook her head in disgust.

"You haven't got the balls to kill anyone. You'd wet your pants if you tried to grab someone and they told you to fuck off."

"I'm not kidding." He lowered his voice as he leaned in. "I've killed people," he said again.

"Yeah, right. You've killed people. Good for you." By her tone, she let him know that she didn't believe him, even though she knew it was true. "Now get out."

"Did you hear about that whore who disappeared? Carrie something . . ."

89

Angela knew who he was talking about. Carrie Stratton was no whore. She was a nurse who worked at the hospital.

The hospital usually used overnight-delivery services, but if it was after the cutoff time for a pickup and there was urgent need, the hospital sometimes used a courier service, and Angela's courier service was usually their choice to rush specimens to one of several labs in bigger cities. On rare occasions they had even sent her to specialty labs in Buffalo, Newark, or New York City.

It wasn't a big hospital, so she knew a number of the people who worked there. She'd briefly met Carrie Stratton a couple of times. Carrie had a son and daughter not yet in their teens. Her husband worked for the power company.

Carrie had taken the night shift to earn extra money for her family. Everyone liked her. Angela had picked up a specimen a few days back and Carrie had been the one who checked it out.

It had been late at night and they told her it was critical that she get it to a special lab for testing first thing in the morning. When she was pulled over by a state trooper on I-86, she showed him the package from the hospital marked "urgent" and got out of a speeding ticket with a stern warning. Angela didn't heed the warning but she did get the sample to the lab on time.

That was the night before Carrie had vanished.

Everyone at the hospital was upset over the disappearance of the young nurse. They knew that she wasn't the sort to run off or something. Her car was still in the parking lot. Everyone feared she had been abducted. Even though lots of people were looking for her, hoping to find her safe and sound, everyone was grimly aware that the search might not end happily.

Right up until the moment Owen had walked into the bar a couple of hours earlier and she'd looked into his eyes, Angela hadn't known, either, what had happened to Carrie Stratton.

"I think I heard something about a woman people were looking for," Angela said. "What about her?"

Owen leaned in a little, lowering his voice. "I killed her."

"Knock it off, Owen," she said as she scanned the wet cars in the dark lot. "People say she ran away with a new lover."

"I was her new lover," he said, snorting a laugh. "But she didn't run away. I fucked the bitch. Fucked her good and hard. She told me that she could identify me and that I was going to go to prison. For what? Fucking a whore? So, I killed her."

Angela let out an impatient sigh. "You're a goddamn liar, Owen, trying to play like you're a badass."

Owen cocked his head to the side. "If I was telling you the truth?"

Angela appraised him in the reddish light from the motel sign. "If you really had the balls . . . but I don't believe—"

"I can prove it."

Angela rolled her eyes. "Yeah, right."

"No, really. I can fucking prove it."

"How?"

"I can show you where I put her body."

"You could show me her body?" Angela ran a black fingernail down his arm as she let her lips spread in a smile. "I've never been with a man who killed someone. Well—other than that guy who killed a man in a bar fight, but that was more of an accident than anything. It wasn't deliberate. It would take some kind of man to set out to do something like that."

"Did you ever watch someone die?" he asked as he stared into the memory. "Watch the life go out of them?" He looked back at Angela. "An ordinary guy wouldn't have the nerve. They couldn't do it."

She knew he was driven to dominate women, to hurt them. He liked to watch them die. It aroused him sexually. That lust was growing ever stronger, and there was less time between his kills. It wouldn't be long before he was aching to kill again. Just recalling it was making him ache to kill again.

"Maybe I had you wrong."

"Come on up to my room."

"Come up to your room?" She withdrew her hand. "Okay, I get it. You heard about the disappearance on the news and now you're trying to take credit. You think it will get you laid if you say you're the guy who killed her. Nice try, asshole. I gave you the ride you wanted, now get the fuck out."

"No really, I wasted the bitch. I killed her and dumped her body." Owen waved a hand in a northerly direction. "Up that way. Up the road that way."

Angela knew that the police and a lot of volunteers were conducting an extensive search of the area around Milford Falls. They hadn't found anything yet.

The first instant she had looked into his eyes when he'd come into the bar, Angela had known exactly what Owen had done. Carrie hadn't told him that she could identify him and he was going to go to jail. That was his just his excuse to justify killing her. In her mind's eye, Angela saw Carrie begging, promising not to say anything if he let her go. She told him that she had two children who needed her. She had cried and begged for her life. She had shown him their photos in a locket. Carrie couldn't know what Angela knew—that begging for her life only amped Owen up.

That was when he felt the most powerful. It got him hard.

Angela had seen all of that. But because it had been so dark and foggy, she hadn't been quite able to discern in her vision the location of where he'd dumped the body.

She tapped the side of her thumb on the steering wheel. "How far up that way?"

"Fuck, I don't know," Owen said, getting a little surly that she wouldn't simply take his word for it. "Far enough that they won't likely find her for a long time, if ever."

"How far is that?"

"From here? From the motel?" He stared off into the fog. "Thirty-one miles," he finally said.

He knew exactly how far it was to where he'd left Carrie's body when he had finished with her. Killers could usually return to the exact spot without any difficulty. Sometimes they visited the corpse to help them relive the excitement of the kill. Sometimes they were curious if anyone had found the body, so they would keep it under surveillance. On occasion they would even volunteer to be part of the search party.

With a tilt of her head, Angela gestured toward the motel sign. "Lots of people passing through stay at the Riley Motel. The police would question those kinds of people. How come the police didn't question you?"

"They did." His smile turned sly. "I stayed around long enough to make sure they did."

"You wanted them to question you? If you really did kill her, and the police questioned you, they would figure out that you did it."

He leaned back and gestured his superiority with a flick of a hand. "Cops are stupid. They don't have a fucking clue. Especially with someone who knows what they're doing.

"They don't got a witness or a body. They don't got shit. I wanted to stick around and see the looks on their faces. They always get this serious look when they're searching for a killer, but they don't know they're looking right at him. Know what I mean? I'm right there in front of them and it's like they're fucking blind. Kind of like you were until I told you. You looked right at me, just like the police did, and you didn't believe I could be a guy who could kill someone."

For Owen, the game with the police was part of the thrill. Killing was the rush, but it faded. He thought he was smarter than the police. Playing games with authorities was his way of keeping the excitement going. That and drinking.

"Yeah," Angela agreed, "I guess it's not like they could tell that you've killed people just by looking in your eyes."

But Angela could.

From that first glance it had been instantaneous knowledge, almost as if she were sharing—experiencing—his detailed memory of everything he had done to Carrie. In fact, in that same instant she had seen all four women he had killed. She knew the details of what he'd done to each of them.

When she had been young, Angela had sometimes been overcome with agonizing pain in her legs. Her grandmother told her it was caused by her bones growing so fast. Looking into a killer's eyes brought her that same kind of pain. It made her bones ache.

She knew that other people couldn't do what she could do, couldn't recognize a killer by looking in his eyes. She knew she was different from other people.

She believed that her mother's chronic drug use when she had been pregnant with Angela had been the cause. That constant soup of drugs swirling around inside her mother's womb as Angela's fetus was developing had resulted in her being a freak of nature.

Her grandmother said that Angela was lucky all those drugs her mother took hadn't left Angela retarded, or blind, or crippled. She said once that Angela was lucky to have been born alive. Angela didn't feel lucky.

She knew that she wasn't normal and never could be.

Angela knew that she had been born broken.

She knew that her desires, the things that drove her—the things that made her feel alive—were not normal.

And now those things that drove her had her focused in on Owen like a laser.

"Easy enough to brag, to take credit, to say you fooled the police," she said. "That doesn't mean you really did it. Lots of losers confess to crimes they didn't do. Maybe the cops believed you're innocent because you are."

"They believed me because I'm smarter than they are," he snapped. "They can't catch me."

"Maybe." She knew she had to push him that last inch. "Like I said, it's easy enough to make up the story. Nowhere near as easy to be a man who could actually do it."

He looked over at her out of the corner of his eye. "I can show you where I left her body."

She stared at him for a moment. "Thirty-one miles. You said it was thirty-one miles?"

"That's right." Owen gestured out into the darkness. "That way. Thirty-one miles. Come on, I'll show you, then you'll know I'm telling the truth." He was beginning to enjoy taking her into his confidence. Unlike other women, she wasn't repulsed or horrified, but actually interested. With a sly smile he revealed more. "She wasn't my first, either."

"You mean to say you've killed people before?"

"Two others." When he looked over at her she could see how bloodshot his eyes were. "She was the third."

No, Carrie was the fourth. In his drunken haze he was forgetting the skinny prostitute he had strangled to death in a flophouse in Pennsylvania. She'd been a heroin addict who had been killing herself for a long time, not unlike Angela's mother. Owen had simply finished the job for her. But this was not the time to refresh his memory.

"I've never been with a guy who actually killed someone, not deliberately, anyway. That's fucking hot. At least, it is if you're telling me the truth." Angela put the truck in gear and drove out of the lot. "You better not be bullshitting me."

"You'll see," he said with smug confidence.

FIVE

Owen directed her onto a little-used, narrow, winding secondary road. The long, backwoods loop off the main roads, called Duffey Road, went to a scattering of houses and camps.

At first, not too far out of Milford Falls, there were a number of squat, ramshackle houses close to the road. Some of them had patches of black tar paper nailed to dingy white siding. More than one had a caved-in roof. A few of those had blue tarps over them to try to hold out the elements, but over time, those too had shredded.

Derelict vehicles, along with old appliances, discarded lawn-mowers, storm windows, bicycles, rusted barbecues, and broken lawn furniture, lay scattered around some of the properties. It all sat silently rusting or rotting away among the weeds and overgrown brush.

A few old houses had such a large variety of discarded scrap that the yards looked more like junkyards than homes. Other properties had outbuildings with old tractors and ancient trucks up on blocks. Some of the places had rutted roads leading back to barns in fields behind houses. More than one place had several no-trespassing signs nailed to trees and fences.

Dim porch lights at a few of the houses gave off an eerie glow in the fog, but most of the places were long abandoned and dark. There used to be a textile mill and a variety of other manufacturing plants in Milford Falls that employed a lot of people, but one by one they shut down, leaving no work, so a lot of people moved out. Milford Falls was not an easy place to make a living, so many residents had simply picked up and moved on.

Past the houses there was nothing to interrupt the forest. In places pine trees crowded right up to the edge of the asphalt road. Some of the switchbacks were barely more than a car width wide as the road made its way through the mountainous countryside. The fog, along with the wet, black asphalt and lack of lane markings, made it hard for Angela to see where she was going. It made the drive nerve-racking—to say nothing of sitting beside a man who had raped and killed women because he got off on it.

The county apparently didn't do much to maintain the road other than lop off any errant limb if it hung down in the way. The road was potholed and crumbling in places. Layers of leaves and pine needles had long accumulated along the sides, obscuring the edge of the pavement. With so many people moved out and leaving abandoned places behind, it felt like the forest was gradually moving in to reclaim the land.

Owen had turned moody as they drove along the lonely road to the spot where he'd dumped the body. She suspected he was resentful of having to provide proof that he'd actually killed a woman. Angela knew that had she not gotten him drunk first, he would not have been as willing to brag about having killed people. She didn't think that he could be getting sober this soon, but it still concerned her.

Angela was also well aware that her companion in her truck had a hair-trigger temper. To keep him content and thus committed, she had to tolerate his hand down inside the front of her shorts as she drove. Having implied she would welcome such treatment from the right kind of man, she knew that if she was too insistent about rejecting his groping at this point it could easily make him angry enough to simply decide to add her to his kill tally.

She needed him to think of her as sort of a coconspirator impressed with his daring so that he would willingly show her the body or else it might never be found.

So, she did what she had learned to do as a young girl when she had no choice about what was happening to her: she let her mind slip away to another place. It didn't matter what was happening to her; she wasn't there. She was gone, her body absently driving on through the drizzly night.

Thirty-one miles up the narrow secondary road, Owen pulled his hand out from the front of her shorts and yelled for her to slow down, bringing her back from that faraway place.

"There!" he called out as he leaned in front of her to point to the left just before they reached an old steel-girder bridge over a more frequently used two-lane road that went to the small village of Bradley. "This is it. Turn in here."

Angela slowed to a stop. She hit the wiper stalk again to clear the windshield as she squinted into the dark. The bridge surface ahead of them was rain-slick wooden planks. Limbs, heavy with wet leaves, leaned in over the road.

"Are you sure this is the place?" She pulled up the short zipper on her shorts. "I don't see any road."

"I never said it was a fucking road," Owen growled. "It's just a place where people pull over to turn around or something. Just pull in here."

Angela turned in to a gap in the glistening green tangle of brush and trees. It was indeed a turnoff. She was concerned that it might be muddy. She definitely did not want to get her truck bogged down out in the middle of nowhere on a seldom-used old road with a killer who could easily get unpleasant ideas.

By the way grasses had overgrown the barely detectable ruts, it appeared that the turnoff hadn't been used for years. Fortunately, it wasn't muddy. There was a weight limit on the narrow old one-lane bridge over the highway, so it might have simply been a place where heavy trucks could turn around if they had to, or perhaps it was once an old fire road.

The turnoff only went in fifty or sixty feet before she had to stop because saplings had grown in, blocking the way forward. Even so, with the way it hooked a little to the right, they were easily far enough in that the trees would conceal them from any passing car, especially at night. That was undoubtedly why Owen had picked this spot to rape and murder Carrie Stratton.

Owen opened his door. "We have to walk the rest of the way."

Before she could get her gun out of the center console, he leaned back in. "What the fuck are you waiting for?"

"Nothing," she said as she opened her door and got out. "How far is it?"

Owen lifted his arm to point through the moonlit fog. "Back that way. Come on. I'll show you."

As they walked into an area of deciduous saplings, Angela could see a small stream to the right down a slight embankment. Some distance away beyond the stream and the trees was the highway that went under the bridge. Back in the expanse of these woods it was possible that Carrie's body would never be discovered. It wouldn't be the first body to vanish in these mountains, never to be seen again, or the last.

It was a lonely, miserable place to die. Especially the way Carrie had died.

"You'd better not be bullshitting me," Angela said to keep his mind on the task of proof as she followed him farther back into woods that grew dense and thick. She didn't want his mind to wander and get other ideas.

The thick boughs of fir trees would muffle the distant sound of any cars going under the bridge and on up the road, so they certainly would have muffled Carrie's screams.

If things went sideways, no one would ever hear Angela's screams, either.

The moon was out, giving the damp, low-lying blanket of fog a faint glow. It wasn't much, but it was enough to see by as she made her way through a stand of oak. Owen stumbled over rocks here and there. Despite being drunk, he knew precisely where his prize lay and he was eager to show it to her.

Angela had lost sight of her truck back in the fog beyond the trees and thick patches of brush. She counted her strides to mark the distance. The farther in they went, the more the forest had grown in to obscure any trace of the old road. Owen wound his way down a deer path through brush and then along ground thick with fallen leaves between maple and birch trees, avoiding the thicker tangles of brush and denser groves of fir trees. Leaves and needles dripped big drops of water they had combed from the fog. The wet aroma of the woods would have been pleasant if not for the reason she was there.

Angela began to hear the stream burbling among rocks. Moss, spongy under her boots, carpeted the ground in low spots. Water oozed up with every step on the beds of moss. She grew ever more concerned by how far back into the woods Owen was leading her.

"Bad things happen in the woods," she murmured, not realizing she had said it out loud.

Owen grinned his agreement back over his shoulder, then pointed. "Just over there."

Not far from the stream, Angela finally spotted the corpse. Owen led her right over to the naked body. It lay on its side, one arm cast out. Angela saw a small pile of bloody blue scrubs not far away. In her mind's eye, Angela saw again what she had seen when Owen had first walked into the bar and looked into her eyes. She saw Carrie trembling, bleeding, and begging for her life as Owen ordered her to take off the scrubs. The true horror of her ordeal had only begun.

In the warm, wet conditions, the body had already begun to decompose. There were places on the soft belly of the corpse where animals, likely ravens, had torn open the flesh to feast on what was within. Maggots writhed in the open wounds. The smell drove Angela back a step.

"See, I told you," Owen said, sounding irritated that he'd had to go to all this trouble to prove it to her.

Besides the wounds inflicted after death by animals, there were gaping cuts in Carrie's chest and neck that had been inflicted by a human animal.

The sight and condition of the body confirmed for Angela the details of what she had seen the first instant she had looked into Owen's eyes. Death had been slow in coming as Owen became ever more intoxicated with the brutality of what he was doing. Owen liked his victims to be alive so that he could dominate them, terrify them, hurt them. Carrie had fulfilled his sickest desires.

Angela held her breath and put a hand over her mouth and nose before squatting down beside the body to confirm one last detail of the vision she got from Owen's eyes. As expected, there was a delicate gold chain hanging from between Carrie's lips, part of it dangling down to coil in the mud by her cheek.

The fine gold chain held a small locket with the photos of her two children. Owen had forced her to swallow it after she had shown him the photos of her two kids in the locket, one in each half, to prove to him that she had children who needed her. She had mistakenly believed it would make her worthy of sympathy. Owen had forced her to swallow the locket to show her he had none. When he pounded his big fists into her gut as she lay on her back on the rocky ground, she had vomited it back up into her mouth.

Angela rose up beside Owen as he gestured to the body. "There's your fucking proof. Just like I told you."

She couldn't even remember how many times growing up when that could easily have been the way she ended up.

"Okay, I believe you. Let's get back."

As she walked beside him, looking over at the size of him in the hazy moonlight, she was all too aware that she was alone out in the middle of nowhere with a monster. A monster who had already killed four women for the thrill of it. They had fought for their lives. They had been no match for him.

Not only did he weigh probably twice what Angela did, but much of that weight was muscle. She felt like she was balancing on a tightrope as she walked beside him.

At the same time, it was a glorious rush of emotion.

As her pickup came into sight, Angela was acutely conscious of where her gun was. She often carried a gun inside the waistband at the small of her back, but dressed in shorts and a cropped top, she had no practical way to hide a gun on her—to say nothing of it being illegal to carry a concealed weapon—so she'd left it in the truck. She knew that to get to it now, she would have to get into the truck before he did.

That was only one more detail swirling in the storm of things already thundering around her mind.

"You seen the body," Owen said as they walked toward the pickup. "Now it's time for me to take it the way you like it."

"I don't want to do it in the mud," she told him in an assertive tone.

He didn't like her tone. Not one bit.

The switch flipped.

In a heartbeat, he snatched a handful of her hair in his big fist and pulled her from her feet.

"I don't really give a fuck what you want, you little cocksucker," he growled through gritted teeth. "Now I get what I want."

SIX

Angela clamped on to Owen's wrist with both hands lest he pull her hair out by the roots as he dragged her across the rough ground. Her weight was no problem for him to handle. With the urgency with which he pulled her along, and with the way he was holding her by her hair, twisting her neck around, she could only get in a half step here and there. Most of the time, she was off balance as she was dragged like a rag doll.

Angela didn't say anything. She knew Owen had done all the listening he intended to do.

When they reached the pickup, instead of pulling her into the cab as she had expected—the cab where her gun was—he went around to the back of the truck. He dropped the tailgate with his free hand, hopped up, and with one swift yank hauled her up by her hair.

Owen threw her down in the bed of the truck. He was done with proving to her that he was no ordinary guy. He had switched into psycho mode and was now intent only on what he wanted. He would now dictate what was going to happen. She knew that she shouldn't expect anything less of him. She had told him, after all, that she liked guys who took what they wanted.

Angela was acutely aware of how very alone they were, and that no one would hear her screams any more than they had heard Carrie's.

In a flash he was on top of her, pawing at her.

"I like your tits," he said in a breathless pant laced with lust. "I don't like those big, fake, plastic tits most whores have these days. I like real tits, like yours."

"Kiss me," she whispered urgently into his ear.

He pushed a knee up between her legs, forcing them open as he pressed his mouth over hers. His breath stank of alcohol.

Angela pressed her mouth back at him, encouraging him. He responded by pushing his tongue into her mouth. She didn't resist. He unbuckled his belt and unzipped his pants, letting his uncomfortable erection spring out before going for the zipper of her shorts.

As his tongue probed deep into her mouth and his hand was busy fumbling with opening her shorts, she reached down to the top of her right boot, her fingers searching blindly.

Once she found what she was looking for and had a firm grip on the handle, she abruptly clamped her teeth down on his tongue as hard as she possibly could and pulled her head back.

Owen cried out in surprise, anger, and pain. His immediate instinct was self-preservation, so he leaned forward, going with her to keep his tongue from being torn open by her teeth should he jerk back.

At the same time as she clamped down on his tongue with her teeth, Angela yanked the knife from its sheath in her boot. She rammed her left forearm against his throat, abruptly pushing him back as she kept her teeth tightly clenched on his tongue, leaving less than an inch between their lips.

In that instant of an opening she swept the knife up between their faces and severed his tongue.

Owen fell back from the sudden release of tension, gasping in shock and confusion. Being as drunk as he was and the blade as sharp as it was, he didn't feel it immediately. She could see by his expression that his intoxicated brain was scrambling to process what had just happened. Angela spit out his bloody, detached tongue.

As the pain began to register, Owen screamed, but it came out as more of a gurgling cry than a scream. One hand came up to cover his mouth as he tried to make sense of what had just happened. Blood seeped out between his fat fingers to run down his chin.

As he grasped what she'd done, anger flashed to the forefront of his mind. He grabbed her by the throat with his free hand. Angela stabbed the blade into his arm between the humerus and his bulging biceps, then pulled forcefully, severing the muscle in half. By the volume of blood spurting out, she knew she'd cut the brachial artery. The warm, wet blood flooded across her chest and bare midriff.

Despite the severity of the injury, his big hand managed to clamp her throat in a death grip. Angela gritted her teeth against the pressure of him trying to crush her windpipe and slashed the straining tendons on the inside of his wrist. As the muscles drew back up into his forearm, his fingers went slack. His arm finally flopped down onto the bed of the truck.

When he made the mistake of taking his other hand from his bloody mouth and again reaching for her throat, she slashed the inside of that wrist, then cut the bundle of tendons at the inside of his elbow before he had time to flinch back.

Just that quick, both his arms were largely put out of commission.

Angela leaned in. "Aren't you glad I didn't wait any longer?"

His eyes wide, he stared at her, confused by the question. He didn't know what she meant.

She grabbed his shriveled penis hanging from his open pants. "Aren't you glad that was your tongue in my mouth, and not your dick?" She showed him a grim smile. "See? Things could always be worse. And believe me, they are going to get worse."

Finally realizing the full magnitude of the danger he was in, Owen raged and managed to prop himself up on one elbow as he banged his heels on the truck bed, trying to gain traction to scramble to his feet so he could at least stomp her to death. Before he could get his drunken balance, Angela turned the knife in her hand, holding it like an ice pick, reached around, and drove the blade into his left kidney from behind.

Owen stiffened from the shock of pain. It locked his breath in his lungs. It stiffened his legs out straight. Eyes wide, he couldn't even scream.

Everything had happened so blindingly fast that he was not only bewildered, but now in the grip of immobilizing pain.

"Just when you thought things were going so good, here they are suddenly going oh so wrong. Right, Owen?"

Angela yanked the knife out and held the double-edged blade up before his eyes. She didn't ever want to have to worry in an emergency if she had the knife turned the right way. With a double-edged blade, that was never a problem. There was always a cutting edge ready to serve her wishes.

"The secret to a good flesh knife is not using it for anything else," she explained to him. "I never so much as open an envelope with my flesh knives. I save them for men like you. That way they effortlessly slice through flesh. I think you can tell that I take exceptionally good care of my blades. Right, Owen?"

As she was talking, at the same time she was gripping the handle of the knife, she reached around him. Using two fingers on his lower spine, she felt for the gap below the L3 vertebra. It was somewhat difficult with the way his legs were beginning to flail.

"What you're thinking right now is 'This is it. It's either me or her.' Right, Owen?" She leaned closer and whispered into his ear. "Isn't that what you're thinking, Owen? Well, I've got to tell you, ever since you came into the bar, I've known all along that one way or another it was going to be you."

Once she found the area of the disk between the L3 and L4 vertebrae, she swept her left arm around his thick neck and pulled his head toward her as she pushed a knee into his gut. Bending him forward arched his back, opening the space between the vertebrae. She plunged the knife between them.

With all the fibrous sinew around that area of the spine it took committed force, but such a sharp, double-edged blade punched right through. She levered the knife handle from side to side. With each sweep, the blade scraped against the bone of vertebrae as it sliced apart the disk and severed his spinal cord.

Owen's legs flopped down, at last motionless.

Each huffing breath as he gasped in pain and shock expelled droplets of blood all over her. She could see in his eyes that he was stunned by how fast it had all happened.

"Do you know what my name means, Owen?"

He looked at her, dumbfounded, unable to answer.

"Do you!" she screamed. "Do you know what it means?"

Terrified, he shook his head, never taking his gaze from her. Owen was not at all used to being on the wrong end of terror. She knew he was trying to assess the damage, trying to figure out if he could still make it out of this alive.

"I told you that my name means 'angel' in Italian? Remember?"

He nodded, panic-stricken at what she might do next.

"Good." She arched an eyebrow at him. "But do you know what 'angel' means?"

Eyes wide, he quivered as he shook his head, unable to give any answer without his tongue except a groaning moan she couldn't understand.

Angela abruptly pushed the knife in just below his rib cage until it found his liver.

Owen gasped, his eyes watering and going even wider as the pain of it reached his brain. He let out a high-pitched, falsetto squeal.

"Angela—Angel—means 'messenger from God,'" she patiently explained to him. "So you see, Owen, you can't really blame me for this, now can you? After all, I'm just the messenger. Right?"

As he struggled, twisting his torso, he only succeeded in slicing up his own liver on the double-edged blade, increasing his level of pain. Blood ran over her fist holding the knife and down her arm. She could feel it dripping off her elbow.

"You asked me before if the tattoo across my throat was some kind of joke. Remember? I told you that maybe one day you could answer that question yourself. I think that you ought to understand the meaning, now. Right, Owen? The meaning of my tattoo? The meaning of 'Dark Angel'?

"So, you see, maybe I really am a messenger from God. An angel. But now you know that some angels are dark angels. Get it, now, Owen?"

"Peege opt." Tears streamed from his eyes. "Peege opt."

Without his tongue, that was the best he could do to form the words he so desperately wanted to get out.

"Please stop?" She cocked her head as she looked at him from under her brow. "Is that what you're saying, Owen? Please stop? You are asking a dark angel for mercy, then?"

He nodded, relieved that she had understood the words.

Angela glared at him a moment before speaking in a soft voice. "That was what Carrie said when you were using your knife on her, isn't it, Owen? When you were raping her? Isn't that what she said to you? Please stop?"

He cried out in agony at understanding.

He may have thought it was revenge for Carrie.

Angela considered it more than that. A great deal more.

Angela considered it justice. Not justice in some abstract legal sense, but human justice.

Clear, cold, unflinching justice.

"There is no leeway for mercy in this, Owen. None."

She slipped the blade in between two ribs, into his left lung. When she withdrew the knife, air hissed out, bubbling blood from the wound as his lung collapsed.

"You're an aberration, Owen. A fucking monster living among normal people. You shouldn't be allowed to live so you can hurt innocent people, like Carrie, or the other three women you murdered. It was their terrible misfortune to have crossed paths with you.

"Unfortunately for you, I'm an anomaly, too. A freak of nature. Maybe I really am a messenger from God sent to eliminate fucking aberrations like you. What do you think, Owen?

"I can't seem to have a normal life, a happy life, like other people. Maybe I'm not meant to. Maybe I'm only meant to kill lunatics like you before they can hurt anyone else. What do you think?

"I mean, I do seem to have a knack for attracting psychos. Seems like I'm a lunatic magnet." She grinned at him. "Maybe that's my reason to exist.

"Then again, maybe I'm just a freak of nature. Know what I mean, Owen? After all, I do so fucking enjoy the hell out of this. I live for it. Kind of like you, Owen. I think only a guy like you could truly understand the pleasure I get from inflicting this kind of suffering and terror, from the blood, from the act of killing another human being."

Owen gasped for air. He had lost a lot of blood. Those gasps hissed and wheezed through the knife wound in his collapsed lung.

By the icy dread in his eyes, she could tell that Owen understood he had run across that rare someone just as twisted as him.

He had encountered the flip side of his own coin.

Angela smiled as she pushed the blade into his gut, slicing through muscle and intestines. Owen stiffened, holding his breath, immobilized by the agony. Tears streamed down his cheeks.

His warm, slippery blood was still running all over the front of her. It felt good. It felt glorious. It made her feel alive.

Angela was in her element. She had this monster right where she wanted him and she was tripping on it the way her mother tripped on drugs. She didn't want it to ever end.

Her mother often told her—Angela thought as a way of somehow justifying what she did—that when you do a line you live forever.

That's what Angela was feeling—like she was living forever in that moment.

Every synapse in her brain was firing to pull it all in so she could savor it, remember it. She wanted the feeling to last forever. Just like her mother when she was rolling.

Angela slammed the full length of the double-edged blade into another spot. It went in effortlessly, deliciously. Her head tipped back as her eyes rolled up in ecstasy at the feeling. She could sense the tip of the blade finding a vital, tender spot inside him.

The pleasure of it ran a shiver up her spine.

Her head came back down. "I have some bad news for you, Owen," she murmured as she pushed the blade in again, just for the exquisite pleasure of feeling it slide through his flesh, muscle, and viscera. "I'm afraid you're not going to be able to be an organ donor. You're not going to have anything left worth donating."

Owen wept in utter agony. For the first time in his life he was experiencing the helpless suffering he visited on others.

Using a knife to kill someone was hard, messy, tiring work. It was also dangerous. A great many people cut themselves badly when using a knife either to defend themselves or to attack someone. A lot of force was required and blood was slippery. More often than not, their hand would slip down off the handle, cutting their palm and fingers on the blade. Because they were using such force, such injuries were usually quite serious.

Angela knew better. Her knife had a cross guard to prevent her hand from slipping up onto the blade. The cross guard wasn't large, but it was big enough to provide a stable place to brace her right knuckle and thumb for leverage. She was always conscious of being careful not to accidentally cut herself whenever she did knife work, and the cross guard helped protect her hands.

Angela knew what she was doing and did it well. She'd never cut herself.

Owen groaned incoherently. Tears streamed from his eyes as he trembled.

"Carrie cried just like you're crying now, didn't she Owen? She didn't want to suffer, to be hurt, to die, just like you don't want those things to happen to you. Right, Owen? The only fucking difference is that she didn't deserve it."

Angela gritted her teeth as she twisted the blade inside him. "You do."

He let out another wet cry.

"Right now, Owen, all you know is pain." Angela peered into his eyes. "But through pain comes knowledge, realization, understanding. Now, in your pain, maybe you can see yourself for what an evil monster you truly are." Her brow drew down. "An evil fucking monster who shouldn't be allowed to live among decent people. Right, Owen? Are you beginning to understand?"

Owen nodded as he wept. She wasn't sure he understood any of it.

Angela didn't really care.

She did.

SEVEN

Even though it seemed like it had gone on forever, it had actually all happened very quickly. But it was getting late. Angela realized that she needed to get on with it. Still, she didn't want it to end.

She drove the knife into his other kidney because she knew how much it would hurt. The excruciating pain made it through the fog of blood loss to widen his eyes so much it almost looked as if his eyeballs might pop right out of his head. He trembled uncontrollably. Just like Carrie and the other women he murdered had trembled.

Owen was no longer capable of posing a threat to Angela or anyone else. No other woman would die to satisfy his twisted desires. No other family would grieve and go through hell because of Owen.

There would always be others like him—there had always been murderers and there always would be—but this was at least the end of Owen bringing pain, terror, and agonizing sorrow into the world.

Angela finally got up and pulled his shredded, blood-soaked shirt off him. He was no longer able to offer any resistance. She went to the toolbox at the head of the truck bed and lifted the diamond-plate lid to retrieve a stout length of nylon rope. She'd found it by the side of the road and knew that one day it would come in handy. Today was that day.

Going to one knee, she rolled Owen over onto his stomach. He flopped down into the blood filling the channels of the truck bed like a half-dead carp. Blood dripped off the frayed legs of her shorts and ran down her legs. It dripped from the tips of her hair.

"Kind of the way you like to do things to women, right Owen? Rough and brutal? Knifing them as you fuck them so they'll scream and thrash? That's what you like, isn't it? Isn't it!"

Although he seemed to show some response, she couldn't be sure if he was capable of hearing her anymore or if it was simply the involuntary reaction of the nervous system. She hoped that somewhere in the dim recesses of his fading consciousness he could still grasp what she was saying. She hoped that her words would escort him into death. She hoped that her words would be with him for an eternity in hell.

Despite how fast it had all happened, with the way he was losing blood from the severed artery in his arm, to say nothing of the other knife wounds bleeding both externally and internally, she didn't think he was going to be conscious much longer. His skin was cold and pallid, so she was sure he was already going into shock.

Angela didn't think there was a trauma center on earth that could save his sorry ass, now.

"Owen, you dumb fuck, you're getting blood all over my truck." She kicked him in the ribs where she'd stabbed him. "But go ahead and bleed all you want. I like it."

As she stood over him, a boot to either side of his head, she used a finger and a thumb to wiggle a black marker pen from her back pocket. She squatted down, sitting on his head to keep him still. He coughed up blood as he tried to breathe with his one functioning lung.

Leaning over, Angela started at the bottom of his rib cage and wrote *I KILLED CARRIE STRATTON*. The words were intentionally upside down from the way they would be if he were standing. *I LEFT HER BODY 320 YARDS UP THE TURNOFF BEFORE THE BRIDGE.* The last words ended up across the backs of his shoulders.

Angela leaned back to inspect her work. It looked to her like it would be perfectly legible from a distance. Since it was a permanent marker, the blood running out of him wouldn't wash away the words. Neither would the rain if it started in again.

She leaned in once more and rummaged around in his back right pocket. She knew from the visions that was where he kept the knife he used on the women he murdered. Once she fished it out she saw that it was a rather cheap Chinese knockoff of a large Buck folding hunting knife. She opened the blade and felt the edge. Owen didn't take good care of his knife. The blade was dull and chipped.

She used the bent point of the blade to cut deeply into his flesh, tracing over the letters of *I KILLED CARRIE STRATTON*. He moaned with each dragging stroke she cut. Those words were the important part. She left the black marker lettering for the rest of the words. She wanted to make sure Carrie's remains were found. It wouldn't bring any joy to her family, but at least they would be able to bury her properly. It would bring closure.

Angela climbed off Owen, leaned down, and put her mouth close to his ear. "Well, Owen, all done. Sorry I had to get to the end so quickly. Ordinarily I would have taken you home to let the fun go on and on for a few days until I turned your brain to mush, but since we're out in the middle of nowhere in the dead of night I'm going to have to wrap it up.

"See, like I told you, things could always be worse. You're getting off easy. Easier than Carrie did. Easier than the other women you killed. I just need to put a period to it."

Angela picked up his shirt and wiped the handle of his knife to get rid of her fingerprints just in case. Holding his knife with his shirt to avoid adding back any prints, she put the blade on the period after *I KILLED CARRIE STRATTON*. She leaned over, putting her weight on the handle to work the dull blade down between his ribs and finally into his heart.

Angela had been tempted to let him bleed out, to suffer in a nightmare dream state between life and death until the end came.

She knew it wouldn't be long until he crossed over into death. Truth be told, she was a bit surprised that he was still alive. But she didn't want the remote risk of him using his dying breath to utter her name to someone.

As the knife irreparably damaged his heart, one last gurgled breath rattled out of his remaining good lung.

Angela left his knife, the one he used to murder Carrie, sticking in his back as she stuffed most of the bloody shirt in his back pocket. She tied the rope securely around one of Owen's ankles before hopping down out of the truck.

She swiped her hair back off her face, then jerked on the rope, checking the knot. She was drenched in blood. It dripped from her hair, looking in real life like the way she had dyed it that morning.

She didn't want to get in the cab of her pickup and get blood smeared all over the inside, so after retrieving her knife off the floor of the truck, she walked back up the path to a spot where the stream was close.

After the violence of unleashing her rage on Owen, it was a wonderful, peaceful walk in the faintly moonlit woods. Owen was dead. The world was rid of a killer.

Angela sat on a rounded rock in the small stream and cleaned her knife in the running water before slipping it back into the sheath in her boot. She splashed water over the laces, rinsing blood out of the crevices in the leather. The suede boots would never be the same after getting drenched this way, but she didn't care.

Angela lay down on her back in the stream, letting the cold water wash over her hot flesh. Despite how cold the water was, she lay in the running stream for a time, staring up at the glow of the moon through the fog.

It was a wonder the way she couldn't see very far ahead when driving through the fog, but when she looked straight up through the blanketing layer of it, she could see all the way to the moon.

She rolled over several times to wash off the blood as best she could. It was dripping from the tips of her hair, so she washed her hair in the running water and scrubbed blood from her face.

It took a while in the cold water but she did a pretty good job of getting the blood off her. Most of it even washed out of her shorts and top. She regretted that. Having his hot blood all over her had been an intoxicating rush.

Being covered in the blood of a monster like Owen was the only time Angela truly felt alive.

Once she was washed as clean as she was going to get in a stream, she returned to her truck and backed out of the turnoff. She spun the steering wheel as she reached the road and backed onto the bridge, parking at an angle in the middle with the tailgate protruding over one of the steel girders.

When she went around to the back of the truck, Owen was, of course, no more than a fresh corpse. Even though it was over, she was still filled with rage. She would need that anger for the final effort.

She tied the rope to the steel guardrail and then hopped up in the bed of the truck. Thick blood sloshed out the end of the bed when her movement rocked the truck. She stood over the slain monster, still seeing visions of the things he had done to Carrie and the other women, and reveled in his agonizing death. She only wished she could have made his end last a lot longer.

Angela let the thoughts of him enjoying torturing and killing innocent women fill her with rage. That rage powered her muscles to help with the last bit of it.

Owen was a big man, making him a lot of dead weight. Freshly dead people were heavy and extremely difficult to handle. She wasn't anywhere near strong enough to lift their weight. Even dragging them for more than a very short distance was almost impossible. She had learned that she needed to kill people where she meant to leave their body, because she wasn't going to be able to move them very far once they were dead.

All the slippery blood in the bed of the truck made it somewhat easier to slide Owen to the end of the bed. She tugged until she was able to spin him around so that his head stuck off the tailgate.

She put her boot against his ass and with one mighty, final push, slid him off the tailgate. Owen nosedived out over the bridge.

Angela stood on the tailgate, holding a steel girder for support, as she leaned out and watched him tumble through the murky, moonlit darkness. The rope snapped taut, but held. Owen flopped and bungeed up and down a bit on the end of that rope, arms flailing outward like a brawny ballerina's as he spun and twisted, until he finally settled down to dangle by one ankle at the end of the rope.

His body swung back and forth slightly over the highway below. The rope wasn't long enough that a car could hit him, but there would be no missing him hanging there, one leg flopped awkwardly out to the side, his genitals dangling through his open zipper, his arms dangling out and down, his knife stuck in his back, a human sign confessing his guilt and telling people where he had dumped Carrie's body.

Angela had gotten blood all over her hands pushing Owen around and on her boots from walking around in his blood, so she went to a puddle at the side of the road and stood in it to wash her boots clean as she squatted down and cleaned the blood off her hands.

She shook her hands dry as best she could before getting up into the cab of her truck. Her shorts and top were soaking wet, but at least it was only water and not Owen's blood she was getting all over the upholstery.

When she turned the key the powerful engine roared to life.

She felt powerful, too.

EIGHT

By the time Angela reached the turnoff onto the long, winding drive up to her cabin back in the mountains, the truck's heater had gotten her warm and mostly dry. There was a gap for her drive in the substantial barbed-wire fence along the road.

The barbed-wire fence, with no-trespassing signs posted at regular intervals, was intended to keep people out, rather than keep anything in. A determined person could, of course, use a wire cutter to cut through the fence. The height of the fence was meant to be a statement that the signs meant business.

Angela put the truck in park at the opening through the fence, unlocked the padlock, and dropped the cable with a sign that had a white skull and crossbones against a black background above the words "No Trespassing." It was a sign not easily missed, and its serious appearance was not frivolous. Once she drove in, she parked again and pulled the cable back across the opening, locking it with the padlock. Angela didn't like visitors any more than her grandparents had.

A half mile up the winding one-lane drive past a meadow and then back into thick forest, the brick cabin came into view. It was tucked into pines growing in the craggy rock that began ascending behind and to each side. The small, hunkered-down building looked sinister in the pale, foggy moonlight. She liked it looking sinister.

Most locals were afraid of the place. Trespassers had, in the past, tended to have "accidents."

Built by her grandparents, Vito and Gabriella Constantine, the place wasn't the usual backcountry cabin. Most of those were little more than wooden or log hunting shacks deep in the woods. But hunting was not allowed in the preserve around the property, and her grandparents had long ago posted no-hunting signs.

Her grandparents called the place their cabin, even though it was built of brick, because that was the local naming convention for places people had back in the woods. The solidly built little house had really been their retreat, their second home.

Vito Constantine had been a bricklayer and a union steward. He'd helped build many of the old, sprawling manufacturing plants in Milford Falls that were now mostly graffiti-covered shells with broken windows. After saving for most of his life, he'd bought the commercially useless sixty-odd-acre leftover parcel of land and put his cabin in the recess between mountains.

The vast, surrounding preserve had been established by one of the wealthy factory owners back when he had more money than he knew what to do with and rocky land could be had for next to nothing. He'd had grand ideas about eventually donating it to the park service, but after the factories closed he left the area and lost interest in the project. The preserve remained intact, managed by a small trust he'd established that nowadays rarely kept tabs on it.

The game wardens and sheriff's officers mostly saw to keeping people from hunting or timber harvesting on the preserve. For the most part, since it couldn't be used for hunting, the extensive tract of land was ignored and forgotten.

For some reason long forgotten, her grandparents' sixty acres hadn't been included in the preserve, and, it being so isolated, they had been able to buy it for a price they could afford. Once her grandfather had the land, he did what he knew best: he built the cabin, as he and Angela's grandmother called it, out of brick.

While he wasn't a big man, laying brick and block his whole working life left him sinewy and strong. Vito Constantine was a gentle man but he possessed an air of quiet authority. People instinctively knew not to cross him.

Since the road going past didn't go directly to anywhere important, people rarely came around their place. Once, a couple of young men who didn't respect the no-trespassing signs ended up with broken bones and memory loss. All they could seem to remember when questioned by the police was having fallen off a ladder.

Over the years, her grandfather's wolverine-like reputation had cast a spell of sorts over the property, so much so that even after his death people continued to avoid "the Constantine place." It also helped that there was no hunting in the preserve, so people rarely had any reason to be in the area. Cars parked along the road running past the property and the preserve were easily spotted by the sheriff and wardens.

The property was a kind of outlier from Milford Falls, for all practical purposes a dead end with few reasons for people to be out there. That was one of the reasons her grandparents liked it. That's the way Angela liked it.

Angela parked at the side, turned off the truck, and sat for a few minutes, eyes closed, enjoying the quiet, forested seclusion of her cabin. After a time, she got out and uncoiled the garden hose from up against the house, then dropped the tailgate and hopped up into the bed of the truck. She hosed out the lacings of her boots before turning her attention to blasting the nooks and crannies of the truck bed to clean out all the blood. She kept hosing water around until the water that ran out ran clear, no longer showing any trace of blood.

Once finished, she unlocked the heavy oak door to the cabin and went inside. The place wasn't very big. It had a living room with a woodstove across the front with a kitchen behind to the left. To the right, behind the living room, was bedroom and bath. It wasn't a big house, but it was all her grandparents had needed, all Angela needed. She liked the small, cozy nature of the place as well as the seclusion.

Between the bathroom and the living room there was a door that led down to the basement—far and away the most interesting room in the house as far as Angela was concerned.

At the back, between the kitchen and bedroom was a small mudroom at a back door. Angela opened an upper cabinet in the small mudroom and retrieved a nearly full gallon jug of bleach.

Back at the truck, she poured the bleach all over the bed, sloshing it into the corners and seams until she had used it all. She tossed out the empty jug, picked up the hose, and once again thoroughly washed out the truck bed.

Angela knew enough about forensics to be aware that there was plenty she didn't know and would never know. She held no illusions that she was smarter than the police, or that she could cover up a killing and never be found out. She knew that there were experts who could recover evidence in ways she couldn't begin to imagine.

That was the risk she had to run.

Her only safety was in being as careful as possible and above all maintaining a low profile. She did her best to fly under the radar by avoiding connections to trouble and avoiding all the various kinds of authorities. Owen's was the only body she'd ever left to be found. She hoped that once the police found Carrie's body they would be focused on the women Owen had killed, rather than on who killed Owen.

Angela knew that if there was ever reason to take a close look at her in connection with deaths, experts could always find something incriminating. So, she did her best not to ever leave anything for them to find. She also did her best not to give them a reason to look in her direction in the first place.

She didn't want to be a needle in the haystack; she wanted to remain a needle in the boundless forest. It helped that she didn't have friends and didn't socialize. People generally didn't know much about her other than what she let them see on the surface.

Once the bed of the truck was cleaned to the best of her ability, she got a spray bottle of cleaner and a rag and went about cleaning the inside of the truck, wiping away any fingerprints Owen might have left. She cleaned the door wherever he might have touched it when getting in or out of the truck, as well as the tailgate and sides of the bed he could have touched.

Angela knew that the police would eventually come around with a photo of Owen, asking if he had come into the bar. She would tell them the truth, that he had. They would want to know what he'd had to say. She would tell them the truth, that he'd hit on her and wanted her to come back to his motel, she said no, and he left after last round was called. Barry would corroborate everything she would tell the police.

Owen had been outside alone with her truck for quite a while, so she didn't know where he might have put his hands. If the police did happen to find his fingerprint somewhere on the outside of the truck, she could always say that for all she knew it was because he had been looking to break into it. How would she know? She had been inside working and then cleaning up after the bar had closed. As long as they didn't find any fingerprints inside the truck they had no reason to investigate Angela any further.

That was the key to her survival—make sure the authorities had no reason to ever look at her any further.

She worked on the truck until she was confident every surface inside was free of Owen's fingerprints.

She let out a sigh as she flicked her rag back to lay it over her shoulder. It had been a long day. She was relieved to be home at her cabin in the woods, away from people.

When she had been a young girl, Angela had stayed with her grandparents often, either at their house in town or more often at their cabin in the woods. The house in town was on a small lot close to other homes that all looked alike. Angela loved being with her grandparents anywhere, but she much preferred the cabin, where there were no other people around and seemingly endless woods to explore.

When she had been younger, Angela's mother, Sally, didn't much care that her parents took care of Angela so often. In reality, a lot of the time Sally was so high she didn't even notice that Angela was gone. Her mother rarely kept track of her.

Her grandparents, on the other hand, were protective of Angela and always knew where she was or at least where she was supposed to be. They were more like parents to her than her mother ever was.

Angela's mother didn't care about much of anything, except getting high. She wasn't picky about what kind of cigarettes she smoked, what brand of beer she was drinking, what kind of booze, or who she slept with. She was much the same with drugs. She had used cocaine since long before Angela was born, and when meth became readily available and cheap she often turned to that. While she would snort, smoke, or shoot just about anything, meth became her drug of choice. But she would happily use cocaine if it was available.

Both would leave her wired for days. After being high for three or four days, she smoked weed to bring herself down so she could sleep. She occasionally shot up heroin to bring herself down enough to sleep. But then she could get into a cycle of using heroin.

The police had been to their trailer many times. When they showed up they frequently ended up arresting Sally and some of the other people in the house. Sally rarely spent more than a night in jail. Vito always refused to bail her out, but he would come pick up Angela. By hook or by crook, Sally always got out. Either the charges were dropped or she was given probation.

She got into heroin at different times, and several times had gone to the emergency room with an overdose. Some of those times it had been Angela who had to call 911. Each time the hospital brought her back to life.

Several times, to stay out of jail, she had gone to rehab. When she got out, and was off heroin, she was almost immediately drawn

THE GIRL IN THE MOON

back to meth. Angela didn't want her mother to die, but she envisioned that if she did, Angela would then be able to live with her grandparents and not have to be near Sally's friends.

The living room of their trailer was often filled not only with a boyfriend but with strangers, mostly men, often snorting drugs from the mirror on the coffee table, or smoking crack, or shooting up. Sally preferred to live her life in a stupefied state.

That often led to trouble for Angela. The people hanging around the house would frequently offer Angela drugs, encouraging her to try this or that, and then laugh when Angela only glared as she went past them to the refuge of her bedroom.

Sally didn't work. She scraped by on welfare checks, child assistance, food stamps, and a variety of other assistance programs. She got all the needles she needed from clean-needle programs. People came around the trailer park handing them out like candy on Halloween. If she had no money to buy drugs, her male "friends" who always seemed to be hanging around their trailer, her sketchy boyfriends, or a dealer was always willing to provide drugs in exchange for sex. More than once Angela peeked out her bedroom door to see several naked men strutting out of her mother's bedroom.

Angela knew that one of those slimeballs, or any one of the random men just like them, had fathered her. Who, exactly, no one knew. It was a matter that was rarely discussed, not because they thought it was shameful, but because it was as unknowable as it was unimportant.

Sometimes, when she had been in bed under the covers, she heard the men drinking with Sally out in the living room joking about who Angela looked like. There was never agreement. Someone would throw out a name and everyone would laugh, or groan "No way!" Angela's father was just one of the random tweaker boyfriends, or a friend of a friend who had some money, or some shady drug dealer her mother fucked for some meth.

That union of two dysfunctional, unstable psychos had resulted in a pregnancy.

The seed that had been planted from that union of degenerates grew and developed in a continual broth of drugs and alcohol.

Angela was the mess that resulted, the little girl born broken.

NINE

Angela's grandparents vehemently disapproved of their daughter's lifestyle, but after a lifetime of trying everything they could think of to straighten her out, they eventually came to the conclusion that there was nothing they could do about it. Sally always refused any kind of advice or help, usually at the top of her lungs. Angela remembered epic arguments and Sally throwing things at her father. She insisted there was nothing wrong with her and that she had everything under control. She said it was her life and she was living it the way she wanted.

Angela knew that Sally was loony tunes.

Sometimes people were simply stupid, and there was no fixing stupid.

Angela loved her mother, yet had been disappointed by her so many times that she had come to love her in an at-arm's-length way, part of it snippets of rare smiles and hugs, most of it fantasies of what it would be like to have a real mother.

On the other hand, she adored her grandparents. She loved nothing more than being with them. They were stability and safety and the comfort of unwavering love.

She was often afraid of the men who always seemed to be hanging around their trailer. Angela hated to have to be in the house when her mother was out of it or unconscious—or getting laid—and there were men about. Her grandparents were her refuge from that ever-present, shadowy threat.

When she had just grown into her teens, one of those men, Frankie, her mother's more-or-less regular drug dealer and boyfriend, began to lose interest in having sex with Sally in exchange for drugs. Drugs and alcohol had taken their toll on Sally's once-good looks. His fixation began to turn to Angela.

That first time it happened was as terrifying as everything Angela had imagined it would be. She lived in fear of those men, always worried what they might do to her.

She found out one night when Frankie came into her bedroom after her mother passed out.

Much like her mother, Frankie was skin and bones. The teeth he wasn't missing were yellow and rotting. High on meth, he grinned like death itself as he pulled her clothes off. He warned her what would happen if she didn't keep quiet. Angela knew Frankie well enough to know he did not make idle threats. He groped her a bit and then stripped down to his bony self. It was like being raped by death without his black robes.

He held a knife up to her face as he was forcing himself into her. After he finished, he leaned in close and whispered that if she told anyone, anyone at all, he'd skin both her and her mother alive. Angela believed him.

While Angela was never close to her mother, she couldn't understand why Sally seemed to care so little about her, or herself for that matter. Even so, Angela didn't want her hurt and she certainly didn't want her to be murdered.

She was terrified of being cut by Frankie. She knew what he was capable of. After all, he'd just raped her.

Rather than leave after he was finished, he sat on the edge of the bed for a while, stroking her hair, whispering to himself how hot she was. Before long, he got it up and was on her again. She pleaded for him to stop. Frankie told her to shut the fuck up or he'd cut her throat.

She cried as quietly as she could through the ordeal. She bit the inside of her cheek to distract herself when he was hurting her. She wasn't sure exactly how long he had her in her back bedroom of the trailer, but she knew it had lasted hours.

When it was finally over, she lay quietly, listening until she heard the screen door bang shut. Frankie had finally left. There was no one else in the trailer but her mother. Angela lay in bed shaking until she worked up the courage to go into her mother's room. Sally lay sprawled on her rumpled bed, dirty clothes thrown everywhere, only barely conscious. Angela shook her mother's arm to wake her. Sally mumbled incoherently.

Angela knew that Frankie had given her mother extra drugs to make sure she didn't interrupt him. Despite Frankie's warning that if she said anything to anyone he'd cut her, Angela's outrage at what he'd done to her was stronger than her fear. He'd already hurt her. She was already bleeding.

She shook her mother harder, crying as she told her that Frankie had raped her. Her mother's answer was to mumble something dismissive before slipping back into unconsciousness.

Angela's tears stopped as she grew angry with herself for thinking that her mother would care what happened to her, much less do anything about it. What was her mother going to do? What could she do? Angela knew the answer. Nothing.

She went out into the living room and called her grandparents, the tears returning, and asked if they could pick her up and she could stay at their house even though it was a school night. They knew by her voice that something was wrong. When they arrived, it felt like she was being lifted out from the depths of hell. In the car, even as ashamed as she was to say it out loud, Angela told them that Frankie had raped her.

Her grandfather drove them to the cabin and told Gabriella to take care of Angela, that he had an errand to run. As horrified as she was, as distraught and physically damaged as she was, it was the most wonderful feeling in the world to be safe at the cabin with her grandmother.

Gabriella cleaned her up, nursed her, had her shower, and gently asked questions. She gave Angela a tea that made her sleepy. Then she took Angela to their bedroom, to their bed, and tucked her in. Gabriella slept with her, holding her all night.

Vito had come home sometime during the night and slept on the fold-out bed in the couch in the living room. He slept there for the next few nights, where Angela usually slept when staying at the cabin, while Angela and Gabriella slept in the bed.

Angela loved being there with them both, being safe at the cabin. She didn't ask where her grandfather had gone that night, or what he had done. She didn't need to. All she needed to know was that her grandparents had rescued her.

Sally eventually said something in front of her father about her friend Frankie being missing. She cast a suspicious look at Vito. It was a wordless question. He said that he suspected Frankie had taken a shortcut to hell.

Sally didn't know what he meant, but she was afraid of her father so she didn't ask. Between the assistance checks she got from the state and the sex she provided for drug dealers and their friends, she was soon back into a suitable stupor. Sally was on to other men. Frankie was soon forgotten.

Angela never forgot him.

Since she was getting to be old enough to do a lot of things to take care of herself on her own, Angela was also gradually drawn into being her mother's servant of sorts. On school nights when not staying with her grandparents, she did laundry and cooked and was always at her mother's beck and call.

Sally would tell her friends, "Go get the girl in the moon. She's in her room. Tell her I need her." Or "Go tell the girl in the moon to run to the store and get us some cigarettes." Or "Tell the girl in the moon to make us something to eat." Or "Tell the girl in the moon to bring us some beers."

Angela never knew why her mother called her the girl in the moon. She assumed it was mockery of some sort.

Angela knew that Sally was growing increasingly jealous of how her daughter was evolving into womanhood, becoming gracefully leggy and inescapably feminine, while Sally, who had once been a seductive beauty, had become skin and bones. The teeth she had left were horribly discolored and rotten. She had scabs and scars everywhere on her skin and needle tracks up her arms. While Sally was busy partying and getting high all the time, before she knew it, she had lost her looks and her sex appeal.

Angela was becoming everything her mother no longer was.

TEN

Even though Frankie was no longer around, Angela did her best to avoid being at home. She feared that one of the other weirdos would rape her. Some of them were scary guys and she didn't like the way they increasingly leered at her. She knew what they wanted. They wanted the same thing Frankie had wanted.

While a few of the other guys who hung around had been reasonably decent, most, like Sally's new boyfriend, a biker named Boska, were just plain psychos.

Worse, they frequently became violent when they drank. When Boska was drunk he sometimes argued with Angela's mother, and then ended up beating her. That was always a frightening experience for Angela. After he was finished with Sally he would storm out. Angela would clean her mother up and put antibiotic and bandages on cuts. Her mother always refused to call the police. She said it was her fault, that Boska was a good man; then she would do a line or smoke some meth that he'd left for her.

More than once there were bloody fights between men drinking at their house. Those fights often spilled out into the street in front of their trailer. People would stand around and watch, but rarely try to break it up. Once it involved knives and one man was stabbed. It wasn't uncommon for the police to be called by neighbors.

Angela spent as much time as possible staying with her grandparents. They were everything her mother wasn't. They were protective, reasonable, safe.

When she was at home and there were people there partying, Angela went out as much as possible, walking the streets, wandering through stores, or sitting in secluded alleys watching the stars and the winos. Fortunately, her legs were getting long and she could easily outrun them if she had to.

Thankfully, sometimes her mother and her friends went out for the night. When they did, Angela did laundry, emptied ashtrays, picked up beer cans, and collected used needles. Sometimes they would be gone for a few days, leaving Angela to wonder if she would ever see her mother again, but she always returned, looking wasted.

After Frankie, Angela was thankfully with her grandparents as often as possible. Angela's grandmother said she didn't like Angela in the house when Sally was using drugs. Of course, since her mother was an addict, that was most of the time. Her mother was rarely sober for long. When she was, she was a bitch on wheels—argumentative and combative.

Sally didn't especially like Angela staying with her parents. She viewed it as her parents' direct denunciation of her and her way of life. When she was sober enough she would insist Angela stay home on school nights. Angela knew that it was out of spite.

Her grandparents talked about taking guardianship and having Angela live with them permanently. With as often as the police had been to the trailer, and as often as Sally had been arrested and Angela handed over to her grandparents until she sobered up or bonded out, Sally was certainly on shaky ground with Child Protective Services. Angela was excited about the idea of living with her grandparents permanently. Being with them made her fears evaporate.

She dearly loved Gabriella and she idolized Vito. After he was dressed in the morning but still in his stocking feet, he would let her come with him into the bathroom to watch him shave. It fascinated her the way he went about it, the way he spread on lather, the careful, measured way he stroked his jaw with the razor, the way he followed the same pattern every time.

Sometimes he would tell her funny stories about his job from before he'd retired. When he was done shaving he would splash on a little aftershave. Angela loved the way it smelled. It smelled like Grandpa and no one else.

She would then follow him into the bedroom and watch while he put on the big, heavy work boots with lugged soles that he always wore. She loved those boots, because they were part of who he was. They were the boots of someone who was strong and trustworthy.

Sometimes she would race into the bedroom ahead of him, slip her feet—shoes and all—into those big work boots, and clomp around the room, putting on a show, imitating him, making him laugh. He would sometimes tickle her to get them back, telling her never to grow up. Angela couldn't imagine why her mother rolled her eyes when she mentioned Grandpa or Grandma.

One day they took her to a thrift store to get some clothes to wear at the cabin when they went fishing or climbing the surrounding mountains. While wandering the store, Angela spotted a pair of hardly used boots almost exactly like her grandfather's. To her surprise, they were only a little big, but they fit her close enough to wear. She wanted those boots more than anything. Her grandmother told her they weren't good shoes for a pretty young lady. Angela said they were perfect for the woods and the mountains. Her grandmother instead kept her busy looking for jeans and shirts and sweaters for school.

But before leaving the store, on their way to the checkout, Vito smiled at Gabriella and picked up the boots.

Angela took to wearing those boots all the time, not just at the cabin, which meant she wore them to school. The other girls made fun of her for wearing work boots rather than feminine shoes. Angela didn't care what they said or what they thought of her. She wore them because she liked them. She thought that a short skirt went well with the boots.

They weren't only good for wearing in the woods, they were good for walking home from school in bad weather. They became part of her the way her grandfather's boots were part of him.

Besides the boots and not dressing like the other kids, Angela didn't act like them. She didn't think like them. She didn't care about the childish things they cared about.

When she refused the drugs and alcohol the other kids were starting to get into, it made her the object of ridicule. Her mother had probably started out like them. Angela had seen firsthand how that had turned out and wanted no part of it.

She had more important things in her life. She had her grandparents and their cabin. She had woods trails to hike, and mountains to climb. She had lakes to fish. Sometimes there was nothing better than skipping rocks across a glassy lake.

The other girls at school often called her a freak, among other things. When it came right down to it, she couldn't really argue with them. She was the offspring of freaks. She had been born a freak. She didn't like being called names but she saw no point in getting into a fight over it. The other girls were even more annoyed when Angela didn't respond to their taunts than Angela was at being called the names.

Because she was so obviously different in ways they couldn't exactly put their finger on, the other kids were wary of her, so it rarely went beyond name calling. On a couple of occasions another girl, emboldened by her friends, would start a fight. If they pulled at her clothes, Angela smacked them. If they slapped her once, Angela punched them on the arm three times. If they pulled her hair, she knocked them down. But it never got to the point of anyone getting hurt, mostly because that was enough to stop them, and if they stopped, Angela stopped.

Such encounters only added to the word around school that you didn't want to make Angela angry. The reason, though, that girls called her names and picked on her was more and more a matter of them being jealous of her looks and because the boys they liked were beginning to pay a lot of attention to Angela. She ignored the boys the same as she ignored the girls, but that didn't stop them from being interested. In fact, it only seemed to make them more interested. At least they didn't call her names.

One day when she was going home from school, three girls several grades above her stopped her in the parking lot of the liquor store she had to pass by on her way to the trailer park. These were not the ordinary girls she was used to dealing with, not her classmates who snickered at her, or whispered names, or even yanked her hair as they ran by.

These three were at least a head taller than Angela, and wider. She recognized them as the popular girls the jocks at school liked. They had perfect clothes and perfect hair and perfect nails. They laughed at Angela, called her trailer trash, and pointed at the work boots she was wearing. The boots that were like her grandfather's.

Angela didn't much care if they laughed at her—she was used to that—and she certainly didn't want to get into a fight with girls who were so much bigger than her. She kept her head down and tried to get past by walking around them.

As she did, the tallest girl stepped in and slammed an unexpected punch into Angela's gut.

It wasn't the typical girl punch Angela was used to. It was a full-force hook by a strong older girl who meant to hurt her.

The blow staggered Angela back. She spiraled down to the grimy asphalt, doubled over in pain. Mouth open wide, she gasped for air but couldn't get her breath. And then, holding herself up with one hand, as the world spun around her, she vomited. All the while they laughed at her and called her a freak.

Then the girl who had punched her kicked her in the side. She yelled out to the other two, "Mess her up good!"

Something inside snapped. Angela spun as she came up, whipping her leg around, and hard as she could landed a boot in the face of the girl who had hit her. She could feel bone break. Blood sprayed across the other two girls.

The big girl went down hard. She was out.

The other two bent down to the unconscious girl lying there on the crumbling asphalt, among the cigarette butts and trash. As they screamed and cried hysterically, Angela simply brushed herself off and went home.

ELEVEN

The next day at school Angela was pulled out of class, taken to the principal's office, and made to sit in a chair in the waiting room. The principal, Mr. Ericsson, came out and said that her mother wasn't answering her phone. Angela wasn't surprised. Her mother usually didn't answer her phone unless she was looking to score something. If she already had, Angela didn't think her mother would even hear the phone.

Mr. Ericsson stood over her, hands on his hips, and asked who else he could call to come get her. Angela didn't really want to get her grandparents involved, or have them see her in trouble, but she didn't know anyone else, so she finally gave the principal their number. Angela waited alone outside Mr. Ericsson's office until her grandfather showed up.

Before he could say anything to Angela, a sober-faced woman immediately ushered them both into the principal's office and shut the door behind them. They sat in wooden chairs before the principal's old wooden desk. Mr. Ericsson drummed his fingers on the desk as he scowled.

"You're Mr. Constantine? Angela's grandfather?"

"That's right. What's she done?"

Mr. Ericsson cast Angela a dirty look before turning his attention back to her grandfather.

"She put another girl in the hospital, that's what she's done. Broke bones in her face. She's going to require surgery."

Her grandfather turned toward Angela, looking at her without saying anything. He didn't need to say anything. She knew what the look meant.

"On my way home, three older girls stopped me in the parking lot of the liquor store on Barlow Street," she explained to her grandfather. "They called me names. I tried to walk away but the biggest one punched me in the stomach. It hurt so much it made me vomit. When I was down on the ground she kicked me hard in the side and I heard her tell the other two to mess me up good. I knew they were going to hurt me bad. I knew I couldn't outrun them.

"So I came up and planted my boot hard as I could in the face of the girl who had hit me. She went down. There was a lot of confusion and screaming. I went home."

Her grandfather gave her a nod, looking relieved by her answer. He turned back to the principal.

"What are we doing here? Have you called us in to file some kind of charges against these three girls?"

The principal's eyebrows lifted in surprise. "Mr. Constantine, Angela hurt another girl badly enough to put her in the hospital. We're expelling Angela from school."

Her grandfather frowned. "Expelling her? Why? You just heard her. She was defending herself. Had she not put that girl down, then the three of them would probably have put Angela in the hospital, if not worse."

"Mr. Constantine, we have a zero-tolerance policy against violence."

"Violence? It wasn't violence," her grandfather said in a calm voice. "It was self-preservation."

Mr. Ericsson sat back and laced his fingers together on top of his prominent belly. "Angela put another girl in the hospital. We can't tolerate such violence. That's why she is being expelled."

"Are you expelling the other three girls?"

He looked confused. "No, of course not. Why would we? Don't you understand? They were the ones Angela hurt. One of them, anyway."

A dark look came over Vito's face. "So you're defending the violent girls who attacked Angela and you're punishing her for being their victim."

"Well, no, that's not exactly—"

"Did you ever see someone's head split open like a melon on concrete?"

The principal's face paled. "Why, no, but what does that—"

"I was a safety steward with my union for sixteen years. We worked around concrete surfaces all day. I saw a deliveryman slip on something one day and fall back. He hit the back of his head on a concrete curb. It cracked his skull. He was on a respirator for two weeks before his family pulled the plug. I was there that day when his heart beat for the last time.

"I saw to it that there were new rules that everyone had to wear a safety helmet anywhere on the jobsite at all times, not just the men mixing mud or laying block and brick.

"When those girls attacked Angela, they could easily have knocked her down and she could have hit her head on a concrete curb in that parking lot. She could have been left an invalid for the rest of her life. She could have died."

"Well, the chances of—"

"Look at her. Look how thin she is. A bigger, stronger person punching a girl like Angela in the gut could easily have ruptured an artery and she could have bled internally and died in agonizing pain. Any number of serious injuries could have resulted from that kind of blow to the abdomen. This wasn't some other girl in her class pulling her hair or throwing a spitball at her, this was a much bigger person—three of them—attacking her with the clear intent of hurting her.

"Angela didn't set out to hurt them. She tried to get away. She was attacked. She defended herself."

Mr. Ericsson fell back on the only line he knew. "But violence of any kind is strictly—"

Vito folded his arms. "So your policy at this school is to protect bullies? Your policy is that Angela should let herself be hurt, maybe very badly, possibly even murdered, rather than defend herself. Is that about the sum of it?"

The principal had clearly expected contrition. He was rattled that he wasn't getting it. "I don't think you understand what—"

"I think you should think *very carefully* about what kind of harm could come from your decision, today. What kind of message it would send to other thugs and their victims."

Angela's grandfather had an intimidating glare that went with a voice that, without him even raising it, could make the blood drain from people's faces.

Mr. Ericsson wet his lips several times and averted his eyes before he spoke.

"Considering the circumstances and what Angela had to say explaining her actions, I think it best if we drop the whole thing about expelling Angela."

"Yes, I think that would be best for all concerned."

"But Mr. Constantine, I must tell you, Angela needs to buckle down," Mr. Ericsson said, changing the subject. Angela had apparently already been on his radar. "She scored the highest IQ scores we've ever recorded at this school. Did you know that?"

"No, she never told me."

"Well, she did. And yet her grades are subpar. She's barely passing. She has great potential but she isn't applying herself. Maybe if she worked harder and tried harder to fit in she wouldn't have to defend herself in the first place. I mean, just look at the way she dresses, at those boots she wears."

Vito lifted a leg and thunked his boot down on the desk. "What's wrong with her boots?"

Mr. Ericsson stared a moment at the lugged sole of the boot on his desk before looking up into Vito's glare. "Well . . . nothing. That's not really my point. My point is that she needs to apply herself."

Angela didn't care about applying herself. When the teachers put problems up on the blackboard, she grasped the entire problem and the answer all at the same time. It bored her to tears waiting for the other kids to figure it out, or waiting while the teachers painstakingly walked other kids through what Angela had seen in the first instant. Her mind would wander away. She didn't feel she needed to go through the motions of explaining it, so she didn't. She knew the answer, and to her mind that was what mattered.

"And I must tell you, this isn't the first time. That's one reason you're here. She's fought with other girls before."

"I know about that," her grandfather said. "That's all been petty kid stuff, just kids tussling. We're not here to talk about petty stuff, or her grades.

"We're here today because three older girls tried to hurt Angela."

"Mr. Constantine, you have to understand my—"

Her grandfather leaned in, his glare darkening. "We're here today to talk about what I should do about you causing yet more harm to Angela."

The principal, his face pale, finally cleared his throat.

"Mr. Constantine, I already told you that after having heard the explanation—which I had been totally unaware of—I can see that there is no need to expel your daughter."

"And you are going to suspend the girls who attacked her for a week and tell their parents why." It wasn't a question.

Mr. Ericsson glanced briefly at Angela. "Well, I guess that would be the right thing to do."

"Yes it would."

Mr. Ericsson leaned forward, folding his hands on his desk. "I'm glad we've been able to clear up this matter, but I must insist that you see to it that she buckles down and applies herself because—"

"Let me tell you what has been cleared up today, Mr. Ericsson. I'm not sure this school is a safe environment for Angela, or for that matter any other decent children. It's clear that you don't have a policy to protect children from becoming the victims of abuse.

"I'll tell you what's going to happen, now. I'm suspending you and your school from Angela's life for a week to give you time to reflect on how you are going to correct the situation."

The principal blinked. "What? You're pulling her out of school?"

"For a week. That will give you a chance to straighten things out. If I have to come back here again I will expel you from her life permanently. Are we clear?"

The principal swallowed. "Quite clear, Mr. Constantine."

In the car on the way home her grandfather rode in silence for a time before he looked over at her. "I'm proud of you for standing up for yourself and not letting those girls hurt you."

"Thanks, Grandpa."

He mulled something over before speaking again.

"I know you're smart, Angela. I don't need any test to tell me that. So, don't you think you ought to use those smarts of yours? Apply yourself? Smarts can help you in life, you know."

Angela thought a moment. "Mom's boyfriends offer me drugs and booze all the time. They try to get me to take a hit off their crack pipes, or snort a line with them. They wanted to show me how to shoot up some of what they called the good stuff. I always tell them no, and to leave me alone."

She didn't say anything else.

Her grandfather got the point and smiled to himself. "I guess you do use those smarts of yours."

TWELVE

When they got to the house in town, Vito told Gabriella to get things together, that they were going to go stay out at the cabin for a time. She asked why, what had happened, and what about school.

"Nothing much," he told her. "Angela was jumped by three bigger girls and she defended herself. I thought it would be safer if I pulled her out of school for a week so things can cool down."

Once they got to the cabin, her grandparents went into the bedroom and shut the door. She could hear them calmly discussing something, but she didn't know what. Her grandparents were very close. They shared everything. Sometimes it seemed they could have an entire conversation just by looking at each other. Angela suspected that Vito was telling Gabriella about the girls who had attacked her, and what she had done to one of them.

When they came out, instead of going hiking or fishing, her grandfather pulled a small handgun out of the cabinet where he kept his guns. He checked that it was empty and then handed the gun to Angela.

"This is a Walther P22. You're plenty old enough to start learning to use it. I realize, now, that I should have been teaching you all along how to defend yourself.

"You did good, this time, Angela, and you weren't hurt, but when I looked at you sitting there next to me as you told me about how you had been jumped by those bigger girls, I was struck by how small and vulnerable you still are. Not just to bigger kids but to people like . . ."

Frankie.

He didn't say it, but that's what he meant.

Frankie had vanished, but that didn't mean that men like him were no longer a threat. She knew there would always be men like him. She'd heard the police tell her mother on more than one occasion that she needed to stop hanging around with the wrong crowd.

To Angela's mind, her mother wasn't hanging around with the wrong crowd. Her mother *was* the wrong crowd.

"Anyway," her grandfather went on, "you're growing up fast and one of these days you'll be on your own." He put four boxes of ammunition in her other hand. "I won't always be there to watch over you and help you out."

Angela didn't like that thought.

She had watched him practice shooting a number of times, but he mostly did it when she wasn't there. She always thought that it was a grown-up thing. She was growing up and ready take on more responsibility. Growing up also meant she understood dangers she had never grasped as a little girl. With her grandfather wanting to teach her to shoot, she suddenly felt older, more mature, and acutely aware of the dangers not just at her mother's trailer, but out in the world—even at school.

"We're going to shoot those four boxes today, and we're going to try to shoot every day until you can shoot the wings off a gnat. That will take time and a great deal of practice, but it will be worth it to have a skill you will carry with you your whole life. Do you think you're up to the challenge?"

Angela smiled up at him. "Yes."

She liked how well the Walther fit in her hand. She'd seen her grandfather use bigger guns. She liked this one.

"Is this gun big enough? I mean, you know, to protect myself?"

"Assassins of every stripe use a twenty-two as their gun of choice."

"Really? Why?"

"Because it's a smaller bullet so it won't overpenetrate. It won't go through people and then through walls. But to be fatal it has to go in the right place. If you put a twenty-two in the right place it kills instantly. Shot placement is more important than the size of the bullet. That's why assassins are so successful with it—because they're expert shots.

"Putting the bullet where it needs to go takes a lot of practice. Is that something you think you're ready to take on?"

With a serious look, Angela nodded.

"You be careful," her grandmother said as they headed for the door. "You do as your grandfather says so you will be safe."

"I will, Grandma."

Her grandfather gave her a set of electronic ear-protector headphones that shut out the sound of gunshots, but not the sound of talking. That day she shot all four boxes of ammunition. Loading bullets by pushing them into magazines left her thumb sore, but the excitement of learning something new, something so serious and adult, made it more than worth it.

They spent that first day and many a day after that practicing nothing but holding the gun rock steady as she fired it into a cliff as a backdrop. Her grandfather wouldn't let her aim at anything. She had trouble holding the gun still, and she flinched in anticipation of the recoil.

It was months before he was satisfied with the way she could unfailingly fire off rounds, fast or slow, with the gun remaining dead still until the round fired, and then after the recoil it immediately returned to the ready position.

Her grandfather told her stories from the news about people, mostly young women, who had been abducted, and how their remains had been found after they had been held captive, tortured, and murdered. These were real people it had happened to.

She knew that he wasn't trying to scare her. He was trying to make target shooting relevant. He was trying to impress upon her the importance of practice. Angela took everything her grandfather said seriously.

Once she learned to hold the gun rock steady he started having her shoot at a paper target tacked to a stump. She shot countless paper targets to pieces.

Once she could reliably hit the bull's-eye, he brought out something she had seen him use a few times in the past when he practiced. It was a target contraption of some kind he had made himself out of parts from junkyards.

The target machine had a heavy metal base with gears and a coil spring. A metal rod stuck up from that heavy base. At about eye level there was a metal triangle welded to the end of the rod. When he wound it up with a key in the base, the rod would wobble and swing from side to side, and back and forth, over an area of several feet.

"There's a reason the target is a triangle," he told her. "Do you know the reason?"

Angela squinted up at him. "To make it harder to hit?"

"In a way," he said. "A twenty-two can easily kill a man, even a big man. Remember when I told you that shot placement was important?"

Angela nodded. "I remember."

"Well, you see, if you hit a man with a twenty-two at the top of his forehead, or off to the side, the bullet will likely glance off the hard bone of his skull without doing much harm. That won't stop him."

"So, you need to aim for his heart?"

He made a face as he considered. "If you had a bigger-caliber gun, certainly. But a twenty-two could glance off the rib cage and not get to his heart. If the guy is big and tough, a twenty-two going into his body without hitting something vital like his heart probably wouldn't stop him. With someone on drugs they probably wouldn't even feel it. They might die in a few hours from internal injuries, they might even live for a few days, or they might even survive.

"But if they're coming to do you harm and you shoot them somewhere nonvital, it isn't going to stop them fast enough. You might not get another chance. That means you will be dead and your death may be horrific."

Angela looked down as she thought it over. She looked up.

"Well, if you put a bullet in their brain, that would stop all brain function. That would stop them."

Her grandfather smiled. "Exactly. But the human skull is extremely thick. A twenty-two will penetrate that hard bone if the bullet strikes it at a right angle. But if it isn't straight on, it's liable to ricochet off the guy's skull. You don't have much time to stop him. If the bullet ricochets off, you may not get a second chance to put him down."

He held his first two fingers in front of her eyes, one in front of each eye. He put his thumb on the tip of her nose.

"This area, this small triangle from eye to eye, to the tip of the nose, is the most vulnerable part of the human skull. If you put a twenty-two into that triangle, the bullet will easily enter the skull. It's instant death.

"If a guy is coming at you and you put a bullet into that triangle it will destroy his motor function so fast that even if he's pointing a gun at you, he won't be able to pull the trigger.

"The base of the skull is another vulnerable spot. Assassins often shoot a person at the base of skull in the back. It destroys the medulla oblongata. It's lights out. But it's virtually impossible to shoot someone there if they're attacking you. The ear is another vulnerable spot, but neither of those spots do you much good if you are being attacked head-on.

"If some guy is attacking you, and your life is in imminent danger, then you must put a bullet in that triangle. If you do, they die and you live. Simple as that."

Angela looked over at the target he'd made. "So that's the reason for the triangle at the top of the rod."

"That's right. It's the size of the kill zone in an average man's head. I made it so that it would move because when someone is intending to abduct you or murder you they're moving as they come at you. If they see you have a gun they might even bob and weave. So, I made a moving target for practice.

"You'll know when you hit it because the bullet will make a sharp ping against the steel."

Angela let out a deep breath. "I don't know if I can hit it when it's moving."

"You have to," he said. "You're going to practice every day until you can hit that wobbling triangle with every shot."

"Every shot?" She shook her head. "I don't know, Grandpa, if I'll ever be able to do that."

"If it's ever necessary, your life will depend on you making that kill shot first time, every time."

Angela nodded her determination. "All right. I'll practice until I can hit it. Well, at least most of the time."

"Every time," he repeated with stern finality.

Angela looked at him for a long moment. "Every time," she said with resolve.

Angela was determined not to quit. After a lot of practice she could hit the triangle every once in a while—when it was still. But once he wound up the device and it started wobbling around, it seemed hopeless. She missed the triangle every time. It was frustrating trying to follow the target and fire off rounds.

He urged her to settle down and not to fire until she was on target, but it was always gone before she could pull off the shot. She didn't see how she was ever going to get good enough to hit it, much less good enough to hit it reliably.

It was several months and tens of thousands of rounds before she hit the wobbling triangle for the first time. When she heard the ping, it surprised her. She stood staring as the sound echoed back from the forest. She wasn't sure if it had been by chance or intent.

Over the months that followed, she would shoot every day they were at the cabin, usually for hours at a time. There was little hiking or fishing, which she regretted, but the shooting had become important to her. It was a challenge, but also fed an inner yearning to do better. The effort of concentrating so hard often left her soaked in sweat at the end of a session.

One autumn night, as her grandfather was taking a shower, Gabriella sat on the edge of the fold-out bed as Angela snuggled under the covers. The fire in the woodstove was low, and the woodsmoke smelled good.

"Can I ask you a serious question, Grandma?"

"Of course. You know you can always talk to me."

Angela turned her head, listening to the shower run through the closed bathroom door. She turned back.

"Why is he doing this? This isn't just teaching me to shoot a gun. This is something different, I can feel it. There's something serious about this, but I don't know what it is."

Her grandmother looked off in thought for a time.

"We think that maybe you're different, Angela."

Angela's brows drew together. "Different?"

"Yes, *piccolo*." "*Piccolo*" meant "little one" in Italian. It was a term of endearment her grandmother used on occasion.

"I don't understand."

She finally looked down at Angela. "We have long suspected that you're different—special. You've shown it in a thousand little ways that we can't really put our finger on or explain.

"But then, when you did what you did to that girl who hit you, we knew. It may seem like you simply defended yourself, and you did, but there was more to it. You're not like other girls, other people, Angela."

"I know. I don't know how to explain it either, but I know I'm different. Sometimes it makes me afraid. Sometimes it makes me glad. I don't know what it is, but I know I'm different than other people."

"We think you are. We think you're meant for something."

"Something? Like what?"

Her grandmother shrugged. "We don't know. But we think you have some purpose to your life. When you put that girl down the way you did, we knew. It was the first sign we could point to. You're different. Your life will be different. We decided that your grandpa should start teaching you what you need to know for that life, for that person you will become."

Angela made a face. "I don't understand."

Her grandmother smiled a sad smile. "I know, child. But one day you will."

"What person will I become?"

"It's too early to say for sure. Have patience and keep being yourself and you will grow into that person you're meant to be. Now, get some sleep."

THIRTEEN

Then, one day the following spring and over a half a year after starting, after thousands upon thousands of rounds fired, as she stood there in the woods, her gun in hand, her gun feeling like an extension of herself, Angela blinked as an unexpected feeling washed through her.

It was as if a doorway had opened in the darkness and she suddenly saw everything beyond in a new light.

She had come upon those mental doorways before. With each one she passed through she would discover that she understood the world in a new light. Things became clear to her. She had always thought of those doorways as simply part of growing up and learning new things, making connections she'd never made before, and maybe they were.

But this doorway was distinctly different, and decidedly more significant.

In that moment of insight, Angela was no longer aiming at a steel target. That was what she had been doing up until then—trying to hit a steel triangle as it wobbled and zigzagged.

Throughout her practice, she had often thought of the steel triangle as the bad guy. But it was always her conscious mind imposing that thought on the target. It was her imagining it.

This was similar, but at the same time somehow profoundly different.

This was a visceral desire to kill those bad guys.

It gave her goose bumps.

She thought about Frankie and the kind of men who abducted and murdered women. In that moment of clarity, it was no longer a target. It had become a man coming for her, coming to hurt her, coming to end her life.

A kind of primal fear welled up from inside. She could taste it in her mouth. This had morphed into life and death.

This wasn't about shooting at a target anymore. This was a savage coming for her. This was about killing him before he could kill her.

Some mysterious piece of a cosmic puzzle that had been looking for where it fit in her life finally snapped into place.

She no longer felt frantic about trying to follow the triangle. Instead, she felt a sense of calm come over her.

The random movements of the steel triangle didn't exist independently. They couldn't. A killer all alone didn't bob and weave. He became connected to his victim. She became a part of that connection.

She no longer chased the target. Instead, it pulled her through that connection.

It was no longer a metal triangle. It was the area between two eyes and the tip of the nose of a killer coming for her. It was the portal into his skull, a gateway for her bullet, the pathway to her salvation.

Her one chance to live.

That understanding gave her a sense of purpose and inner calm. At the same time, in that calm she held on to a core of rage at a killer, letting that fire burn deep within her.

It all came together in a heady rush. It gave her goose bumps and took her breath. The frustration was gone. It felt as if she had passed through a hidden doorway into a new kind of connection with the target.

She was able to lock on to the target so solidly, so reliably, that no matter which way it jumped, the gun went with it. The bullet found it.

She heard the salvation of *ping, ping, ping* with every round fired.

Angela couldn't hear the birds anymore, the wind in the trees. The steel triangle wasn't wobbling every which way anymore. It was instead moving with her in slow motion.

Time seemed somehow suspended.

Time was hers.

The target was hers.

Whether she was shooting fast or slow, every round pinged the steel triangle. Sometimes she fired with a slow rhythm, sometimes she fired as fast as she could pull the trigger.

Each time the gun emptied and she dropped the magazine, she slammed home a new one, racked the slide, and in a flash she was back on target. When that magazine was empty, the next one went in and was emptied in a heartbeat. From months of practice she could reload with a new magazine so fast that there was hardly any pause between one magazine and the next one feeding bullets into the chamber as she fired.

What mattered, what was important, was the connection she felt with that small area where the bullet had to go. The bullet went where she sent it, where she saw it going before she even pulled the trigger.

It all seemed to fall into place so unexpectedly, so profoundly, that she had to stop for a moment as tears rolled down her cheeks. It was almost like magic.

She felt that she had just mastered—not a skill, but her life in a new way. She had a new kind of vision. A new sense. All her senses keyed in to this singular purpose.

Angela knew it was somehow connected to what her grandmother had told her about her being different. She didn't know how, but she knew there was a connection.

This is what her grandparents had seen in her. She now saw it in herself.

When she realized that she had used up all the ammunition for the day, she stood in the ringing silence for a long moment. She finally looked up at her grandfather. He was standing back, watching her with a strange, penetrating look.

He finally smiled and nodded. In that moment, in that look, they shared a silent understanding.

"This is the next step"—her grandfather snapped his fingers as fast as he could—"to fire this fast and hit that moving target every time."

Angela had been immensely pleased with what she had just achieved. Now she was stunned at the impossible.

"Grandpa, I can't think that fast."

He smiled knowingly. "That's the part you need to learn next— to do it without thinking. Thinking slows you down. Once you learn not to think, your subconscious will take over and do it. Like riding a bicycle without thinking of how to balance. Your subconscious can fire and hit the target as fast as I can snap my fingers."

Angela nodded. "If you say I can do it, then I will."

He put a hand on her shoulder. "How about some dinner."

She pulled off her hearing protectors and looked around. It was nearly dark. She had been able to hit the target every time even as the light had faded and was almost gone.

The cabin smelled wonderful. Her grandmother was in the kitchen, and Angela saw that she was making Angela's favorite meal: Italian bread torn up into chunks, soaked in scrambled eggs with basil, oregano, and some other spices, then fried up in olive oil in an iron skillet.

"How did she do?" her grandmother asked as she turned the bread and eggs with a spatula as they cooked.

"She's got it."

"Like you?" Gabriella asked without looking up as she stirred the sizzling dinner.

"Like me," he said at last.

Angela didn't know for sure what she had, but her grandmother lifted an eyebrow at the skillet.

Angela sat at the table spread with a white tablecloth with red strawberries on it, her head still spinning from what she had done. It didn't seem real, and at the same time it felt more real than anything else in the world. It felt as if a whole new world had opened up for her.

As her grandmother leaned in and put a heaping pile of bread soaked in eggs on Angela's plate, she looked up at Vito.

"In that case," her grandmother said, "then maybe it's time you showed her the basement?"

What? The basement?

The basement door was always locked. She had never, ever, been down in the basement. It wasn't even talked about. She had absolutely no idea what was down there. She had always been curious about it, but now she felt an unexpected sense of apprehension about going down there.

Angela looked between her grandmother and grandfather as they shared a long look. In that moment, they looked like, to them, they were the only two people in the world.

Her grandfather nodded slightly. "I think you're right."

Angela was still looking between them. "What's in the basement?"

FOURTEEN

Not long after that eventful day when a new doorway had opened to her, another closed.

Her grandparents were found by the side of the road, both shot in the back of the head with a .22-caliber bullet.

It was a sensational murder mystery on the local news for a few days and then it was gradually forgotten. Angela didn't know if the police were looking hard for the killer, but it didn't really matter because even if they were, they never found him and no one was charged with the murders. What mattered, though, was that her grandparents were dead and even if they found their killer that wouldn't bring them back.

Angela was beyond devastated. She stayed in her room and cried for two days. She felt totally lost. She didn't want to eat, or for that matter, to live any longer. She wished she had been there with her grandparents and that the killer had put a bullet in the back of her head first so she wouldn't have to endure the agony of losing them.

Sally took it mostly in stride.

She spent the morning of the funeral smoking meth. She drove them to the funeral in her ratty old Pontiac GTO, a car that had been a fixture in the dilapidated trailer park since long before Angela had been born. Angela sat in the backseat crying. The sky cried, too, with a steady drizzle.

Standing beside the open graves, rain plastering her hair to her head, Angela felt numb. Nothing seemed to matter anymore. All she wanted to do was to hold them and be with them. She didn't think she could go on without them.

In their will, they left money to pay for their funeral and burial. They left their home in town to Sally. But they left the cabin to Angela, along with an endowment she would receive when she turned twenty-one.

Sally was angry about the cabin and the endowment going to Angela. She ranted and raved that her parents hadn't left everything to her. She was their only daughter, after all. She resented her parents for it. She hated them for it. She was consoled by the fact that the house in town was worth more than both the cabin and the endowment together.

It didn't take her long to sell the house. It would have been better to move into the house and sell the trailer, but Sally didn't see it that way. Selling the house got her more money.

Angela wished she could escape to the cabin, but it was way too far to walk there, and she wasn't yet old enough to drive.

Once Sally had what she thought of as a fortune from selling the house in town, she started spending it on drugs. Angela knew that her grandparents would not have wanted their house to be turned into money for drugs. But she also knew that it was more important to them that the cabin go to Angela. In a way, Angela thought that giving the house to Sally, even though it would go for drugs, was a way to distract her from what they thought was more important—that Angela have the cabin.

On many a night, the trailer became party central. Friends, neighbors, and strangers smoked, got drunk, and were rowdy late into the early-morning hours. Some did lines of cocaine on a mirror on the coffee table in the living room. Most of them smoked, either cigarettes, meth, or pot. A few shot up heroin. Even when there wasn't a party, there were frequently tweakers hanging around to share the meth her mother scored, or to supply it.

When Angela left her bedroom in the morning to go to school, there were often people asleep on the couch, in the chairs, or in their own vomit on the floor. She knew most of them, but it wasn't uncommon for strangers to be there in the house when she left for school.

After Frankie had vanished, Sally had gradually become more and more involved with a new guy, Boska. Boska was some kind of shadowy supplier to dealers, so he had no problem satisfying Sally's needs. More often than not he spent the night.

Boska was a big man, thick-boned and barrel-chested. He rode a Harley and had a scraggly beard. He hung out with other bikers and sometimes brought them to parties at the trailer. They were the scariest guys Angela had ever seen, but it was Boska who made the hair on the back of her neck stand up.

Angela would shut herself in her bedroom when there was anyone other than her mother in the trailer. One night, Boska broke the door so it wouldn't latch anymore. Then, when her mother was sleeping, he would come in, sit on her bed, and ask her stupid questions, like how she was doing in school or what she wanted to be when she grew up. All the while he leered at her. Boska scared her to down into her marrow.

With her now-ample supply of drugs, Sally was out of it much of the time. She would be up for days, strung out on meth; then she'd smoke pot for hours to bring herself down so she could sleep. Those periods were less like sleep and more like a coma.

It was during those periods of her mother's comatose sleep that Boska came into her room and the serious abuse began.

Sally's continual quest for oblivion had earned her badges of scabs. The teeth she had left were rotten. Her eyes were bloodshot and ringed with red. Her once-beautiful face looked like badly crinkled paper plastered down over a skull.

Even though Sally was only in her midthirties, she was used up.

Angela, on the other hand, was maturing into a leggy young woman blossoming with the femininity her mother had lost.

Sally was an easy lay, but Boska preferred Angela. Each encounter was accompanied by threats of what would happen to her if she didn't keep her mouth shut. Angela was so afraid of Boska that she often lost her voice when he asked her questions. When he smacked her, she could only get out the words she knew he wanted to hear.

In order to stay alive, she submitted to him.

With no one to protect her and no way to escape her new hell, Angela learned to survive those encounters in her bedroom by letting her mind go to another place. What Boska was doing to her dimmed into insignificance. She wasn't there. She was gone.

While Boska was on top of her and her mind was in another place, she was nearly as comatose as her mother.

When Boska was finished, the threats at knifepoint, and on occasion gunpoint, brought her back from that distant peace and scared her witless. She knew that if she angered him, he wouldn't hesitate to slash her face, or cut her throat. He promised her a face full of acid if she ever crossed him.

One time when she did say something snotty to him as he was zipping up his pants, he said that if she ever smart-mouthed him again he would give her as a gift to the motorcycle gang that sold drugs for him. She could see in his eyes that he was not making idle threats.

After he left her room and then went to sleep with Sally, Angela would tremble for hours, unable to go to sleep, knowing that there was nothing she could do about it, no one who could help her, and that there would be more to come.

Her fear of Boska kept her from telling anyone at school about the things he did to her. She also knew that Mr. Ericsson wouldn't be inclined to believe her, and would be even less inclined to help her. She was quite sure that Mr. Ericsson would be pleased to hear that she was getting what was coming to her.

She knew the police wouldn't help her—Boska had been arrested dozens of times for all kinds of things and he always got out. He was released for time served, the charges were dropped, the charges were reduced to a misdemeanor, or he received probation. He never went to jail for the things he did. He always got away with it. She knew that if she went to the police, Boska would get out, and then when he had her alone she would pay the price for snitching. As far as Angela was concerned, the law was meaningless.

It all left Angela feeling totally alone and helpless. Frankie had been once, but Boska seemed perpetually aroused. He was an ever-present threat.

At one point she began to spend nights sleeping in hidden places in alleys, or in bushes behind other trailers, shivering in the cold but glad to be alone. One day when she came home from school, Boska grabbed her hair in his big fist and warned her that if she didn't stay at home at night he'd come looking for her, and she sure as hell wouldn't like what would happen to her when he found her.

After that, Angela stayed at home where he would have ready access to her. Her mother wouldn't help her, the school wouldn't help her, and the law wouldn't protect her. There was nothing she could do but endure it while her mind drifted away to distant places.

She knew that the worst thing in the world would be to get pregnant, so she started on the pill. She got a supply each month from a women's health clinic in a run-down rented storefront. She had just turned fifteen, and they thought she was too young to have sex, so at first they turned her down. She asked them if they thought she was old enough to have a baby. They relented and let her start on the pill.

Because they knew that some girls had difficult, and even dangerous, situations at home, it was their policy not to call the parents if the underage girl asked them not to. Angela asked them not to.

She seriously doubted that her mother would care if she thought Angela was screwing boys, but Angela knew she would be blamed if she told her mother the truth. She knew it was all too likely to blow up into a screaming fit. Sally would say that Angela had asked for it, and then, when her mother was out of it, Boska would do his worst to her for saying something.

Angela wasn't sure she cared if he killed her, as long as it was quick, but she feared his threat of acid in her face.

She was relieved when the women's clinic agreed to provide her with the pill and confidentiality.

After the money from the sale of her grandparents' house ran out, Angela often became the unspoken source of payment for her mother's drugs, so she knew that her mother would have a vested interest in looking the other way. If the men got what they wanted, Sally got what she wanted. That was all there was to it. Oftentimes Boska was the gatekeeper for which men could have her in exchange for what Sally received. He told Angela that he was protecting her from the guys who had diseases.

More days than she could count, Angela walked to school spitting out the taste of semen.

As time went on, she slipped into a deep depression. She felt like a trapped animal. There was no escape from the situation and no hope.

She did as she was told by men she dared not cross. She did as her mother told her as well, shopping for groceries and cooking, taking care of chores around the house, and in general doing her mother's bidding.

She was the girl in the moon passing silently through the gloomy trailer, at the beck and call of psychopaths.

She knew that the only way the abuse would stop was if she were able to get totally out of her mother's place. If she had a car, she could drive to her grandparents' cabin—her cabin—and live there. But it would be nearly a year before she was old enough to get a driver's license. The fact that she had no money to get a car even then only left her feeling even more hopeless.

She lost all interest in everything. She didn't care about anything or anyone. She only did the minimum to pass her classes at school. Every person she knew used her for one thing or another. She wanted everyone to leave her alone.

At fifteen and a half, Angela started dyeing her hair different colors. In a way, it was the only thing she had any say over. She got piercings. With change she collected from the floor and couches in the trailer she could buy clothes from the thrift store and put them together in a way that in addition to her dyed hair and piercings gave her a forbidding look.

The kids at school were already leery of her. She was the girl who had messed up the face of a much older, popular girl. Now she, too, was older, and bigger. She didn't take crap from anyone. On top of that, they thought she was a freak, and, because of the standoffish way she acted, possibly crazy. She had no friends. All of that kept them all far away from her.

As far as Angela was concerned, mission accomplished.

She knew that no one was going to protect her. No one was going to help her. She was going to have to protect herself.

In the back of her mind, she knew she had to get away from her mother and the trailer park. To do that, she would need to get older. When she turned sixteen she could get her driver's license. But she would need a car. Realizing that a car was ultimately her only real salvation, getting money to buy a car became her central goal.

She was able to get a job with a housecleaning service, working a few hours every day after school without being missed much at home. She saved every dime she earned toward a car. Once she could drive and had a car, she would be able to get away.

Because she worked hard at the cleaning service, a manager at a clothing store offered her a job on weekends stocking shelves. Her savings continued to build. She gladly accepted tips she received from some of the people she cleaned house for.

The only money she wouldn't take was the cash some of the men who abused her would push at her. It was their way of taking the crime out of what they did. If she was selling herself, then they weren't really raping her. She always refused the money they offered. If they left money in her room, she put it out on the coffee table. She was not about to absolve them of their crime.

Her school had a driver education course, and when she turned sixteen she got her license through the course. As soon as she had her license, she went to a car dealership she had visited a few times previously. With the money she saved, she bought the car she had been eyeing and could afford. It was a well-used silver Honda, but to her eyes it was the most beautiful car in the world, not because she cared about the car itself, but because it meant escape from the abuse.

The day she picked up the car, she drove to the trailer park and packed up her things while her mother was sleeping off a party. There wasn't much she really cared about, and she didn't want Boska to come home and catch her, so as soon as she had the basics together in a couple of black plastic bags, she left for the cabin.

Before she left, she wrote a brief note, telling her mother that she was moving away and would not be back.

Driving up to the cabin and seeing those two mountains, one to either side, felt like the warm embrace of her grandparents. She knew she was at last safe. The first thing she did when she got inside the cabin was to load the Walther P22. If they figured out where she was and Boska came to haul her back to the trailer, she intended to blow his brains out.

Angela didn't worry about her mother coming to bring her home. She was a lot stronger than her mother, and besides, her mother was more likely to smoke some crack as her reaction to the situation than come get her. Drugs were her answer to everything.

Once she put her things away in the bedroom, Angela sat down on the bed and cried with grief that her grandparents weren't there, and cried with joy that she had finally escaped the abuse at home.

As it happened, there was no need to worry about Boska. He was unexpectedly killed in a motorcycle accident. He ran a stop sign running from the police and was broadsided by a woman in a minivan.

Karma was a bitch.

FIFTEEN

The next time one of those unexpected mental doorways opened was several years after she had moved to the cabin. She had made sure to keep her grades high enough that she was able to graduate high school. Being out of high school was a huge relief. Graduation was a joyful event, because it meant formally leaving the misery of childhood behind.

Angela had always thought of herself as an adult trapped in a child's body. At long last, her body and mind had reached parity. She was truly an adult, even if not legally until she was twenty-one.

Being done with school and on her own, she was finally able to work full-time. One of the houses she cleaned was for a couple who were both lawyers. Mr. and Mrs. Bollard appreciated the job Angela did at their house, so they asked her to clean their office as well. Since they were pleasant and treated her fairly, Angela was happy to do it.

One day, as she was emptying wastebaskets, she overheard Mr. Bollard telling his wife that he needed to get some papers across town. They were debating how they would do it, since it was urgent they get some signatures but neither could leave the office right then.

Angela straightened. "I'll do it."

The both looked up at her. "What?" Mr. Bollard asked.

"I'd be happy to do it." When they stared at her for a moment, she added, "I have a courier service," she lied. "I can deliver the papers for you."

They shared a "why not?" look with each other. Mrs. Bollard slid the papers into an envelope, wrote a name and address on it, and handed the manila envelope to Angela.

"Ask him to sign the papers. When he's done, please bring them right back here."

"No problem," Angela said.

After that, they gradually came to depend on her to deliver things like court documents on a regular basis. One day when she brought a package to them, Mr. and Mrs. Bollard asked her to sit down.

"You do know that you're charging half the going rate other courier services charge, don't you?"

Angela shrugged. "It's enough to cover my costs and make me some money. I appreciate the work and I'm satisfied with what I make doing it. It's an attractive enough price that you keep using me instead of anyone else. You're happy, I'm happy."

Mr. Bollard leaned back in his leather chair and tapped a finger on the armrest as he studied her face.

"You're more than you appear."

Angela frowned. "Excuse me?"

He shrugged. "You look . . . well, you don't exactly look like the determined and meticulous young woman you really are."

Angela frowned. "Are you unhappy with something I do?"

"No," he said. "No, not at all. It's just that we've learned we can depend on you. You don't screw up. You get contracts and papers where they need to go, when they need to be there."

"So, what's the problem?"

"You don't have a business license, do you?"

"Well . . ."

"Insurance?"

"I have insurance."

"I don't mean on your car. I mean, do you have a business license and business insurance? Are you insured and bonded? Did you post a bond to have a courier service?"

Angela let out a sigh. She didn't have any of that. She imagined that the money she made with her new courier service was about to evaporate.

"No," she admitted.

He appraised her for a time, considering something.

"You do a good job, Angela, taking care of our house, and the office, as well as the other places you clean, and you always get documents where they need to go on time, and get them back to us on time. But you need to have a business license if you are going to do this kind of service for us, and you need to be bonded to have a courier service. We're lawyers. We can't use you without everything being legal."

Angela could feel herself sinking into her chair. "I see."

"I'll tell you what. My wife and I can handle all the legal matters. You'll need to have an official business name and the money for the bond, but we can take care of the paperwork and filings for you so that you don't get into legal trouble."

Angela sat up straighter. "You would do that for me?"

"Sure," Mrs. Bollard said. "You've helped us out of spots enough times."

"What would the bond cost?"

Mr. Bollard smiled. "We'll make you a deal. We'll handle all that and in return, you just deliver documents for us for two months for no charge. That should cover the costs. After you're legal, then we can not only use you, we can recommend your courier service to other lawyers and people we know."

"That would be great. Thank you both."

With that deal, Angela moved up from maid service to courier service. Once she had a business name that played on the meaning of her name, and her license, she bought herself a plastic, magnetic sign for the door of her car. ANGELA'S MESSENGER SERVICE. GIVE YOUR PACKAGE WINGS.

Some of the clients the Bollards dealt with were people in a variety of legal trouble. Some were criminals. The people in legal trouble started to ask her to deliver documents for them as well. Besides the lawyers she handled, she became known among people in legal trouble as a trustworthy courier service. They liked that she made a point of her service being confidential.

She never asked questions and she never talked about her other clients. She discovered that the more confidential she kept everything, the more business she got. Not only from people in legal trouble, but even from places like the hospital, where the law required patient privacy.

It was the end of one hot summer day, during one of those deliveries, that the new mental doorway opened for her.

Mrs. Bollard had given her a package of legal documents to deliver to a seedy little bar at the edge of town, called Barry's Place. The plain block building was rather dark inside. There were people at small tables and a few at the bar. A rotating ball in the ceiling projected sparkling light over everything.

When she spotted a man behind the bar, she crossed the room, weaving her way among the patrons. He watched her out of the corner of an eye as he dried glasses.

She leaned in over the bar to be heard over the rock music.

"I'm looking for Barry."

"I'm Barry. I own the place. What can I do for you?"

Angela handed him the envelope with legal papers.

He looked at the return address of the law firm. "Ah, good. Thanks."

Angela turned to leave, but he told her to hold on. She turned back.

He smiled, but not in a slimy way. Angela knew slimy smiles filled with meaning when she saw them. Barry's smile was pleasant and respectful.

"I don't mean this in a sleazy way," he said, "but you have some damn fine legs."

Angela was wearing low-rise shorts. She knew he had been look-ing at her legs when she walked across the room.

"Thanks," she said cautiously, fearing a proposal.

"Have you ever thought about tending bar?"

That wasn't what she had been expecting. Angela made a bit of a face. "No. I don't know anything about being a bartender."

"It's not all that hard." He gestured around. "This isn't a fancy place. I can teach you all you need to know. Besides, you have the most important part down pat already."

She frowned. "The most important part?"

He gestured with the hand holding the rag. "Those legs of yours. I mean . . . damn. Legs like that bring in business and they could earn you more in tips than you could ever make delivering packages."

"Really?"

"How old are you?"

"Twenty."

Barry sighed. "Crap. You need to be twenty-one. How long until you're legal age?"

"Five months."

He made a face as he considered the obstacle. "You come back here on your birthday and I can give you some part-time work. If it doesn't make you at least double what you make with your courier service, I'll make up the difference, but I guarantee you, it's not going to cost me a dime."

Angela thought about it briefly. She would certainly like to make more money. If she worked at the bar at night, she could get a better car and still have her courier service. She didn't want to give that up.

"My name is Angela. I'll see you on my birthday."

Barry flipped the towel back to lay it across his shoulder. "Cut those shorts shorter when you come back, Angela, and you'll make triple what you make now."

Angela smiled. She always thought her legs were too long. If they could make her more money without having to wrap them around some scumbag, she thought that she might as well do it.

"Deal. I'll be back just as soon as I'm twenty-one."

"See you then." Barry smiled, but in a friendly, nonthreatening way, before picking up a few empty boxes and heading into the back room.

When Angela turned around, she met the gaze of a man sitting close by at the bar.

He was a bull of a man, at least six-four and 250 pounds. His sandy-blond hair had been pulled back in a ponytail. His hairline was just starting to recede, the way it sometimes did prematurely with men in their late twenties. He had on a sleeveless denim jacket that showed off not only his tangle of tattoos that colored both arms, but his muscles.

All the tattoos were grim. There were skulls, snakes, reptilian monsters, and graves with ravens overhead. A snake tattoo coiled up from beneath his denim jacket to bare its fangs on the side of his neck.

He had a diamond, or maybe a fake diamond, in each earlobe. Although, just his presence told her they had to be real. He was the kind of man who would not appreciate having it pointed out that he was wearing fake diamonds.

For the first time in her life and with absolute certainty, she realized that she was staring into the eyes of a killer.

In that instant, she was sucked through that doorway and her life changed irrevocably.

Besides comprehension, fear also flashed through every fiber of her being. She was frozen in place. Sweat felt like ice on her skin.

In that instant, gazing into the man's eyes, she had a vision. It was something that had never happened to her before. She saw this man straddling a girl with short red hair. They were in one of the old, abandoned factories with broken windows. Angela knew that place. It was just getting dark in that vision. He pulled off the girl's jeans and panties so she was naked from the waist down. She was begging him not to hurt her. She promised not to tell anyone if he would let her go.

She trembled in terror. Angela knew the feeling well.

169

In her mind, she could see how excited he was becoming by her begging. It thrilled him. He got off on her fear. He ripped open her blouse. She screamed and begged. He suddenly stabbed her in each breast. It was a quick, one-two jab. It wasn't deep enough to mortally wound her. He didn't want her to die yet. He wanted to terrify her.

Her screams excited him even more than her begging.

He started stabbing her, making her scream all the louder. He held the knife in both hands, lifting it over his head and then driving it down over and over as fast as he could. He continued stabbing her in a frenzied fury even after she had gone still.

As she was gurgling her last few breaths, eyes wide open, he undid his pants and penetrated her. He didn't orgasm until she was long dead. He liked that. It gave him a sense of triumph to fuck her into death.

When he finally pulled out of her, he went wild, slashing her face repeatedly until it was unrecognizable. He found a nearby piece of iron and used it to bash out her teeth. When he was done he wrapped her in a piece of burlap that had been lying in a pile of rubble in a corner. He then carried her outside to an old cistern with a concrete lid. He was muscular and had no trouble lifting it aside. He threw the girl with red hair down into the lonely darkness and then replaced the lid.

He doubted that anyone would ever find her before she rotted away to nothing, but if they did, with her skull crushed and without her teeth he figured they would have a hard time of identifying her. He would later throw the pieces of teeth into the woods.

"Well, well," the man sitting there at the bar said. The man whose visions she'd just had. "Aren't you just the prettiest little thing."

Angela stood paralyzed by what she had just seen in her mind's eye, what she had seen this man do to an innocent girl with red hair.

The whole thing had all come to her in a millisecond. It was as if she were recalling a vivid memory.

His memory.

She could even feel the shiver of his sexual gratification as he'd come in the freshly dead corpse.

She didn't know how she knew the whole thing was true, but she knew it just as surely as if she had been there when he had done it.

"What's the matter," he asked. "Pussy got your tongue?"

"Fuck off," she said to the guy, her gaze still locked on his. She knew saying that would bait the guy. She wanted more than anything to bait him. "Asshole," she added for good measure.

Angela had no idea how she could have recognized a killer for what he was. She didn't have any idea how she could have had visions of him murdering the girl with short red hair.

Angela knew in that moment that there was no going back through that doorway.

Not ever.

She knew that her life would never be the same.

The only explanation that made any sense to her was that she truly was a freak of nature. Her mother's constant drug use, along with that of the tweaker who had fathered her, had left Angela to grow and develop in a toxic broth of what was flowing around in her mother's veins.

Angela had been born broken.

The only thing she knew for sure was that she had, for the first time ever in her life, come eye-to-eye with a killer.

It terrified her.

But more than that, it excited her.

SIXTEEN

For the next few days, Angela couldn't get the guy out of her head. She couldn't keep the horrifying details of what he had done out of her nightmares.

She knew with every fiber of her being that it was true.

She did her best to put him out of her mind as she went about delivering and picking up packages. All the while she kept thinking about how much more money she could make tending bar. There weren't many good paying jobs in Milford Falls. She decided that she would get some books on bartending so she would be prepared when she turned twenty-one.

But in the background there was always the memory of the man in the bar and the haunting images she had seen in his eyes.

As Angela went about her deliveries, she searched the people she saw, looking for him.

She didn't know how she knew it, but she knew for certain that she had not seen the last of him.

That thought made her queasy with fear.

At the same time, it excited her in a way that nothing had ever excited her before.

She dreaded the thought of ever seeing that monster again.

And yet, she felt intoxicated with the thought of encountering him.

She finally decided that she was going to make herself crazy thinking about him, so she did her best to put him from her mind. She thought instead about the bartending job Barry had offered her. None of the people there were anywhere near as scary as the people who had hung around her mother's trailer, so she was sure she could do it. When she finished all her deliveries for the day, she stopped at a bookstore and picked up two books on bartending.

She deliberately selected the simpler books, with basic drinks and lessons on the trade rather than how to make fancier drinks. Barry's bar was decidedly not fancy.

On the highway before reaching the road that turned off to the north and eventually went past her cabin, she saw a blue muscle car parked off the side of the road. She remembered seeing a car like that in the parking lot of the bar.

Angela did not believe in coincidences.

It would be a long walk to her place from where the car was parked, but on the other hand the distance served to diminish suspicion.

When she reached the drive up to her cabin, she scanned the bushes and trees beyond the meadow as she lowered the cable. When she put the cable back up after entering, she looked around but didn't see any footprints in the dirt. Of course, someone could have walked in from a different direction to avoid leaving footprints.

When she parked and then went into the dark cabin, she knew he was in there, somewhere.

She could feel him.

Her gaze searched every dark corner, but she saw no sign. Heart hammering, she unlocked the basement door, then returned to the living room and turned on a single light.

After turning on the light in the living room, she deliberately calmed her thoughts. Once she set aside the mental distractions, she began to feel his presence radiating from her bedroom. She found that as she focused on him, she could feel him crouching there in the bedroom, waiting for her.

She did not intend to play into his plan of walking into her bedroom so he could jump her. Instead, she flopped down in the chair at the dark end of the living room. She yawned and made some noise pulling the footstool closer and plunking her feet down on it.

Then she waited.

He was waiting too.

For nearly an hour he waited, until his lust for her got the better of him. She could feel his hatred of her, of her raw femininity, and the way it taunted him. She could feel his rage building to the point where he had to do something about it.

He stepped quietly into the living room.

It wasn't a big house. The hall from the bedroom entered right into the center of the living room, so he wasn't far away from her. In his mind he measured the few strides and big lunge it would take for him to be on her. Because of the isolation of her cabin and with him being so much bigger than her, he felt safe and in complete control. He knew he had her where he wanted her. His mind was already filled with visions of the things he intended to do to her.

Those thoughts petrified her.

When he took another step into the living room, he saw her arm resting on her leg. He froze when he saw the gun in her hand that she had leveled at him.

When he took a closer look and saw that it was a .22, he grinned and put his hands half up in fake surrender.

"Whoa there pretty lady. You aren't going to blast away at me with that little peashooter, are you?"

His grin reflected the sinister thoughts filling his head but revealed absolutely no fear.

"Could be," she said. "We'll have to see how it goes."

He lowered his hands. "I don't think a pretty little thing like you would have the nerve to shoot someone, especially someone who only means to get to know you a little better."

She calmly stared, gun still pointed at him.

"Besides, even if you did have the nerve to shoot at me," he said as he gestured at her gun, "and even if you could manage to hit me, that little thing wouldn't do me much harm before I got over there and took it away from you."

"It would do enough harm if I shot you between the eyes."

Her gun barrel followed every slight movement he made.

He glared for a moment before his grin returned. "I don't think you're that good of a shot, especially in the dark. How about I take that thing away from you and shove it up your pretty little ass?"

"How about I shoot those diamonds out of your earlobes just to show you how good a shot I am." She cocked her head. "You know, most guys with an earring only wear one."

He reflexively touched one of his ears before letting his hand drop. "Yeah? Well I'm twice what most guys are." His expression turned murderous.

He suddenly started to take a lunging stride toward her.

Angela had the gun up in both hands and pulled off two shots before he'd finished the stride. She could see the splash of blood as his earlobes, along with their diamonds, were blown off.

He lurched to a stop as he put his hands to each ear.

"Goddamn it!" he screamed. "You motherfucking little cunt!"

His right foot started forward. Angela fired before his left foot could leave the ground. The round blew apart his left kneecap like a clay pigeon. He crumpled to the ground, clamping both hands over his knee as he screamed and rolled and cursed.

Angela, still sitting in the chair, her feet propped up on the footrest, hadn't moved yet, except to fire her gun those three times.

"You goddamn little bitch! I'm going to break your arms off and stuff them up your fucking cunt!"

He managed to pull himself up, hopping on his good leg to get his balance. He yanked a knife from a sheath at his belt under his vest. When he lifted it over his head, Angela put a round through the joint in his wrist, shattering the bones. The round left a splatter of blood as it went through the wall behind him. The knife clattered across the floor.

"Fuck!" he screamed. "What the fuck's wrong with you! You got no fucking right to do this!"

Angela didn't answer. She got up and walked around him toward the hallway between the kitchen and bedroom. He was cradling his injured wrist.

On her way past, without a word, she fired a round into his other knee, shattering the patella. He fell over on his side, clamping his good hand over the freshly wounded knee.

Angela opened the basement door. She gestured with her gun. "This way. Move."

"Move? Are you fucking crazy? I can't stand up!"

"I didn't tell you to stand up, I told you to move. You've still got a good hand. Use it to drag yourself in here."

She saw him look toward the knife on the floor. She walked around him, just out of reach of his good hand, her gun pointed at his face the whole time, and picked up his knife.

"I think by now you ought to know that I don't miss. Now drag your sorry ass over to that doorway. I'm not going to tell you again."

Panting as the pain was beginning to bear down on him in earnest, he finally did as she ordered and propped himself up on one elbow and his good hand to drag himself across the wooden floor. He grunted with each pull, leaving a smeared blood trail behind. He reminded her of a wounded seal.

He stopped, propped up on his one good arm, halfway into the dark doorway.

"Keep going," she said.

He looked back over his shoulder. "I can't see! It's pitch black! How the fuck do you expect—"

Angela slammed her boot solidly into his back between his shoulder blades. It was enough to topple him in and down the stairway. She could hear him thudding and thumping as he tumbled down the steep steps. When he finally smacked onto the floor at the bottom and came to a stop, he let out a groan.

Angela flipped on the lights and saw him crumpled at the bottom of the steps, only partially conscious. Without wasting a moment while he was dazed and out of it, she raced down the steps and, before he regained his senses, pulled a law-enforcement-grade zip-tie restraint from a box of them she had on a shelf. She twisted one arm behind his back and pressed her knee on it to hold him down while she collected his other arm and twisted it back behind him. She used the zip-tie cuffs to secure his wrists.

He howled in pain when she grabbed his bleeding wrist and yanked the plastic strap tight. For good measure, she put another pair of the zip-tie cuffs on his ankles. With his blown-out knees, she didn't think he would be able to do anything, even without the handcuffs—and she could always put a bullet in his brain if things got out of hand—but she wanted to make sure he was immobile for what she had planned. She also wanted him to feel completely helpless, the way the red-haired girl had felt.

It was frightening to be in the presence of such a brutal killer. But at the same time she felt more alive than any time since she had been with her grandparents.

Angela rolled him over and waited patiently until he regained consciousness. Once he did, he turned his head, looking around. He twisted and flopped around trying to get free, looking like a fish out of water. He was strong, but not strong enough, especially with his injuries.

"Goddamn you!" he screamed at her. "Why the fuck are you doing this?"

Angela lifted an eyebrow at him. "You broke into my house and hid in my bedroom waiting to jump me while all kinds of nasty thoughts danced through your head, and you ask why I'm doing this?"

"I didn't mean anything by it! I wasn't going to hurt you!"

"Yeah, right."

"You can't just shoot someone like this! It's illegal! I'm going to call the police on you. I'm going to sue your fucking ass for everything you've got!"

Ignoring his threats, Angela went to one knee beside him, the wrist of her gun hand resting over her other knee.

"I'm bursting with questions," she said. "I'd like you to give me answers."

"Fuck you!" he yelled. He was so angry he was drooling spittle. "I'm not telling you a fucking thing!"

"Really?"

Angela got up and went to a shelf, where she retrieved a handheld propane blowtorch and a flint igniter that had belonged to her grandfather. She opened the valve on the propane tank, put the steel cup of the igniter up by the tip of the blowtorch, and squeezed the spring steel handles to strike the flint. After the blowtorch lit, she adjusted the flame and then carried it over to her houseguest.

Angela again went to one knee beside him and plunked the blowtorch down beside him where he could see it.

"Like I said, I'm just full of questions."

He screamed and flopped trying to get away. "Fuck you! I'm not telling you anything!"

Angela picked up the torch. "Oh, I think you are."

"If you know what's good for you, you'll let me go!"

"Tell me about the girl with red hair."

He froze, his panicked eyes turning up at her. "What?"

"The girl with red hair. I want you to tell me everything you did to her."

"I don't know any girl with red hair!"

Angela swiped the flame across his face. His flesh blackened. He screamed and shook his head to get it away from the torch, so she put the tip of the flame to his upper arm. The fat beneath the flesh bubbled and the skin crackled. The whole room smelled like cooking meat. He panted and squealed.

It was exhilarating.

"Every detail," she repeated as she held the flame up before his eyes.

His gaze went between the hissing flame and her eyes. "I didn't mean anything by it. It was an accident. It was just rough sex, that's all."

Angela shoved the tip of the flame toward his left eye. It burned his eyelashes off. He howled with a bloodcurdling scream as he jerked his head violently from side to side.

She planted a boot on his jaw to keep his face still. In order to find out if her vision was accurate, if it had really happened the way she saw it, she needed him to tell her the details of what he had done. She knew without doubt that he was a killer, and yet she still had a hard time believing that she could actually have visions of such things. She had to know for sure if he really did everything to the red-haired girl that she saw in that vision, or if she had only imagined it.

With her boot on his jaw and using all her weight to hold his head still, she burned out his left eye.

She took her boot away and let him scream and flop for a while. As he shook in pain, Angela leaned in closer.

"Every detail. Start at the beginning."

He looked again at the flame with his good eye. His jaw trembled uncontrollably. She saw him not as a man, but as what he really was—a monster who murdered women. He might as well have been a rabid dog that needed to be put down. What he once might have been, he no longer was. He was now a killer who would kill again given the chance. In fact, he had intended to murder her this night and have sex with her corpse.

"I took her to an abandoned building. I told you—we had rough sex. That's all."

Angela lifted the torch.

"The next time you lie to me I'm going to burn out your other eye, and that will only be the beginning. I want every detail. Beginning to end. The time has come for a full confession. Don't leave out any-thing." She thumped the propane torch on the floor to make her point. "Start talking."

With the blowtorch sitting close, he finally abandoned all resis-tance and began spilling out everything he had done. He almost seemed relieved to confess his sins.

Every detail matched exactly the vision she'd had that first instant she saw him in the bar and knew that he was a killer.

It felt somehow amazing, but at the same time it sickened her to be in the mind of a killer, to see what he saw, what he had done, to be there and witness the terrifying, lonely helplessness of his victim. Angela was now that young red-haired girl's only advocate.

It had been his first kill. It had been an orgy of rage that unlocked all his pent-up hatred and urges. It was his initiation to becoming a killer. Angela had put an end to it.

She still wasn't sure how she was able to do such a thing, but that melted away into insignificance once she had confirmed that she had gotten every detail right. All that mattered now was that she could do it.

That night, something snapped in her, the same way it had snapped when that bigger girl had punched her.

She had passed through that mental doorway to become some-thing she had never been before. She felt a new purpose in life. She had a new reason to live.

There were killers, and then there was her.

She was chaos among them. She was a disrupter. She was the unexpected, the unanticipated, the fly in their ointment. She was imbalance in their perfect equation of evil.

Angela had found purpose.

She spent the next three days down in the basement with the killer. He spent the next three days in hell on earth.

She had wanted it to never end.

SEVENTEEN

Rafael stood watching through the window in the small office as the team out on the dock loaded the metal cylinders into containment chests. It was exciting that after all the decades of planning and hard work the mission was finally getting under way.

He glanced to the clock and saw that they were behind schedule. There were long overland drives ahead of them, and then a journey aboard a freighter that would make several stops before reaching South America. Many other members of their team were already on their way. They would infiltrate in separate groups.

He and his team had been training for this mission nearly their entire lives. It seemed surreal that the real thing was finally happening.

He looked up and saw a cylinder slip from José's arms when he turned to tell a joke to some of the other men. The cylinder bounced twice and then rolled across the floor of the loading dock.

José ran after it, tripping over his own feet along the way. When he stumbled, his foot hit the cylinder and sent it racing away even faster. Fortunately, Ronaldo planted his boot on the cylinder to stop it as it rolled past.

Those cylinders were quite strong, but if they were mishandled who knew what might happen? José, laughing, thanked Ronaldo, and then hoisted the cylinder up onto his shoulder, as if it weren't the least bit dangerous, to carry it back to the crate.

"*Idiota*," Rafael muttered under his breath.

Rafael couldn't hear through the window what José said to the other men when he brought the canister back, but some of them returned a weak laugh. Others shook their heads. José was the joker of the group. But this was hardly the time or place.

Alejandro, Rafael's second-in-command, glanced up and gave Rafael a look as if to say he'd about had it with José.

Rafael's jaw clenched tight. Like Alejandro and many of the others, he was sick and tired of José's antics. This was the mission of their lives, the mission they had trained for since early childhood. Now that the most critical parts of the plan were finally in motion, he didn't know how they could any longer afford to have such a fool involved in the operation.

He wished they had cut José from the team years ago. But even then it would have been far too late to bring anyone else in. Even if there was no one to replace José, José was far more of a liability than an asset. José put everything at risk.

Rafael turned when he heard the door. Hasan stormed into the room. His face was red. His *thobe* swirled around his legs when he came to a halt. He raised his shoulders and then lowered them to make slack to pull his *bisht* together in front. The rich brown cloak edged in gold was distinguished looking, as it should be for someone of Hasan's importance.

"*Que te trae aquí hoy?*" Rafael asked.

Hasan waved a hand. "Farsi, please. You know I don't speak Spanish."

"Sorry. I forget. I asked what brings you here today?"

"I wanted to let you know that everything should be ready for final assembly by the time you get there."

Rafael folded his arms. "How are you getting the exploding bridgewire there so the team on site can continue the build without any delays?"

The exploding bridgewire was of concern to Rafael because it was a vital component that had to be sent on ahead of them, and if it was intercepted or lost it would jeopardize the entire mission. Like many of the critical parts, exploding bridgewire was usually illegal to possess in America and closely tracked.

"Couriers," Hasan said. "We have MOIS intelligence officers in foreign missions and embassies in most of the countries we need to send it through. They're waiting to hand off the package with the EBW from one of our trusted agents to another."

"That makes sense," Rafael said. "But what about in America? That is the most dangerous link in that chain. Do you have trusted agents who can make the final delivery?"

"We can't risk using any of our agents to deliver the package because it's possible they are known to American intelligence and under surveillance. The Americans have electronic communication techniques we don't always know about. Using our people for this delivery would risk everything. This is the operation that will make history. We can't afford to let it be compromised.

"To eliminate suspicion, we won't use our people or even sympathizers. We will instead use small, commercial couriers. They will hand the package in a chain from one to another. None of them know the contents or the destination. Each courier has only sequential instructions to deliver the package to another courier. In this way, only the final courier will open the instructions with the final destination—your team there run by Miguel."

"But that final courier knows where the package is going," Rafael said. "He has to deliver it there. That knowledge is a threat to us."

Hasan smiled. "You and I think alike, Rafael. That is why I had instructions placed in the box along with the EBW. The instructions order them to kill the courier and make the body vanish. No one will know what happened to that last courier so there will be no connection to our team. In that way, the link is broken. I used your name on the orders. Those are your men, so they will not hesitate to carry out the instructions."

Rafael nodded as he sighed with relief. "Good."

"What about you? You are behind schedule."

"We have the most dangerous part done and we will soon have the rest of the components loaded. All that is left is to load the power unit. We are close to having the shipment on its way. I have calculated that if we push we can be back on schedule by the time we reach Brazil. Our people are keeping a watchful eye over the route until we arrive at each transfer point."

Hasan nodded. Rafael thought he looked distracted.

"Is there some problem?"

Hasan swiped a hand across his mouth and then smoothed down his black beard. "You remember me telling you that we sent Wahib into Jerusalem?"

Rafael cast about in his memory for a moment. "Wahib, the assassin? Is that who you mean?"

Hasan nodded. "He was recognized."

Rafael leaned in with a frown. "Recognized. How could he be recognized? As far as anyone knows, the enemy did not know of him. That is why he is so valuable. He was unknown to them, invisible, a ghost among the infidels."

Hasan glanced about as if the walls might have ears. "You recall me mentioning my suspicion?"

Rafael tapped his thumb on his leg as he thought a moment. "You mean that the Mossad have people who can tell if someone they see has killed before?"

Hasan nodded again. "From our intelligence reports, it sounds like that may have been what happened. Our people say that they saw two men together. One of them must have made a sign of some kind when Wahib turned his face in the man's direction, because soldiers and men in plain clothes immediately swooped in out of nowhere and seized him."

Rafael found it a troubling notion. "You are certain of this? I mean, certain that he was recognized as having killed the enemy before simply by this man looking at his face?"

"Not his face. His eyes."

Rafael's expression twisted. "It's hard to believe that such a thing is actually possible."

"I believe it is." Hasan gave him a troubled look. "Wahib was a valuable man. No one there ever knew who he was. We are certain of that much."

"Where did you come up with this idea about people who can recognize in someone's eyes that they have killed before?"

Hasan smoothed his beard again. "Wahib told me that when he was once on his way to an assignment, he encountered an old woman—one of our women carrying home a jug of cooking oil so she could prepare a nightly meal for her family. As Wahib was making his way down the crowded alleyway, when she looked up into his eyes she gasped." Hasan held up a finger to make the point. "The old woman recognized he was a killer.

"He said that this had happened to him once before, and that he, in turn, was able to recognize in her eyes that she was one of those very rare people who just by his eyes knew that he had killed before.

"He said that both he and the old woman possessed a rare ability, each the counterpart of the other, and that was how she recognized him as a killer."

Rafael was dubious. "Just by looking at him?"

"By looking into his eyes," Hasan corrected, holding up the finger again to make his point. "Fortunately, he was able to calm her and assure her that he only killed Jews. She was very relieved and happy to hear this and went on her way, wishing him success and many more kills.

"Wahib said, though, that he had heard talk that the Mossad used people like this, people who were able to recognize killers. He believed that it was an ability like this old woman had. I am worried that there may be truth to what Wahib said."

Rafael lifted an eyebrow. "So, then you think that one of these people recognized him in this way and that was how he was captured?"

Hasan let out a heavy sigh. "I believe so." He adjusted his robe again. "Because of how serious this situation is, it is a high priority that this person working with the Mossad be eliminated. There is no telling what harm he could do to us, or what plans this enemy snake could ruin." He gestured out the window to the dock. "Who knows, even plans such as this. We cannot afford the risk. We need to eliminate this person."

"How in the world could we find this Jew with such vision?"

Hasan regarded him with a sideways look. "That's the problem. You or I would not recognize a person with such special ability. It takes a very high-level killer to recognize them—a killer like Wahib. In order for them to tip their hand, it needs to be someone this Jewish devil would recognize as a killer.

"An ordinary assassin might not be aware they had been identified for what they are. We need a man who can recognize in their eyes that they can identify killers. That means we need someone like Wahib, but unfortunately he is now in the hands of the enemy."

"So, it would have to be someone who has killed before, but also a high-level killer, a special man, who could recognize this ability in the eyes of the enemy?"

"That is it exactly."

"Allah willing, how in the world are you ever going to be able to find a man like that?"

Hasan met Rafael's gaze. "We have a man, Cassiel, that I believe to have this ability to identify such an enemy."

"What makes you think so?"

"This man, Cassiel, is a wolf in a *thobe*. He's a ruthless killer. Highly intelligent. Clever. Cunning. He speaks five languages fluently and several more well enough."

"He is one of our men?"

"No. He is a murderer captured by the SSF."

"Why would the State Security Forces be involved with a murder case? They usually only handle internal security."

"They became involved because this was a special case and in a way it did involve internal security. This man was preying on women, mostly, but also some men, slaughtering them for no reason or pattern we could understand. One of his most recent targets was an imam and his relatives. He killed the relatives as he worked toward the imam."

"And the imam?"

Hasan pulled a finger across his throat. "The Ministry of Intelligence and Security isn't sure where he was born, but they learned that for many years he has moved about from country to country. We know he has killed people from Italy to Tajikistan. I'm sure there are more victims. For some reason he sometimes slaughters entire families. He is an international serial killer."

Hasan tilted his head closer. "I believe the seeming random nature of his victims means that they must have something in common. I suspect he was hunting those rare people who could recognize a killer—recognize him as a killer."

"He was eliminating possible threats to himself?"

"In a way." Hasan arched an eyebrow. "No wolf likes the sheepdog watching him hunt. I think that this man, Cassiel, was hunting sheepdogs."

"That's a disturbing thought."

"Anyway, he was to be executed shortly after he was captured. I went to him and made him an offer. I told him that we would release him on the condition that he worked exclusively for us, killed for us, going after people we selected, rather than going after victims of his choosing. We told him that he could kill them in any way he wished as long as he killed them.

"The man is an animal, though. He is dangerous. I told him that if he killed any but the enemy we selected, we have agents everywhere—eyes everywhere—and we would put him down as we would any rabid dog. He liked the idea of not being put to death, and even more the idea that we would let him continue to kill, even if it is those on our target list, so he agreed to the terms.

"I believe he has the ability to spot that person we are looking for, the man who recognized Wahib as an assassin."

"So then you will send him after the Jewish snake who identified Wahib?"

"Yes, but it is not that easy," Hasan said. "From what our informants tell us, the Israelis always have this special man under heavy guard. With the Mossad handling him it will not be easy to get close to him, but he must be eliminated. He puts too much at risk." He gestured out the window again. "Even this."

"How do you intend to do it, then?"

Rafael was beginning to wonder why Hasan was bringing him into his confidence about the whole affair. After all, it was not Rafael's area of responsibility, and besides, he had critically important work ahead of him with his own team. They soon needed to be leaving on their mission.

Hasan clasped his hands in front as he rocked back on his heels for a moment.

"For Cassiel to get close to the target and eliminate it, we will need to use a distraction."

"What sort of distraction?"

"A martyr. Someone who wants to serve Allah by carrying a bomb that will kill as many Jews as possible. We need someone who wants to be a martyr and bring honor to themselves. Someone who has never killed anyone yet so they can't be recognized in the same way Wahib was recognized.

"That bomb will be the distraction Cassiel will need."

Rafael suddenly looked out the window to the people loading canisters. José was making stupid faces for the other men to see as he was screwing on the inner lid. He wasn't watching what he was doing and cross-threaded it. Once he saw what he'd done, he cursed at the lid, as if it were to blame.

"I think I have just the man for such an important mission."

Hasan saw where Rafael was looking.

"Those are incredibly valuable men," Hasan said. "We have trained all of you since you were babies just for this mission. We have much invested in all of you, and much hope lies with all of you."

It didn't sound like Hasan was objecting so much as he was testing the strength of Rafael's suggestion.

"It is because we have so much invested in this plan that I believe this one must be culled. He makes too many mistakes. Our leaders of course had no way of knowing when we were still young children, but he isn't very intelligent.

"I fear that because he is so clumsy and ignorant he could accidentally put the entire effort in jeopardy without even intending to. As valuable as each of those men are, I think it would be better to select this one as the martyr you need. It would solve two problems at once."

Staring out the window, Hasan considered Rafael's suggestion.

At last, he smiled. "Bring him in and I will let him know that, because we have so much faith in him, he has been selected for a very special honor: he is to become a martyr far earlier than he had anticipated."

Rafael finally smiled himself. "He will be in awe that you have personally selected him for this mission."

EIGHTEEN

After she finished cleaning the truck of Owen's blood and finger-prints, Angela went inside the cabin and unlocked the door to the basement. Her grandparents had always kept the door locked. Angela did as well.

She flicked on the light and then descended the steep wooden stairs. The basement had a low ceiling and was only about half the length of the house. Granite ledges sloping down from both ends formed a shallow V under the house. The floor of the house spanned that V, resting on the rock ledge at either end.

The teak floorboards of the basement were spaced about a quarter inch apart so that the floor could be washed down with the hose stored on the wall at one end. Water would run through the spaces and down the sloping stone underneath and then into the chasm under the far side of the basement.

That chasm was carefully concealed with a good-size hatch. Her grandfather called that chasm the hell hole.

She suspected that it had been created by a split in the gigantic granite formations of the mountains to either side, as if the mountains had pulled apart and the ground had cracked open, leaving a fissure that went down into the bowels of the earth. Her grandfather had put the geological oddity to use. Angela suspected he had chosen to build the cabin on that particular spot specifically because of that rift in the earth.

After clearing away the trees, accumulated deadfall, and brush that had originally covered and concealed the opening, he built his place resting right over that abyss.

Angela liked to think of the two mountains, one to each side, as her grandparents watching over her. Grandmother Mountain to the left and Grandfather Mountain to the right, their spirits always there stoically sheltering her.

Angela knew that there had to be a bottom to the hell hole under the basement floor, but everything she'd tried to measure the depth had been unsuccessful. She once bought rolls of string, tied a big bolt to the end of one, and then fed the string down the hole, tying on the end of new rolls when one ran out, until she ran out of rolls. It surprised her that she hadn't hit bottom. In all, the string she had used had been over five hundred feet long.

The metal bolt at the end of the string had swung around, near the top bouncing off wide walls as it descended, but lower down it hit nothing, so she knew the abyss wasn't constricted. She was even more surprised when she let the string go and watched the end flutter away down into the darkness. She counted the seconds until it hit bottom. She never heard a sound. As far as Angela knew, it might as well still be falling.

When she'd aimed a powerful light down into the hell hole, the light revealed smooth granite walls that sloped inward a bit, then widened again, then got crooked for a bit, and then opened wider yet as they descended until the light simply evaporated in the darkness.

Her grandfather had told her to be careful around the hell hole because if she ever fell in she would never be seen again. There were no shelves of rock, stone spurs, or roots to grab hold of if you fell in, no corners to wedge a foot, nowhere to get a grip to climb back out. Greasy layers of moss grew in places and covered the flat stone where moisture seeped through fine cracks. It was nothing but basically a slippery smooth and somewhat crooked granite shaft down into a great abyss.

She knew that her grandfather was right. If you fell in, there was nothing to stop you. No one would ever hear you screaming for help on the way down, and you would not survive the fall. Even if you somehow did, you would never be able to climb out. You would die in the cold blackness.

Angela suspected that over the thousands of years before her grandfather had built the cabin, all sorts of animals had probably slipped on the sloping ledge and fallen to their death. She imagined that there were prehistoric predators down at the bottom of the abyss. Sometimes she wondered if there might even be a saber-toothed tiger down there.

Angela had once tossed a flare down into the bottomless pit. She watched it fall until the shrinking dot of flickering reddish light had gradually vanished into nothingness.

Another time she had held several smoking pieces of incense over the hole to see if air was moving up or down through the opening, which would indicate another entrance somewhere down in the hole—a side shaft—but the smoke revealed absolutely no air movement. The hole was not the entrance into a subterranean cave system. It was just a hole. A very deep hole, but just a hole.

When her grandfather had shown her the hell hole, she had asked him if Frankie was down in that hole. He said only that men like Frankie belonged in hell. As far as Angela was concerned, that told her everything she needed to know.

Frankie was no longer alone in the hell hole. That first man Angela had recognized as a killer had joined him after his three-day introduction to hell. Other men had followed, all killers she had recognized by what she had seen in their eyes. They were killers who would never again harm anyone. Their remains would never be found. They would be down there forever with the other, ancient predators.

Owen would have joined them except that it was more important to Angela that she find out where he had left the body of Carrie

Stratton, the last woman he had murdered. Her family needed to know. Owen's corpse would reveal her location.

Angela pulled the sheath with the knife out of her boot. She tossed the knife, in its sheath, down the hell hole. She heard it skip against the stone walls a few times on its way down, and then there was nothing but silence as it descended.

Next, she sat on the metal chair off to the other side of the basement and removed her boots and socks. She tossed them down the gaping black hole. Next, she shed her shorts, underpants, and top, dropping them down into the darkness.

Everything she'd had on went down into the abyss.

She didn't want to have to worry about some forensic scientist finding blood in a seam of her boots, or a speck in the fabric of her shorts or top. Part of the way she kept anyone from finding any evidence was to get rid of it in a way that it would never be found. That included the knife. Owen's blood was all over that knife. For all she knew, there were seams in the knife's construction that held blood evidence.

The only way she could be sure the authorities never found any evidence was if they never found any evidence. Simple as that. The only way she could do that and be safe was if everything always went down the hell hole. She never made exceptions. It wasn't worth the risk.

From one of the cabinets, Angela retrieved a new knife in a new sheath. It was just like the one she'd used on Owen. There were a dozen and a half more of them, all the same, all razor sharp, lined up in a row in the cabinet.

Completely naked, with the new knife, she went back upstairs to shower and get some clothes. She wished the experience of killing Owen could have lasted longer. She would have loved to have given him more of what he deserved. At least he was dead, now, and couldn't ever hurt anyone again.

But already, that glorious, intoxicating high was fading.

After she showered and put on some clean clothes, she checked her phone on the nightstand.

There was a missed call from Hospice.

She could have called them back—there was always someone available. Instead she sent a text.

Sorry I missed your call. I had to work.

She deliberately didn't provide any other information or say when she would have time.

She tossed the phone back on the nightstand and retrieved her Walther P22 and the Gemtech suppressor. Most people called them silencers, but her grandfather had told her that they were suppressors because they suppressed sound, they didn't completely silence it. She pulled out a couple of boxes of subsonic ammunition and loaded ten magazines.

She liked using the suppressor when she practiced, especially at night. Night, and fog, seemed to carry sound for miles. She didn't like to unnecessarily attract attention, especially attention from gunshots.

Gunshots drew sheriff's deputies and game wardens. She'd found that out a long time ago and decided that she didn't want to repeat it. There was nothing illegal about shooting on her own property, but they still had come to investigate the reports of gunfire. Also, when using a suppressor she didn't need to use hearing protection, which allowed her to be more alert for anything out of the ordinary, like someone sneaking up on her.

Suppressors required federal licenses to be legal, the same as fully automatic weapons. She didn't want a machine gun, but she wanted suppressors, and she didn't want to go through the long and arduous process of getting a federal license for them. That process would surely raise suspicions and put a red flag by her name.

One good thing about knowing drug dealers and their friends was that they could usually get you just about anything illegal you wanted if you had the cash. Angela had the cash, and bought a large number of suppressors, no questions asked, no ID, no background check, no paperwork, no waiting.

Even with a suppressor, gunshots emitted a loud *crack* when the bullet went supersonic. The subsonic rounds avoided the ballistic *crack*, so with those subsonic rounds and a suppressor the gun was virtually silent. Most of the sound was the slide cycling as it ejected the spent round and loaded a live one.

Even though those subsonic rounds were slower, they were still lethal. A bullet needed to be traveling at only two hundred feet per second to penetrate the human skull, providing it hit relatively squarely. If it hit that deadly triangle, it was guaranteed to kill.

Outside, Angela wound up her grandfather's triangular target. She practiced nearly every day. She practiced so much that she could just about hit the target with her eyes closed.

Practice was also a form of focused violence, which helped extend the high of dispatching Owen.

Angela took shooting practice seriously. That very first man she had recognized as a killer opened her eyes to her strange ability. He would have added her to his kill tally when he snuck into her cabin had she not been such a good shot. Her grandfather had taught her well.

She missed her grandparents. Some killer had put a bullet in the back of their heads—some killer that she knew she could now recognize by looking into his eyes.

He had better pray to God that Angela never found out who he was.

NINETEEN

Jack Raines watched as Ehud worked his way through the people moving along the pedestrian mall near a corner café. Police in light blue shirts and dark blue flak jackets watched over everyone as they walked in pairs along the street. Soldiers in the distance kept watch from their posts.

Jack paused to wait as Ehud, the Mossad team leader in plain clothes, approached. Ehud stepped back out of the way momentarily for a gaggle of older women in a tour group, chatting and laughing among themselves as they moved up the street, all of them loaded down with bags from recent purchases. They were all in a cheerful mood, giving little thought to any danger that might be among them. That was human nature. It was the job of Jack and those watching with him to think of little else.

There were tourists of every variety and speaking a variety of different languages visiting the pedestrian malls in the Jerusalem Triangle. Shops along the stone streets were busy selling artwork, clothes, shoes, religious souvenirs, fresh fruit, housewares, and baked goods. Once the tight knot of tourists had passed, Jack signaled with a tilt of his head for the man to come closer.

"We have everyone in position," Ehud said as he joined Jack. "We're ready to begin again."

Jack nodded. "I'll get Uziel and start a sweep. Stay close. He's already nervous. I don't want anything spooking him. And I certainly don't want him getting hurt. He's too valuable."

Jack scanned the people all up and down the street. The Triangle seemed unusually crowded. Maybe it was just his anxiety playing mind tricks. The plan was to go up Ben Yehuda Street, past the colorful shops, sidewalk cafés, and food stands where the heaviest concentration of tourists visited. Crowds drew threat.

Jack and his team were hunting threats.

"Don't worry, we will keep in constant contact with both of you," Ehud said.

"Be ready for my signal if Uziel spots anyone."

Jack watched for anything out of the ordinary as the light rail cars swept by, carrying a whirling rush of sound with them. Once they were past, the sound of shuffling shoes and conversation seeped back into the sunny day. Jack could hear music in the distance, and closer in, some bubbly laughter.

In the street beyond, three green buses lined up at the curb to let people out for the Triangle area. Squadrons of white taxis prowled the surrounding streets, waiting for fares or to drop people off. Soldiers, police, and men and women in plain clothes watched over everyone, hoping that the visitors had a pleasant, uneventful day in the Triangle.

Not long ago Uziel's rare vision had been spot-on and they had captured an assassin before he could do any harm. They didn't know where he was from, or what his target had been, but they knew by the way he kept his mouth shut that he was well trained. Jack thought that it would be quite a while before they got much of anything out of him.

It took time with men like that. The Mossad would have to find an angle, a crack they could exploit to open him up. Jack knew that they would eventually succeed, at least to some extent, but it would take time. For now, what was important was that he was off the streets.

With the heavy crowds in the area the difficulty of identifying threats was increased. The more people there were, the easier it was for a terrorist to hide among them. But that was why they were using Uziel. He could see what none of them ever could.

"Keep your eyes open," Jack said. "I'll go get him."

Ehud melted into the people perusing the rows of bread on display in a shopwindow next door. He and his team would be close by at all times.

Inside the café, Jack saw Uziel standing off to the side, next to a tall wrought-iron table where a couple of Americans were talking. The tabletop was only big enough for a few people to rest their drinks. Uziel, one forearm resting on the table, idly turned a cup of coffee round and round as his gaze darted about, looking at everyone.

He was nervous and with good reason. Those very rare individuals with his ability to recognize killers were often the targets of rare predators who could recognize them for that ability. Human predators, just like the four-legged kind, didn't like any interference with their hunting. If spotted, the four-legged kind would usually move on and come back to hunt another time. The human predators, on the other hand, sought to eliminate anyone who could recognize them to give themselves free rein to hunt as they pleased.

More than that, though, Jack knew that Uziel was tense for other reasons. His young wife had recently died of a brain tumor. They had been married for only two months when the tumor had been discovered. Her health went downhill rapidly from there. Three months after the tumor had been discovered, she was dead. Uziel was left dazed by the trauma and feeling lost.

That was when Jack discovered him. He had been shopping for dinner and saw Uziel doing the same. Jack couldn't tell if someone was a killer by looking at their eyes, the way Uziel could, but he had the singular ability to recognize those who could. He struck up a conversation with the young man, and eventually Jack filled a void in Uziel's life, giving him a purpose.

To an extent, Jack understood Uziel's pain. A woman he had once been fond of had that same special ability as Uziel. Jack had tried to convince her of the danger she was in, but she wanted nothing to do with Jack's help. At least, not until it was too late. One of those predators had recognized her for her ability and murdered her. That experience had made him realize that in his calling he couldn't afford the risk of emotional entanglement.

But that was before he had met Kate. Kate was different. She had of course been confused and skeptical at first, but she quickly came to grasp everything Jack had told her. He had helped teach her how to survive. Together they worked to stop a highly unusual nest of predators bent on hunting and killing those with her ability.

Over time, Kate had come to mean more to him than he thought anyone ever could. Every line of her face, her mannerisms, the sound of her voice, were now stitched into his soul.

Her ability far outstripped that of anyone he had ever found before. Not only was she able to recognize killers, but she had vague visions of what those killers had done. This was the ultimate type of person Jack searched for. From years of research he was sure they had to exist, but Kate was the only one he'd ever found with that higher-level ability.

Unfortunately, in a battle with that nest of murderers, Jack had been gravely wounded. He had died for a time even as a team of Mossad combat medics worked on him. No one thought he would make it. He didn't remember anything after that hail of bullets, except the fading vision of Kate's horror-stricken face.

That memory still haunted him.

He never regained consciousness before being flown to Israel to see if there was anything the doctors there could do to keep him alive. To save Kate the trauma of what they believed would be his inevitable death, and at best a vegetative state even if they were able to save his life, they told her that he had died. Everyone thought it best.

After he'd eventually come out of the coma, Jack had spent seven months in the hospital recovering from his injuries, and then there were more months of physical therapy. By the time he had been aware enough to do anything, Kate had vanished.

She was highly intelligent, as those at her level of ability were. She had come to understand both what her ability meant, and the danger it put her in. She had done what Jack had taught her to do—what he'd told her she would need to do. She had gone off the grid and disappeared. Not even his friends in the Mossad could locate her.

For people like Kate, who could recognize killers, the safest thing to do was to be invisible. Their kind were always hunted by rare super-predators. Since the ability ran in families, that kind of killer often murdered the entire family to make sure that none with the ability survived.

Jack circled an arm around Uziel's shoulders. "How are you doing?"

Uziel forced a smile. "I'm fine."

He didn't look fine. He chewed gum with his mouth open as if his life depended on it while his gaze darted around at the people outside on the street.

"Let's not draw attention, all right?" Jack put a finger under the young man's chin to close his mouth. Uziel smiled self-consciously and spit the gum into his empty coffee cup.

"How about we get going?" Jack said. "You did good before spotting that last killer. Just remember what I told you—don't fixate. Scan and take in as many different pairs of eyes as you can."

Uziel swiped a lock of straight brown hair back off his forehead. He leaned a little closer.

"I'm fine, Jack. Really." He let out a deep breath to calm himself. "I want to do this. I want to stop anyone else from losing a loved one."

Jack pressed his earpiece, listening to his team calling out their location, before leading Uziel out of the café. The streets in this area of Jerusalem, known as the Triangle, had long been closed to automobile traffic and turned into an open-air pedestrian mall. It was a beautiful area, with trees in planters down the center of some of the streets and a wide variety of shopping along with a vibrant nightlife.

The nightlife also drew crowds, which were also a target for terrorists. But with Uziel's talent it was easier to spot killers in the daytime. Uziel needed to be able to see their eyes. Darkness provided cover. Of course, so did sunglasses.

TWENTY

Jack kept Uziel moving at a leisurely pace. They paused at shops along the way to give him a chance to scan the crowds. It also helped the two of them to look like nothing more than a couple of tourists or shoppers. He didn't want to look obvious to any potential threat seeking an easy terrorist target.

They made their way through some of the narrow connecting streets packed tightly with vendors or shops with their wares on display outside. Uziel occasionally glanced at the racks with hanging scarves, necklaces, and rosaries, or tables of fruits, pastries, and tourist trinkets, trying to look like an ordinary shopper as he watched the faces that continually streamed past him going in the opposite direction.

Uziel suddenly stiffened to a stop.

"What?" Jack asked, looking up.

"Faded green T-shirt," Uziel said with a nod of his head indicating someone across the street.

Jack looked over and saw the older, heavyset man in the faded T-shirt. The faded T-shirt had what looked like a lifetime of stains. The man's heavy jowls and hanging double chins were unshaven. He looked to be in a daze.

Jack just couldn't picture the guy as a murderer, but then, he didn't have Uziel's ability and murderers were often quite unremarkable looking.

"Heavy, older man, faded green shirt, walking past the Jamin Jewelry store," he said into the microphone under the collar of his shirt.

Two men in plain clothes emerged from the crowds, each grabbing an arm of the older man, bringing him to a halt. Two police officers immediately swept in and took over. The man twisted his head around, looking at the two policemen as he protested in Hebrew. He was still protesting as he was rushed away. People in the nearby crowd stared at the apprehension.

All the people in Jack's team melted back into the crowds as people watched the police taking the man away. The whiff of danger in the air was palpable as people switched from a fun day to murmuring about the possibility of danger. It became clear rather quickly that it was a criminal arrest and not a threat of terrorism. Within a few minutes of the man being taken away to jail, people returned to enjoying their day out. They would have a story for the dinner table.

Uziel and Jack returned to their reason for being in the Triangle and were soon back to searching the crowds for trouble. With the sun high in the sky, it was becoming a hot day. Uziel and Jack stopped at a shop to buy a couple of bottles of water. For a time they sat on a bench, drinking water, engaged in the very ordinary act of people watching. Except their form of people watching was quite out of the ordinary.

In the early afternoon, Ehud came on over the radio. "The man we arrested is a murderer," he said into Jack's earpiece. "The police had been looking for him. He murdered his wife last night. Apparently, he has been wandering the streets since then."

"Okay, thanks," Jack said quietly toward the microphone.

"Well," he told Uziel, "you were right. The guy you pointed out killed his wife."

Uziel shook his head as he took in the news. "Doesn't seem fair."

Jack frowned. "Fair?"

Uziel tossed his empty water bottle in a trash can. "To have a wife you love taken from you, while someone else blessed with life doesn't appreciate what they have."

"I see what you mean," Jack said. "Anyway, the guy wasn't the kind of threat we're hunting, so let's get back to it."

They walked on down the street to an area overlooking a plaza of sorts where several streets intersected. The area was filled with people going in all directions. They slowed as Uziel gazed out over the crowds below them.

As they stood in the river of people slowly drifting up the street, they suddenly heard screaming.

It was a soldier, pointing as he yelled.

"Bomb! Bomb! Bomb!"

Soldiers suddenly ran in from every direction, guns at the ready. They screamed orders for people to get back.

Jack stretched up to see over the heads of the crowd. He saw a man in the street not too far away, shirt thrown open, frantically jabbing a finger at what was clearly a bomb vest, trying to detonate it.

The word "bomb" had flashed through the crowd like wildfire. Almost instantly all the people in the streets started stampeding. What had been a quiet shopping afternoon turned into loud, screaming panic. All at once thousands of people began to flee the danger.

Uziel and Jack, standing at the end of a table in front of a shop that sold sunglasses, were sheltered from the crush of people racing past them trying to escape the danger. The mood of the shoppers had instantly switched from convivial shopping to mass hysteria.

Through gaps in the mob of people bolting past, Jack saw two soldiers dive in and grab the suicide bomber by his arms. They took him to the ground while preventing him from detonating his bomb. More soldiers rushed in to help.

Jack stepped behind Uziel, getting ready to shepherd him into the flood of people rushing past to get him away from the danger.

Jack just caught a glimpse of a cowboy hat beyond Uziel abruptly pause.

Uziel gasped in recognition.

Jack flicked open the blade of the knife in his right hand as he swept his left arm around Uziel's waist to pull him back.

In the next instant, as Jack was beginning to yank Uziel back away from danger, the man slammed a knife into the center of Uziel's chest so hard it toppled Uziel back on top of Jack.

In that fleeting instant, Jack saw the back of the killer disappearing into the mad dash of panicked people. All Jack could tell was that the man had short black hair and a beard. He never saw the attacker's face.

Before Uziel and Jack both hit the ground, the assassin was already gone. Jack caught sight of the cowboy hat on the ground being trampled by the stampede of panicked people.

"Medic!" Jack yelled into the microphone. "We need a medic!"

In the mad scene, three of his team in plain clothes were already there, protecting Uziel down on the ground.

When Jack saw the wound in the center of Uziel's chest and the amount of blood, he knew that the young man was beyond help. Two army medics rushed up, going to a knee on either side of Uziel, but Jack knew it was no use. The assassin had only needed to strike once.

Jack knew that Uziel's heart had been torn apart by that knife. Uziel had been dead before he hit the ground.

Jack wanted to scream in rage. He wanted to get the man who had been wearing the cowboy hat, but he was long gone. Jack knew he wouldn't even be able to recognize him—he had barely caught a glimpse of the hat and a beard.

Uziel, though, had recognized the man as a killer, if only an instant before the man had murdered him.

The assassin had obviously recognized Uziel for his rare ability.

Jack wanted to tell Uziel how sorry he was that he hadn't protected him. He had promised that he would do his best to keep Uziel out of danger. He gritted his teeth in rage at himself for failing to stop the attack.

The medics had not given up, but Jack had seen enough killings to know that the man was beyond help. There was a lot of blood, but it was no longer spurting from the gaping wound. That was because the heart was too damaged to continue pumping.

Ehud rushed up, breathless. He stopped in his tracks when he saw Uziel on the ground in a spreading pool of blood, medics to either side. One started an IV as the other was doing CPR.

"What happened?" Ehud asked.

"That suicide bomber was meant to be a diversion," Jack said. "The real target was Uziel."

"How do you know?"

"As soon as someone yelled 'bomb,' the crowd started running. The killer was apparently in that crowd, using it as cover. He recognized Uziel for his ability before Uziel saw him. When he did, it was too late.

"I wish I would have gotten a look at his face, but I only caught a glimpse of a cowboy hat. I was under Uziel's dead weight as he went down and tried to snatch a quick look, but the killer had vanished into the panicked crowd. I never got a look at his face."

Ehud ran his fingers back through his wavy hair as he looked around, clearly frustrated and angered at the same time.

One of the plainclothes members of the team rushed in close. "We got the bomber before he could detonate his bomb vest," he said to Ehud. Of course, they knew that, because there was no explosion.

People still rushing away from the scene gave a wide berth to the dead man in the pool of blood and the soldiers around him. Police officers had appeared and were already pushing the crowds back.

Jack stayed with Uziel as the medics worked on him. He could hear an ambulance in the distance. He felt useless. He felt sick.

These people had saved Jack's life when he had been shot and was, for all practical purposes, dead, but he knew that Uziel's wound was different. He was beyond the same kind of help. The assassin had known what he was doing, and he had not failed.

Jack stood back when the ambulance arrived, letting the medical people do their job.

Once Uziel was on a gurney and loaded into the ambulance, Jack turned to Ehud.

"I'm going with him."

He could tell that Ehud wanted to object, but in the end he only nodded. "It's not your fault, Jack."

"I'm the one who recognized his ability," Jack said as he hopped up into the ambulance. "I recruited him."

It was a somber ride to the hospital in the wailing ambulance. Jack thought that he must once have looked as hopeless as Uziel did now when he had been the one riding in an ambulance. He wished that Uziel could have the same chance at life that had been given to Jack by the Israeli doctors. He held on to a thread of hope, even though he knew better.

When they raced into the ambulance bay at the hospital, there was already a team of doctors and nurses waiting. Uziel's lifeless body was rolled in through double doors, surrounded by a medical team running beside the gurney.

Jack hoped against hope they could perform a miracle, the same as they had done for him.

He waited all alone on a bench in a hallway, wishing he had never found Uziel. Wishing he had never told him that he might be able to save lives. Uziel had wanted to do it, though. Jack wished he had said no and left Uziel to live his life.

But finding those rare people with Uziel's vision was Jack's calling in life. It was what he could do that none other could.

It was late that night when the doctor came out to see Jack. As he expected, there was no saving the young man. Jack nodded and thanked the doctor. With no sense of urgency, the doctor went back in through double doors, leaving Jack all alone on the bench. People rushed up and down the hall, past the green-painted walls, past Jack sitting on the lonely bench.

He didn't know what he was going to do. He felt lost. He missed Kate, and at the same time hoped that she had vanished off the grid and that a killer hadn't found her as well.

Sometime in the night, as he was sitting on the bench, mourning Uziel, lost in his own thoughts, Ehud arrived.

He sat down on the bench beside Jack.

"Any word?"

Jack stared at the floor. "He didn't make it. The doctor said there was nothing they could do."

Ehud nodded. "I'm really sorry, Jack."

"It was planned out, you know. That suicide bomber was a distraction. Uziel had been the real target. At least no one was killed by that bomb. We're lucky it was defective."

"It wasn't defective," Ehud said.

Jack frowned. "What do you mean, it wasn't defective? I saw the guy pushing the detonator over and over."

Ehud arched an eyebrow as he leaned in. "That wasn't the detonator he was pushing. It was the arming switch. He kept hitting the arming switch over and over, thinking it was the detonator. The bomb was live. If he would have instead hit the detonator it would have gone off. He would have been a martyr."

Jack leaned back and folded his arms. "You've got to be kidding me."

"Nope. The guy was probably panicked that he was about to die, panicked that the bomb strapped around his body was about to blow him apart. In the confusion of that wild emotional state he kept hitting the arming button instead of the detonator."

"Do you really think so? That seems pretty odd. That kind usually want to die."

"Yeah, but right at the last instant, it has to be traumatic. I imagine the human mind doesn't think clearly in that last moment when it knows it is about to die."

"I suppose. What did the guy have to say for himself?"

"That's the weird part," Ehud said.

"What's the weird part?"

Ehud glanced up and down the hall, making sure no one was standing within earshot.

"The weird part is that he doesn't speak Arabic, Farsi, or Hebrew, or any other Middle Eastern language or dialect."

Jack made a face. "What does he speak, then?"

"Spanish."

Jack leaned in a little more. "Spanish? He's from the ETA?"

Ehud shook his head. "No, he's not part of the Basque separatist movement. He'd never heard of them."

"Who, then?"

"The only thing we could get out of him is that he's from Santiago de Querétaro, in Mexico."

"Mexico!" Jack looked up to make sure no one nearby had heard him. "He's from Mexico?" he asked in a lower voice.

"That was about all we could get out of him. He's here from Santiago de Querétaro, in Mexico."

Jack heaved a sigh. "So he's a Mexican suicide bomber?"

"It appears so."

"Did you find out anything else?"

"Just that his name is José."

"José. Why was José from Santiago de Querétaro in Mexico trying to blow himself up all the way over here in Jerusalem?"

Ehud shrugged. "All he would say was that he wanted to martyr himself for God. But I've got to tell you, Jack, the guy is dumb as a rock." He tapped his temple. "I don't think he's all there."

It suddenly made sense. Terrorists often recruited the mentally handicapped and convinced them that it was the right thing to do, that it was the right thing to do for God.

Jack rubbed his aching knees. "Do you think that maybe he was recruited because he's easily persuaded?"

"Possibly."

Jack sat back against the wall and folded his arms again. "A Mexican suicide bomber. I don't get it."

"I don't either," Ehud admitted as he stood. "How about I give you a lift home."

Jack stood and went with Ehud. "A Mexican suicide bomber?" he muttered to himself as he walked down the hallway.

TWENTY-ONE

It was a warm day for autumn, so Angela was wearing the same low-rise cutoff shorts she intended to wear to her bartender job later. She had delivered a half dozen courier drop-offs for lawyers, and was about to head to Barry's Place to work until they closed, when she got a call from Mike's Mail Service.

Mike handled a variety of mail-related services for people, including collecting drop-offs for UPS and FedEx. When people occasionally brought him something that needed to be delivered locally by courier, he would call Angela. It wasn't often, but it all added up to make ends meet.

When she walked into Mike's place, he was making out UPS shipping labels. "What's up?" she asked.

Mike came to the counter. "A courier came in from Syracuse. He's never been down here and doesn't know the area. He couldn't locate the address for his package. He said he's a small courier service and he's really outside his element down here. He needed to get back and asked me if I could have a local courier finish the delivery. He left some cash with the package."

Angela shrugged. "Sure, no problem."

Mike pulled the box from under the counter. It was long and light. She thought it might be long-stemmed roses.

When she saw the address, she immediately understood why the courier couldn't find the place. It was in the industrial area where most of the abandoned factories were located. The area was a maze of streets, alleys, vast concrete expanses, buildings, loading docks, and train tracks with sidings beside old factories, as well as fenced areas guarding corroded, outdated factory equipment and heavy machinery parts slowly rusting away.

Many of the buildings had collapsed roofs, leaving only standing walls. Several of the buildings were still in good enough shape to be used for things like equipment storage. A few offered small office or business space. Those office areas were dingy and crude, but they were cheap and used only occasionally by the people who stored equipment there long-term.

Even though a few of the buildings were occasionally still used, Angela had never seen anyone in the area.

Because the old industrial tract was a labyrinth of derelict buildings, the addresses were confusing and for the most part missing. None of it was accurately located on any GPS. You just about had to be familiar with the abandoned area to find anything. The city didn't care to spend money maintaining what was, in essence, a ghost town, so street signs were rare. She suspected they were stolen for souvenirs or for decorations in teenagers' bedrooms.

Her grandparents had often taken Angela with them on a Sunday drive. Usually those rides went through the countryside, to be followed with getting an ice cream cone, but on occasion her grandfather would take them through the old industrial area, pointing out factories he had helped build. More than once Angela had listened to his stories of where a man had once died, hit by a girder swinging past him, and where another man had a heart attack and fell into freshly poured concrete footings, and where a fight had broken out over a dice game and one of the men had been stabbed to death.

"The guy left this as well," Mike said. He laid two twenties and a ten on top of the long package. "He said this should cover it for finishing the delivery. He was insistent that it was supposed to be delivered quickly. He said he was a small one-man service, and his income depended on his reputation remaining good. I told him I had the right courier."

Angela was much the same way—her courier business was built on good word of mouth. She gave the ten to Mike for handling the job. Paying him a commission kept him using her messenger service when he needed one.

"Thanks Mike. Catch you the next time."

Once in her truck with the package, Angela pulled out an old map of Milford Falls that her grandfather had given her. She studied the map, trying to figure out where the address for Hartland Irrigation would be. She had a pretty good idea and the map confirmed her initial thought.

When she reached the old industrial area, rolling along among the abandoned factory buildings, she didn't see any people or cars. There weren't any new business in Milford Falls looking for factory space, so there was nothing keeping the industrial area from continuing its slow decay.

She recognized one of the businesses she passed. The space was rented by an old guy who welded together pieces of junk steel he scavenged from the abandoned buildings. He created fanciful animals out of the junk and sold the pieces at art fairs. The building he was in was perfect for that sort of thing—concrete, steel, and brick. Nothing to burn down with his torch and no one to interrupt him as he worked. But he was getting old and in ill health, so he was rarely there anymore.

Angela passed a building with rows of high windows divided up into small squares. Most of the glass had long ago been broken out. She recognized the place.

When she had first encountered the man who killed the red-haired girl, she had seen that particular building in the vision she'd had. That was the first time she had recognized that a man was a killer by looking into his eyes. He was also the first man she had killed. She had sent that killer down the hell hole after she'd made him confess every detail of what he'd done in order to confirm her vision.

As she drove past, she saw the cistern where that killer had put the body. It was sad to see such a place, and to know that the body of an innocent victim had surely rotted away down in the lonely, dark, wet hole long before Angela had encountered her killer.

Angela drove on among the buildings, looking for Hartland Irrigation. She didn't see signs for it anywhere. That was hardly unusual. The place being so isolated and desolate was also probably why the sender didn't mail the package, or send it by UPS, and instead sent it by courier.

Many of the buildings were covered with graffiti. Taggers, like the rats, came out at night. It was a sketchy area. Fortunately, she always carried a gun in the center console of her truck. But the graffiti was old. There was no one to see their work, so the taggers had moved back to bridges, walls, and businesses in town.

She at last spotted the address painted on a lonely, dented, tan steel door. There were no windows, and there was no name to go with the address. There was an older, beige, four-door Toyota Camry parked by the door. Out of habit when she delivered packages in rough areas she committed the license plate number to memory.

The black paint of the address did look somewhat fresh compared to all the other peeling paint. She parked next to the Camry and hopped out of her truck.

When she pounded on the metal door, she heard someone inside yell to come in. The door scraped on buckled concrete when she pulled it open. Inside was a small room without a ceiling or furniture, lit only by the high skylights and windows in the open area beyond. Long chains on geared rollers hung down to tilt the windows open at the top.

No one was in the small room. Voices echoed from out back.

Angela went through the opening in the front room, into the vast area of the old factory floor. Gray metal shelves stood to the right, sectioning off a smaller area from the open factory building beyond. To the left was another room.

There were several stained folding tables in front of the shelves. Old, dirty blankets covered lumpy shapes on the tables. She noticed that items on the shelves were also covered in ratty old blankets or greasy moving pads. Other than a few small work lights clamped to the tables, most of the light came from the high windows on the far wall. Dilapidated wooden rolling chairs were pushed up to the tables with the lights. It was a dingy work area for whatever Hartland Irrigation did.

Not far beyond the shelves there were several types of milling machines and a pair of red gas-powered generators to run them and the minimal lighting.

"Hello!" Angela called into the empty factory. "I have a delivery." Her voice echoed back from the darkness.

A man in work overalls rushed out from the room to the left, wiping his hands with a filthy rag.

Angela recognized him.

Three other men followed him out of the room.

She recognized all four men. They were the four Hispanic men she had waited on at the bar the night Owen had come in.

"A delivery, yes, thank you, come in," one of them said in a heavy accent. He gestured with a hand, inviting her in closer.

As the other three came forward she got a good look at their eyes for the first time. It had been dark in the bar and the rotating ceiling light made it difficult to see anyone's eyes unless they were close, the way Owen had been.

After Angela learned that she could recognize killers by looking at their eyes, she came to learn to recognize a range of threat in the eyes of people who hadn't yet committed murder.

Frankie's eyes had been like that. Not a killer's, but something close. Boska's eyes had been even worse. They were the eyes of someone extremely dangerous, someone with a violent temper, someone who would hurt you, even though he had not yet killed anyone.

Both Frankie and Boska had the eyes of men who could at some point easily cross that line into murder.

The eyes of these four men were like that. Cunning. Calculating. Cruel.

Boska had a certain cast to his eyes when he wanted her. A look of focused lust. A look of commitment to getting what he wanted. It was a look that made the hair on the back of her neck stand on end and paralyzed her with fear.

These four men had that look in their eyes.

Mole-face moved off behind her and into the front room.

She heard the dead bolt on the front door click home.

Angela was a rabbit in the center of a pack of rabid dogs.

TWENTY-TWO

The man with the rag finished wiping his hands and tossed it on a table.

"You have something for us, no? Something for Hartland Irrigation?"

"That's right," Angela said, trying sound official. She wanted to give them the package and be gone.

He put his fingers to his chest. "I am Emilio. Here, come put your package on the table." He held his hand out toward the table beside him.

Angela couldn't imagine anyone sending long-stemmed roses to these men, so she knew the package had to contain something else. At the moment, that was the least of her concerns. She tossed the long package on the table.

"There you go." She backed away. "Thank you."

"No no," Emilio said, waving a hand back and forth, "wait for us to see if everything is . . . is . . ." He turned to one of the other two. "*Que es la palabra?*"

"No damaged," one of them said.

"Yes, that is the words." Emilio turned back to her with a smile. "No damaged. We will see first if the things inside is no damaged."

"I'm running late," Angela said as she continued backing away. She gestured to the package. "There is no damage to the outside of the box. I'm not responsible for what's inside or how it was packed. If there is any damage inside you will have to notify the shipper."

"The shipper!" Emilio said, looking at the others briefly.

His gaze returned to glide down her bare legs.

When his eyes turned up, he gave her a sly smile. "But they are very, very far away, so let us first see that there is no damage inside."

She could sense Mole-face up close behind her, making sure that she didn't try to leave. She could smell him—a combination of some chemical smell and stale body odor. She didn't let herself turn to look at him. She wanted to break and run for the door, but she knew that he was waiting for her to try that. She also knew that he had locked the door, so it would take her precious seconds to unlatch the dead bolt.

Emilio pulled a big combat knife from a sheath under his waistband and slowly ran the blade down the length of the box. He returned the knife to its sheath and lifted the flaps of the box to look inside. He pulled out a folded piece of paper along with a long plastic tube, hardly thicker than his thumb. Inside the tube was what looked to be a long, folded, very thin wire with a red cap at one end. After inspecting it, he put it back in the box with the others and then set the box on the table.

He then unfolded a piece of paper and read it in silence, his smile widening as he reached the end. He showed it to the men to either side, pointing out something.

"Miguel, I think you should see this," he said to Mole-face standing behind her. "These are orders from Rafael."

Emilio stepped forward to give Miguel the paper. It gave him the chance to move in close in front of her. Closer than she liked. She was sandwiched between the two men.

Angela glanced around, looking for another way out. The front door wasn't a good option because it was locked with a dead bolt. She didn't like the odds of four against one, and decided that if it came down to it, her best option would to make a break for the empty factory floor. She was sure that out in the open she could run faster than these men, giving her time to try to find another way out.

She was acutely aware that her gun was out in the truck. A gun would even the odds, but carrying a concealed weapon was illegal, so she always had to leave it in her truck. Lot of good it did her there. With the door bolted, and these four close to her, there was not going to be any way for her to get to the gun if she ended up needing it.

A sickening sense of dread washed through her. Her knees felt weak. A voice in her head screamed for her to break and run, but she knew that predators were driven to chase prey when it ran. If she ran and didn't find a way out, she would be trapped. Still, against four men, running was her best option.

With no time to waste, Angela suddenly bolted for the space between the men. She elbowed one of them aside as she made a mad dash toward the opening between the standing shelves.

Mole-face yelled to the others, "*Agarrala! Agarrala!*"

Everything seemed to move in slow motion, her legs feeling as if they were mired in molasses. As Angela knocked one man aside, two of the other men blocked her escape route. They each seized an arm before she could go for her knife as a third man, the one she had elbowed out of the way, swept an arm in around her waist from behind. With three men holding her there was no way for her to run or fight. She tried but couldn't break their hold on her arms. The man with his arm around her waist snatched her hair in his other fist. Panting in fury, she tried to twist out of his grip around her, but he was too strong.

She kicked at them, trying to get them to let go. They danced around with her, avoiding her heels as she kicked. She squirmed and fought as they all tightened their grips on her, controlling her arms. As Miguel put his hands around her throat, she tried to use her head to smash his face, but the one holding her hair pulled her head back, preventing her from striking.

When one of them adjusted his grip on her arms, she landed a kick in the kidneys of the man to the other side. He immediately punched her in the gut to take some of the fight out of her. It worked. Besides struggling to get away, she now had to struggle to get her breath.

Angela didn't know if they had a plan to begin with, but when they saw her—recognized her from the bar—and realized she was alone and vulnerable, they saw their opportunity to take something they all wanted.

"Hold her tight," Miguel shouted as he went to a shelf and pulled down a grease-covered moving pad. He threw it on the floor.

He came up in front of her and put his face close to hers. He grinned. "I felt your leg before, remember? In the bar. I liked what I felt. I told my friends how good it felt. Now I am going to feel much more."

Angela's fear at what these men were going to do to her made her struggle frantically to get away. She tried with all her strength to break their hold on her arms. Not having the use of her arms only increased her sense of helplessness. She tried to kick Miguel. The men to each side locked a leg around one of hers, preventing her from kicking. Miguel slapped her hard across the face. The three men holding her had her completely locked down and unable to fight back.

Miguel sneered as he hit her again as if out of some deep-seated contempt.

He leaned in to whisper in her ear. "You are all the same. American women think they should have a say, but in the eyes of God you are all Satan's whores. Women are dirt in His eyes, and the eyes of all devout men."

Angela wasn't sure what he was talking about, but it fit her first impression of these men when she had seen them in the bar. By the look in their eyes now she could see that they all shared some sort of fundamental disapproval of her, of her way of life. They were all somehow viscerally offended by her, and yet they were also sexually aroused by her.

Miguel unbuttoned her shorts and then slowly unzipped them. He sank down before her, pulling her shorts and panties down her legs as he went. Angela gritted her teeth as she growled in rage.

With the way the others were holding her, there was nothing she could do to stop him. He pulled her shorts and underwear off over one boot, then did the same to get them off her other leg. He threw her shorts and panties to the side.

Angela could feel her face going red with rage as well as humiliation.

Mole-face, still down on his knees, leaned in and kissed her belly. "It would be good for you to be with my baby, but you will not live long enough for that to happen." He reached up and pushed her top up over her breasts. "Yes, you could be a good mother to feed my baby." He squeezed a breast. "One day all American whores will have our babies to man our great armies."

Angela strained and twisted, trying to get away, but it was hopeless. Even one of these men was stronger than she was. Four were easily able to control her. She was furious at her own helplessness, at her own inability to do anything to defend herself.

Even though she intellectually realized she would not be able to stop these men or get away from them, her fear and panic kept her struggling as hard as possible. She'd had enough visions from killers to know how this was going to end.

Miguel slid his hand up between her legs as he stood. He let out a moan of satisfaction at what he felt.

Angela gritted her teeth. "You are all going to die."

Miguel, with his finger up inside her, smiled. "Really? And how are we to die?"

"I'm going to kill every fucking one of you, that's how. You have my word on that."

"I think we are the ones to do the fucking, no?"

The other three laughed.

Miguel punched her in stomach for her insolence. It bent her face down. His fist came up into her face. He called her an American whore and hit her in the middle again for good measure. It knocked the wind out of her. The pain was staggering. She gasped, trying to get her breath. She thought she might vomit.

He pointed at the moving pad on the floor. "Put her there," he told the others. "Hold her legs. We will show her a woman's proper place as a servant for men."

When they got her down on the ground, two of the men pulled her legs apart while a third held her arms up over her head with her wrists held tightly together. The man holding her wrists punched her in the face, apparently to make her stop struggling. When she twisted again, he hit her again, but harder. It made her vision start to go dark. He grew angry and kept hitting her face as hard as he could. Grunting with the effort.

Angela drifted in and out of consciousness, at times hardly feeling the blows.

Miguel stood between her open legs as he unbuttoned his work overalls. He wasn't smiling anymore. His expression was an odd mix of lust laced with loathing. He pulled his arms out of his overalls and then pushed them down enough to free his erection.

In a daze from being hit so many times, Angela struggled weakly, more out of a frenzied sense of helpless fright than any belief that she could escape. Miguel knelt between her legs, leaned in, and punched down into the gut a few more times. Her screams turned to tears of choking agony. He lay down on top of her.

If she had learned anything from the visions of the killers she had found, this was more about hatred, humiliation, and control than sex. But they still wanted the sex.

Angela struggled to breathe with the weight of him on top of her. He made no effort to hold his weight off her to give her enough space to breathe. She gritted her teeth as tears streamed from her eyes. She had to swallow the blood in her mouth to keep from choking on it.

She had been down this road enough times before, and seen enough visions of men like these, to know what she was in for.

In that moment she became a young girl again.

It became Frankie and Boska again. It became the same terrifying ordeal all over again, the same ordeal she could never escape. It again simply became the way her life was going to be.

Her instinct was to beg them to stop, but she knew that never did any good. If anything, it only excited men like this and made them feel more powerful. Screams were a reward to men like this. She vowed not to reward them with screams.

But then she did.

And then, in that moment as she became that young girl again, she felt as if she left her body. She could see herself there on the floor, her legs being held open. While one monster was top of her the others held her, pawing her breasts, eager for their turn.

Her mind drifted away and she was gone to another place.

What was happening to her there in that filthy factory didn't matter. It couldn't really touch her, touch who she was.

She was outdoors with the peaceful woods all around. It was her grandparents' place, near the cabin, on a rock ledge where she often went to sit because it was so achingly beautiful.

It was night.

The moon was out, watching over her.

As she cried somewhere back in another world, the moonlight took her away.

TWENTY-THREE

When Miguel was finished, he traded places with one of the men holding her legs. When he punched her again as he got up it brought her back in a rush from that distant place. It was an unwelcome return.

She struggled, teeth gritted, still trying without success not to give in as each man took his turn. She knew that struggling was useless, but she couldn't stop herself. She didn't want them to remotely think that she had given in, or worse, that she was willing.

She wanted to kill them. She promised herself that one day she would kill every one of them. Kill them dead.

It was different this time than with Boska. She had never fought against Boska. He would have hurt her bad, and hurt her mother to further punish Angela. He was the ever-present brute. She knew he would always be around. As long as she lived at home, he could always come into her room. If she didn't come home, he would always come and find her. Fear of Boska paralyzed her. But she always knew that if she gave in to him, he would eventually finish and let her go.

She knew that these men had no intention of letting her go.

She was a woman, now, not that helpless little girl. While there was still fear, the emotion that overrode everything now was rage.

She fully expected that these men were going to do something horrific to her. Her visions when looking into the eyes of killers had shown her what sorts of things men like this liked to do to women to show their power over them. Those visions from killers had opened her eyes to a world of degradation, pain, and horrifying death.

She was now in the hands of men like that.

She could see in the eyes of these men that they were not yet killers. She knew by what she saw, though, that they were on the cusp and this was the night they fully intended to cross that line.

For some reason their murderous desires had been building but they had lived lives of restraint. Now those restraints were off and they felt they had license to do whatever they wanted. She could tell by the way they hit her that they were finally free to live out long-held urges.

By the time the last man was done, Miguel had recovered his erection and was lusting for another turn. He pulled her up by her hair and then punched her in the gut a few times—fast and hard. It doubled her over, leaving her limp. He lifted her like a rag doll and threw her facedown over a table so he could take her from behind. He grabbed her hair in his fist and pressed her face down against the table while he was violating her.

Lying there helpless as he grunted and slammed into her from behind, she could see blood, lots of blood, her blood, smeared on the table. Her face throbbed from the blows.

She could also see under the edge of the blanket that covered the things on that table. As if in a dream, she saw the oddest, whitish yellow geometric-shaped objects, several inches thick. There were a half dozen cell phones under the blanket as well. It didn't make any sense to her.

When Miguel finished and pulled out of her, one of the other men took his place. He held her head down on the table the same way. Blood ran out of her mouth onto the table. As he was going at her, Miguel used a blanket to scoop up the things on the table and then carried them out. She could hear the door scrape open. A few moments later, she heard the trunk of the car slam shut.

When the last man had finished, he wrenched her up by her hair and threw her down on the floor. She didn't have the strength to try to break her fall. He kicked her in the face, his heavy boots stunning her. Instinctively, she curled into a ball, arms around her knees, hands covering her head as she shivered. She held her breath against the blows as the men kicked her.

Angela knew that after the raping would come the killing.

She heard an odd sound. She realized after a moment that it was the sound of her teeth chattering.

The last man stood over her, watching her, gloating with his power over her, satisfied they had put her in her place. As he watched her, he pulled up his overalls, stuffed his arms through the sleeves, and buttoned it back up. Angela stared ahead at their feet.

Defeated, she couldn't bear to look up at any of them.

She heard the front door slam as Miguel came back in. He stood over her a moment and then went to one knee beside her. He leaned down, putting his mole-covered face close to hers. She didn't want to look into his terrible eyes, but she did.

He had the paper that had been in the box she had delivered. He waved it in her face.

"Do you know what this paper tells us?"

Angela looked away from his eyes toward the paper, but it was in Spanish, so she couldn't understand it.

When she didn't answer, he told her anyway.

"These are our orders from Rafael, our team leader. We are getting close to the day we will finally destroy the Great Satan. These orders tell us that when the courier delivers these parts we need for that glorious day, we must kill the courier. That is you." He flicked a hand against the paper. "You are this courier. It says we should kill you so that no one knows where you took this package, or who was here to take it from you. Dead people can't talk, no? Americans are stupid. You make it easy for us. You are all easy to fool. So, you see, you were dead the moment you picked up this package. You should be happy that we are merciful and let you have one last fuck to enjoy."

The others chuckled.

Angela hadn't expected that, exactly. She expected that they were planning on killing her when they had finished, but simply for the lust of killing as well as to cover up their crime. She hadn't expected that they would receive orders to kill her. She especially hadn't expected that she would be the one to deliver her own death warrant.

Angela accepted her fate with grim resignation. As she was growing up she had always expected that one lunatic or another would eventually kill her. That sense of destiny had always shadowed her. She had always thought she was living on borrowed time. She was ready to die. Life held little for her. Death promised more. Death promised release.

The only time she felt truly alive was when she was killing men who killed, when she was making them suffer for what they had done to women who couldn't fight back, women who could never seek justice for themselves. When she was killing a man who had done things to his victims like these men were doing to her, it gave her a high. It was ecstasy.

That was all she lived for. That was all that her life was good for—bringing death to men like these, bringing justice down on them, preventing them from ever again harming anyone.

It seemed ironic that this was to be the way she died.

Death, though, held the quiet offer of everlasting peace. If there was a God, then maybe He would let her be with the only ones she had ever loved—her grandparents.

In a way, she was surprised she had lived this long. She took chances she knew could get her killed, like with Owen, because she didn't really care if she died, and being that close to the edge made it all the more exhilarating.

Those risks enabled her to get closer to the pure ecstasy of vengeance.

Angela had grown up around dangerous men. Now she hunted dangerous killers. She'd always known that death could come at any time.

Miguel abruptly snatched her by her hair and hauled her to her feet. She stood before him, before all four men, naked, shivering both in pain and in helpless fear of what was coming. She didn't really care if she was about to die, but she feared the agony of how they would do it. Men like this didn't like to make a quick kill. They liked to make it an agonizing death.

Miguel spoke in Spanish to the others. They discussed something for a moment, and then Emilio ran off into a room to the side. He came back with a rope.

Emilio held the coiled rope he'd retrieved up before her. "A rope can kill quick, no?" He held a hand up above his head and did an impression of being hanged and the rope snapping taut. His tongue flopped out to the side of his mouth. "See? Break the neck and it is quick."

"But quick is too good for Americans," Miguel said.

Juan and Pedro nodded their agreement. By now, she had learned all their names, and the name of the man who gave the orders: Rafael.

"We have something better in mind for you," Emilio said.

A wicked smile grew on Miguel's face. "Hold her."

As the other men held her arms and hair again, Miguel tied one end of the rope around her neck. The rope was coarse and hard. It hurt as they tied a knot at the back of her neck and jerked it tight. It was already starting to choke her. Angela didn't know much about hanging, but she did understand that they didn't want it to be an easy death by breaking her neck.

"Should we tie her arms?" Emilio asked.

"No," Miguel scoffed. "Let her have her hands free so she can claw at the rope that will be choking her to death. Let her be free to struggle. That will make it worse that she cannot get the rope that is strangling her from her neck."

Emilio peered up at the ceiling for a moment and then tossed the rope up and over one of the iron beams.

The men all let go of her to grab hold of the end of the rope. They quickly pulled together and hoisted her up off the ground by the rope around her neck.

Angela took one last gasping breath as her feet were lifted off the floor and her weight tightened the rope. The men pulled together until she was about four feet above the floor. It might as well have been a mile. Already she was panicking from not being able to breathe.

One of the men tied off the end of the rope on a post.

Angela kicked and twisted. She wanted to scream at the men, but she couldn't. Desperation took control of her. She clawed at the rope that was strangling her, just as Miguel said she would.

"Let's go," Miguel said.

"Don't you want to watch the American whore die?" Emilio asked.

"Now that we have the parts we need, you know that we have other things we must do. It is already getting late. We will come back for her truck later. When we do, we will dispose of her body as well. We already took too much time with her." He grinned as he smacked her bare bottom. "But it was worth it, eh?"

Angela kicked at his head, but he easily dodged to the side. She desperately wished that she could reach a table with her feet, but the tables were way too far away. Her body rotated around and around as she kicked, all the while desperately clawing at the rope strangling her. Tears streamed down her cheeks, mixing with all the blood that was dripping off her jaw.

She was still kicking and struggling as she watched the four men hurry toward the door carrying more bundles from the shelves. She couldn't see it, but she heard the front door scrape the ground and then slam shut. She heard the car start as doors shut and then the tires chirp as it raced away.

Angela was completely alone in a dark, deserted factory her grandfather had helped build. No one was going to save her.

The rope around her throat held all her weight. The pain was horrific. She desperately needed a breath.

Her vision was narrowing down to a dark tunnel.

As she twisted, the world was starting to go black.

TWENTY-FOUR

Hanging by her neck at the end of the rope, Angela twisted and spun as she struggled. She could only imagine the shock when her corpse was eventually found hanging there, naked, her tongue bulging out of her mouth, her skin blue.

What a sensation—a naked girl found hanging by her neck.

Naked.

The word seared through her panic-stricken mind.

She was naked—except for her boots.

They had pulled off her shorts and underwear and then ripped off her top to get at what they wanted, but they hadn't bothered with her boots.

Even as she realized that she was still wearing her boots, Angela knew she was rapidly running out of time. A desperate plan was forming in her mind, but being unable to breathe she knew that her window of time for a chance to do anything to save herself was very small and closing fast.

If she wanted to live, she knew she had only seconds to act.

Move, Angela, she told herself. *Don't let them win. Move!*

She frantically reached up with her left hand and grabbed the thick, coarse rope above her head. She pulled with all her strength to at least take some of the weight off her throat, but more importantly it gave her the ability to more easily twist her shoulders so she could reach down with her right hand. She wasn't able to keep the rope from strangling her, but it at least helped ease the excruciating pain a little so that she could focus on what she needed to do.

With her right shoulder tipped downward, Angela bent her right leg at the hip and knee, as if she were squatting, to get her boot up closer to her hand. She tensed her neck muscles as hard as she could to try to help blood get to her brain before she blacked out.

Although her whole arm was tingling like it had fallen asleep, nerve pain shot down the length of it, so moving it was difficult. She wanted to scream at how hard it was to reach down. She needed to reach down if she was going to save herself. Her tingling fingers were going numb.

Holding her leg up with the little strength she had left, she felt around blindly, desperately, until the tips of her fingers found the handle of the knife down inside the top of her boot. It was a moment of giddy success amid the icy dread of death cloaking her in darkness.

She reminded herself that she was going to lose consciousness and die if she didn't hurry.

As frenzied as she was at not being able to breathe, Angela forced herself to be as deliberately careful as possible as she worked the knife up out of the boot. She knew that once she got it partway out of the sheath, if the knife slipped and fell from her numb, tingling fingers, she would lose her only chance to live.

It was so frightening to be hanging by her neck, and so difficult to try to pull the knife up, that part of her wanted to give up. It seemed so inviting to simply let the darkness smother her. It would be over, then. If she gave up, she would have everlasting peace. There would be no more pain. No one would ever again be able to hurt her. As her vision and her mind dimmed, that option seemed ever more inviting.

It felt as if the peaceful realm of the dead was calling to her, whispering promises that if she simply gave up, she could be forever at peace and safe. If she just stopped struggling it would only be a moment longer and there would be no more pain.

A moment longer and she could be with her grandparents again.

But some part of her deep down inside wanted to live.

Move!

She didn't want to be one of those women who died, never to see their killers punished. She didn't want this to be the way she died. She wanted her life to be more, to mean something.

She didn't want those men to win. She had made a promise that she was going to kill them. She couldn't do that if she gave in to the sweet whispers.

Even as the specter of that inviting end to the pain called to her, with her last, waning bit of strength, Angela's weak fingers kept working at the knife until she wiggled the end of the handle up far enough to be clear of the top of her boot. She struggled to muster the power to lift her heavy leg up even more, to bring her boot up closer to her quivering fingers. It felt as if it were made of lead.

Her lungs burned with pain. Her brain could hardly think of anything other than the desperate want of air and the simultaneous desire to give up. She had never known how much it hurt to strangle to death. She knew now what the women in those visions felt when their killers strangled them to death.

Tears ran down her cheeks as she felt herself losing the battle.

She was so close, yet so far.

She just didn't have enough left in her to do it.

And then, her fingers closed, almost reflexively, around the handle and she pulled the knife free.

She would have screamed in joy as she finally grasped the handle in her fist, but she wasn't able to breathe, much less make a sound. For a very brief instant she held the blade up before her eyes in her trembling hand just so that she would believe she truly had it in her fist.

And then, her eyes closed.

She no longer had the strength to keep them open.

Eyes closed, she clenched her teeth, straining the muscles in her neck in an attempt to keep the noose from crushing her windpipe and from cutting off the blood supply to her brain. Once she had stretched her arms above her head, she held the rope with her left hand as she started dragging the blade across the rope with her other hand. Her knives were always razor sharp. She heard some of the fibers make a snapping sound as they tore. That sound urged her on to find the strength she didn't think she had to keep sawing at the tough rope.

Even though Angela sawed as fast as she could, it wasn't very fast, and consciousness continued to fade away. Tears of frustration seeped from her closed eyes.

Then, when the blade had cut partway through, the rotting fibers of the rope that were left couldn't hold her weight and they suddenly ripped apart.

Angela dropped heavily to the ground. Her legs were unable to hold her weight. She collapsed to her knees.

The pressure was off, but she found that the rope was still choking her. When they had hoisted her up it had tightened the rope around her neck as well as the knot.

She was horrified to realize that cutting herself down wasn't enough. She still couldn't get any air. Her eyes felt like they were bulging out of her head.

She told herself that she had done her best.

It just wasn't good enough.

With that thought, she remembered the smug faces of the men as they looked back at her as they were leaving, knowing that they had won.

She didn't want that to be it. She didn't want them to win.

On her knees, bent forward, Angela felt blindly behind her neck until she located the knot. With the trembling fingers of her left hand she guided the blade onto the knot. She carefully but urgently worked with both hands to saw back and forth to cut the knot, the fingers of one hand grasping the sides of the blade and helping to push as she pulled the knife back and forth with the other hand.

The fibers of the straining rope finally started to pull apart. She could feel it in her neck when some of the strands popped apart; then at last they all separated, undoing the knot and finally releasing the pressure on her throat.

Angela flopped back onto the moving pad, arms splayed out, loudly gasping in breath after breath.

She lay there for a long time, simply breathing in and out, with hoarse gasps, letting the life come back into her. Once she had gotten the air that she so desperately needed, she was finally able to pull the remainder of the noose away from her neck.

The men had left her to die. Instead, she was alive—in crippling pain, but alive.

TWENTY-FIVE

For quite a while, Angela lay on the greasy moving pad where she had been raped, gasping in air, sucking in life, getting her breath, both from the hanging and from the sheer terror of the ordeal.

Tears ran down her face but this time they were tears of joy. She had beaten her would-be killers. She had beaten all four of the bastards.

After a time, she made herself get up on wobbly legs. She couldn't straighten up all the way because her abdomen hurt so much from the blows. She feared something inside was broken. Blood dripped from her chin to the concrete floor, leaving growing pools of vivid red. Her face throbbed in pain. She looked around and finally saw her shorts and panties lying against one of the shelves where Miguel had thrown them.

Angela shuffled over to her clothes. She pulled a blanket from the gray metal shelf. Blood was splattered all down her legs from the beating.

She stood for a few minutes to regain enough strength, then used the blanket to wipe off the semen running down her thighs before she pulled on her underpants and shorts. Her top had been torn off. She put it on with trembling hands and tied the front shut as best she could.

She almost shouted with excitement when she found the keys to her truck still in the pocket of her shorts. She wasn't sure she could drive, but she knew she had to.

The door grated on the buckled concrete when she slowly pushed it open just enough to carefully poke her head out. She was worried that one of the men might have remained behind to stand guard.

She didn't see anyone. It was dark and lonely outside. Her truck was still there.

The craziest thought came into her head. Barry would be wondering why she wasn't at work. He had always been good to her, treated her well.

She pushed the door open a little more so she could put her head out farther into the night and get a better look around. She didn't see any of the men. Their car was gone. They must have all left. They wanted her dead, but they hadn't stayed to see her die. She supposed that they figured she didn't have a chance in hell of escaping.

The abandoned factory area was dead quiet and pitch black. She didn't see any lights anywhere. Overhead the moon shone down on her all alone among the ghostly buildings, giving her enough light to see.

Angela unlocked the truck and with an effort climbed up into the driver's seat. Her abdomen cramped in pain, her face throbbed, and her throat burned with every breath.

Her phone was in one of the cup holders where she'd left it. She briefly thought about calling the police, but she knew they would take forever to find her. That would waste a lot of time.

Angela didn't think she could afford to waste any time.

Her fingers were shaking so badly it took her several tries before she was finally able to get the key into the ignition. She turned the key and her faithful truck roared to life—her chariot ready to carry her away and help her escape. She backed away from the building, put the truck in drive, and laid rubber away from the death trap.

Her fuzzy thoughts kept wandering. She didn't know where she was going. She was having trouble focusing enough to keep a train of thought as to how she had found the address in the first place.

It wasn't long before she realized she was completely lost. Nothing looked familiar. In the dark, the dark shapes of the buildings all looked the same. Getting lost in the old industrial complex was easy enough to do in the day, but at night, without any lights or landmarks, it was easier to lose your way. On top of that, she was in so much pain she was having trouble thinking at all.

Angela leaned forward against the steering wheel at the end of every building, looking left and right for the four-door Toyota Camry the men were driving. The last thing she wanted to do was get caught by them again. Of course, if she was in her truck, they would never be able to catch her. But if they were armed they could shoot out her tires, or more likely, shoot her. Being in the truck was no protection from guns. Her truck wasn't bulletproof. She wasn't bulletproof.

But now she had a gun and she could shoot back.

The industrial district wasn't laid out with regular streets. The entire area was acres and acres of concrete with buildings placed in what seemed like random places. The expanses of concrete were broken, cracked, and overgrown with weeds. Even though it seemed random, there was a pattern to the way the buildings were laid out, such as to take advantage of the rail lines, and routes among them with occasional streets.

The problem was, Angela wasn't familiar enough with that pattern. Here and there larger buildings blocked the way she thought she needed to go, making it necessary to detour around them. Without streets among the maze of old buildings, and in her foggy mental state, it was maddening trying to find her way out.

At last she saw a familiar building in the moonlight. It had a partially collapsed roof. Beyond that building she found the road she knew led back into town. She wanted to go home to her cabin in the woods. That was all she wanted to do. Go home and shower off the filth from those men.

But she knew that wasn't the smartest thing to do. Instead of heading for her place, she headed into Milford Falls. It was a relief when she reached streetlights again and areas she knew well.

She encountered traffic but it was light because of the late hour. In a way, seeing other cars was a relief, because for a time it had seemed like she was the only person left in the world. When she saw no cars at intersections, she rolled through stop signs and red lights. She didn't want to waste time to stop unless she had to.

When she finally saw the glowing red sign for the hospital, she pulled in and came to a crooked stop at the emergency entrance. She knew there was no parking allowed where she stopped. She didn't care.

The emergency entrance had double glass doors. She could see activity inside. She didn't see any patients. She knew that the emergency department was usually quiet this late at night. The drunks who had been in car accidents or fights had already been treated, so the hospital usually quieted down until the early-morning rush started in.

Angela slid out of the driver's seat. When her feet hit the ground, she found she was so dizzy she didn't know if she would be able to stand, but the light from beyond the glass doors drew her onward. She made up her mind that if it was the last thing she did, she was going to make it inside. If she could get inside, someone would help her.

The automatic doors slid apart as she stumbled through the entryway. Once in the light she saw that she was dripping blood all along the tan linoleum floor. She could feel it dripping off her chin and running all down the front of her.

The chairs for patients coming in with an emergency were empty, but there were people ahead at the desk. She knew the place well from picking up courier packages. She knew many of the people who worked in the hospital.

They would recognize her. They would help her.

When the nurse at the desk saw her shuffling in, she immediately called for help and then rushed out from behind her desk. Two more nurses emerged from a side hall. An orderly poked his bald head out from behind a curtain. None of them ran in a panic, but they all hurried with professional familiarity with medical emergencies.

One of the nurses came up and put a hand under Angela's arm and the other around her waist just as she started sinking toward the floor. The orderly shoved a wheelchair at her from behind and helped pull her into it.

"Good lord, young lady—is anyone else with you?"

"I'm alone," Angela managed. Her voice sounded garbled. Her tongue felt swollen.

The orderly started wheeling her toward one of the treatment areas, a nurse to each side.

"What's your name, dear?"

Angela looked up. "Julie, it's me."

"Me? Me who?"

"Angela."

The woman looked stunned. "Angela? Angela Constantine? Our courier?"

Angela nodded. She realized her face must be pretty messed up for Julie not to recognize her.

"What happened? Were you in a car accident?"

"No. I was raped by four men," she said. "They tried to kill me."

Angela was only dimly aware of being lifted onto a bed in the treatment room as people rushed around. Everyone seemed to have a job and knew just what to grab.

A short Asian woman leaned in. Angela realized she recognized her. It was Dr. Song. One nurse put a blood-pressure cuff around her left arm as another worked at getting a needle into her other arm. Once the nurse had taken her blood pressure, she bent in with a pair of scissors and cut off Angela's shorts and panties, then quickly unlaced her boots. She pulled off the boots and set them aside.

"What happened to your neck?" Dr. Song asked while listening to her heart.

"They tried to hang me."

237

Dr. Song turned to one of the nurses. "Call the police. Ask for a female officer. Then get a rape kit."

Angela started to cry.

One of the nurses patted her on the shoulder. "No need to cry, Angela. We're going to take good care of you."

That wasn't why Angela was crying.

She was crying because she was at last safe.

TWENTY-SIX

Julie glided into the room like a ghost, or maybe an angel, and touched her fingers to Angela's shoulder. "How are you feeling?"

"What's going on?" Angela asked in a weak, hoarse voice as she squinted up at the nurse.

"They had to give you some medication to relax you. It put you to sleep for a while."

Angela had never seen Julie doing her job as a nurse, caring for patients. She had only seen her with paperwork for samples that needed to go to a lab. She seemed so professional, so competent and caring as she looked over the readings on the monitors.

Julie reminded her of Carrie Stratton. She had been a nurse here, too, until Owen had murdered her. They were about the same age and their hair was similar.

Angela's throat hurt. Her jaw hurt. Her abdomen hurt. In fact, she hurt all over. Her voice sounded raspy to her.

She looked around and realized she was in a hospital room, rather than the emergency ward. She was aware that she had been in and out of consciousness. She remembered the exam, and the CT scan, but little else. She didn't remember being brought up to the room. She vaguely recalled them injecting something into the IV line they'd put in the back of her hand, and then the world fading away.

"If you need more pain medication, Dr. Song left orders that you could have it," Julie said. "Just ask."

Angela nodded. "My cheeks feel numb. There's something crusty inside."

"You're feeling the stitches. They had to stitch up the inside of your cheeks," Julie said.

Angela squinted in disbelief at the woman. "What?"

"They got cut on your teeth when you were hit. The doctor used medication to numb the area where she had to put in stitches, so it's going to feel a little strange for a while."

Angela remembered the way the men kept punching her as if it were a game. Even though she was still in pain, she didn't want any more drugs. The ones they'd already given her were probably what was making her feel nauseated. She hated drugs. She had been born a freak because of drugs.

Angela was more than glad to be finished with the embarrassment of the examination. She had immediately agreed to it. In fact, she had insisted on it. That was a main reason she had come to the hospital in the first place. She wanted those men to be prosecuted. To do that, the police would need DNA evidence. At least the CT scan had been easy enough. Now, after the ordeal of the examination, she just wanted to be left alone so she could go to sleep.

As Julie was making notes on a chart, Dr. Song appeared at the side of the bed. "How are you feeling? Is the pain better?"

Angela reached up with her right hand to touch her left shoulder. "My left shoulder hurts. Did they break something?"

Dr. Song smiled as she rubbed Angela's arm in a reassuring manner. "No, your shoulder is fine. That's referred pain from your spleen."

"My spleen?" Angela found it hard to believe. "That can't be it. Are you sure?"

"Yes, the CT scan showed that you have some bruising and possible injury to your spleen from blunt-force trauma to your abdomen. That is what's causing the pain you're feeling in your shoulder."

Angela found it difficult to believe that a problem in her abdomen could cause such aching pain in her shoulder.

"We need to keep you here under observation for a couple days," Dr. Song said. "I want to do another CT scan after twenty-four hours, and then, depending on the results, possibly another one the next day to make sure your spleen isn't ruptured and that everything is okay. We're hoping to avoid the need for surgery. The best news is that the CT scan didn't show any internal bleeding and your brain doesn't show any signs of injury."

"I want to go home."

Dr. Song smiled. "Don't worry, we want to get you out of here as soon as possible."

"The police are waiting outside," Julie said to the doctor. "They want to know if it's okay for them to talk to her."

"I think so," Dr. Song said. She looked down at Angela. "Is that okay with you?"

Angela nodded. Julie checked the flow on the drip and then left. Dr. Song went out to update the police.

After a few minutes, the female police officer came in. Her expression creased with concern when she saw Angela's condition. Angela wasn't sure what she looked like, but the alarm on the woman's face gave her a pretty good indication. Angela could see a male officer out in the hall, talking to a nurse at the station.

The female officer, in her late thirties, looked both impressive and authoritative in her uniform. Her light brown hair was pulled back into a loose ponytail. When she approached the side of the bed and leaned over a little, Angela saw that her service weapon was a Sig Sauer.

"Ms. Constantine, I'm Officer Denton. Can you tell me anything about the men who did this to you? Do you know who they were, or their names?"

She sounded professionally sympathetic. Angela didn't want sympathy. She wanted the bastards caught and put in jail forever.

Or else down the hell hole.

"They came into the bar where I work, once." Angela's voice sounded strange to her. "Do you have a pad and pen?"

Officer Denton pulled a small pad out of a pouch in her black leather equipment belt and handed it over along with a pen. Angela wrote down the names of the four men—Miguel, Emilio, Juan, Pedro—and the license number of their car.

She handed the pad back to the woman. "That's their names and the license number of the car they're driving."

Officer Denton looked at the pad a moment, then looked up. "Okay. Do you know the kind of car, or at least the color?"

"Beige Toyota Camry. Probably six or seven years old."

The policewoman arched an eyebrow. "You have a good memory."

"I tend to remember people who try to kill me."

"Can you tell me what happened? Anything you remember would be helpful."

Angela met the officer's gaze. "I have a courier service. I had a package for Hartland Irrigation. When I made the delivery the four of them overpowered me. They pulled off my clothes, raped me, beat me, and after each of them finished having a few turns at me," Angela said in a bitter tone, having to look away and pause to control her rage, "then they put a rope around my neck, hanged me from a beam, and left me to choke to death hanging there a few feet above the floor while they drove off. They wanted me to suffer as I was dying. They fully expected me to choke to death."

Officer Denton wrote down what Angela had said on a report on a clipboard. Finally, she spoke again.

"Where did this happen?"

"In the old industrial area." Angela gave her the address.

"Can you describe these four men? What did they look like? Height, weight, that kind of thing."

"They were all Hispanic. Darkish skin, dark hair, average build. Under six feet. All of them probably between five-eight and five-ten at the most. Each had a little facial hair, but not what you would call beards. They were in their mid- to late twenties, maybe early thirties.

They were wearing work overalls. Medium bluish gray. Miguel seemed be the one in charge. He has a zillion moles all over his face."

"Okay, that's good," Officer Denton said as she wrote.

She finally looked up. She stared a moment at the tattoo—DARK ANGEL—across Angela's throat.

"By the look of those bruises and the abrasions from the rope around your neck, you're one lucky girl to be alive."

Angela didn't answer.

The woman's penetrating gaze moved to Angela's eyes. "How'd you get the rope off your neck?"

Angela saw her boots standing on the bottom shelf of the hospital cabinet at the side of the room. She could just see the tip of the black handle at the rim of the boot. The knife, in the sheath, was down between the lining and the leather. Angela always put the sheath of her knife in her boots that way. It kept it from chafing against her bare skin.

The police were sure to go to the address Angela had given them to collect evidence. She knew that if she said that the rope was old and rotted and it simply broke from her weight, she would be caught in the lie when they saw that the rope had been cut.

Angela had two rules about police. First rule, don't talk to the police. Second rule, if she had to talk to the police, don't lie. The police remembered being lied to. She didn't want to give the police any reason to remember her.

"I was able to cut the rope with a knife," Angela said.

A frown twitched across Officer Denton's face as she looked up from her report. "A knife." She glanced down at her notes on the clipboard. "You said they pulled off your clothes. You said you were hanging several feet off the floor. How did you get a knife?"

"They hadn't pulled off my boots. I had a knife in my right boot. After they left I was finally able to get to it and cut the rope."

Officer Denton looked over her shoulder to Angela's boots. She finally turned and went to the little cabinet. Squatting down, she used a finger and thumb to pull out the knife. She held it like it might bite her. Angela could see that there was blood all over it. At least it was only her blood and not Owen's. She was glad she had followed her rule about disposing of anything she used on a killer.

The policewoman returned to Angela's side. She held up the knife by a finger and thumb.

"This is illegal."

Angela frown. "My knife is illegal?"

"Yes. It's clearly over the legal length."

Angela ran her tongue over the stitches in her cheek. "I have kitchen knives that are longer than that."

"Maybe so, but this is a knife made to carry. It's clearly a weapon, not a kitchen knife. For that reason, it's illegal. Worse, you had it hidden in your boot. That makes it a concealed weapon. It's illegal to carry a concealed weapon."

Angela briefly wondered if she was imagining such lunacy.

"I sometimes make deliveries to high-crime areas," she said. "I only have the knife to protect myself."

"Looks like it didn't do you any good this time, did it?"

"They grabbed my arms and legs so fast I couldn't get to it until they left me there hanging by my neck."

"Concealed weapons usually only make matters worse and get people killed. If you would have pulled it on those men, they likely would have taken it away from you and stabbed you to death."

Angela wanted to say that it had saved her life, but her instincts told her to keep quiet and not argue.

Officer Denton pulled a manila envelope from inside her thin aluminum clipboard and slipped the sheathed knife into it. "The people of New York State have made it clear that they don't want anyone carrying a concealed weapon. A knife this long is a weapon, so it's a crime for you to carry it, and it's a much more serious crime to conceal it."

"But it's not a gun. I thought only a gun was a concealed weapon."

"This is classified as a concealed weapon, the same as a gun."

The same as a gun. Angela could feel her face going red with rage. She had been raped, beaten, and nearly murdered, and here this woman was, not relieved that the victim had managed to cut herself down and give information that could lead to the apprehension of the criminals, but instead was growing hostile because Angela had a knife to protect herself. Officer Denton hadn't shown that much anger toward the four men.

Angela would have loved to say all of that, but the last thing she wanted to do was to get on the wrong side of the police. They sometimes came into the bar asking about patrons. Whenever Angela spoke with them she always tried not to make herself noteworthy or memorable. At least other than the way she dressed. She wanted to stay under their radar. If they never investigated her, they couldn't find any evidence of anything.

"I'm sorry," Angela said, trying to sound contrite. "I didn't know."

Officer Denton's expression softened a little. "I can't give this back to you."

Angela had dozens just like it. She had no reason to try to hold on to this one. They were meant to serve a purpose and then be discarded down the hell hole. This knife had served its purpose. It had saved her life.

Angela nodded. "I understand."

Officer Denton stared at her for a long moment. Her expression was unreadable.

"Constantine. You live in the trailer park. Your mother is Sally Constantine. She uses meth."

"I used to live there," Angela corrected. "I moved out a long time ago."

"There's been a lot of drug activity there for years. The police have been to your trailer a number of times. Made a number of arrests there."

It was an accusation of some sort. Angela didn't say anything.

Officer Denton finally gestured at Angela's throat. "I'm beginning to wonder if maybe this whole thing with these men may have been a drug deal gone bad. Is that it? Does this somehow involve drugs? They bringing you a supply up from Mexico and you couldn't pay what you promised them? That sounds more like what really happened."

Angela blinked in disbelief. "I don't do drugs."

"You just sell them. Smart. Lots of people who sell use. That eats into their business and gets them in trouble. The smart ones sell but they don't use their own inventory."

It was all Angela could not to tell the woman to go fuck herself, but she knew that would only convince her that she was on to something.

"I don't do drugs," Angela said as calmly as she could. "I don't live there with my mother anymore. As soon as I was old enough, I moved out. My mother's a meth-head and that brought a rough group of men around the place. When my mother was high some of those men abused me—raped me—when I was just a girl. I hate drugs. I don't want anything to do with drugs. I have a courier business and I tend bar. That's how I earn a living.

"If you don't believe me, they have plenty of my blood around here, test it all you want. Go out and search my truck if you want."

Officer Denton tapped her thumb on the railing of the bed, still showing no emotion.

"I'm terribly sorry for what happened to you, Ms. Constantine," she finally said. "With the information you've provided I'm sure we will be able to capture these men."

With that, she turned and left.

TWENTY-SEVEN

Three days later Angela was still in the hospital, but she was hopeful they would release her soon. A lot of the swelling had gone down. Everything was still sore, though.

She wanted to go home to her cabin and crawl into bed there where people wouldn't come in and wake her up at all hours of the night to take her temperature and blood pressure and give her pills. She was tired of having to roll the IV stand along with her when she went to the bathroom.

She had just returned from another one of those tricky bathroom trips and settled back into bed when two men in plain clothes came up to her room and stood in the doorway. They knocked on the doorframe and at the same time identified themselves as detectives Preston and Vaughan. They were both middle-aged. Both were dressed in suits. They had police badges hung on chains around their neck. The badges rested over drab ties.

"Are you up to talking with us?" Detective Preston asked. He was the older of the two, heavyset, with a buzz cut.

"Sure," Angela answered cautiously, fearing they might have come with more accusations about her selling drugs or that they might even want to charge her with carrying a concealed weapon. "What is it?"

"We'd like you to take a look at some photos of some men," Detective Vaughan said. He was thinner, taller, and with even shorter hair. His eyebrows and eyelashes were a light color that looked weak against his penetrating blue eyes.

Angela was relieved to hear that and gave them a nod. They rolled the food tray in over the bed and positioned it in front of her. She used the buttons to elevate the top half of the bed until she was almost sitting up. They laid out two rows of three photos each. The six photos looked like they had been made on a black-and-white copy machine, but the men in the photos were recognizable enough.

"Take your time," Detective Vaughan said, "and tell us if you recognize any of these men."

Angela looked at all six faces only briefly. A brief look was all she needed.

"No. None of these are the men who tried to kill me."

Detective Preston took them away and Detective Vaughan laid down two more rows of three photos each.

Angela pointed at the last one before he had even finished laying it down. "Him. That's Emilio."

"None of the other five look familiar?" Detective Vaughan asked.

When Angela shook her head, Detective Preston took the photos away, keeping Emilio's mug shot to the side.

After Detective Vaughan laid down six more, Angela pointed at the one in the middle of the top row. "That's Juan," she said, her anger rising. "He was one of the four men who tried to kill me." She pointed at the photo beside it to her right. "That's Pedro."

Angela held out her hand as Detective Preston took them away, keeping two of them aside. "Just give me the rest of them and if Miguel is in there I'll know his mole-covered face when I see it."

The two detectives shared a look and then Detective Vaughan handed Angela the rest of the photos. She went through them quickly, one at a time, laying them facedown on the tray in front of her until she got to the photo of Miguel. She would recognize his face anywhere. Angela plunked the photo down for the two men to see.

"That's Miguel. That's all four. If you have their mug shots, does that mean you have them under arrest?"

Detective Vaughan nodded. "They were just picked up a couple hours ago. We wanted to make sure we had the right men. From how certain you are, it appears we do."

"When is the trial? I want to testify. I want to help put them away forever."

Detective Preston smiled at her eagerness. "We'll be in touch and let you know what happens at the arraignment." He laid his business card down on the tray. "In the meantime, if you have any questions or think of anything else here's my card."

"And mine," Detective Vaughan said as he laid his down beside it. "A lot of victims are afraid to testify. We're glad to hear that you would be willing."

A short time after they left, Barry stopped in to see how she was doing. It was his second visit. He assured her that the bruises on her face looked better, as did her neck. She didn't know if he was just trying to cheer her up or if he was being honest.

Barry was a nice guy, but he wasn't the type who was comfortable expressing sympathy. He didn't know what to do with his hands as he stood beside the bed. Before long he said he wanted to let her rest, so he didn't stay long. Angela appreciated him stopping in.

He told her not to worry about her job, that once she was better it would be waiting for her. He smiled, then, and said that she was the best bartender he'd ever had and he wanted her back.

The next afternoon, Dr. Song stopped in. It was earlier than she usually came by.

"This morning's CT scan looks better," she said. "If you feel up to it we could release you today. But only if you feel up to it. I can tell you, though, that the less time you spend in a hospital, the better."

Angela sat up. "I'm good. I'm ready to go home."

Dr. Song smiled at Angela's impatience. "I'll send down the release orders, then. A nurse will come by in an hour or two and take out your IV and sign you out."

"All right," Angela said, already eager to leave. "Thank you for everything you've done for me."

"Happy to help," she said with a smile. "But I want you to take it easy. No strenuous activity. No physical exertion. It would be best if you got a lot of rest for the next couple weeks. Eat light meals. No aspirin—we'll give you a few pain pills to take home and a prescription for more, but if you feel any increase in abdominal pain you need to let me know right away."

Angela simply nodded. She didn't want to tell the doctor that she had no intention of taking pain medication. The drugs made her feel sick. She'd rather have the pain than the nausea.

By later in the afternoon, she had been unplugged from everything and had signed all the paperwork. Julie brought her a shirt and jeans from the lost and found and told her where she had moved her truck into the parking lot. Angela thanked her for all her help and promised to buy her a drink if she stopped into the bar once Angela was back to work.

Julie paused for a moment. "Do you remember Carrie, the nurse who worked here? She gave you samples to be taken to the lab not long ago."

"I remember her," Angela said. "I heard about her being abducted."

Julie smiled, even though her eyes watered up. "Somehow, God intervened, or something, and they were able to find her body along with the guy who did it. We all wish she was still with us, but at least it's some comfort for her family that they were finally able to give her a proper burial."

"I'm so sorry . . ." After an uncomfortable silence, Angela finally spoke again. "Thank you for taking care of me while I was here."

Julie wiped a tear away, smiled, and rubbed Angela's arm. "Glad to watch over you."

As she left the room to get an orderly with a wheelchair, Angela thought, *You all watch over me, and I watch over all of you.*

It's what they did. That's what Angela did.

Julie finally brought back an orderly with a wheelchair. As they wheeled her to the door, and then out into the parking lot to her truck, they offered to call someone to drive her, or to call her a cab. Angela thanked them, but insisted she was fine. When she carefully climbed into her truck, relieved to be free at last, the first thing she did was check that her gun was still there in the center console. It was right where she'd left it.

She drove through town slowly to be sure she wouldn't have to slam on the brakes for anyone. She felt a wave of relief that she had survived the attempt on her life and that she had finally gotten out of the hospital. The four men who had raped her and tried to kill her were finally behind bars. She would rather have them down the hell hole, but at least they were in jail. She hoped they spent the rest of their lives in prison.

When she reached the drive up to her cabin, she let the cable drop to the ground so she could drive in. She would have liked to leave it there and simply drive up to the cabin, but she wanted it back across the drive.

Her four attackers were in jail, but she didn't want anyone else coming up to her place uninvited. She struggled to pull the cable tight across the drive, but she finally got it locked back on, happy that she would be left alone.

TWENTY-EIGHT

Even though it was still light out, Angela went right to bed. She was relieved to finally take off the baggy jeans and shirt from the hospital lost and found, but more than that it was a relief to be in her own bed and to at last be completely alone.

Before climbing into bed, she resisted the temptation to look at herself in the mirror.

Several mornings later, when she finally did look in the mirror, it was worse than she had hoped, but it wasn't as bad as she had feared. The bruises had lost their sick-looking deep violet color, but now they were an ugly dark yellowish black. The stitches inside her cheeks were a continual annoyance, but they would dissolve as the wounds healed. She was thankful that they hadn't gone all the way through her cheeks and that she wouldn't have scars across the outside of her face. It was going to be a while, though, before she was in shape to tend bar.

After she got dressed and made herself some soup, she went down into the basement. The quiet of the basement was different from the quiet of the house. The basement was deathly quiet. She thought about the killers she had put down the hell hole, and promised herself they would not be the last.

Angela retrieved another knife from the cabinet and fit its sheath into the pocket in the lining of a new pair of boots that hadn't been covered in blood. She had never known that it was illegal to carry the knife. She had carried the knife because she knew it was illegal to carry a gun. She thought she was taking on an extra risk by carrying a knife instead of a gun in order to stay legal.

Since it was illegal to carry the knife, too, that changed everything.

Angela went back to the cabinet where the supplies were stored and retrieved her grandfather's inside-the-waistband leather holster for the Walther P22. She tried the gun in it. It fit like a glove. But that wasn't exactly what she needed.

Angela put the leather holster on the counter and used a utility knife to cut off the bottom end of the barrel pocket to make an opening. She screwed on a suppressor and tried putting the gun into the holster. She had to cut away some extra leather until the suppressor fit down through the hole and the gun sat snug in the holster.

She undid the button and zipper on her jeans and fit the holster to the inside of the waistband in back. It would stick out and be too visible if she wore it on her hip. Wearing it in the back she could wear a top to help conceal it.

The suppressor made for a long weapon, but she found that with the barrel of the suppressor resting partway down into the crack of her ass, the gun was well concealed.

She often wore a short top that showed her midriff when she tended bar. She decided that her cutoffs revealed enough to keep men buying drinks and leaving tips without needing a cropped top as well. A longer top would allow her to carry the gun with the suppressor already attached.

Ever since she had killed that first man, who had murdered the girl with red hair and dumped her body in an old cistern in the deserted industrial tract, she knew she had found her calling in life. It seemed like the more men she killed, the more she wanted to kill. It was addicting.

Fortunately, she seemed to be a lunatic magnet. Killers were drawn to her like wolves to a lamb.

Angela figured that if she was breaking the law carrying the knife, then she might as well carry a gun. Better to break the law than to be murdered. The next time she wouldn't have to worry about it being out of reach in her truck.

Even if she did have a gun on her, she was concerned by how fast those men had gotten control of her. She wasn't sure that even if she had been carrying a gun she would have been able to get it out fast enough. She wasn't sure yet what she was going to do about that problem. There seemed to be a piece to the puzzle missing.

Satisfied with the way the holster fit, Angela collected a few boxes of ammunition and went out to practice. Having the gun holstered at the small of her back added a challenging new dimension to shooting. She would have to get used to drawing it quickly, even with the suppressor attached. That was not going to be easy. It was a trade-off of speed for stealth.

First, she needed to master drawing it quickly and then getting off rounds accurately. It didn't matter how fast you could shoot if you missed the target. Her grandfather often told her that you couldn't miss fast enough to save your life.

She soon became good at drawing the gun from a concealed position and getting off the first round with dead accuracy. Once she could draw and every round pinged the steel triangle, her confidence grew that having the gun concealed on her would be worthwhile.

Her abdomen was finally feeling better and the bruises were healing. When she went for a checkup, Dr. Song was pleased with her progress. The stitches inside her cheeks were beginning to dissolve, too.

Confident she could cover the remaining bruises with makeup, she felt good about going back to work for Barry. To celebrate being alive and going back to work, she dyed her hair a stark platinum blond with blue tips. Her hair and her cutoffs showing off her legs always brought in good tips. For all she knew, maybe the tattoo across her throat did as well.

Since she was carrying her gun in the waistband at the small of her back, she had to wear a longer top to cover it. Because the suppressor made it hard to wear her gun when driving, she decided that for now she would carry the suppressor separately. With no pockets big enough to hide a suppressor, she put it down the inside of her left boot, much the way she did with her knife in the right boot. It wasn't too comfortable, but it worked well enough for the time being.

While she was concerned that it was illegal to carry the gun and knife, and doubly illegal to have a suppressor, she was far more realistically concerned about suddenly finding herself looking into the eyes of a killer. That happened far more often than she had ever encountered the police.

At least with the four men who tried to kill her in jail, she wouldn't have to worry about encountering them.

Pleased that she was going to be well armed, and just as she was about to leave to bartend, she got a call.

She pulled out her phone as she was heading for the front door, keys in hand. "Hello, this is Angela."

"Hi, Miss Constantine. It's Detective Vaughan."

Angela used her shoulder to hold her phone to her ear as she locked the front door. "Have they set a trial date?"

The detective cleared his throat. "I hate having to give you this news, but the charges were dropped and all four of the men were released."

Angela straightened, keys in hand. For a moment, she couldn't seem to form a thought.

"I don't understand. Why would they be released?"

"I'm afraid it was the prosecutor's decision."

At first, Angela felt like she might faint. It took only seconds, though, for rage to take over.

"But I identified them. I said I would testify. You have the DNA evidence they collected at the hospital. It's all in the rape kit."

"Rape kits from all over the state are backlogged for years. There's not enough funding to process them. It will be at least three years, more likely four or maybe even five years, before they can get to yours for processing and DNA analysis."

"But I'm willing to testify. They have the rope. My blood was at the location. There's a hospital report of what they did to me. None of that has to be processed."

"Look, Miss Constantine, I'm on your side. I'm angry about this, too."

"Oh yeah? Did those bastards rape you? Did they put a fucking rope around your neck, hang you from a beam, and leave you to strangle to death?"

The line was silent for a moment.

"Of course not. I realize there is no way I could feel the way you do. I'm just saying that I'm on your side. I wanted those four assholes to go to prison. I was pretty angry when I heard that they'd been released."

"Who ordered them released?"

"John Babington, the assistant district attorney."

In her courier job delivering legal documents, Angela had met John Babington a few times. He was a prick.

"Can't you—"

"There is nothing I can do about it. It's over my head. The reason for my call is to inform you, but more importantly I wanted to warn you. Those four are out of jail and since they had intended to kill you, it's possible they could decide to finish the job. I asked if we could provide protection, but since there is no specific threat, the chief said we don't have the manpower."

Angela scanned the surrounding woods.

They could be anywhere.

"Do you have any idea if they left town?"

"I'm sorry, but I don't. If I get any word on their whereabouts or if they left town, I will certainly let you know right away."

"All right, thanks," Angela finally said.

Her thoughts were already elsewhere, already on that pompous prick, John Babington.

One time in the hall of the Municipal Building, when no one else was around, John Babington had put his hand on her ass. It wasn't tentative or fleeting. It was deliberate and forceful. In the same way she handled drunks in the bar, she simply glided out of range without making an issue of it as she handed him the documents she was delivering for one of her attorney clients. He had flashed her a smile that was both lewd and condescending at the same time.

Instead of going into work at the bar, Angela called Barry and told him she would be a little late, that she had to make a stop, first.

TWENTY-NINE

After calling Barry, Angela drove straight in to downtown Milford Falls. The whole way she kept trying to think of a reason why they would have let the men go. It didn't make any sense. These weren't petty shoplifters. These men had beat her senseless and left her hanging by a rope, fully expecting she was going to die.

Having been to the Municipal Building before, Angela knew that they had metal detectors. Once she found a parking place in a commercial lot about a block away, she did as she always did—she pulled the knife out of her boot and slid it under her seat. Since she was now carrying a gun, she removed the holstered weapon and hid it, along with the suppressor, under the back end of the floor mat in the passenger foot well, where it went under the seat.

Going up the broad steps, she realized that she wasn't exactly dressed properly to see the assistant district attorney. Most of the other people going in and out were dressed in business suits, even though there were some messengers and lower-level workers who were dressed somewhat more casually. Angela had been on her way to work to tend bar, so she was wearing cutoffs and boots. Her attire earned her some inviting smiles from men and murderous looks from women.

Inside was the usual entry to a public building: a large, bland chamber that echoed voices and footsteps. A small line had formed at the security checkpoint as people laid briefcases and purses in tubs on a table before going through the metal detector. Angela slipped her purse off her shoulder and slung it up into a gray plastic tub. She knew the routine from delivering documents to the prosecutors who had offices in the building.

Once past security, she took the elevator up to the fourth floor. Down the hall, past people who paused to stare at her, she came to the office of the assistant district attorney. The receptionist was a thin young man with perfectly styled hair. His blue shirt, offset with a coral-colored tie, was too big for him. He asked if she had an appointment to see Mr. Babington. When she said no, he told her he was in a meeting and she would have to make an appointment and come back. She said she wanted to wait to see if he would have time to see her after his meeting. Annoyed, he asked her name. Angela told him that she was a courier and had delivered packages to Mr. Babington before. Pouting, he told her to have a seat.

Just before 5:00 p.m. John Babington opened his office door to let out a couple of men. They hurried past him on their way out. He paused, putting on his suit coat.

The guy at the front desk smirked his disapproval as he pointed at Angela. "I told her she would have to make an appointment, but she insisted on waiting."

John Babington stood frozen with one arm in the sleeve of his jacket, taking in her bare legs. There was no question in her mind that he remembered her. He pulled his suit coat back off and gestured with a tilt of his head for her to come in to his office.

Angela closed the door and then sat in one of the two maroon leather chairs in front of his wooden desk. He swung his coat over his taller chair behind the desk and sat down.

"What can I do for you . . . "

"I'm Angela Constantine."

He leaned back in his chair and with one hand slicked back his long, thick, dark brown hair. "What can I do for you, Ms. Constantine?"

"Four men tried to murder me. I was told you dropped the charges and let them go. I want to know why."

Recognition showed in his eyes and then he smiled to himself as if she were a child who had asked something naive.

"It's not that simple."

Angela nested her hands in her lap. "It is to me. They tried to murder me."

"Didn't you say they raped you, as well?" He leaned in with a hint of a smile, wanting to hear the juicy story.

A simple "Yes" was all she gave him.

His extra chins oozed over his collar and tie as he tried to glance down at her legs, but she was too close to his desk for him to see much, so he took a long look at her chest instead before he shifted his attention to the stack of folders to the side. He fingered through them until he found the one he was looking for and then tugged it out.

He dropped the folder on the desk in front of himself and then flipped it open. He turned over papers, reading, making small sounds in his throat. She saw the photocopied mug shots of the four men. He flipped those four pages over, then wet his thumb and picked up a page, studying it for a moment.

He finally looked up over the top of the paper. "What exactly was it you wanted to know?"

"I told the officer who came to see me in the hospital that I was willing to testify against all four men. I can identify them. I gave the officers the license plate number. I want to know why you would drop the charges and let them go."

He gave her a long, cold look. "Are you prejudiced, Ms. Constantine?"

Angela blinked. "What?"

John Babington gave her a haughty smirk. "They're undocumented Mexican immigrants, Ms. Constantine. This state has a policy of giving sanctuary to undocumented immigrants."

Angela leveled a glare back at him. "They tried to kill me."

"The good people of New York State"—he lifted his arm to twirl his hand in the air over his head—"and all the elected officials above me, have made it abundantly clear that this is to be a sanctuary state for undocumented aliens. That means we protect them. There are standing orders not to cooperate in any way with federal officials—"

"This isn't a federal case," Angela said, cutting him off. "This is a criminal case. I don't want them deported, I want them prosecuted." With a finger, she pointed out the bruises around her neck. "They hanged me and left me to die. They attempted to murder me. You're the one who is supposed to speak for victims and prosecute criminals."

He stared at her throat a moment before looking up into her eyes. "Are you into Satanism, Ms. Constantine?"

"What?"

"Satanism. You know, Devil worship." He gestured toward her neck. "Your tattoo, there. It says 'Dark Angel.' Do you worship Satan?"

Angela frowned her incredulity. "No. And even if I did, which I don't, what does that have to do with those men raping me and trying to kill me?"

He briefly looked back at the paper he was holding and then looked up with icy contempt. "It says here that the men said the sex was consensual."

Angela stared in astonishment at the accusation. "That's a lie. Of course they're going to say it was consensual—they're trying to get out of going to jail for what they did. I suppose they also claimed that the attempted murder was actually assisted suicide?"

He arched an eyebrow at her sarcasm before going back to silently reading the report in his hand. "I have the testimony of all four men saying the same thing, that it was consensual. They claim that you wanted to have an . . . 'experience.' "

"What are you talking about? What 'experience'?"

"They all say that they met you at Barry's Place, where you're a bartender. They say that after work, out in the parking lot, you got friendly with them and then told them that you had a rape fantasy. They say you asked them if they wanted to play along and help you have that kind of experience."

After work that night Angela was busy killing Owen. But she could hardly say that.

"They put me in the hospital."

He nodded as if he knew all about it. "They claim you wanted it to be rough sex, so that, as they say, it would feel real to you. They say you told them beforehand that you wanted them to hang you by a rope and leave you so as to complete your fantasy. When they were reluctant to go that far, you told them not to worry, that you had a knife in your boot and you would cut yourself down."

Angela sat stunned. The men didn't know she had a knife when they'd left her there to die. That knife was only discovered by Officer Denton at the hospital. That could only mean that someone fed that information to the four men and helped them craft their statement, or crafted it for them.

She realized that since the state's policy was to provide sanctuary to undocumented aliens, he needed to find an excuse to drop the charges and let the men go, so they fabricated a story to discredit Angela.

He cocked his arm and pumped his fist as he gave her a knowing wink. "You enjoy a little gang bang, now and then, Ms. Constantine? Is that it? A bit of hard, fast, and rough?"

Angela could barely contain her rage. But she knew she had to. She knew her face was going red but she couldn't stop that.

"I'm telling you what happened," she said as calmly as she could. "I'm the victim of a crime, of attempted murder."

John Babington regarded her with an imperious expression. "I'm just letting you know the statement the four men gave. It certainly is at odds with what you say. Their account would come out in court, of course. There are four of them and one of you. Their side of it would be a sensation in the press. It would be all over the Internet with sympathy pouring in from all around the country for the poor, innocent, undocumented immigrants. You would be hounded as a bigot, a racist, and worse.

"That's why, in my view, I had to drop the charges. It protects everyone, including you."

"They're criminals," she repeated. "I'm not a criminal."

He flipped over a few more pages. "Well, let's see. I have a report here that you were carrying a concealed weapon." He looked up over the paper and arched an eyebrow. "Is that true?"

Angela swallowed. She knew better than to lie. "Yes. I carried a knife for self-defense. I was unaware it was illegal."

"Ignorance before the law is no excuse, Ms. Constantine. You do realize, don't you, that because the officer found the weapon and seized it, we have the evidence needed to prosecute you for carrying a concealed weapon?" He gave her a threatening smile. "At the discretion of this office, of course."

Angela didn't say anything. She was getting the bigger picture. They intended to let the men go, period. He was letting her know that he would bring charges against her if she made a fuss about it. He would charge her with a crime and suggest that it hadn't been rape at all, but consensual sex. He would say that after the romp she wanted to charge the men to cover up the true nature of her behavior and because she was a racist.

His gaze went from her hair as far down as he could see. "It's rather self-evident that you were asking for it. Right?" he said to make a point of it. "I mean, why else would you dress the way you do? Anyone can see by looking at you that you're the kind of woman who is always looking to get laid, right?"

"The way I dress does not make it okay to rape me."

He smiled as he winked at her. "Come on, now, tell the truth. You liked it."

Angela knew she was in a dangerous situation with a powerful man, the kind of situation with authorities she always tried to avoid.

She simply said, "That's not true."

He shrugged off her denial and flipped over the page. "It says here in this report that the officer who interviewed you at the hospital suspected that the incident might have been some kind of drug deal gone bad."

Angela blinked. "I don't use drugs."

"It doesn't matter what you say. It only matters what the jury believes."

He flipped over some more pages, mumbling a list of things under his breath as he read. He finally straightened the papers and laid them back down in the folder, then leaned back in his chair and locked his fingers behind his head. His big belly flopped out over his pants.

"Despite what you say, young lady, the evidence shows that you are likely heavily involved in drugs. The Constantine residence—where you lived—has long been the scene of visits from the police for drug activity, including possession with the intent to distribute. Your place is well known to police. There have been fights there, stabbings, and any number of arrests on various charges, most of them having to do with drugs. All of that is very incriminating to a jury."

Angela did her best to control her voice. "I don't do drugs."

It didn't matter. She was guilty for the sins of her mother.

Hands still laced behind his head, he shrugged. "All the people I prosecute for drug possession and for dealing say the same thing. They don't do drugs. They don't deal drugs. We have the wrong person. The police planted the drugs on them. All that kind of bull crap. You're all the same."

"You would prosecute someone you know is innocent?"

"It's not up to me to say who is innocent and who is guilty. It's up to a jury to make that determination."

Angela stood, fists at her side. "I don't have anything to do with drugs."

"Well, what we're left with is the word of the police . . ." His gaze glided down to her cutoffs for a lingering look. ". . . against the word of a whore the cat dragged out of a trailer park."

His gaze came up to glare at her with cold contempt.

By the way he kept looking at her body, Angela realized that he had something important in common with the four men. Like them, he thought he was better than her. More than that, he had an elitist disdain for her, and yet, he couldn't help lusting for her. It left him with the confused emotion of hatred mixed with desire.

Angela didn't say anything as she sat back down.

He shrugged. "Maybe what we have here is a simple case of a woman dealing drugs and known to be carrying a concealed weapon."

He leaned forward, pointing at her with a pen he picked up off his desk as his voice got louder. "Like I said, we're a sanctuary state and we are not going to unfairly prosecute undocumented aliens on the word of a fucking little trailer tramp!"

With great effort, Angela kept her mouth shut.

"So," he said, his voice returning to normal levels. "I think that you should consider yourself fortunate that I'm not inclined to press concealed-weapons charges against you. Don't you agree?"

Angela swallowed back her anger. She knew she had to be very careful in her answer. This was not a battle she could win. Worse, she knew she would be in great peril if she said the wrong thing.

"Yes . . . I agree."

His politician smile returned. "I'm so glad that I could explain it and learn that we see eye-to-eye about this whole matter."

There was an urgent knock at the door. When Babington looked up and called "Yes?" the door opened just enough for the young man who had been at the front desk to stick his head in.

"Can I have you for just a minute, Mr. Babington? A critical matter."

Babington shut the folder on his desk and rose. "Excuse me for a moment, Ms. Constantine."

He hiked up his pants as he went to the door. He leaned his head out, discussing something with the young man. Babington's side of the discussion sounded heated.

Angela watched him a moment, watching as his ill humor revealed itself. Babington had one hand on the doorframe and the other on the edge of door as he leaned his head out asking pointed questions and giving angry orders. She couldn't see the young man. He had withered back under his boss's temper.

Angela leaned in over his desk and lifted the cover of the folder, then the papers, until she found the four mug shots. She quickly snatched them out of the folder, folded them up, and stuffed them in a pocket. She closed the cover of the folder.

When Babington finished talking to the young man and came back into the room, Angela lifted her purse off the other chair and put the strap over her shoulder. He gave her that lewd, condescending smile she had seen from him before.

She returned a phony smile she sometimes had to use at the bar to avoid trouble with fragile male egos.

"Thank you for your time, Mr. Babington," Angela said on her way past him.

"Any time, my dear," he called after her. "Any time."

THIRTY

Angela sat in her truck, gripping the steering wheel as if she were trying to strangle it, panting, her heart pounding as she stared down at nothing. She knew better than to go to the authorities. She knew better. She should have expected it. When she heard that the charges had been dropped and the men released she should have known that the fix was already in and there was nothing she could do about it.

The system always blamed the victim.

She remembered something her grandfather told her that day on the way home after he had come to her school. Principal Ericsson had been about to expel her for fighting back against those bigger girls who had attacked her. She wasn't expelled, but only because Principal Ericsson was more afraid of her grandfather than of any criticism for not expelling her.

In the car on the way home, her grandfather had told her that every form of authority, from the school system to the justice system, was far more concerned about protecting itself than the innocent. He said that was why he was proud of her for standing up for herself. He said that was the only true way to insure justice.

He had been right. The prosecutor's office didn't care about justice. Like all forms of authority, from the smallest to the largest, they only cared about protecting themselves and their political agenda. It was always dangerous to go against what had already been decided by the authorities. People like Angela were a petty annoyance, a minor obstacle to their ends. If need be, the system would crush them if they got in the way.

Angela, though, cared about justice. It was all she really cared about. Vengeance was the only thing that made her feel alive. It was the only thing worth living for.

In a way, Angela was glad the self-centered prick had let the four men go.

It meant that Angela could hunt them.

Although the men had been let go because they were undocumented Mexican immigrants, Angela didn't really believe that the four men were Mexican. She didn't think Mexicans talked the way these men talked, or thought the way these men thought. She didn't think Mexicans thought of America as the Great Satan.

She knew who did.

She could see it in their eyes that they genuinely despised America. They radiated a visceral hatred.

They were going to kill her, so they had nothing to hide.

She also didn't think the things she saw in that room were parts for irrigation systems. Irrigation systems didn't use cell phones, or piles of machined, geometric-shaped parts, or wires that came in by courier.

The four men weren't who they pretended to be. They were up to something.

She briefly considered calling the authorities—the FBI or Homeland Security—and reporting what she'd seen. But with John Babington's accusations still burning hot in her mind, and seeing how laws created by lawyers protected criminals, not victims, she dismissed the thought.

Everyone would accuse her of being a racist who hated the men because they were Mexican. If she reported them, the most likely outcome would be that she would be the one who got in trouble.

They would check with Babington about the men, he would brush off the accusations, and then he would likely charge her with carrying a concealed weapon. More frightening, he would come up with a large quantity of drugs and charge her with dealing. It was easy for a man like that to put someone like Angela in jail where she would be silenced and forgotten.

She repeated her rule to herself. No good could ever come of talking to the authorities or trusting in them—whoever those authorities might be.

Angela picked up her phone and called Barry. He answered on the second ring. "Barry, it's Angela. Would it be all right if I didn't come in tonight?"

"What's up?"

"It's nothing."

"It's something. I can hear it in your voice. What's wrong?"

Angela cleared her throat. "I just found out that the charges against the four men who attacked me have been dropped."

"What? That doesn't make any sense. How in the world could that happen? Who dropped the charges?"

"The assistant district attorney. John Babington."

Barry huffed the name. "Figures. Do you know that when Babington was running for office he came by the bar and asked for a campaign contribution?"

"No, you never told me."

"Well, he did. He said that it would be nice if I could help with a contribution to his campaign—you know, to continue his strong record on law and order. He said that it would be a good idea to help get him elected because if he lost, before the new man was sworn into office there are always a lot of pending charges against bars that came across the desk of the assistant district attorney and he might finally have to pursue them all as a last duty to the people of the state.

"I told him that I didn't know anything about election campaigns and I asked what the suggested amount of a contribution would be. Do you know what that asshole said?"

"No, what did he say?"

"He said that the suggested contribution was fifteen hundred dollars. Fifteen hundred dollars!"

"So you made a 'contribution' to his campaign."

"Damn right I did. I know a shakedown when I hear one. Sometimes, even when you know it's not fair, you gotta do what's right for you. Know what I mean?"

Angela's grip on the steering wheel had her knuckles white.

"Yeah, I sure do."

He paused a moment. "I'm sorry, Angela, talking about my petty shakedown. That's nothing like what the fucking asshole did to you. Listen, it's not that busy. Take the night off. In fact, take the rest of the week off. This must be rattling you. Hell, it has me fuming and it didn't even happen to me."

"Thanks for understanding, Barry. I'll call you in a few days and see what the schedule looks like."

When she hung up, she called the missed number that had called half a dozen times.

"Hello, this is Betty with Hospice Services," a woman on the other end of the line said.

"Hi, Betty. This is Angela Constantine."

"Angela! I've been trying to reach you."

"I know. Something happened."

"What could have happened that you wouldn't—?"

"I was attacked by four men. They raped me, beat me, and left me for dead. I've been in the hospital, recovering."

Her heated tone turned to apologetic shock. "Oh my God! I had no idea! Are you all right? I'm so sorry that I've been calling you so often—"

"Don't worry about it. Listen, Betty, the reason I'm calling is I need to know something from my mother."

There was a momentary pause. "Well, it's getting difficult, you know? She's in and out. She doesn't seem to be able to process talking on the phone anymore."

"That's fine—I don't expect her to be able to talk on the phone. I just need you to ask her something for me. It's important. I need the last name of a guy who used to come around our house. His first name was Nate. I need to know his last name. It was foreign sounding and I can't remember it. Ma should remember him—she always said he was cute and she wanted to pinch his ass. He came around our house for a while until he went to prison for manslaughter."

"Nate. Went to prison for manslaughter. That's terrible. Okay, hold on and I'll ask."

She was gone for quite a while. At last she returned to the phone.

"It was difficult. She has a hard time, you know?"

"I know."

"But she remembered him. His name is Nate Drenovic."

Angela snapped her fingers. "That's it. That's the guy. Thank you, Betty. I'm sorry but I have to go for now."

"Half the time, with the medication, I don't know what she means, but she does ask for you. Just now she asked something kind of strange."

"What did she ask?"

"She asked me just now if it was the girl in the moon. It was kind of strange. Eerie. You know?"

Angela didn't know what to say.

"When will you be able to come see her?"

"Soon," Angela said. "I have to take care of some things first. . . ."

"I understand. You take care of yourself, dear, and get better. Do you hear me? Get better."

"I will. Thank you, Betty."

THIRTY-ONE

nce she hung up, Angela started doing a search on her phone for the name Nate Drenovic. Surprisingly, there were a number of entries, but they were in other cities. Then she found one in Milford Falls: Drenovic Tactical. Under the name it said "Combat Martial Arts." From what she remembered of him, that sounded like the same guy.

Angela knew roughly where the address was located. She replaced the knife in her right boot, the suppressor in the other boot, and the gun inside her waistband at the small of her back. It was uncomfortable leaning back in the seat of the truck with the gun there.

She reminded herself that the gun was not meant to be comfortable. It was meant to be comforting.

She felt safer having the gun on her, rather than left in the truck where it had been useless to her when she had needed it most—all because she had been following the law. But she knew that even having a gun wasn't the whole solution.

She found Drenovic Tactical in a seedy strip mall set back from a busy four-lane street. She didn't know if Nate would remember her. She'd been fifteen, maybe nearing sixteen at the time. She didn't know if he was still into drugs, but since he had a business she was hoping not. If he was, she would simply find someone else.

With all the scary men at her mother's place, she had thought he was one of the more decent guys who hung around the trailer. But he wouldn't have hung around unless he did drugs or ran with people who did. At the least, though, he hung around with the wrong crowd.

There was also the matter of his manslaughter conviction. That worried her. She wondered what she might be walking into.

At the moment, though, he was the only one she could think of for what she needed. At least it was a place to start. If she didn't like what she found, she could always walk.

Angela parked in front of the storefront window painted black from the inside, with the name DRENOVIC TACTICAL in gold lettering outlined in red. Because the window was painted over, there was no way to see what might be inside. She opened the typical strip mall aluminum and glass door, which was also painted over in black.

Inside, the place was basically all one open room. While not big, it looked like plenty of space for martial arts training. The bottom six feet of the walls were painted black, with a red band above the black running around the room, and white the rest of the way up to a high ceiling with exposed ductwork and vents. There looked to be a bathroom in back, and there was a desk with a few folding chairs up against the blacked-out window in front. Wooden benches lined one wall. Most of the room was covered with mats.

Two men were practicing some sort of arm locks and escapes in the center of the room. One of them pretty much fit her memory of Nate.

The other was older, more muscular, with a buzz cut, a wife-beater undershirt, and lots of tattoos upon tattoos upon tattoos. He was doing the kind of steroid-induced sniffing and shoulder twitching that made her wonder if she'd made a mistake coming into the place. The guy was clearly amped up. His eyes were bugged out. From lots of experience at quickly judging men as she had been growing up, she knew that he was trouble.

Both men disengaged from grappling and came over to Angela.

Nate was a ruggedly good-looking guy, at most maybe five or six years older than her. He had short brown hair that was pleasing in its disorder. The tight, black, short-sleeved T-shirt he had on showed that he was ripped, but not muscle-bound like the other guy.

"Hey, hot stuff," the tattooed guy said as he circled in close beside her. He aggressively grabbed her ass cheek. "Nice."

In an instant Angela had the barrel of her gun pressed up under his chin, lifting his head back a few inches.

He froze.

"Did you hear that click?" she asked.

"Uh . . . yeah?"

"That was the safety coming off. I've had a very bad day and I'm in a really, really bad mood. Right now I'd like nothing more than an excuse to pull the trigger.

"If you so much as fantasize about touching me again I'm going to send a bullet ricocheting around the inside your thick cranium. Do you know what 'cranium' means, dumb fuck?"

Her tone of voice turned him cautious. "Yeah, I know."

"What? What 'cranium' means? Or that you're a dumb fuck?"

He didn't seem to know what she wanted him to say. "Uh . . ."

"All right, Malcolm," Nate said, "listen to me—I know what's going through your head right now and believe me, you're just starting and you haven't had enough lessons yet to even think of trying to disarm this pissed-off young lady before she could pull the trigger."

Nate gently put his fingers on Angela's forearm. "It's all right. I swear I won't let him touch you again, so why don't you put the gun away?"

Angela glanced at his eyes. They were calm and confident. She put the safety back on as she pulled the gun from under Malcolm's chin. She slipped the weapon back into its holster.

Nate put a hand against Malcolm's sweaty shoulder, right over a tattooed nuclear radiation symbol, backing him away a few steps. "I think we should call it a day. We'll pick it up from there next week." He pointed a thumb toward the door. "See you then."

Malcolm frowned in confusion at what had just happened and his quick dismissal. His bug eyes twitched back and forth between Nate and Angela.

"Fucking little cunt," he finally said.

Angela glared at him. "Sticks and stones."

"All right, that's enough," Nate told Malcolm as he started forward. "You know that one of the things I teach is when to walk away. This is one of those times. You don't need to prove that you can beat up a hundred-fifteen-pound girl. You've made your point. I'll see you next week."

Malcolm looked between them once more and then finally snatched his shirt off the back of a chair. With the shirt clutched in his fist, he stormed out the door.

When she looked back, Nate had a puzzled frown as he stared at her. "Do I know you? You look familiar."

She could see in his eyes that he was a killer, but in some mystifying way it was different from the eyes of every killer she'd ever seen before. Looking into his eyes brought on that same primal, bone-chilling fear of a predator, but at the same time there wasn't the vicious quality to go with it. She also didn't have any visions of him killing, only vague shadows fighting. It was oddly disorienting, because it was alarming but at the same time calming.

"Kind of. I'm Angela Constantine. Sally's daughter. You used to come around to the parties at our trailer."

He snapped his fingers. A pleasant smile spread across his features as he pointed at her.

"Right . . . Sally's daughter." He gave her a quick look down and back up. "Damn, girl. When you grew up, you did it right."

She was not in the mood for flattery. "Are you still doing drugs?"

The question momentarily threw him off. He recovered quickly.

"Nah," he said with a dismissive gesture rather than get defensive, "that was a phase. I was hanging out with the wrong crowd."

"In my experience, people who say that *are* the wrong crowd."

He turned a little more serious. "If you really must know, it had to do with a girl named Becky that I thought I was in love with at the time. I would have walked off a cliff if she asked me to. I was young and stupid back then." He waved off the subject. "So, what brings you here?"

"I'm interested in learning some self-defense."

He smiled as he shook his head. "Are you sure that you need it? You're pretty damn fast with that gun."

Angela didn't return the smile. "Guns can't always save you. Sometimes you don't have a gun when you need it most. Even if you do, you might not be able to get to it fast enough. Even worse, some people know how to take a gun away from you before you can use it to save yourself. . . . Sometimes you simply get overpowered."

He turned more serious when he saw that she wasn't smiling.

"You're right. Not Malcolm—not yet, anyway—but there are people who can take a gun away from you before you know what happened and then you're in a whole lot of trouble. If it's a bad guy, you're dead."

Angela studied his eyes for a moment. "You went to prison for killing a guy. Why did you kill him?"

He lifted a hand as if in defense. "Whoa, there. What kind of question is that?"

"The kind of question I have to ask before I agree to let you teach me anything."

"Before you agree . . . ?" He planted his fists on his hips. "What if I don't want you as a student?"

"Then I'll find someone else. I started with you because I always thought you were a decent guy, despite the people you were hanging out with. I'm a pretty good judge of character. I wanted to come to you first because I thought you would remember me and might be willing to help me."

"I see."

"So why did you kill a man?"

He chewed his bottom lip as he stared off for a moment, apparently considering if he wanted to answer her. Finally, he looked back at her.

"Becky—that girl I told you I was in love with—discovered meth. She was getting wasted on it more and more often. Whenever I asked her to stop she would call me a chickenshit loser. So, for a while, I went along with it. I didn't want her to dump me so I smoked pot when she did meth or when we partied. At your house when she smoked crack and I would smoke weed. I was trying to fit into her world and be part of her life.

"But I finally grew up enough to realize that I deserved better, so I told Becky we were through and I quit seeing her. Quit cold turkey. It hurt and at the same time it was a relief, you know?

"Anyway, she was royally pissed. Becky was damn good looking and no one had ever dumped her before. She didn't like it. She wanted revenge.

"She told this other guy—a guy she was two-timing me with but I hadn't known about—that I beat her up all the time so she'd left me for him. The guy was always getting wired on angel dust. One night he came looking for me to avenge the damsel.

"He caught me leaving a convenience store. I told him he could have Becky with my blessings, but the guy wouldn't listen to anything I said. I didn't want to fight him. He wasn't having it and he got really pissed when I simply kept him off me and wouldn't fight him.

"Then he came at me with a knife. I could tell by his eyes that he was flying on angel dust, and that he was serious about intending to kill me.

"He was a big guy and he kept swinging that knife at me. I tried to hurt him enough to make him stop, but he was so high on PCP that he wasn't feeling any pain. Finally, when he lunged at me, I put him down hard to buy me enough time to leave.

"The thing is, when I flipped him down on the ground he landed on the stub of a signpost that had been broken off by a car. It was a freak thing. It severed his spine at the base of his skull and killed him instantly."

When Angela had lived at home there were people who did Supergrass—marijuana combined with PCP. She knew how much it messed people up. The ones who did straight PCP called it Rocket Fuel. It made them behave like they were insane. Angela hid from them.

"That sounds like self-defense to me."

Nate lifted his arms in frustrated agreement. "It was! I was going to be cleared of any wrongdoing. But then this fucking asshole of a prosecutor came across the case. He was running for reelection at the time and he wanted to look tough on crime.

"He wanted a murder case to puff himself up to voters. He had a dead guy and me. So he said it was a love triangle and charged me with second-degree murder. He got that bitch, Becky, to testify against me. She loved that. She wanted revenge for me dumping her.

"Fortunately, the jury didn't entirely believe her and they convicted me of the lesser charge of manslaughter. I served a little over two years. So there it is. That's how I ended up killing a guy and serving time. Becky got to gloat to her friends how she'd put me away."

"Who was the prosecutor?"

"John Babington. Jobs are scarce in Milford Falls to start with, but on top of that, being a convicted felon makes it nearly impossible to get hired. I've studied martial arts almost since I was in diapers. So, I decided to put it to use and open my own martial arts studio to make a living."

"Could you have killed that guy intentionally, if you needed to?"

He looked like he couldn't believe she doubted his ability. "In the first second he came at me I could have broken his neck. I could have killed him a dozen different ways if I had wanted to mess him up. No problem. But I wasn't looking to kill him, or even hurt him. I was simply trying to leave. I was done with that drama queen and I didn't want to get dragged back into a soap opera.

"But Babington was happy to fuck up my life as long as he could use my case to help him get elected."

THIRTY-TWO

"**A**s it just so happens," Angela said, "I met John Babington today. It did not go well."

He looked surprised, and a little suspicious. "Really. What were you doing with Babington?"

Angela pulled out the mug shots. She unfolded them and handed all four to Nate.

"I have a courier business. I delivered a package to these four men. They overpowered me, raped me, beat me nearly to death, then hung me by my neck from a beam and left me to die."

"Yeah . . ." he said quietly, "I saw what's left of the bruises and abrasions around your neck from the rope. I wondered what that was about. I'm sorry you had to go through that."

He gave her a puzzled look. "But if they left you hanging there by your neck, how the hell did you get out of it?"

Angela pulled her knife from her boot and held the blade up briefly, then slid it back down into its sheath. He looked a little surprised to see that besides the gun she also had a knife.

"I gave the police their license plate number along with their names and descriptions. All four were arrested. John Babington dropped the charges and had them released."

Nate made a face. "Why?"

"They're illegal aliens. This is a sanctuary state. Babington didn't want to be accused of being a racist for prosecuting illegal aliens, or get in trouble with the politicians above him for violating that policy. It would be bad for his career. So, he dropped the charges.

"When I objected he said I was a whore and implied that I probably got what I deserved for enticing the men. The police had confiscated my knife when I was in the hospital. He threatened to prosecute me on concealed-weapon charges, along with invented drug charges, if I made a fuss over it. He's a pompous prick. I knew better than to cross him."

Nate let out a sigh. "That sounds like Babington. I'm glad you were smart enough not to test him. He would have carried out the threat. Believe me, I know." He folded his arms. "So, what do you want from me?"

"Those four men overpowered me in an instant. I had this knife on me, but they grabbed my wrists before I could even try to get to it. I tried as hard as I could to get out of their grip, but I couldn't. They were a lot stronger than me. I was at their mercy and they had none. I was helpless. I don't like being helpless."

His expression reflected his understanding as she went on.

"I know that people who don't have a weapon, but who know what they're doing, can get out of it when men grab them, and even turn the tables on them. I know that there are people who know how to put down the threat, even though the men are stronger. But I didn't know how to do it.

"I spent hours being abused and beaten by these men. You can't imagine the degrading things they did to me, or how they hurt me. I nearly died. I thought for sure that I was going to die, hanging there."

"Thank god you survived. At least it's over."

Angela shook her head. "I know them. These aren't regular bad guys. They're something more. They would know by now that I escaped the death they had planned for me, and now that they're out of jail they will come after me to finish what they started. Besides

that, it's also a matter of their masculinity, their imagined superiority. A woman bested them. They can't have that.

"But it's not just those four. I tend bar and that can be risky at
times. I'm a woman, and I'm not as strong as most men. On top of
that, for some reason I seem to attract bad guys. I want to know
how to stop killers like these four—or any man, for that matter, who
intends me harm.

"Can you teach me that?"

Nate shrugged. "Sure. I'm strongly in favor of women knowing
how to protect themselves. But it takes—"

"You don't understand. I don't have a lifetime to devote myself
to learning some kind of higher way of life. I don't want a hobby or
inner peace. I don't want to learn forms and ritual moves that have
fancy names. I'm not a bored housewife. I'm not a gullible girl looking for the meaning of life. I don't have time for any of that crap.

"I'm not interested in learning to protect myself the way you
teach women to protect themselves. This isn't about empowerment.

"I don't want to learn martial arts and get colored belts. I want
you to teach me down-and-dirty street fighting. I want you to teach
me how to hurt people who need hurting.

"Those four men are out there somewhere. I want you to teach
me how to put them down when they come after me. I don't want you
to teach me how to simply get out of their grip so I can run away."

Nate cocked his head. "But there are a number of steps—"

"And I also don't want to go to classes with other women. I'm not
looking to compete in stages or any of that stuff. I'm only interested
in one thing. I want you to teach me how to fucking kill them.

"I know how to do it with a gun or a knife and if I can I will, but
I need to know how to do the same thing if I can't get to a weapon in
time. I don't want to be defenseless if all I have are my bare hands.

"That's what I need you to teach me."

He studied her eyes for a moment as he considered. "You're
talking about something very different than my standard self-
defense training."

"Like I said, I don't need a hobby."

"You're talking about some serious, game-ending moves."

"Exactly."

"I don't ordinarily teach those to idiots like Malcolm. You're talking about things that can break bones or even kill. You only use deadly force in life-and-death situations, when it's you or them—the same as with a gun."

"I understand."

He looked dead serious as he considered her for a few moments longer. "You would have to come in for a few hours every day for a while. That would give you a good variety of effective moves—the kind of things you're talking about. You can learn those moves fairly easily, actually, if that's all you're interested in learning. You're not interested in advancing through martial arts, so you can do without most of the rest of it. You won't understand the totality of it, but you will know how to seriously hurt people."

"As long as I'm able to put a guy down so he can't get up. If necessary, not ever."

He appraised her for a moment longer. "I'm a convicted felon. I'm not legally allowed to teach anything like you're talking about, so it would have to be kept strictly confidential. You can't ever let the authorities know where you learned it."

"Not a problem."

"It also means it would need to be private sessions—just you and me—so that no one else would know about it. That's time I can't teach classes. Private lessons like that are going to cost you."

"My grandparents used to protect me from the kind of men who hung around my mother's trailer. When they died they left me a little money. I'm sure they would love nothing more than for some of that money to go toward me learning how to better protect myself."

Nate nodded. "If you're sure you're serious, I'll cancel some classes. That time will be for you exclusively. You will be my only student. I'll lock the door. I'll leave some time on both sides of your time here so people won't see you come and go. No one will see you train or see you in here, and no one will know about this."

"Perfect."

"I'll skip all the forms and traditional instruction. It's basically repetition practice of game-stopping moves. I'll just teach you what you need to know to escape from the grip of an attacker and cripple him for life if you need to, and if necessary, to kill him." He smiled to lighten the grim mood. "And when you're done with a lesson, you can always go next door and get your nails done."

"When do I start?"

Nate shrugged. "Right now if you want."

"I do. Do I have to change?"

"Are you planning on changing your clothes before someone tries to kill you?"

For the first time since coming into the place, Angela smiled. "No, I guess not."

He smiled with her. She liked his smile.

"Well all right then."

"How do we start?"

"First, I want you to listen to me. Going over that line with the clear intent to kill is not something that most people can do. Even seriously hurting someone is something a lot of people aren't willing to do. You have to realize that the things I'm going to teach you can seriously mess someone up. Some of these moves can kill. Most people, when it comes right down to it, can't bring themselves to kill.

"These moves can be just as deadly as using your knife on someone. Dead is dead. I want you to think about it—could you actually stab someone if you had to?"

Angela almost laughed, but she didn't. "If someone comes at me to kill me, then they are going to get what they deserve. I don't have a problem with that. So how do we begin?"

Nate's arms were folded across his chest. He let them slip to his sides.

"A guy is almost always going to be bigger and stronger than you. You're not going to be able to overpower a guy like that with strength, but you can overpower them with technique."

"Okay, how?"

"Your objective is to disorient, disable, destroy. That requires intent, aggression, momentum."

Now he was talking her language. Angela was quite familiar with "disorient, disable, destroy." She'd had plenty of practice at that. She was beginning to feel good about her decision to come to Nate.

"Show me."

Nate reached out and gripped her wrist. "Let's say a guy grabs you like this."

Angela nodded. "That was how one of them grabbed me."

"Okay. You must first get out of his hold on you. I'm going to show you how to do that by converting his hold to a position where you can break his wrist. Unless the guy is on PCP or something, like the guy I killed, pain is your best tool."

"I can't argue with that."

He let go of her wrist and looked up to her eyes. "We're going to start by focusing now on how to break the bones in a person's wrist. That takes the fight right out of them and immediately puts you in control. But the sound of breaking bone is revolting. You can't afford to hold back. You need to do these moves with the conscious intent of breaking bones. Are you squeamish?"

If he only knew . . .

"I'll try not to puke." Angela lifted her arm out toward him again. "Show me."

She was already feeling good about this. It felt kind of like when her grandfather started teaching her how to shoot.

THIRTY-THREE

Rafael sat quietly as the cab of the truck rattled and rocked in concert with the idling engine. He'd been in the commercial-vehicle line at the border checkpoint for a little over three hours. That was about what it normally took to cross into the United States from Mexico at the Oeste Mesa border checkpoint. He idly scanned the details of the crisscrossed girder elements under the catwalk connecting all the booths just ahead. He was close. It wouldn't be long.

When the truck ahead of him moved up a space, he released the air brake and put his truck into gear to inch ahead. The cab sprang up and down a little as his rig lugged into the load he was pulling and began moving forward. Once the gap was closed, he set the brake and put the transmission in neutral, letting the diesel engine idle again.

The sprawling facility at the Oeste Mesa border crossing was crowded with lines of trucks of every kind. The vehicles were backed up for miles behind the broad delta of lanes spreading out for the booths staffed with border agents. Any suspicious trucks, or trucks the agents wanted to inspect as a precaution, or even random trucks, were guided to the Commercial Vehicle Enforcement Facility down a short side road beyond the booths. There, they would receive more intensive scrutiny.

Rafael had been through that extra facility twice. Of course, nothing had ever been found on those practice runs. If they only knew what he was carrying this trip, the place would not be at all so calm with the monotony of a routine day.

Rafael rested his arm out the open window as he looked out over the massive numbers of trucks waiting in lines. In the big rearview mirrors he could see hundreds of trucks waiting in the sweltering sun for their turn to cross over into California. Farther back, vendors had tried to sell him everything from ice cream, to food cooked on small carts, to puppies, to Christian religious goods on tall displays the vendors wheeled in wagons among the waiting trucks.

There were no Islamic religious goods for sale. This was the land of the nonbelievers. For now. He gripped the wheel tighter in anger at being among so many Christians. Someday all nonbelievers would be slain and the world would be united under Islamic rule and Sharia law.

He watched border agents in dark uniforms up ahead going about their work of checking loads, looking over, under, around, and inside vehicles for drugs and other contraband. They also inspected the trucks for safety violations and looked through paperwork.

Infidels.

Years of surveillance and research had finally brought them to choose the Oeste Mesa facility. Part of the reason behind that decision was that it was a large commercial border crossing into Southern California. California was a sanctuary state. When advance team members had been caught after crossing into California they had been routinely released to go on their way. Although even in Texas it wasn't much of a problem if you were determined to get into the States, you spoke only Spanish, and you looked Hispanic.

The Americans expected to see Mexicans coming into the United States, both legally and illegally. Rafael and his team worked very hard on every detail to make sure the Americans saw what they expected to see: just some more Mexicans.

That was the reasoning behind the entire team having been raised from very early childhood speaking Spanish almost exclusively.

While some of them spoke Farsi and English, most spoke only Spanish. That was central to their mission. Perfect language, proper hair, appropriate clothes and they melted right into the teeming masses from south of the border. Even though they were Iranian, they were easily taken for Mexican as long as all the details fit. No one had any reason to take a second look at them.

After almost three decades being raised solely for this mission, it seemed surreal for the final phase to be under way.

Rafael and the rest of the team had spent the last month working as drivers taking cheap office furniture from a factory in Mexico to a warehouse distribution point in San Diego. The factory was owned through a series of Iranian shell companies. Their jobs, like all the other details of their mission, had been prearranged.

Those jobs as truck crews had given Rafael and his team the opportunity to run through practice missions dozens of times as they took loads across the border, all the while checking on how everything worked. They even got to recognize some of the border staff by name. All those trips gave them the opportunity to refine their timing, which was critical. Everyone on the team knew exactly where to be, and when. In such a complex mission, it was critical that they get it right.

Those practice runs with furniture loads also gave Rafael and his team ample time to assess the methods of the customs and border agents as well as the way the California Highway Patrol worked. Sitting in line for hours allowed him to closely study the surveillance and detection equipment, and to take note of the numbers and placement of personnel, booths, computer monitors, cameras, the X-ray machines that scanned every load, and most importantly the neutron and gamma detectors.

Until today they'd never had anything to detect.

Today, his truck had no office furniture. Today, the real mission began.

When the truck ahead inched forward, Rafael put his truck in gear and started slowly rolling forward to take up the gap.

Cassiel, in the passenger seat, stuck his head out the window, checking ahead, trying to have a look around the truck they were following. He had an AK-47 resting across his lap, as did Rafael. Both men had long banana magazines taped together in opposite directions so that when one ran empty they could be turned around to use the second, fully loaded magazine. It had been Cassiel's idea to carry the guns, not Rafael's.

They had never dared to carry weapons in the past, of course, but today it was the real thing, so Cassiel had insisted they carry the guns. The mission had been planned for years in every detail. If anything went wrong, decades of work would be for nothing. If that happened, a couple of AK-47s would not save the operation.

A lot of people had spent an enormous amount of time on planning to make sure nothing would go wrong. They'd run through every scenario. There were hundreds of people involved in the operation. Everyone from workers in the enrichment facility in the ancient city of Qom running the thousands of centrifuges, to the brave reactor crews, to the software engineers, to their allies in North Korea and Pakistan who helped provide the technical expertise they needed. They even had computer-operations personnel embedded in Russia.

But Cassiel wanted to bring along a fucking gun, as if that could bring down America.

While not tall, the man was thick-boned and powerfully built. His head looked like it had been carved from a block of stone. Deep wrinkles and creases gave the impression that his head had been pressed into a cube shape. It almost looked like he had no neck, as if his head had been placed directly on his shoulders. At least his complexion and close-cropped black hair and beard made it easy enough for him to pass as Mexican.

From what Rafael knew about him, the man was skilled with every kind of weapon. Even if you saw him without a weapon, he was a man who looked dangerous. People tended to look away and become busy with their own business when Cassiel looked in their direction.

Cassiel was of course not an original member of their team. He spoke fluent Spanish, among several other languages, including English, so that, at least, helped him fit in.

The members of Rafael's team had grown up together since childhood. They were all like brothers. Their having lived together, schooled together, trained together, and prayed together in such a closed group since childhood made infiltration by informants or spies impossible. There was simply no way for an outsider to get into their midst, and no way for any of the team members to talk with an outsider. That was one of the foundational principles for making this portion of the attack undetectable beforehand.

While they all spoke Spanish and some English, most of them didn't speak Farsi. Rafael and several of his team spoke Farsi fluently so that they could communicate and coordinate with commanders. It was also necessary for much of the technical training that they'd needed.

This was a mission they had been practicing and training for their entire lives.

Cassiel, though, had not been part of that. Rafael did not like having such a stranger along on the mission. As far as Rafael was concerned, he might be a gifted assassin, but he was not one of them and so he did not belong with them.

Hasan had told Rafael that Cassiel had been saved from execution because he was such an expert at lethal skills.

Hasan had been impressed with how quickly and efficiently Cassiel had killed the Israeli snake with strange vision that could recognize men who were killers. That would allow the men they would send in to kill Israelis and tourists to be successful without being detected the way Wahib had been. The assassination of the man responsible for Wahib's capture only added to Hasan's apparent awe of Cassiel's kill history. Hasan thought that a man of his ability was invaluable.

In return for being allowed to live, Cassiel had been assigned to go on the mission with Rafael's team to help them in any way he could. Hasan might have considered him valuable, but Rafael considered him nothing more than hired muscle.

Cassiel didn't talk much, although he did follow Rafael's orders. He knew the consequences if he didn't. He seemed perpetually in a sour mood. It probably grated on Cassiel's nature to be indentured to his Iranian masters.

Rafael wondered how dedicated he was to their mission. He wondered if the man was prepared to die, as were the rest of them. Somehow, Rafael didn't think so.

Some of them, in fact, were going to die this very day. Rafael was a bit disturbed that some of his lifelong brothers were going to give their lives to their cause this day, but Allah would richly reward them for their martyrdom.

One of the phones beeped. It was Javier, one of those who was to become a martyr this day.

The message asked how close Rafael was to the gamma detector.

Rafael told him he was several trucks back. Javier said that he was in the perfect place, then. Rafael could see Esteban's truck, so he knew that he, too, was in position and ready for the go command.

Rafael put the phone back in the tray with the others, each with a piece of tape on the back with a name or a function.

Rafael smiled at the collection of iPhones. Apple was a valuable, unwitting partner, providing the very best encryption, which made successful attacks with high death tolls possible. They even refused to give the FBI and other intelligence agencies any help stopping or identifying terrorists.

The team also used a messaging app that had end-to-end encryption, which prevented even the technicians who developed it from reading messages. No Western spy agency would be able to know anything they communicated.

It was amazing that here they were, at a high-security checkpoint, and they could communicate without fear of being detected because American companies provided the means and protected their secrecy. None of the border agents running around all over the place and checking everything for the slightest hint of a problem had any idea of what was about to happen, any idea that they were about to die, and they could not intercept any of the messages coordinating it all.

Rafael thought that Silicon Valley was probably the only place in the world completely safe from an attack, because it provided the tools that were so necessary for killing as many Americans, Jews, and other infidels as possible. No jihadist would harm such a valuable resource—the people and companies that made the secrecy and security of jihadist operations possible.

The truck ahead moved up to the neutron and gamma detector.

Rafael picked up the phone in his lap.

THIRTY-FOUR

Rafael pressed the send button of the message to the team overseeing the operation back in Iran. It was a single, simple word.

NOW.

He watched and waited. A moment later he saw the computer screens in the string of booths go dark. Border agents leaned closer, peering at monitors, then looked around at the rest of their equipment, looking for the cause of the problem. Some of them typed in commands on their keyboards, trying to bring them back to life. Others checked connections, all to no avail. There was nothing for them to find and nothing they could fix.

On the command from Rafael, hackers had initiated preloaded routines to shut down every piece of electronic equipment at every border crossing with Mexico and Canada. Shutting them all down prevented the authorities from realizing there was an attack at any one specific spot. They might assume that the hack of the border crossings was in and of itself the attack. Every part of the attack was designed to keep them from knowing what was eventually to come.

It wasn't just the computers that went dead. All the handheld devices they depended on for everything from logging data to taking readings also went dead. Every reader and scanner linked to their system went dead.

The computers that ran the X-ray scanners, neutron detectors, and gamma detectors and logged the data also went dead.

The electricity to the entire facility simultaneously went down. The lighted message boards with lane numbers and other information that changed throughout the day went dark. Every bit of equipment went quiet.

Rafael smiled as he watched the confused faces of the border agents. Some leaned out of their booths to ask others if their systems were down as well, or if it was only them. They yelled their frustration from one booth to another. Other people were busy attempting to reboot systems to try to fix the problem. Of course, their systems would not reboot. The roving agents who checked paperwork and looked over equipment and loads returned to the booths to see why their handheld devices weren't working.

Many of the agents in the booths picked up phones to call in, but the landline phone systems that connected them to the operations center had gone dead as well. Finding the phones not working, they turned to their cell phones, but those phones weren't linked directly into the centers, so it would take them time to get through to the right individuals, and those people would be swamped with calls not only from this border crossing, but from them all. To make matters worse, their computer screens showed only ransom demands. Those ransom demands were of course fake, but it would be quite a while, possibly days, before they came to realize that it wasn't really ransomware.

Even if the people Rafael was watching did get through on their cell phones, there was nothing the center would be able to do. It would take time to uncover the hack and then to regain control of their systems.

And their time had just run out.

Rafael picked up the phone with Javier's name written on the tape on the back. It was time to begin their part of the mission. Javier would be waiting for his encrypted orders.

Rafael set the message that said *GO WITH GOD.*

Rafael tilted his head back to look between the lines of waiting trucks. Javier was in the lane on the far end of the facility. Although the border checkpoint was relatively level, it was somewhat higher at that far end.

Javier was driving a regular tractor trailer, but hidden inside his ordinary-looking trailer he carried a two-thousand-gallon steel tank filled with gasoline. The trailer had hatches below valves on the tank. Once he received word from Rafael, Javier hit a switch that dropped the three hatches in the floor of the truck. When those hatches sprang open, they automatically opened the gravity valves on the tank above. Gasoline poured out of three wide-opened valves and began spreading across the pavement as it ran downhill under all the waiting trucks.

Border-patrol agents smelled the gasoline and began coming out of their booths to look for the source.

Rafael picked up the phone with Esteban's name. He could see Esteban out of his truck, standing near the rear of his trailer. Many of the other drivers had emerged from their trucks as well, because of the apparent failure of the electricity and computers, so none of the security officers thought anything of Esteban being out of his truck.

At least half a dozen officers finally converged on the truck spewing gasoline. At first, they ran around the truck, looking for the source of all the gasoline. When they saw the open gravity feed valves, they drew guns and pointed them up at Javier in the cab of his truck.

Rafael pressed send for the message to Esteban. *GO WITH GOD.*

Esteban, only two lanes over from Rafael's truck, had been waiting for the order. He glanced briefly at the message for confirmation, then deliberately dropped the phone in the river of gasoline. He put a foot up on the rear crash bar that kept cars from submarining under the back end of the truck in the event of an accident, and hoisted himself up. He quickly pulled open the latch and then lifted the roll-up door. Lining the sides of the trailer's interior were over a hundred cages. Esteban pulled the handle on a steel cable that sequentially unlatched all those doors.

The doors of the cages had springs, so once the latches were released they sprang open, one after another. Over a hundred dogs, most pit bulls, bolted from their cages and spilled out of the back end of the truck. All the dogs had been bred and raised in Mexico to be vicious. They had all been trained for one thing: to attack anyone in a border agent or highway patrol officer uniform. They had been trained to ignore gunfire and loud explosions.

All the dogs were also wearing bomb vests packed with high explosives, ball bearings, screws, and nails.

Some of the dogs began fighting each other, but most single-mindedly charged toward border agents and highway patrol officers. The dogs storming around all the standing trucks at the border checkpoint created confusion and disarray. Tactics used in the training of border agents and police for gaining control of a situation suddenly became worthless. While prepared for an assault by men, they were not prepared for an attack by dozens of vicious dogs.

Some of the dogs raced in and latched on to a leg with their powerful jaws. The dogs would never release the leg they had in their jaws, so the men now had a heavy dog anchoring them. Men drew guns and shot the dogs clamped on their leg, but the damage had already been done.

Other dogs clamped on to arms held up defensively. Once they had that arm in their teeth, they shook it for all they were worth. The stocky dogs had powerful neck muscles, and when they shook their prey it tore muscle from bone. Other dogs, running at full speed, leaped up at the men, knocking the wind from them as they knocked them down. Once they had their prey on the ground they went for the throat or face. There was no effective way to physically fight them off. Only guns could stop them.

One dog leaped onto and grabbed a female officer by her breast. As she toppled back with the dog on top of her she drew her gun and shot it, only to have another dog race in and clamp her face in his powerful jaws. When he shook her head, it tore neck muscles and ripped flesh from her face.

People everywhere, both agents and truck drivers who had gotten out of their trucks, screamed in terror or pain. Some of the drivers who had been waiting at booths saw the erupting chaos, put their trucks in gear, and took off to escape before they were caught up in the attack. Men in other trucks leaped out and ran, leaving their trucks blocking the lane between booths.

While some dogs attacked the same man, most of the angry animals raced throughout the facility, looking for people in uniforms to attack. They spread out as they ran, going after any uniformed officer they saw.

It only took seconds for guns to be drawn. Officers everywhere began shooting at the dogs. A few took down a dog, but many shots missed the racing animals as they zigzagged through all the trucks and people. The shooting diverted their attention from the true danger.

As officers tried to shoot the dogs, the timers on the vests the dogs were wearing ran out and the bombs exploded. Everywhere throughout the entire facility the dogs' bomb vests started going off. It didn't matter if a dog had been shot dead. The vests had already been armed, and they exploded by their internal timer, sending shrapnel streaking out in every direction.

People close enough but not directly taken down by the explosion were shredded by the ball bearings and nails. People farther away were hit with shrapnel and went down. Others were wounded but still able to run. They did their best to stop the bleeding of injuries as they ran. Many ran directly into another explosion, where they were blown limb from limb.

While some detonators went off almost immediately after the attack started and created mass confusion, others had delays of anywhere from ten to sixty seconds, adding to the confusion. As bombs were going off, the dogs left alive continued their attack, until their bomb vests in turn exploded. Those explosions spread the pandemonium and death out to those who had not been in the original danger zone.

Several of the officers around Javier's truck turned to shoot at the dogs that raced in toward them. Others held their weapons pointed up at Javier, since he was the driver of the truck dumping thousands of gallons of gasoline all over the ground. They yelled at him to get out of the truck or they would shoot.

Javier was holding a dead man's switch.

Rafael knew that Javier yelled "Allahu Akbar" back at them. They grasped the meaning and immediately began retreating even as they opened fire.

A few seconds later Javier's truck exploded with a ground-shaking thud.

The men in close, climbing up to open the driver's door to the truck, were vaporized when the massive bomb in the sleeper compartment of his truck cab detonated. The huge explosion sent debris flying in every direction. The expanding shock wave from the explosion knocked people from their feet. It rocked all the trucks trapped at the checkpoint. Rafael's truck rocked in turn as the blast wave raced past.

The catwalk above the booths came apart and parts of it blew high into the air. Half of the booths and personnel in them were blown to pieces, adding to the flaming debris flying through the air. The big axle and tandem wheels off a truck sailed out over the row of booths and into California.

A massive ball of red flame laced with orange and yellow tendrils expanded from the initial explosion. Rafael squinted at the bright blast. Fire boiled over the surrounding trucks. Black smoke swelled up into the air.

Almost simultaneously the gasoline vapor from all the fuel that had poured out across the area caught fire with a chest-pounding thump, igniting the gasoline that had poured across the ground.

Trucks to the side couldn't even attempt to escape by driving around, because they were hemmed in by natural terrain that rose up in most of the area around the checkpoint. Where there wasn't a natural obstruction, massive cement barriers had been placed to prevent anyone from trying to drive around the checkpoints to get into the United States. Those barriers now created a tightly confined trap that was rapidly becoming a killing field.

All the while more of the vests on the dogs kept exploding in a deadly drumbeat, creating a continual cacophony of earsplitting booms. The air everywhere was filled with shrapnel. Men still standing went down.

With the dogs released, Esteban started into his truck to detonate the bomb in the front of his trailer.

He only made it two steps before he was brought down by a hail of bullets from a few of the California Highway Patrol officers still alive.

Rafael had been expecting it. They had planned and trained for it. He picked up another waiting phone and immediately pressed the send button. As he did so, he ducked.

Almost instantly, Esteban's truck blew apart in another massive explosion, bigger than the first. But this one was to a large degree a shaped charge meant to expend most of its energy to the right side. The blast blew apart the truck beside it, and the one beside that one that had been sitting at the gamma ray detector in front of Rafael's truck.

Flaming debris ripped down poles and power lines. The metal siding off one of the trucks spiraled up into the air. A massive chunk of metal hit the hood of Rafael's truck with a bang and bounced over the cab. The air was filled with smoke trails left by burning, unrecognizable bits of wreckage sailing through the air.

Trucks that were trapped and unable to move were engulfed in flames from the burning gasoline that had spread under them. Blazes whooshed to life all throughout the standing vehicles. Men screamed as they were burned alive in the cabs of their trucks. Others tried to escape by running through the rivers of burning gasoline. As they ran, their shoes and then their pants ignited. Flames roared up to engulf their shirts and then their hair. Screams came from faces inside swirling columns of fire.

Many of those running figures succumbed to the smoke or breathed in the flames and collapsed in the inferno. People ran in every direction, trying to skirt flaming trucks and flying debris, trying to find safety. There was none.

Acrid, thick black smoke rolled across the scene, obscuring the lines of trucks. Orange flame licked out from the wall of inky smoke. Throughout it all, the bomb vests on the dogs with delayed fuses continued to explode. Explosions shocked the air.

If ever there was a scene of hell, this was it.

Trucks at the front up near the booths that were not caught up in the fire or destroyed by the explosions sped away to escape the mayhem. Most of the border agents were dead. The few that weren't were tending their own wounds or trying to find a way to fight back. They were not worried about trucks that began fleeing in a panic from the death and destruction. As they picked up speed going for the few openings in the debris and wreckage, they collided with other trucks also trying to escape. Other drivers tried to maneuver between the damaged vehicles, or around crippled trucks, driving over smoldering bodies and leveled border check booths.

The explosions from the dogs' bomb vests finally trailed off. Rafael checked his watch to make sure the timers had all run out. He didn't want to get caught by an explosion from a dog running from the scene. The dogs were trained to be unafraid of gunfire and explosions, but in some their natural instincts took over and they were panicking to get away from the flames. He didn't see any of them still around the immediate area.

Finally, the time had arrived. Rafael jammed his truck into gear and released the brake. With the truck in front that had been blocking his way at the neutron and gamma detectors now mostly obliterated, Rafael began gathering speed and plowing aside torn pieces of the trailer. An axle with tandem wheels still attached spun like a top as it was knocked off to the side. Large sheets of metal siding toppled as he crashed through remaining pieces of the truck beds.

All around trucks burned and people screamed—some in pain and some for help. Some of the other drivers and the border agents tried to rescue people trapped in burning trucks. Fuel tanks continued to rupture and pour diesel fuel on the fire, creating thick clouds of black smoke. Even though he had rolled up the window, Rafael could feel the withering heat radiating from the fires.

As he gathered speed, he rammed into what was left of one of the truck cabs that had been in line ahead of him. The shell of the body and tires had been mostly blown away in the explosion. He used his truck to push it, trying to get it out of the way. Instead of being pushed aside, it rotated sideways ahead of Rafael's grille, sliding sideways on bare rims in front of his truck. With no bodywork left, the dead driver could be seen hanging in his seat belt, his left arm blown off from the explosion.

Rafael kept pushing the skeleton of the truck cab until they were past the booth area. Once clear he spun the wheel to turn his truck to push the smoldering wreck of a truck cab off to the side.

Throughout the entire attack and aftermath, Cassiel had sat quietly watching. He said nothing and took no action. Fortunately, he didn't attempt to lift his gun to shoot out the window at the enemy when he had a chance. Rafael had told him beforehand that their job was to play the part of innocent victims caught in a terrorist attack.

The last thing they needed was to have anyone who was still alive, or any of the officers rushing to the scene from nearby areas, see someone shooting an AK-47 out of the passenger window of an escaping truck. That would instantly tip them off that Rafael's truck was part of the attack. It would ruin years of planning. The plan was for Rafael to look like one of the many innocent trucks frantically fleeing the scene of death and destruction.

There were trucks that, once past the carnage, pulled over. Drivers jumped out to render assistance to the scores of injured. But many more trucks simply fled in a panic, too horrified by the carnage to want to stay.

Rafael wanted to be in among those innocent people fleeing the scene. He wanted to look like any other Mexican truck driver racing away for fear of his own life.

THIRTY-FIVE

As they drove north, away from the carnage at the Oeste Mesa border crossing, flames leaped up from the carcasses of dozens of trucks burning in the distance behind them. Thousands of burning embers floated through the air. An ever-growing mass of black smoke rose into the air until the higher-altitude winds tore the top off the sinister column in a long dark smudge against the bright blue sky.

Emergency vehicles on the other side of the divided highway raced south toward the scene. Rafael could see flashing lights converging from roads to either side. It looked like every police car in Southern California was streaming toward the border crossing, creating a river of flashing lights. They were too late. They always were. They only showed up after an attack.

Ambulances in ever-increasing numbers sped toward the massacre. They would not be able to save many lives. They would have to search through piles of burned bodies to find anyone still alive. There would be some they could help, but they would waste their time taking the large numbers of gravely injured to hospitals, only to have them die on the journey or over the next few days while ones still undiscovered expired.

Rafael smiled to himself. The relatives of all the infidel dead would weep this night and for many more. They would think it was over.

They would think this was one of biggest terrorist attacks ever. They would have no idea that this was not even the real event. The time was rapidly approaching for all the nonbelievers to die.

Several times Rafael had to pull his truck over onto the shoulder for police cars racing down the wrong side of the highway in their urgency to get around traffic and to the scene. But every time, once they had passed, Rafael quickly pulled back out and kept going. He needed to be lost in the mass confusion to escape the scene.

Cars and trucks had pulled over all along the highway. People stood beside their vehicles, a hand shielding their eyes from the late-afternoon sun, as they stared southwest to the fire and smoke. None of them could possibly imagine what had just taken place. They would all be following the news for days and weeks to come as they gossiped about what they had seen.

Other people in cars, SUVs, and pickups continued heading south, following the emergency vehicles, to see for themselves what was happening at the Oeste Mesa border crossing. The determined, ghoulish sightseers would slip through the confused police lines or go around overland to take countless photos and videos of the wreckage, the fires, and the smoldering bodies. They would rush breathlessly to post them on the Internet.

Those photos and videos would also find their way to all the Islamic jihadi websites. Many would wrongly take credit for the attack and promise more to come. Those images would spread across social media, and in a matter of hours people all over the country— all over the world—would be able to see the results of the attack. Everyone would express shock at the number of dead.

People all over America would get a sobering taste of how weak they really were, how blind, how foolish.

What no one realized at the moment, though, was that there were simultaneous attacks being carried out all over the United States and even in a few countries overseas. Bodies would be left after every kind of attack, from stabbings at malls, to trucks used to run over pedestrians, to bombs at airport checkpoints, to poison-gas attacks in three different subways. Cities from Seattle to Las Vegas to Chicago to Miami to New York would all be caught up in the grip of terror.

Everyone would remember this date . . . at least for now.

Everyone would think that this day that cities burned and victims bled and died was the big event, the biggest strike ever against the Great Satan. Even as the dust settled there would be demands for investigations to find out where so much had gone wrong. There would be hand wringing. Every intelligence agency would blame a lack of adequate funding.

But it would all be about what had happened, not about what was going to happen. Everyone was blind to that. America itself had helped Rafael and his team keep the secret of what they planned. Rafael had used the tools, both the physical tools and the political tools, that America had so willingly provided, to get him, his team, and their supplies into the country.

Authorities across the country would be kept investigating the attacks and trying to identify those involved. They would be focused on peeling back layers and networks. They very likely would eventually trace information on everyone involved. They would come to know the names of those who were captured, or killed, or who had escaped and were being hunted, and the names of their organizations. It would be all over the news.

They would collect all the surveillance data of conversations from people involved in those attacks. They would scour all the social media postings of everyone involved. As always, it was after the fact and too late to make a difference.

There would be endless reporting about how these people had somehow escaped scrutiny, or had been on watch lists but not arrested, or had slipped into the country on visas or as refugees and no one had done anything about it. They would get mountains of intelligence from informants. They would analyze the chatter and discover the scope of it all.

They would also find pieces of the bodies of Javier and Esteban, but it would do them do good, because they wouldn't be able to identify the charred remains or link them to any group.

Unlike all the other groups involved in all the other attacks, Rafael and his group were unknown to any intelligence agency. Over the decades of their training, they had never interacted with any terrorist group or movement. They were ghosts.

Many of the people who were also part of that ghost group and who had helped give logistic support to the mission were long since on their way out of the country. They would vanish in the wind.

That kept Rafael and his in-country team, unlike everyone else in the many attacks, not only undetected, but completely unknown.

He was the ghost who had slipped through the chaos, unknown, undetected.

All the other jihadist groups who carried out the other attacks around America also believed this was the big attack. Not even they knew the truth.

That secrecy was necessary to prevent anyone involved with the other attacks, if captured, from disclosing anything about Rafael's group. They had never even heard rumors of Rafael and his group. They couldn't reveal what they didn't know.

Rafael kept his speed in check to match the other trucks leaving the scene. He didn't want to give nervous, trigger-happy police officers any excuse to notice him or stop him for questioning. With all the traffic they were mingling into, the risk of discovery was continually melting away.

The big worry was that they would be stopped to have their load inspected. It would be a very bad thing if any of the authorities looked in the trailer he was hauling. That was the whole reason behind the destruction at the Oeste Mesa border crossing. There they had X-ray equipment, neutron detectors, gamma ray detectors, as well as very savvy border agents. Rafael and his group had just nullified all of those safety measures and the entire system behind them.

Although it was highly unlikely anymore that they would be stopped, it was always possible that Cassiel could handle them, but it was also much more possible that he couldn't. Cassiel was an assassin, a killer, to be sure, but he was not a commando or soldier. It wasn't his specialty. If the police started shooting, it took only one bullet for Rafael to be killed or disabled. That would end their entire mission.

They had to rely on their years of careful planning, not on Cassiel. As far as Rafael was concerned, Cassiel was just excess baggage he had to drag along.

Rafael took the first exit to the westbound connector into San Diego. Before long they merged into masses of heavy late-day traffic. In a little over an hour they reached the industrial area where the rest of the team would be waiting and they could at last ditch the truck that had been through the border crossing.

Rafael phoned Fernando as they turned off the main road into the maze of small office parks and warehouses. Streets lined with palm trees reminded him a little of home. As he pulled up to the building they owned through a shell company, the big overhead door rolled open. Rafael drove the truck right inside and parked at the far end of the building.

He sat for a moment after he shut down the engine, relieved to at last be hidden in a safe place.

Forklifts were standing by to begin transferring the material they were carrying to the smaller cargo van. Behind the important materials they would load into the van, they would place some household furniture to hide what they were carrying on the off chance a police officer opened the rear door. From a professional truck driver, Rafael was now to become a new immigrant with a used van, driving cross-country with a friend and their furniture to settle in another state.

The other members of the team would be in cars escorting them in a loose convoy. Alejandro, Rafael's second-in-command, would ride in a car that would always be right behind him. The other team members would take a variety of other vehicles. No one would be able to tell, but it would be a convoy that would always protect the cargo van Rafael was driving.

Rafael had told Cassiel that he was to ride in the van with him. Rafael thought it best if he kept an eye on the man.

Members of their team broke the seal and opened the big swinging doors at the back of the semitrailer. Men climbed up into the truck to assist in off-loading the critical parts Rafael had been carrying.

"How did it go at the border?" Fernando asked.

Rafael held his head up a little higher. "Javier and Esteban became martyrs today. God has welcomed them home with rich rewards. Many infidels died. It was a good day."

Fernando nodded and climbed up onto a forklift to start unloading Rafael's semitrailer truck.

The first thing they loaded into the front of the small cargo van was the generators and batteries that would produce the five kilovolts needed to charge a high-energy capacitor to fire the detonators. They had already assembled platforms to anchor the most valuable part of the load.

Next, they carefully pulled the two cases, each holding a pair of half spheres of plutonium-239, surrounded by tungsten carbide bricks and beryllium reflectors, from the semitrailer and placed them on the platforms in the cargo van and secured them down.

Over those cases they placed the steel shells for the outer casing. They would help protect the cases should they have any kind of accident.

When the time came, the two halves of the plutonium spheres would be assembled along with a polonium-beryllium neutron initiator placed in their hollow centers. Those initiators would help kickstart the chain reaction to prompt criticality. The pit would be placed inside a heavy lead tamper several inches thick. That in turn would be surrounded by explosive lenses made of Semtex.

The Semtex explosive lenses, fired with the EBW, would create a shock wave designed to collapse the lead tamper inward. The tamper's inertia would spherically compress the plutonium-239 pit to critical mass.

Miguel's team had been in place for a while now and had been forming the Semtex into precisely shaped geometric pieces that later would be assembled into a sphere to surround the lead tamper and the inner shell. They had established their operation in a deserted industrial area that had proven to be a perfect source of the nearly thousand pounds of lead they would need for each bomb.

Their Iranian shell company had bought the entire building as well as another smaller building and machining workroom with old but workable milling machines. Once finished with the machining at the smaller workspace, Miguel's men would move to the larger building to begin working the lead into the spherical tamper that would surround the plutonium pit.

Miguel's team had also machined the brass chimney sleeves that would hold the detonators. Conventional detonators didn't have the precision needed to make all the explosive lenses go off simultaneously.

To make those explosions highly symmetrical, the detonators would need to be connected by exploding bridgewire that had already been delivered to Miguel's team by courier. When the proper voltage hit the EBW, the high current would melt and vaporize the wire in microseconds. The resulting shock wave would fire all the detonators in the same instant.

While precise yields were very difficult to determine, calculations done by Iran's nuclear engineers along with the help of North Korean scientists suggested a little over one hundred kilotons.

Once Rafael and his team reached Miguel and his men, they could begin the final assembly.

The test of Iran's first atomic bomb would not be conducted in some remote desert location.

It would be conducted in America.

This would be the Great Satan's Hiroshima and Nagasaki.

THIRTY-SIX

This particular Mossad operations facility had always reminded Jack of a mission control center for spacecraft launches. Like the seating in a mini amphitheater, rows of curved counters with workstations descended toward a small stage with a wall of monitors behind it displaying up-to-the-minute information. Those monitors were alive with everything from maps, to scrolling lists of information, to video feeds of demonstrations going on at different locations. One of the feeds showed a speech being given at the United Nations. Another was a live feed of an interrogation of a prisoner.

Dozens of controllers, managers, and coordinators tended monitors of their own, along with their own sets of switches, buttons, and knobs. Many of them were talking on headsets. These operators tracked, and were in communication with, agents in the field. When Jack had been in the United States and called in, he talked to Dvora in this very operations center.

As Jack made his way across the surprisingly quiet room, he immediately noticed that all the controllers seemed especially tense. Some of them pored over reams of paper readouts in their laps. Others were talking into headsets. The lighting in the room was muted, to make it easier to see all the information both at their own screens and on the large monitors against the wall. It gave the place a kind of foreboding atmosphere.

Jack spotted Dvora Artzi and stopped at her station. When she saw him she broke into a sudden smile as she pulled off her headset and then stood to squeeze him in a warm hug.

"How are you, Jack?" she asked, holding his shoulders as she looked up at him with a broad smile.

"I'm okay," he said without much enthusiasm.

Ehud saw Jack stopped at Dvora's station and rushed over to meet him.

"Jack!" he said as he extended a hand. "Where have you been? Didn't you get my messages? I've been trying to reach you for weeks! It's not like you to be out of communication."

Jack shook hands with the man as he looked around.

"Sorry, Ehud," he said, returning his attention to the man. "I just didn't want to search for another subject right now."

"It's not your fault that Uziel was murdered."

Jack flashed him a weak smile. "Nice try, Ehud. But if I wouldn't have found him and convinced him to help us, he would be at home and safe right now."

"Safe at home mourning his wife. You gave him a reason to care about living. You let him be part of something bigger than himself. You didn't force him to help us. He wanted to do it."

Jack sighed. "I suppose." He didn't want to debate it, so he didn't. "But I'm thinking I may take a break from our work. I'm a little sick at heart of finding people who can recognize killers only to watch them be murdered."

"Jack," Dvora said, "these are special people. They are hunted by those who want to kill their kind. You save many of them by finding them first. You saved Kate. If not for you, she would have been slaughtered without ever knowing the reason. She never knew about her ability until you found her and helped her understand what she could do. If not for you, she would be dead. Not just her, but others as well."

Jack smiled more sincerely. "True enough. I just wish I could find her. I taught her a little too well how to go off the grid and become a ghost to hide from those killers."

"Anyway," Ehud said, interrupting the conversation about Kate, "that's not why I've been trying to reach you."

Jack folded his arms and devoted his full attention to Ehud. "Okay, what's up?"

"What's up?" Ehud looked a little surprised. "Haven't you been listening to the news?"

"No, I've had my phone off. I'm a bit sick of listening to all the problems in the world. I wanted to be left alone to do some background research on some of the super-predators I've been hunting. I've been thinking about taking some time away from all this to go do that for a while."

Dvora frowned with concern. "You don't know about the attacks?"

Jack looked between Dvora and Ehud. "Attacks? What attacks?"

"In America," Ehud said, lifting his hands out in exasperation. "There were also some terrorist attacks in the UK, one stabbing at a nightclub in France, and a truck attack in Brussels. But there were a great many more in the US and they were much worse."

"Worse?" Jack's arms unfolded. "What happened in the US?"

Dvora sat down at her station and pulled up video of a massive hotel fire. Ehud gestured to the monitor.

"That's a hotel in Las Vegas. They still don't know the death toll. Right now it's thirty or so, but it's expected to climb over a hundred. It could even go much higher. It was started by a large incendiary device that probably contained jellied gasoline. It went off on a lower floor, taking out elevators and trapping people on higher floors. The stairs were destroyed by explosive devices so that people couldn't escape as the fire climbed up inside the building."

Dvora switched to another scene. "This is the airport in Tampa." The surveillance video showed people walking along, then debris and smoke exploding out, leaving bodies littering the terminal. She pulled up another video showing rescue personnel with gas masks carrying people out of a subway station in New York City. Another video showed the aftermath of a car bomb in a big United States city, but it could have been a scene from Baghdad.

"Who claimed credit for all the attacks?" Jack asked as Dvora kept pulling up different videos, different scenes of destruction and victims.

"Each attack was claimed by a different group," Ehud said.

Astonished, Jack glanced down at the monitor. "Has that ever happened before? A series of attacks all carried out at once with different groups claiming credit?"

Ehud clasped his hands behind his back. "No, not like this. To tell you the truth, we don't know what's going on, but it's obviously very troubling."

"Here's one of the worst," Dvora said as she pulled up what looked like a war zone in Syria. Shells of burned-out trucks littered the scene. "This is Oeste Mesa, the big commercial border crossing between Mexico and California."

"This attack was accompanied by a cyber attack that took down the entire US network for their border stations," Ehud said. "Besides this attack, here, there was also a mass shooting—several people with machine guns—at a crossing into America from Canada. The terrorists killed five agents and almost two dozen civilians before they were shot dead. This attack at Oeste Mesa was much worse."

"There are several terrorist groups that have been working on that kind of cyber warfare," Jack said. "Sounds like they chose this time to strike."

"There were also cyber attacks on air traffic control, as well as power plants and other infrastructure." Ehud glanced at Dvora before looking back at Jack. "US intelligence services leaked to the press that the cyber attacks were Russian."

"The Russians!" Jack put one hand on a hip as he swept his hair back with the other. He held the hand against the back of his head as he paced a few feet away and then returned. "That doesn't make any sense at all. The Russians doing something like that—especially in coordination with terrorists groups—would cause the Americans to jump to a war footing."

Ehud arched an eyebrow. "They did."

Jack cast about for some answer that made sense. "You have to know that it's possible to make a cyber attack look like it was done by anyone—Russia, China, even Israel. All it takes is a team inside Russia to set up servers using Russian credit cards to pay for hosting services and then use a VPN to remote into those servers from access machines inside the country. That would make it look to all the world like the hack had been done by Russia. The evidence would seem irrefutable—unless you really understand how it can be done."

Ehud waited until Jack had paced back. "The problem is, US intel leaked information to the press saying that the Russians carried out the cyber attack. People are used to things like this on a smaller scale from Russia or China. Ransomware attacks have crippled large companies, hospitals, and government agencies for some time now, so this being done by the Russians makes perfect sense to many in the American intel community. Of course, the news media and thus the public are absolutely convinced it was the Russians, so they're up in arms. They're demanding action. Some are even demanding a strike at Russia."

"But it doesn't make sense. It's most likely not true."

"Perception is reality," Dvora said.

Jack paced off again, thinking, looking at the wall of monitors. Many of the scenes of destruction and panic were the attacks in America. Something was bothering him.

"The Mexican bomber you captured in Jerusalem," he said when he realized what was nagging at him. "That has to be connected to these attacks." He pointed at Dvora's monitor showing the carnage at the Oeste Mesa border crossing from Mexico into the United States. "That's too much of a coincidence. Your Mexican bomber isn't really Mexican, is he?"

313

"He says he's from Santiago de Querétaro, Mexico. He doesn't speak any language except Spanish—we're sure of that much. We questioned him about Santiago de Querétaro and growing up in Mexico. Once we got into the details, he knew a lot of the basic information, but he wasn't convincing. When pressed, he came up with the name of a street where he says he grew up. He described a pretty standard Mexican slum, but we don't believe the street exists. There were other things as well that lead us to believe he's lying."

"What do you think he's covering up?"

Ehud pinched his lower lip as he glanced around the room and lowered his voice. "We found something on one of his boots."

"Okay . . ." Jack said. "What did you find?"

"A speck of plutonium-239 stuck in the lugs of the sole."

Jack stared at the man for a long moment. "He certainly didn't pick that up walking around in Santiago de Querétaro."

"Nor did he get his suicide vest there, either. The materials that were used in it are common throughout the Middle East, but not Mexico."

"Any suspicions where he picked up plutonium?" Jack asked.

Ehud shrugged unhappily. "Pakistan? Iran? A terrorist group bringing material out of Russia? Hard to tell."

"Were you able to get anything useful out of him?"

"We told him that we found nuclear material in the sole of his boot. We pressed him about where he could have picked it up. We pressed him hard. He seemed confused about everything, including how to answer our questions.

"He seemed lost and disoriented. He started to cry. He cried for hours and hours as we continued to ask him questions in Spanish. It seemed like being captured was something that had never crossed his mind before and now that he was away from the people he knew, he didn't know what to do or how to answer. He knew, though, that he wasn't supposed to cooperate.

"We put him back in a cell to let him think about it and get a little sleep before we questioned him again. Captives expect torture.

Letting them get some sleep instead often helps soften them up so they will begin answering a few questions. A few answers eventually lead to a few more, and so it goes.

"Sometime while the guards were changing, he managed to kill himself."

"He killed himself?" Jack was stunned. "How could that happen? You know quite well that these terrorists are suicide risks. You take precautions to prevent it. Wasn't he in a straitjacket or something like that to prevent him from killing himself?"

"Yes, of course." Ehud sighed. "You won't believe it. He apparently stood up off the floor—likely on the toilet—and did a backflip to come down on his head and break his neck. He was fine one minute, the next minute his neck was broken and he was dead.

"But he did unwittingly leave us one clue before he died."

"What's that?" Jack asked.

"His arms and hands were restrained, so he rubbed his nose until it was bleeding and wrote 'Allahu Akbar' on the wall."

"That doesn't sound very Mexican," Jack said.

"We're running DNA analysis to see if we can come up with his country of origin," Dvora told him.

THIRTY-SEVEN

Jack leaned in next to Dvora to look more closely at her monitor. It showed a map of America with little circled numbers and corresponding information points down the right side.

"You know, it feels to me like these attacks might be a smoke screen," he said. "I suspect that there is some overriding objective, and all of this is meant to obscure that objective."

"A smoke screen." Ehud considered for a moment. "Many of those groups are competitors for money and resources. Terror attacks gain them status. Status gets them money, resources, and recruits. They are not going to cooperate with each other."

Jack lifted an eyebrow. "They would if they didn't know they were merely a diversion and if the whole thing was promoted to them as a competition of sorts—a chance to show off what they are capable of. A big game day of sorts."

"Put to them by who?" Ehud asked.

Jack shrugged. "Take your pick. But only a state sponsor would have the weight and authority to be able to bring all these different Islamic terror groups together for a chitchat and convince them to attack at the same time. What if these groups thought they were taking part in an audition of sorts to see who should receive that state's financial support?"

Ehud hooked a thumb behind his belt. "You're connecting a lot of dots that we don't see, at least not yet."

"Maybe. But it worked to get José to try to blow himself up. He thought he was doing something great. I'm sure they didn't tell him the truth that they were only using him as a diversion to accomplish something they wanted more—getting rid of Uziel. After all, because of Uziel, we took Wahib captive. I think someone might be doing the same kind of thing here—creating a diversion."

"I'm listening," Ehud said.

Jack gestured at the monitor. "These attacks were carried out by different groups. Right? It seems like the coordination and lethality of Islamic terror groups have reached an entirely new level."

"It certainly has the US up in arms," Dvora said.

"But could it be a diversion, like José was?"

"All right," Ehud said, "I like the way you always think outside the box, but a diversion for what?"

Jack thought a moment. "Can you pull up any photos from the American cameras at the border crossings where the attacks happened?"

"Why the border crossings?" Dvora asked. "What about the rest of the attacks? Do you want them as well?"

"For now I just want to see the border-crossing attacks." Jack gave them both a meaningful look. "José was simpleminded. I think he became more useful to them as a diversion, but when he walked away to do their bidding, he walked away with a bit of plutonium stuck in his shoe. Where would they want to go with plutonium?"

Ehud and Dvora shared a look.

Jack gestured to the screen. "Let me see the photos you have from the border attacks."

"There's surveillance photos and video from the Canadian-US border attack," Dvora said. "The terrorists' timing was off. They started before the cyber attack brought down all the systems. That means the cameras were still in operation during the attack, so we have some good visuals."

First, Dvora clicked through dozens of facial-recognition photos of people in cars waiting in line. She stopped at a young couple in a pickup. The woman had a black scarf on her head.

"This is the couple that carried out the attack. The facial-recognition software didn't hit on them, so they weren't on a watch list. Nothing about them triggered alarms."

"A lot of homegrown terrorists don't show up on any watch list," Ehud said. "They only become known to authorities after they kill people. That's why the people you find, like Uziel, are so useful."

Next Dvora showed Jack a video overlooking the lanes of traffic, with the man and woman's truck waiting in line a few vehicles back from one of the booths. Suddenly, the man and woman both sprang out of the truck with AK-47s and started spraying bullets at the border agents. The attacking couple looked to have no intention of trying to get away. They didn't fire from cover. They were there to the death. Jack could see several agents go down and smoke from gunfire off-camera being returned.

They both screamed "Allahu Akbar" as they killed surprised people. Some of the people in cars leaped out and tried to run, only to be cut down. Some people tried to hide in their cars, only to have the couple spray their vehicle with a deadly hail of bullets, killing them where they hid.

They fired their weapons in sequence, alternately switching full magazines for empties while the other fired. That indicated practice and planning. It also kept up constant fire, with lethal rounds going everywhere to make it more difficult to return fire. They stood in the open on either side of the truck, shooting at officers in the booths as well as through the windows of a building off to the side. Armor-piercing rounds went right through the bulletproof glass, vehicles, and vests.

A well-placed shot to the head abruptly took out the man. The woman was wounded in the leg and left arm but kept firing her weapon until she was killed by a bullet through her throat. When she went down, a bomb in the truck went off and took out the camera.

318

"They weren't refugees or illegal aliens who had slipped into Canada to carry out an attack," Dvora said. "They were both identified as children of Syrian parents, both born and radicalized in Canada. They left a lot of online rants. Chatter from American authorities indicates they believe that the woman convinced the man to devote himself to jihad, along with her."

"What we're looking for wouldn't be homegrown terror," Jack said. "Show me what you have from the Oeste Mesa border crossing with Mexico."

Dvora pulled up files, then clicked on one of them. It was a video from a surveillance camera that showed a normal day at the border checkpoint. Vendors could be seen in the distance walking between trucks, hawking their wares.

"As you can see, everything looks routine," Ehud pointed out to Jack.

Dvora nodded. "All the video is from before the cyber attack shut everything down. Everything went dead some time before the attack began, so there isn't any video showing where the attack came from or how it unfolded."

She showed him a series of photos of the aftermath. It looked like a war zone in Mosul. Pieces of truck frames, heavy parts like axles and engines lay scattered. The checkpoint facility was in ruins and bodies lay strewn everywhere. Rebar stuck up from broken concrete barriers. All the skeletal remains of the trucks were blackened from the intense fires.

"It was a horrific attack," Ehud said in a tone of voice that sounded as if it were in reverence for all the dead.

Jack had seen carnage plenty of times. It didn't tell him anything. "Do you have any of the facial-recognition photos, like the ones at the Canadian border?"

"Sure. But those cameras went down a while before the attack just like all the rest of their equipment, so they don't show anyone the Americans suspect of being involved. They believe the attack came from people waiting in trucks farther back, before they could be captured on the cameras."

Dvora started opening files of one face after another of men sitting in their trucks, waiting in line. Nothing Jack saw looked out of the ordinary. It struck him that many of the faces he was seeing of people waiting in line would die that day.

After a few minutes, though, something caught his eye.

"Stop!" He pointed. "Right there."

Dvora halted on a photo of a driver sitting in his truck. It was a photo similar to all the others taken by cameras at every lane at the border crossing, the same way every truck then had to go through X-ray machines and neutron scanners.

The photo showed a driver who looked Mexican. He was yawning so that you could see that he had a gold molar.

Jack tapped the screen. "There. Blow that up."

Off to the side of the truck that was the subject of the photo, just barely in frame, was a face in the background. It was a man on the passenger side of the truck behind.

He was sticking his head out the window to try to see what was going on ahead of the truck he was in.

Dvora clicked a key several times, enlarging and centering the face on her screen.

"Shit."

Ehud leaned in. "What is it?"

Jack pointed at the blocky face of a man with short black hair and beard. "Him. I recognize the trim of his beard above his jawline. It's not quite cut square. I didn't see his face at the time, but I'm almost positive that's the guy who killed Uziel a few weeks back."

"I wish we had a name," Dvora said with a sigh.

"We do," Jack told her. "Cassiel Aykhan Corekan."

Dvora looked back over her shoulder. "You know who he is?"

Jack straightened as he ran his fingers back through his hair. "Cassiel Aykhan Corekan is one of the super-predators I've been trying to find for years. He's a proficient killer. Like other men I track, he's a serial killer. Killers like that are wolves. They don't like being seen by sheepdogs, so he also hunts down and kills people like

Uziel—people who have the ability to recognize killers for who they are.

"That rare ability to recognize killers is genetic and usually runs in families, so once Cassiel recognizes one of these people for their ability he will often slaughter their entire family. He has murdered people in several family lines that I'm aware of. I'm sure there must be others."

"Well, it appears he has taken up a new interest," Dvora said. "He must be working with this terrorist group that wanted Uziel dead, and who also attacked the Oeste Mesa border crossing."

"A man named Cassiel a terrorist?" Ehud made a face. "Cassiel is an old Hebrew name. It seems unlikely that Islamic terrorists would trust a man with a Hebrew name."

"Old Hebrew is its primary origin," Jack said. "But the name has other meanings, especially in certain countries."

"Like where?" Dvora asked.

"Like Azerbaijan, where he was born. Azerbaijan is a mix of cultures, but they are a people for whom names hold great meaning. Children are not named because the parents like the sound of a name. Names are given because they are meant to impart a certain nature upon a person. Bravery, health, strength, tenderness, beauty. Babies are expected to grow into their name."

"So . . . what do you think is the meaning of his name, if it is not a Hebrew name?" Dvora asked.

"A few old texts sometimes describe 'Cassiel' as the angel of tears. He is sometimes regarded as the ruler of the moon."

"Well," Ehud said, "he certainly has brought tears to many people."

Dvora didn't look convinced. "If it's typically an old Hebrew name, what makes you think the obscure, alternate meaning 'ruler of the moon' applies in this case?"

"Because of his middle name, Aykhan," Jack said. " 'Aykhan' means 'king of the moon.' I think his parents used Aykhan for his middle name to indicate the intended meaning of 'Cassiel.' "

"Okay, so let's say we believe all that," Dvora said. "What do you think this business about ruler of the moon means? What did his parents mean him to grow into?"

"I wish I knew." Jack pulled over an empty chair. "Here, let me use your console so I can get into my files and see what I have on him."

Jack had a number of super-predators he was trying to locate. He gathered intelligence on them whenever possible and added it to their file. Eliminating any of these killers would save countless lives. But, by their very nature they were difficult to track, and each case was time consuming.

So, he did his best to instead find people with the kind of vision those predators hunted. Sometimes he could help them stay alive. Kate had been like that. Sometimes, though, even when he did his best, he couldn't help them. Some people didn't want to face the truth of what would be coming for them.

"Wait—" Dvora said as she started typing. "Let me send the name to some of the other stations, first. The more people looking for information, the more we'll be able to dig up."

Ehud snapped his fingers to get the attention of nearby operators. "Dvora is sending you a name. Find out everything you can about this man. We believe he was involved in the terror attacks in America."

People at nearby monitors nodded as they looked at the name before beginning searches.

"He was born in Azerbaijan," a man to the right said.

They already knew that, but Jack let the operators search as they would, rather than try to direct them.

"Interpol suspects him in murders in several countries," another operator said. "He has been questioned on several occasions by authorities in those countries, but there was never enough evidence to charge him in connection with any of the murders."

Again, Jack was aware of that. He had a few photos of the man from those interviews, and it was clear it was the same man he was staring at on the monitor. After Dvora finished, he typed in his credentials and opened his cloud account.

"He is believed to have killed several members of the Al-Saleem family in Jordan," a woman two stations over to the left said, "and—get this—eleven members of the Maarouf family in Egypt."

"The Italian authorities believe he murdered several members of the Constantine family," another operator said.

Jack paused in his search through files. He looked up. "Constantine . . . That name rings a bell for some reason."

He went back to his own search as other agents called out a few names of victims associated with Cassiel.

"Here it is," Jack murmured to himself as he sat back, staring at the screen. "There was an older couple in New York State who were shot execution style. Twenty-two-caliber bullet in the backs of their heads. My cross-reference tools had pulled up the name of that murdered couple because they had the same last name as the family in Italy that was thought to have been murdered by Cassiel. Last I checked, the police in New York had no clues or leads. The murders are unsolved. That's why you don't have a link to them for Cassiel."

But Jack had a photo in his physical files of Cassiel that the Italian authorities had taken when they questioned him before letting him go. It was a real photo printed on photo paper from an actual negative. Those were like gold for Jack's particular calling.

"Another one of those troubling coincidences?" Dvora asked. "Cassiel murdered Constantine family members in Italy, and a couple by the same name was murdered in New York State?"

"It's more than a coincidence," Jack said, "it's a connection."

Ehud rubbed his chin as he frowned off in thought. "But why would this serial killer, Cassiel, be right there as a terrorist attack is about to take place?"

"Beats me. Find out what you can about the Constantine couple in New York State," Jack said to Dvora as he rolled back out of the way to give her room to get at her monitor again.

"Cassiel is a hunter," Jack said, "a wolf. He likes to go after families to eliminate anyone with the ability to recognize killers. See if there are any more Constantine family members of the murdered couple in New York."

THIRTY-EIGHT

"I've got a pair of hits," Dvora said. "Sally Constantine is the daughter of the murdered couple. Then there's an Angela Constantine, granddaughter of the murdered couple and daughter of Sally. Birth dates for both. No death certificates. Both must still be alive. Angela would have been young at the time her grandparents were murdered."

"That's certainly a close family connection," Ehud said. "I wonder why Cassiel didn't also kill the mother and daughter when he was there and killed the older couple?"

Jack leaned back in his chair. "It may be a tactic he uses to confuse anyone looking for him. He doesn't follow any patterns that I can figure out. He sometimes randomly returns to hit other family members, so you never know where or when he will abruptly reappear. A lot of killers work in an area. He works all over the world.

"Sometimes the time span is so long you never know if he will ever return to kill relatives, so you waste a lot of resources waiting to see if he will be back. In several cases he hasn't returned. That may be his method of operation, or it may not be a tactic at all.

"He's a brutal serial killer, so it could be that he simply gets distracted by a woman he has abducted. He has a thing for abducting young women and keeping them in homemade dungeons where he can torture them for prolonged periods of time. Easy enough to pull off that kind of thing in a lot of the third-world countries where he likes to prey."

"Look at this," the man at the next station to the left said. He gestured to the monitors on the big wall in front of them all. "This was a very strange killing in Milford Falls, where the older couple was murdered and those two Constantine women live."

Everyone looked up at a big monitor to the right side of the wall. While other nearby monitors flickered with videos of everything from speeches to riots, a static police photo showed a man dangling from a bridge by a rope tied around one ankle. He had no shirt. His torso was covered with knife wounds and streaked with blood. It looked like there was something carved into the flesh of his back.

"Can you enlarge the words, please?" Jack asked.

"Sure," the man said as he clicked keys and the image got bigger until they could all read what it said.

I KILLED CARRIE STRATTON.

Dvora twirled a lock of her curly black hair around a finger as she stared at the big monitor. "That's pretty damn weird."

"It sure is," Jack agreed. "But I don't see how it has anything to do with either of the Constantine women and certainly not Cassiel. He doesn't torture and kill men. Any idea who Carrie Stratton is?"

"She was a nurse in Milford Falls," the man who had put up the image said. "She was abducted and murdered. The writing on the dead guy's back led authorities to her body. DNA analysis of the semen and material under her fingernails confirmed that he was indeed the man who had killed her."

"Damn strange involuntary confession," Dvora said.

Jack had to agree. "What do you have on the Constantine women?"

"The mother is a longtime drug addict," Dvora said as she scanned a series of police reports on her monitor. "Methamphetamine is her drug of choice. She has a long history of arrests. They all look to be drug related, nothing violent. Most of the time the charges were dropped for a variety of reasons. She does have a string of drug convictions, though. Looks like she always got off with time served, probation, or drug rehab. She appears to be a user, not a dealer. From the sequence of arrests, it's obvious that rehab never worked.

"A good many people have been arrested in raids at her residence on other charges. Drunk and disorderly, possession with intent to sell, possession of firearms by a felon, and some fights—a few with serious injuries."

"What about the daughter?" Jack asked as he leaned back in his chair, twirling a pen around his fingers as he listened.

"Angela . . ." Dvora murmured as she went through several pages. "Let's see what we've got." She finally stopped on a page.

"Well this is interesting."

Jack looked up. "What is it?"

"She was recently hospitalized."

"For what?"

Dvora leaned in as she read the report on her screen. "She was raped by four Hispanic undocumented aliens. They beat her nearly to death, then hanged her by her neck with a rope and left her to strangle to death. She managed to escape and get to a hospital. Looks like she was in bad shape. Cuts and abrasions, some damage to her spleen, things like that."

"How did she escape the hanging?" Ehud asked.

"Doesn't say. She identified the men and they were arrested but released."

"Released. Why?" Jack asked.

"It just says that the charges were dropped by the assistant district attorney," Dvora told him. "Doesn't say why."

Jack tapped his pen on the counter. "I don't like the sound of that."

"Charges are often dropped for a variety of reasons," Ehud said from behind Jack.

"Maybe, but something about it doesn't sound right. She was seriously injured, she identified the men, they were arrested. Seems pretty cut-and-dried. How do they not at least get tried? Do you have an address on her?"

"Sally has an address in a trailer park, but Angela's address is listed as a box at something called 'Mike's Mail Service.' "

"That's kind of odd." Jack sat up and rested an elbow on the counter beside Dvora. "Let me see what her social media looks like. We should be able to get good information from that. Let's see her Facebook page, first."

Dvora typed, looked at the screen, typed some more, clicked on a few places, looked some more.

"Nothing." Dvora shook her head. "She doesn't have a Facebook page."

Jack was now fully focused. "What about other social media?"

Dvora did brief searches, reporting after each one. "No Instagram account. No Twitter account. No Google Plus. No LinkedIn." She typed and clicked some more. "She doesn't have a YouTube account. Nothing on Pinterest. No Tumblr. She doesn't use Reddit. No Snapchat. Nothing on Swarm or Flickr or Kik. No WhatsApp account. Nothing on Quora, Vine, or Periscope. She doesn't visit Digg."

"Maybe she's using something more obscure," Jack said, "some smaller site."

Dvora looked over at him. "I'm using our proprietary scanning tools. If I can't find her by using these tools, then there's nothing to find."

"Maybe she uses another name online," Ehud suggested.

Dvora shook her head. "Our tools would have found a link to an alias or fake name. There is none. There are no photos of her online—dressed or nude. I can't even find so much as an online review posted by her. She has zero footprint online."

The hair at the back of Jack's neck was standing on end.

This was a marker of an unusual type of person. The kind of person he tried very hard to find.

If her relatives were killed by Cassiel, that strongly suggested that she had that kind of vision that got her relatives—both in Milford Falls and those back in Italy—killed, the same kind of vision that got Uziel killed. People who had that kind of vision tended not to be social creatures.

Jack gestured at the screen. "Let me see her driver's license."

Dvora pulled it up. Jack looked back at a young woman staring out at him.

"Angela, Angela, Angela," he murmured as he stared at the stunningly attractive young woman. "What do you see with those eyes of yours?"

Dvora moved the photo to one of the big monitors on the wall ahead and then started looking for more information.

"Tax records show that she's employed as a bartender at a bar called Barry's Place. She makes really good tips—and reports them, believe or not. She also has a courier business—Angela's Messenger Service. It does well, too."

Dvora paused, clicked a few places, and then started scanning down through a page of listings. She swiped the cursor back and forth over one in particular to highlight it.

"Remember that woman who was murdered in Milford Falls? Carrie Stratton? Well, the hospital where she worked uses Angela's Messenger Service."

"It sounds like a small city, so that may not mean anything," Ehud said. "And maybe the young lady doesn't have a social profile because she works so much."

Jack was seeing too many connections for it all to mean nothing. "I think she's one of those with the vision to recognize killers," he said, half to himself.

Ehud frowned. "How do you know that?"

"It's what I do, Ehud. I'm very good at it." He looked up. "I need to get a plane ticket to the US. I'm starting to get the feeling that time is of the essence."

Ehud seemed perplexed. "What makes you think all this?"

"Connections are part of what I do, part of why you pay me. There are starting to be too many suspicious connections.

"I need to be able to look at this Angela Constantine in person to tell for sure if she is able to see killers for who they are. I will recognize it in her eyes if she has the ability. But I also need to go there for bigger reasons."

"Like what?" Dvora asked.

"We captured that supposedly Mexican suicide bomber because he failed to complete his mission. He only spoke Spanish, and at some point he came in contact with plutonium. Had he completed his mission we wouldn't know either of those two things that don't make any sense. Had he detonated that suicide vest, we would have assumed he was just another terrorist.

"He was being used as a diversion so that an assassin—Cassiel—could kill Uziel. The thing that disturbs me the most about this man pretending to be Mexican is that he had plutonium-239 stuck in his boot. That links Cassiel to nuclear material. Now, Cassiel just happens to be right there at the scene of a massive terrorist attack at Oeste Mesa. He is on his way into the US. That can't be a coincidence."

"What does the Mexican connection have to do with anything?" Ehud asked.

"Muslims in America might be noticed. They stand out. Mexicans, though, are largely invisible in America."

"That's true . . ."

"I think there might be something bigger behind the terrorist attack in the US, and it involves plutonium-239—nuclear material that can be used for a bomb." Jack stood. "I presume you're going to brief American intelligence agencies on what we've learned? An attempted suicide bomber posing as a Mexican who had plutonium-239 on his shoes and the rest of it?"

Ehud pinched his bottom lip as he thought about it. "I will talk to people higher up, but no, I don't think we would wish to do that."

Jack was surprised. "Why not?"

"Because the American intelligence agencies would leak all of this to the press like juicy gossip. That would send people to ground and make it all the more difficult to find out what's really going on."

"Leaks are an unfortunate fact of life these days," Jack admitted with a sigh.

"It's been getting worse. American intelligence agencies have gradually become more dedicated to a political agenda than a security agenda. They increasingly view spying on Americans citizens and politicians—including members of Congress and the Senate—as their mandate and a legitimate objective."

"Legitimate objective? Where did they get that idea?"

"Political operatives have increasingly swelled the ranks of the agencies. Their attitudes and agendas have gradually infected the intel community. Leaking top secret information is a tool and a weapon they use with increasing frequency.

"It helps the Deep State grow in power all the time. Just look at this latest leak about the Russians being responsible for the cyber attack. Congress is calling for heavy sanctions and some even want a declaration of war because of that leak—and the information is almost certainly wrong. That leak was crafted to further a political agenda, increase the budgets of the agencies, and thus increase their power. It has nothing to do with protecting America against terrorism.

"It is becoming more and more dangerous for us to share certain information with agencies that increasingly view Israel as an enemy. These days many in the US intel community would not be upset if Israel were to be wiped off the map. They actually think that would solve the problem of terrorism."

"Do you really believe the situation with American intelligence is getting that bad?"

Ehud arched an eyebrow. "Why are you no longer working with them to find people who can recognize killers—the way you now do for us? Because it is politically incorrect, that's why," Ehud said, answering his own question. "They care more about being politically correct than protecting lives."

"In that case," Jack finally said, "I think I better get to the US in a hurry and see if I can fit some of these pieces together." Jack pointed up at the big monitor showing Angela Constantine's face. "And she is one of those pieces of the puzzle. I don't know where she fits in, but I think she does."

Ehud frowned suspiciously. "I thought you wanted to take a break from this never-ending war."

Jack gave him a look. "The war seems to want me back."

Ehud nodded. "We will send you on a diplomatic jet."

Jack clapped the man on the shoulder. "Thanks, Ehud. I better go pack a bag. I'll stay in touch."

He gestured down at Dvora. "Stay by your phone."

"Always. And Jack, please come back in one piece this time?"

THIRTY-NINE

As she turned down the long hill out of Milford Falls, Angela spotted the police cars in the distance at Barry's Place. Seeing police cars at the bar was not entirely out of the ordinary. Guys would frequently get belligerent, typically over a woman, and cause trouble.

It could be anything—a word, a look, or the wrong gesture. Sometimes women helped instigate it. Some women got off on men being jealous over them. With some booze, men's inhibitions tended to evaporate and they would decide to settle scores.

If it looked like it was going to come to blows, and especially if it did, Barry would push such fights outside into the parking lot. If he thought it was serious enough, he would call the police. Angela wondered what sort of jealous nonsense it was this time.

As she got closer, Angela spotted an ambulance backed up to the door at the rear of the building. Because the ambulance was at the back door, she became more alarmed, worrying that maybe Barry had been hurt in a robbery. As hard as he worked all the time, it could even be that he had a heart attack or something.

There was a small crowd standing around in addition to at least a half dozen police. Some of the police, their pads and pens out, were questioning people in the crowd. A second ring of people stood farther back, out of the way of the police. They appeared to be curious onlookers. It was now obvious to her that whatever it was, it was serious.

Angela rolled quietly into the parking lot and parked away from the crowd and the police. She recognized some of the gathered people as locals who frequented the bar.

As she sat in her truck watching the police talking to several women who worked in the bar, the ambulance pulled away, its emergency lights strobing the scene. It turned on its siren as it pulled out of the parking lot and headed up the hill toward the hospital.

As the ambulance went up the hill, a white crime-scene van pulled into the parking lot and parked by the rear of the building. Several people with equipment emerged and went inside.

Angela needed to find out what was going on, so she carefully pulled out her gun, then the suppressor, and hid them under the floor mat where it went under the seat. She hated having to do it, but she also pulled her knife out of the sheath in her boot and slid that under the passenger floor mat.

All she needed was to have an overzealous cop—like that bitch from the hospital, Officer Denton—spot the weapons and arrest her. Getting caught carrying a concealed weapon was trouble enough, but having a suppressor in her possession would be much bigger trouble. That prick John Babington would love to prosecute her for that.

Angela spotted Tiffany, one of the girls who served drinks, all by herself some distance back from the crowd watching the police. She was in high heels with ankle straps and a skirt so short it barely covered the bottoms of her ass cheeks. Her heels and knees were pressed together as she hugged her bare midriff. Most of her hair was piled up on top, with some strands hanging down strategically, along with lots of stray wisps going everywhere. Tiffany always said that it gave her that just-fucked look that guys liked, which made her better tips.

When Angela quietly approached her, Tiffany turned to see who it was. It wasn't cold out, but she was shivering as she cried. Tears dragged long streaks of black mascara down her face.

"Tiffany—what the hell is going on?"

Tiffany swallowed. "It's Barry. I don't know if he's going to make it."

Angela put a comforting hand on Tiffany's back. "What happened? Did he have a heart attack or something?"

She didn't want to ask if he'd been shot in a robbery for fear of making it be true.

Tiffany took a tissue when Angela offered it. She pressed it under her eyes.

"No. Someone beat the shit out of him."

"Is that what the police said?"

"No. I'm the one who found him when I came in to work just a little while ago."

"Do the police know who did it?"

Tiffany shook her head. "I don't think so."

Angela gave Tiffany a suspicious look. "Do you?"

Tiffany stared off at the gaggle of police and onlookers. "Yeah. When I found Barry on the floor, I rushed to help him. His face looked like raw hamburger. That white T-shirt he always wears was soaked red with blood. It had holes burned in it and he had burns, like from a cigarette. He had a rag stuffed in his mouth. They'd been torturing him. I pulled the rag out so he could breathe."

"Was he conscious?"

"Barely." Tiffany sniffed back a sob. "I asked him what happened. All he was able to say was 'Those Mexicans,' then he lost consciousness."

Angela felt goose bumps race across the bare flesh of her legs and arms. She knew without a doubt what Mexicans he was talking about.

"Did you tell the police?"

Tiffany huffed her contempt. "Fuck the police."

"Well . . . who called them?"

"I did."

"Didn't they ask your name?"

Tiffany gestured toward the simple block building. The beer sign in the window glowed its perpetual invitation.

"I didn't use my cell phone. I called from the phone behind the bar. That's where Barry was laying. They asked what was the emergency. I told them that someone robbed Barry's Place Bar, and that Barry was hurt real bad. Before they could ask anything else, I hung up. A stayed with Barry until I heard the sirens and then I got out before they saw me."

Angela frowned. "Why didn't you want to tell the police what you knew?"

With a finger, Tiffany carefully wiped the lipstick from each corner of her mouth. It was a long moment before she answered.

"I never told you about it before, but I was arrested not long ago."

"You? For what?"

"Prostitution."

Tiffany dressed like a slut, but Angela had always thought that was just to get better tips.

"I didn't know."

Tiffany's expression drew down into a scowl. "I don't hook. All right? This off-duty cop—Officer Palinski, a real mean motherfucker—was in here one night. He wanted me to come out to the parking lot and give him a blow job. I didn't know he was a cop. I told him to fuck off. He came back in his blues later that night and arrested me for solicitation. Took me to jail and had me booked—said I had solicited him. My mother had to come down and bail me out." Tiffany shook her head in anger at the memory.

Guys asked Angela to suck their cocks often enough, but so far none of them had been a cop, so she'd never feared getting arrested when she said no.

"But that ain't the worst of it," Tiffany said. "The prosecutor called me in. He gave me that smug smile like he knows I'm a whore, know what I mean?"

"Yeah, I know the look."

"And then he says to me, he says, if I want, he could help me out of the jam I was in and maybe drop the charges. I said I'd appreciate that because they weren't true." She looked over at Angela. "It's not good for your health to go accusing cops of shit, know what I mean? So I said it was just an honest misunderstanding."

Angela nodded.

"So this prosecutor—he's still got this shit-eating grin on his fat face—says to me that his officer has pretty good taste in cocksuckers. He told me then that he could add on some drug-dealing charges so that I'd spend at least six months, maybe even a year, in jail."

Tiffany glared off at the police. Silent tears started rolling down her cheeks again. "I got a kid, you know. A daughter. This fucker says that he could make sure that when I was convicted the county would take away my kid." She wiped the tears from under her eyes with the tissue. "She's only three."

"Jeez, Tiffany, I had no idea."

Angela had been taken by the county once when they sent her mother to rehab. It had been a fresh kind of hell—one invented by the legal system. They had Angela in their clutches for six months before she was tossed back into the frying pan.

"He asked what I'd be willing to do to get the charges dismissed so I could keep my kid. I thought he meant community service or something. So I told him I'd do anything, ya know? He says to me, then, that all I had to do was to come around to his place a few times a week for a month or so and give him a blow job, and if I did it good enough he'd drop all the charges. He said I'd need to give Palinski his blow job so that he'd be willing to go along with the charges being dropped."

Angela didn't have to ask if Tiffany agreed to the deal.

"What was the prosecutor's name?"

Tiffany made a face. "Assistant District Attorney John Babington. Why? You know him?"

"I know the prick," Angela said under her breath.

"Yeah? Sorry to hear that you had a run-in with that mother-fucker."

After a time, Angela asked, "Did Barry say anything else?"

"No." Tiffany shook her head. "Alls he mumbled when I asked him what happened was 'Those Mexicans,' before he passed out. I hope to God he makes it. Barry's a good guy, ya know?"

"Yeah, I know."

As Angela listened to Tiffany's story, she was trying to figure out why in the world the four men who had attacked her would have done this to Barry.

Tiffany trembled as she hugged herself. "I gotta pay my rent. I got a kid. What am I going to do?"

"Well," Angela said, thinking out loud, "some of us girls have keys to the place. Why don't we keep the bar open? Barry has bills to pay, too. We don't want him to lose his bar. Most of the girls are like you—they can't afford to be out of work. It would help all of us out and it would help Barry out until he got better if we all pitched in and kept the place up and running."

Tiffany started smiling for the first time. "Yeah, we could do that." Her eyes widened when she had the spark of an idea. "We could start a ladies' night, offer them a free drink. That would bring in women, and women bring in lots of men."

"Barry never wanted to have a ladies' night," Angela said.

"Well Barry ain't here to say no." She snapped her fingers. "I could bring in a string of Christmas lights and we could hang 'em up behind the bar or something. It would class up the place, make it look fancy. We could even paint the ladies' room, ya know? Make it look better so women would want to stay around.

"Until Barry gets better we could do some things to make the place more money than it brings in now. I'm sure of it. And if we do it right—bring in the ladies—we'd all make a lot more tips from the men who would come in."

Angela thought about it for a minute. It sounded like it was worth a try. It certainly would help Barry out if the bar pulled in some money for him while he was in the hospital and until he could recover. *If* he recovered.

"I think that sounds like a great idea. You'd be able to make more money to help out with your little girl."

Tiffany considered a moment. "With just us girls, I think we'd need a man around to watch over things. Like a bouncer or something, so there wouldn't be trouble we couldn't handle."

"I think you're right. Barry always watched over everything. Him and that baseball bat he keeps behind the bar. But I guess it didn't help him tonight."

"Any idea who we can we get?"

Angela shook her head. "I don't know. We'll have to give it some thought."

Tiffany looked over. "Hey, wasn't it some Mexicans that almost killed you, too?"

Angela stared off into the darkness. "As a matter of fact it was."

Tiffany frowned. "But they're in jail, so it couldn't be the same ones."

"They're not in jail. The charges were dropped and they were released."

"Dropped? Why?"

"Babington let them go."

"Fuck," Tiffany said under her breath.

Angela didn't believe in coincidences. It had to be the same four. She suddenly realized why they had tortured Barry.

FORTY

The city they drove through, like many cities in America, seemed run-down, neglected, and devoid of hope. Many of the places where Rafael had grown up were old, but they were old in a different way. They were old in a historic way, with buildings, monuments, and mosques that were many hundreds of years old. Some were thousands of years old. In his land, history lived in all of them. History never died.

Everything in these cities looked merely decades old and already they were unkempt and rotting. The people in America were weak. Their lives were aimless. They did not accept Allah.

Soon many would die under the withering light of the sun Rafael and his brothers would unleash on them.

Rafael spotted the beige Toyota off to the side of the parking lot of the convenience store. Because the building they owned where they would assemble the bomb was remote and difficult to find, Miguel had suggested they meet at the convenience store and then he would guide them to the building just outside town.

Rafael pulled his used cargo van into the lot and tapped the horn once. The cars that were escorting the van and protecting its cargo were spread out all around them. Some waited out on the street. Some were behind. Some were out ahead making sure they would not encounter any problems.

A hand extended up in recognition from the front passenger window. The four-door Toyota Camry turned on its headlights and pulled out in front of Rafael to lead the way.

As they left the lights of the city behind, the countryside became dark and forbidding. Rafael had never seen so many trees in all his life as he saw driving across the country. They came right up to the road all around. It was claustrophobic.

As was typical, Cassiel hadn't spoken for hours. He silently watched the American landscape go by out his window.

"So," Rafael said, "what do you think of America so far?"

Cassiel continued looking out the passenger window as he spoke. "I have been to America before."

Rafael briefly glanced over as he turned a corner, following the Toyota onto a different road. "You have?"

Cassiel nodded. "As a matter of fact, I came to this very city, Milford Falls, several years back. It looks the same."

Rafael was surprised to hear it. "Why were you here?"

Cassiel was still looking out the side window. "I came here to kill some people."

Rafael glanced over to meet Cassiel's gaze. "You should rejoice, then. You are about to have the chance to be part of killing many more people."

Hasan had told him that Cassiel was a killer. In fact, he had been about to be put to death for killing a family in Iran, but Hasan thought that a man like that would be useful for their mission. Rafael didn't agree. Every detail of their mission had been painstakingly planned and every need supplied. He didn't see what Cassiel could add to their mission.

It felt more like he was babysitting a moody child than having the fellowship of a brother-in-arms.

The Toyota led them through a dark countryside until they entered what appeared to be an industrial area, but it looked long deserted. Rafael saw no cars, no people, no signs of life. The buildings were decaying and looked to have been abandoned for many,

many years. Windows were broken out. Many of the walls had spray-painted words or symbols that made no sense. Where Rafael came from, people who did this kind of thing would be put in jail, or in work camps, or might even be put to death. But America was a land devoid of morality.

As they made their way through a maze of crumbling buildings, he saw sprawling areas surrounded by chain-link fencing and barbed wire. The whole place was a maze of ruins. Rafael realized that Miguel was right to suggest leading them in. He would never have been able to navigate the concrete labyrinth of American industrial decay on his own.

As they pulled up to the end of a large building with a curved roof and almost no windows, one of their men waiting outside jumped up and rolled a big door to the side. He waved the Toyota, Rafael's van, and all the escort of vehicles inside. Because the building was so large, it swallowed all the cars and trucks, so that no one going past would have any idea that there was any activity inside.

There were only a few battery-powered work lights on, leaving most of the cavernous building dark. One of their men motioned to Rafael where to park to be in position for unloading. The Toyota parked off to the side.

When Rafael climbed out of the van, Miguel rushed up to greet him. The smiling man gripped Rafael by the sides of his arms, leaned in, and ceremonially kissed each cheek.

"We are so relieved that you have made it here safely, brother," Emilio said. "We followed with great interest the glory you brought to us at the border crossing. It was a tremendous strike against the infidels."

Rafael nodded. "It was everything we have planned for all these years. Esteban and Javier brought great glory to themselves and are now with Allah."

A cheer went up for their martyred comrades.

Miguel regarded the stranger suspiciously. "Who is this?"

Rafael held out a hand. "This is Cassiel. Hasan assigned him to come with me. Cassiel has special talents that may be useful. He is an expert in a variety of weapons. I have been assured that he is lethal with all of them."

Cassiel bowed his head to the men.

"You can all introduce yourselves later," Rafael said. "For now, I would like to see your work."

Miguel held out a hand in invitation. "I am sure you will be pleased to find everything ready for you. Here, on the floor, as you can see, we have the lead sections prepared."

They looked just like the ones they had practiced making many times back in Iran under the watchful eyes of their technical trainers. Miguel moved on to a row of shelves.

"Once we completed the machining we moved everything here to be ready for final assembly."

He handed Rafael one of the geometrically shaped pieces of Semtex. Assembled in a sphere around the outside of the lead tamper, they would form the explosive lens that would implode the plutonium pit to critical mass.

Rafael noted that they were as well made as those they practiced making many times.

"And here are the brass chimney sleeves. As you can see, the connectors for the detonators are already installed and awaiting the attachment of the EBW."

"The exploding bridgewire arrived safely by courier?"

"Yes, of course," Miguel said. "We laid it into the wiring loom. It is ready now for the final connections."

Rafael caught Miguel's brief sideways glance to Juan, Emilio, and Pedro, who were standing not far off to the side.

Rafael leaned in a little. "You did follow my instructions, didn't you? Hasan wanted the courier eliminated. You followed the orders included with the EBW and killed the courier?"

"Well," Miguel said as he fidgeted with the brass sleeve he was holding, "we certainly did follow your instructions. The courier was a woman who works for herself." He gestured offhandedly. "We hanged her."

"You hanged her." Rafael looked to the sheepish faces of the other three. "But you didn't say if you killed her, as instructed."

"We beat her so she was hardly conscious and then we put a rope around her neck. We hanged her up by her neck"—Miguel gestured off to his right—"over at the other place where we did the machining. We had things we needed to do over here, so we left her hanging there by her neck to choke to death."

"Did that kill her? Did you see her dead?"

"Actually, no." Miguel turned his palms up. "Who could know that a person could escape from that? It was impossible for anyone to escape from that rope. We were sure of it."

"So then this woman you say could not possibly escape, escaped."

Miguel shrugged self-consciously. "There was no way for us to know."

Rafael took a settling breath as he gritted his teeth while looking around at the four men. "Well yes, there is a way to know. You stay there until she is dead, or, better yet, you cut off her head."

"We were working hard on finishing the job so that we would be ready for you, Rafael—that was what was most important. The woman went to the police but they let us go because they believe we are Mexican immigrants. The police are not interested in charging us with a crime. We know that we must fix this, so we went to the bar where this American whore works to find out where she lives. At first, the man who owns the bar wouldn't tell us. In the end he told us how to get to her house."

"And did you kill him so he couldn't tell the authorities you were the same men who tried to kill this courier?"

Miguel nodded furiously. "Yes, Rafael. Of course we killed him. I'm pretty sure he was dead when we left him."

"Pretty sure. Not sure, just pretty sure."

"He was not breathing."

"And I thought José was the stupid one," Rafael said under his breath as he shook his head in frustration. "So, who is this woman that you hanged?"

"Her name is Angela Constantine. She is an American whore." He flashed a brief smile. "We used her as a wife to us before we hanged her."

Rafael noticed that Cassiel had come closer. The man's hands had fisted at his sides.

"You say you know where she lives?" Rafael asked.

Miguel nodded furiously before repeating the directions to her house.

Rafael grabbed the man's shirt and yanked him close. "I want you, Juan, Emilio, and Pedro to go to her house—right now—and finish the job, as you were instructed. Do you understand?"

Miguel nodded again, afraid to speak.

Rafael looked at the other three, standing self-consciously together. "Do you all have knives?"

They all nodded.

"Shouldn't we take some guns?" Pedro asked.

"Why? So that if you're stopped by the police you can be arrested for carrying AK-47s? So that you can be interrogated about being heavily armed illegal aliens? So that the authorities can discover our operation and put a stop to our decades of planning? They let you go before because they thought you were simply undocumented Mexican immigrants. They won't let you go if you are caught with guns."

"Sorry, Rafael," Miguel rushed to say. "No guns. We can do what is needed with our knives."

"I think I should go with them," Cassiel said in his gravelly voice.

Rafael thought the man looked a little too eager to go back to his personal fetish. "No. This is not your responsibility. Miguel and his men should be the ones to take care of it."

Miguel nodded again. "We will, Rafael. I swear."

Rafael swept a finger back and forth, pointing at the four men. "I want you to cut off her head and bring it to me. Do you think you can do that correctly this time? Do you think that you four strong men with knives can handle this one woman who escaped from you already once before?"

THE GIRL IN THE MOON

"Yes, Rafael," they said as one.

"We handled her easily before," Miguel added. "She is not big enough to cause us any problem." He dismissed her importance with a casual flick of his hand. "Our only mistake was being too eager to get on with our work and not staying to see that she was dead, that's all. We will take care of it."

"Then get going and finish it before she can cause any trouble."

The four men all scrambled to get into the Toyota.

"All right," Rafael said to all the other men standing around him as the door rolled to the side and the Toyota drove off into the night, "you all know what to do. You all know what this means for us, for our cause.

"Our computer team in Russia successfully launched the cyber attacks, so that we might be able to succeed with our part of the mission. American intelligence agencies have blamed the Russians for the cyber attack. America is angry and demanding retaliation.

"Our comrades running those servers in Russia are standing by for the second phase. Just before detonation they will launch a second wave of cyber attacks. Those cyber attacks will hopefully cause US defense agencies to assume that the nuclear attack that we launch was the second phase of a Russian attack on America.

"This will hopefully result in the US launching a nuclear strike at Russia. Once those missiles are in the air, Russia will counterattack with their own missiles.

"This all means that within a matter of minutes, World War Three may be under way.

"The Great Satan will be destroyed.

"But even if such a nuclear war does not develop, America will never recover from the blow we strike. Hundreds of thousands of infidels will die. Vast territory will be uninhabitable. The electromagnetic pulse will take out much of America's infrastructure. The US will be thrown into chaos. Many millions more will starve to death as they shiver in the darkness we have brought upon them.

346

TERRY GOODKIND

"Our strike, carried about by those of us in this room, will be a turning point for the Islamic world. We now know how to get nuclear material into America. Others will follow the path we have laid out.

"Israel will be next.

"With what we do, the final destruction of the Great Satan will be under way, and then Israel will at long last be wiped from existence. They cannot destroy the entire Islamic world. We are used to surviving in darkness. They are not.

"Once this new nuclear phase of our war against the West is under way, nothing will stop it. We will change the balance of power. Islam will become the new ruling superpower."

The men all around listening to his speech thrust a fist into the air as they let out cheers. These men had devoted their entire lives to this mission and this cause. They had trained in every field necessary to make plutonium bombs, both in Iran and Pakistan, and a few of them in North Korea.

They had worked their whole lives at being able to pass as Mexican immigrants who so easily moved into and throughout American society. No one would suspect the darkness they were about to bring to America.

"Now, put on your protective clothing." He gestured to his second-in-command. "Alejandro, see to the material that is to go into the cargo van. You will oversee this crew, here. I will take the van to the second location."

Splitting up the material increased the chances they would remain undiscovered until it was too late.

He looked to his second-in-command. "You have the entire place wired with explosives, just in case?"

Alejandro bowed his head. "Yes, Commander."

"Cassiel, you will come with me and my half of the team. The rest of you know what to do. If we work hard we should be able to complete the assembly and be ready in a few days. The countdown can then begin. When that hour is upon us, we will bring the Great Satan to its knees."

FORTY-ONE

As Angela dropped the cable in front of her driveway, a car pulled off the road and across the drive at an angle. Gravel crunched under the tires as it rolled to a slow stop. It was hard to see in the dark with the headlights blinding her, but she thought it looked like a government-issue sedan.

She was reluctant to draw the gun she had in its holster at the small of her back, because it might only be someone who was lost. More than that, though, it would be a big mistake to draw a weapon if it turned out to be an unmarked police car. But out here on this lonely stretch of road, it could easily be trouble of one kind or another, so as she walked around to the driver's door when she heard the window rolling down, she was ready to draw the weapon at the first sign of trouble.

Angela leaned down a little but stood back to give herself room to draw her weapon if she needed to, and enough room that the person in the car couldn't grab it. The door popped open just enough for the interior light to come on and show John Babington grinning up at her. His suit jacket and tie were lying over the passenger seat. His shirt collar was unbuttoned.

"I need to have a talk with you," he said.

Angela was sick about what had happened to Barry. If Babington had prosecuted the men who had tried to kill her, they would have been in jail and Barry would be fine. It was this man's fault that Barry was in the hospital near death.

"About what?"

"About the serious charges against you."

This was new. "What charges?"

"Well," he drawled, "that's what I'm here to talk to you about. Took me some digging to find out where you live. Why don't I follow you up to your house and we can talk about it?" He winked at her. "I'm sure we can work it out."

This was not the way legitimate prosecutors conducted business, but Angela knew better than to flat-out tell him to fuck off, even though that was what she really wanted to do. John Babington was about the last thing in the world she wanted to deal with at the moment.

She knew, though, that sometimes you just had to take opportunities when they presented themselves.

She smiled down at him. "Sure, okay."

Angela got back in her truck and drove up the road to her house. Babington followed and pulled around to park next to her. As she unlocked the front door, he stood uncomfortably close behind her. She turned on the living room light as she walked into the house.

She was still wearing the low-rise cutoff shorts for her job tending bar. She knew he was watching her ass. There was little doubt about what he had on his mind. She expected that he wanted to make her a similar offer to the one he'd made Tiffany.

Angela turned around and tried to sound apprehensive. This time, she was not in his office in a building full of police and security. This time, he was on her ground, and he had no idea who he was dealing with.

"So . . . what did you want to talk to me about?"

"You don't want go to jail, do you."

"No, of course not," she said, deliberately elevating the concern in her voice. "Can you keep that from happening?"

He made a face to indicate "Maybe."

He ran a finger up and down the side of her arm. "You rub my back, I rub yours, so to speak. Know what I mean?"

"No," she said, playing dumb so that he would spell it out.

He finally dropped the pretense and reached down to put his hand on her crotch. He felt confident because there was no one to see him doing it. Angela didn't move. He reached around with his other hand and grabbed her ass so that she was sandwiched between his fat mitts.

"Does this help you get the picture?" he asked.

"Are you making me the same kind of offer you made to Tiffany?"

He grunted his displeasure. "I'm going to have to teach that little cocksucker to keep her mouth shut—at least when she's not with me."

"You know," Angela said as he fondled her ass, "your cell phone can be tracked. Not saying that I would, but if I were to report that you came here to proposition me under threat the state police could trace your phone's locations and see that you were here tonight."

"That's why I left my cell phone at work," he said with a smirk. He tilted his head as if to say he was one step ahead of her and she was outsmarted.

She gave him a coy look from under her brow. "I guess, then, that I'm kind of in a spot."

Babington arched an eyebrow as he wormed two fingers under the crotch of her shorts. "Yes, you are, little lady. Now, I'd hate to have to see you sent to jail, so maybe we can work something out to clear up these pending drug and weapons charges?"

Angela pushed his hand away from her crotch. "I can't think with you doing that."

"What's to think about?" he asked. "A little trailer park whore like you screws different guys all the time. None of them can keep you out of jail, but I can."

"You swear that if I agree you would make sure there are no charges? You swear that will be the end of it?"

He shrugged. "I come over for a visit from time to time, you take care of me, and I will keep charges from popping up."

"You mean this is something ongoing? I'm always going to be under threat of going to jail?"

He rolled his eyes back as he smelled the fingers he'd had inside her shorts. "I don't think you have anything to worry about."

"You're saying I have to give you sex or you will bring me up on false charges?"

His look darkened. "Look, I'm not playing games, here. I could easily put you in a great deal of legal jeopardy. It will cost you everything you have and then some to fight it. You will still end up in jail in the end and have a mountain of debt as well. I can keep that from happening. I'm getting tired of the questions. I suggest you agree before I change my mind."

Angela reached down and grabbed his erection through his dress pants. She pressed herself up against him.

"If you would handle my legal problem, then I think I could handle your problem."

His grin widened. "Now you're talking. We start tonight. Right now."

"All right." Angela tilted her head. "I like to get all crazy with guys down in the basement. I have a special room set up." She squeezed his erection as she smiled up at him. "Know what I mean?"

The thought clearly excited him. "Lead the way."

Angela looked back over her shoulder and smiled as she unlocked the basement door while he felt her up from behind. She flicked on the light and skipped down the stairs to get away from his hand. He wasted no time in following her.

At the bottom he looked around, trying to figure out what kind of sex room she had set up.

Angela flashed him a flirtatious smile. "Why don't you have a seat, Mr. Babington, and I'll handle everything."

He flopped down onto the metal chair, his head still swiveling around. Angela swung a leg over him to straddle him as she sat on his lap facing him.

Without saying anything, she unbuckled his belt and unzipped his pants. That seemed to reassure him and get his mind back on track.

She rested her arms on his shoulders, locking her fingers behind his head so that her face was mere inches from his. "This kind of what you had in mind?"

He was sinking into a trance of desire. "Uh-huh."

"You know," she said in an intimate whisper, "I've found that justice is often an illusion."

He grunted. "Indeed it is."

"In fact, I've found that the law has little to do with justice, that laws are merely a way for some people to have power over others and that if you want justice sometimes you have to make it happen yourself. Know what I mean?"

He frowned, trying to figure out where she was going with this. "I'm an officer of the court. I represent the law."

"Uh-huh," she said. "That's what I'm talking about."

"Get on with it," he said, his impatience showing.

"Oh, don't worry, you're going to get fucked real good."

"Hurry up and get on with it, then."

Angela kissed his cheek. "As you wish," she whispered in his ear. His erection throbbed against her.

Angela got up off his lap and drew her gun from her grandfather's holster at the small of her back and pointed it right between his eyes.

She stepped back far enough so that he couldn't reach up and try to grab it. "You're right about one thing. You are an officer of the court. You are supposed to represent the law, but you instead represent what most people in authority have—power for themselves."

"What is your problem, woman?"

"My problem? Well let's see, I was beaten, raped, hung by a rope around my neck and left to choke to death. You let the men who

352

did that go free for your own personal political gain, and the gain of the system and politicians you represent. Those criminals went on to beat my friend and boss nearly to death. He may not live the night. You, Mr. Babington, made all that possible. You were an accessory to both crimes."

Clearly not intimidated by her gun, he zipped up his pants. "Put that gun down or I'll see to it you go to jail for the rest of your life for pointing a firearm at an officer of the court!"

"Then I guess, if I'm going to serve the time, I might as well do the crime."

"I followed the law with those undocumented aliens. The people of this state want them protected. That's what I did—the people's bidding."

"What you did, Mr. Babington, was side with killers rather than their victims."

He stood in a huff. "I don't know what kind of game you're playing, young lady, but I'm leaving. You're a fool to think you could get away with this. People would miss me and come looking. You harm me and you will go to jail for attempted murder."

She tilted her head. "How do you suppose anyone is going to know where to find you? You left your phone in your office so that no one would know you were going off to blackmail yet another innocent woman. How many times have you done this? How many women, Mr. Babington?"

He scowled defiantly as he gestured dismissively. "You're only the second. You and Tiffany—that's all."

"Why is it I don't believe you? Hmm?"

"I don't care if you believe me or not. I'm leaving. Expect the police to be here within the hour."

"Move either foot and I'll pull the trigger."

She could see in his eyes that he was trying to decide if he believed her and if he dared to try to leave.

His gaze went from the gun to the tattoo across her throat. When he saw the words "DARK ANGEL," his confidence faltered.

"You let those four men go," she told him. "Those men are killers. This isn't only about me. It's about all the other victims you condemn to suffer, like Barry tonight. How many people have been brutalized or even murdered because you let killers go, or you let them plea-bargain, or you lowered the charges as a favor to their attorney? How many monsters have you let go back on the street to kill again?"

"I only follow the law."

"The laws you represent are as corrupt as you are."

"All right, you win," he said as he held up his hands as if to ward her off. "I'll file charges of attempted murder against those four men. I'll have them prosecuted. I'll see to it that they go to jail for a good long time. How about that? Do we have a deal?"

"Is that how the law works, Mr. Babington? That the way it's done? You only enforce it when you're afraid for your life? Not when the victims of violence are afraid for theirs?"

Angela had gone to sleep many a night having fantasies about torturing this man to death. It would be easy enough, and he would certainly deserve what she could do to him.

But she was worried for Barry and she just wasn't in the mood. This man sickened her. The system he represented sickened her. She was sick of looking at him, sick of listening to him.

While keeping the gun on him, she lifted open the hatch.

Angela gestured with her gun. "Kneel over here."

He frowned. "Why?"

"Because I said so, that's why."

He reluctantly knelt, thinking it might somehow get him out of this. He peered down into the darkness below.

"Take everything out of your pockets and toss it to the side."

"Please," he said as he followed her instructions with trembling hands. There was no longer any trace of arrogance in his voice. "I've learned my lesson—I swear. Let me go and I will just forget this whole ugly incident. I'll have those four men arrested and I will charge them with attempted murder, like you want. Just let me go."

Angela didn't answer. She walked around behind him and without further ceremony fired a bullet into the back of his skull. A .22 could easily penetrate the thick bone of the skull if fired at a direct angle. Angela's fired at a direct angle. The sound of the shot echoed around the small basement, making her ears ring.

John Babington tumbled forward into the hell hole.

Angela leaned over, watching his lifeless body descend into the darkness.

"Karma is a bitch."

FORTY-TWO

After John Babington had vanished into the darkness of the hell hole, Angela tossed the gun down after him. She watched it fall, glance twice off the granite walls on the way down, and finally fade away into the darkness until she could no longer see it. She had learned long ago not to bother waiting to hear things hit bottom.

Once she had used a gun to kill someone, that gun became forever tainted with the potential for all kinds of trouble. There was forensic evidence she could only begin to imagine—blood spatter, serial numbers, as well as distinctive marks left by the magazine, the firing pin, and gun barrel rifling.

Once she had used a gun on someone, that gun would never be used again. It always went down the abyss along with the killer. Owen was the only man so far that had not ended up in the hell hole. Of course, the knife she had used to kill him had, along with everything she'd been wearing that could have had any blood evidence on it.

Angela could easily have enticed Owen to her house and spent several days initiating him into hell. But it had been more important to her that Carrie's remains be found so that her family would have closure than it was for Owen to be sent down the hell hole. She hoped that he was in hell, the real one, for the rest of eternity.

Angela removed her boots, with her knife and sheath inside the lining, and tossed them down into the hell hole. Like the gun, they could potentially have a wealth of forensic evidence on them. After her boots, she removed her shorts, underwear, and her top and threw them in as well.

Even if they never found John Babington's body, a bullet penetrating the skull created internal pressure that often blew blood droplets, as well as tiny specks of brain matter and hair, back away from the hole. It was inevitable that some of that, even minuscule amounts, would end up on her clothes. He'd had his hand in her pants; they could probably find skin cells from his fingers on her thong.

If any tiny speck were to be found on her clothes, the police forensic department could test DNA from his relatives and tie it to Babington. Even without a body, they could probably still convict her of killing him on circumstantial evidence alone.

Truly evil men often got away with their crimes because of legal technicalities, or things like Babington dropping the charges for political reasons. Even when politics weren't involved, the victims were routinely ignored as unimportant while thugs like Boska were granted favors and leniency. Time after time they were let go for any reason someone could come up with. Rap sheets of violent crimes grew to multiple pages with nothing done to stop, much less punish, the violent criminal. Babington was part of that whole corrupt system. It took something like a minivan to finally end the injustice.

But Angela knew that if it was her they would go to the ends of the earth to make sure she spent the rest of her life in prison. They couldn't have people killing prosecutors, no matter how much they might deserve it. That's the way government officials were. Protect their own at all costs.

So, rather than try to outguess what forensic scientists might be able to find on her shorts, or underwear, or top, or boots, or gun, or knife, everything she had on when she executed Babington went down the hell hole along with his body. Her best protection was to make sure there was never any evidence to be found.

She sometimes wondered if an archaeologist tens of thousands of years in the future would discover the hell hole and all the remains of predators at the bottom. She could only wonder at what theory they would come up with about what it all meant.

Angela knelt and went through everything Babington had emptied out of his pockets. She tossed the change down the hole. He had nearly five hundred dollars in his wallet. She pulled the cash out. She couldn't see the point in throwing away cash. She looked through the photos. There was a picture of a boat, and a photo of a middle-aged woman, presumably his wife.

"I just did you a big favor, lady."

Angela tossed the wallet down the hell hole. She threw his whole four-leaf-clover key ring full of keys down into the darkness. His luck at getting away with the things he did had run out. She stuck her little finger through the key ring with his car keys and remote and set them up on the counter.

After she had thrown everything of no use or potentially incriminating down the abyss, she took the garden hose off the wall and thoroughly washed down the floor to get rid of any trace of blood. The water was freezing cold on her bare feet. She promised herself that after she was finished she would take a hot shower. She also needed the shower to make sure that any speck of blood or brain tissue was washed out of her hair.

After winding the hose back up on the reel at the end of the basement, she took a new pair of boots out of the lower cabinet where she kept a dozen pair. She'd used two pair between Owen and then Babington. She made a mental note to order some more. She pulled out a new knife, in its new sheath, and slipped it into the pocket she had already created between the lining and the leather of the right boot.

Once she had new boots prepared, she took a new Walther P22 out of its box. She tossed the box, with the serial number and the shell inside from the manufacture's test firing, down the hell hole.

She loaded one new magazine with ten rounds, the second with nine. They were supposed to hold ten rounds, but she had learned over years of practice that the magazines didn't always feed reliably with ten rounds. If she was just target-practicing, she might load ten rounds. It gave her practice at clearing random jams. But when her life depended on the reliability of the gun and magazines she carried, she loaded those spare magazines with nine rounds.

She shoved a magazine loaded with ten rounds into the gun and cycled the slide to chamber a round, leaving nine in the magazine. Having one chambered and nine in the magazine gave her ten rounds the first time around, and nine thereafter if she needed to reload with a fresh magazine to keep firing.

So far, with the murderers she had killed, she'd never needed a second magazine, but she always carried extras just in case. Her grandfather always told her that you could never have too much ammo.

Naked, holding new boots loaded with a new knife under her left arm, her holster and a few full magazines in her left hand, and her gun in her right hand with her finger along the side of the slide, she went upstairs to take a shower.

As she clicked off the basement light and then the living room light switches with the back of her hand, she heard a car drive up.

Angela froze.

No one ever drove up uninvited past all the no-trespassing signs. She remembered that she had left the cable down after Babington had driven in, so it was always possible that it wasn't trouble arriving at her door. It could be some innocent visitor looking for directions.

Angela didn't think she could be that lucky.

She dumped everything she was carrying, except her gun, on the couch. The hall light was still on, but otherwise the place was dark.

She peeked out the door. The beige, four-door Toyota Camry that she knew all too well was just coming to a stop.

Angela held the gun behind her back and stepped out onto the porch, naked.

FORTY-THREE

All four car doors popped open. The two men on the passenger side stepped out first. In the moonlight she could see that it was Juan and Pedro.

Angela, gun in hand, was already in a near trance, the same as when she practiced with her grandfather's target. She had put thousands of rounds into that steel triangle. Tens of thousands of rounds. Hundreds of thousands of rounds. That triangle haunted her dreams.

An ear-to-ear grin grew on Pedro's face. "Ah, I see the American whore is naked and eager to—"

She put a round through the center of his face, stopping him cold.

The bullet entered through the soft area of that triangle formed by the points between the two eyes and tip of the nose, the triangle her grandfather had told her about when she was younger and had her practice hitting.

The bullet ricocheted around inside Pedro's skull, turning his brain to pulp and instantly ceasing all neurological function. He dropped where he stood before he had been able to complete the sentence. The way he went down, it looked as if his bones had dissolved.

Even as Pedro was still falling, Juan pulled a knife and screamed some sort of battle cry in Spanish that she didn't understand.

He charged for the porch. Angela was in no hurry. Her aim had locked on to him. He was that target, wobbling, moving, swaying.

Angela shot him between the eyes. He fell dead at her feet.

Even as the sounds of the two shots were still ringing through the night air, and the two men were hitting the ground, the other two men realized they were in trouble and slammed their doors shut. The driver threw it into gear and matted the gas pedal. Wheels spinning, the car reeled around, throwing up a cloud of dust as it raced back down the driveway and into the darkness.

Angela didn't shoot at the escaping car. She didn't think a .22 bullet would penetrate the metal of the car reliably enough to kill the driver. A shot through glass at an angle would deflect a bullet. She doubted that the small-caliber slug would blow out a spinning tire. Shooting at the car would be little more than random shots in the dark. She didn't like low-probability shots.

Besides, she didn't want the shot to be luck. She wanted to look into their eyes when they died. She wanted her face to be the last thing they saw as they knew they were an instant away from death.

Angela's immediate urge was to go after the two men, but she was naked. By the time she threw on some clothes and grabbed the keys to her truck, she knew they would be long gone and she would be unlikely to find them. It would be a series of choices—left or right—and in the end they would probably be gone.

She would find them, and when she did, she would kill them, just as she had promised that night in that filthy room on the greasy moving pad. They were not going to get away. They had come back to kill her. They were not going to give up. Neither was she.

The most important issue at the moment was the two dead guys in her front yard and the car of the now officially missing Assistant District Attorney John Babington sitting in front of her house.

She believed that she knew generally where she could find the other two men. She thought they were up to something in the old industrial area, so they weren't likely to leave town. They weren't going anywhere for now.

She had been out to the deserted industrial area many times, looking for them, so far with no luck. But they were still out there, somewhere. She knew they were. The fact that they had just shown up at her door to finish the job they had started that night proved it. She would find them sooner or later. And if they showed up at her house again, all the better.

Angela squatted down beside the two dead men. Her address was listed everywhere as a box at Mike's Mail Service. The address of her house was not listed anywhere or easy to find. They had tortured Barry until he told them where she lived. She didn't blame him for talking. In fact, she wished he had told them what they wanted to know before he had been so badly hurt.

Anyone was going to talk under torture. Holding out during prolonged torture wasn't going to accomplish anything, because they would give it up in the end anyway. She knew that well enough.

Angela found a knife on Pedro. It was inside a sheath tucked down in his pants. It was a serious combat knife. It was big enough to decapitate someone. Other than that, he didn't have so much as pocket change. No ID, no keys, no nothing. The only thing in his pockets was some lint.

Juan's knife was still in his fist where he had fallen on the steps. It was the same kind of combat knife as Pedro's.

His fist was still clenched around the handle from that instant when his brain function ceased. A person who died that fast couldn't even unclench their fist. They couldn't even pull the trigger if they had a gun in their hand.

He didn't have anything in his pockets, either. The only way she knew the men's names was because they had used them when they had been raping and beating her. They had not expected her to leave that abandoned building alive.

Neither one looked so smug, now. Since they had both died instantly when the bullets had shut down their brain function, each man's eyes were open, staring, in death, looking up at her. She smiled back at them.

Angela knew that moving dead men was damn near impossible, and yet she couldn't leave them both sprawled in front of her house. She had to do something. She quickly went back inside and retrieved a new plastic shower curtain. She managed to roll Juan onto it, and then she was able to pull him the rest of the way up the steps. Once she got him inside, it was relatively easy to drag him—rolled up in the plastic shower curtain—across the floor to the basement door. There, she rolled him off the shower curtain and let him tumble down the steps. She used the same plastic shower curtain to drag Pedro to the basement doorway and dump him down the steps as well.

She flicked on the light again and went down to find Pedro's lifeless corpse sprawled atop Juan. Fortunately, neither man was big. She opened the hatch, then grabbed Pedro's wrist to drag his body close. Once she had him to the hatch, she rolled him into the hell hole. She did the same with Juan.

There was a little blood on the shower curtain, but like anything else with evidence on it, it had to go. Rather than let it billow out on the way down and possibly get hung up on something, she folded it up to make a relatively heavy, compact bundle and then threw it in after the men.

"Two down, two to go," she said under her breath as she tossed the second gun that day into the hole. She closed the hatch.

Using a .22 kept the bullets contained within the skulls. That meant a minimal amount of blood. Lots of guys thought big guns were best, but a .357 would blow out the back of the skull and spray blood, bone, and brain matter all over the place. It made a huge mess that left evidence everywhere, and, importantly, the victim was no deader. That was why assassins liked to use a .22.

But even with only a .22's small entrance wound, there was still some blood. The shower curtain contained what blood there was as the men were dragged through the house until the bodies were in the basement. The outdoor hose and then rains would wash away what little there was outside.

Angela again pulled out the hose and washed down the steps and basement floor. By this time, her feet were freezing.

She still had the problem of what to do with Babington's car.

FORTY-FOUR

Angela went back upstairs and finally took a hot shower. She shivered under the stream of water until it banished the chill. She took special care to wash her hair thoroughly. She dressed in jeans and a longer top to hide the gun she holstered in her waistband.

Worried about leaving any evidence in Babington's car, she put on a hoodie and drew the drawstring tight around her face. She wanted to make sure she didn't leave any of her hairs in his car. She picked up the car keys with a little finger through the key ring. Not wanting to leave any fingerprints, she retrieved a pair of disposable gloves and stuffed them in a pocket.

She left her phone at home on her nightstand for the same reason Babington didn't bring his phone. She didn't want anyone to be able to track its position to where she would leave his car.

After she locked her front door she pulled on the gloves, opened the car door, and started Babington's car. She stopped at the entrance to her drive and put the cable back up to make sure no one wandered up her drive.

It was late in the evening, but not so late that people driving around would be viewed suspiciously. There was no traffic on the road leading away from her house—there rarely was—but once she got into town the traffic started getting heavier. She didn't want to take the chance of having someone recognize John Babington's car with her driving it, so she took side streets, rather than four-lane roads where people could pull up beside her at traffic lights.

Once she reached an upscale motel near downtown, she parked on a side street right around the corner. The parking lot of the motel was likely to have surveillance cameras. She didn't want to be recorded driving or getting out of Babington's car. She kept her hood up over her head in case there were any cameras pointed out at the street she intended to walk down just around the corner from the motel after leaving the car.

She hoped that when the car was eventually found the police would theorize that John Babington had been going to a late-night liaison and parked where his car wouldn't be seen on the motel's cameras, and that he was then robbed, taken somewhere else to be murdered, and his body dumped. With the density of the surrounding forests just outside town, that happened occasionally and the bodies were rarely found.

That was, in fact, what Owen had done. He had dumped his victim's body like trash. If not for Angela seeing in his eyes what he had done, Carrie Stratton likely would never have been found. Angela might have been born broken—born a freak—but at least she could use that for something good.

Angela locked Babington's car with the remote. She peeled off the disposable gloves and put them in the pocket of her jeans along with the car keys. Later, she would toss the keys and gloves down the hell hole.

She kept her head down, hood up, and started walking.

When the strip mall finally came into sight, Angela was relieved to see that the lights were still on at Drenovic Tactical. She had ditched the car where she had because that motel was only a mile and a half from Nate's place. Nate had done a good job teaching her what she needed to know. But now she needed him for something else.

She pushed back the hood and opened the door. Nate was sitting alone at the desk doing paperwork. He stood in surprise.

"Angela! What are you doing here at this hour?"

Angela stuffed her hands in the pockets of the hoodie. "I need a favor."

Nate shrugged. "Sure, anything. What do you need?"

"I need a ride home, if it's not too much trouble."

"No problem. But what are you doing here? Did your truck break down or something?"

"No, it's not that. I had a date. The guy turned out to be a real jerk. I didn't want to do what he had had in mind, so I dumped him. Now I find myself without a ride home. I can walk if it's too much trouble."

A cab would have left records, so that was out. It would be an awfully long walk, so she had been hoping Nate could drive her home. But she had also been prepared to walk if he hadn't been at work or couldn't give her a lift.

Nate opened a drawer and retrieved his car keys. "It's the least I can do."

"What do you mean?"

He gestured around the empty room. "Business has been slow. Seems like every strip mall has a martial arts school next to a nail salon. Even Malcolm stopped showing up. Teaching you kept my head above water."

"I should hope so. You were charging me enough."

He smiled. "I was. I hope it was worth it?"

"It was," she hastened to add, along with a smile.

"I wish you were still taking lessons. It paid some bills." He held a hand out toward the door. "My car is right outside."

Nate didn't know where she lived, so Angela had to give him directions as they drove out of town and toward her house. When they finally reached her driveway, she had him pull off the road and stop just before the cable. He was surprised to see that she lived outside Milford Falls in such a remote place.

"Thanks for the ride, Nate. You're a lifesaver."

"Stop seeing jerks and you won't need rides home."

Angela couldn't help smiling.

"I'm glad that at least I was able to teach you how to handle trouble if you end up in a bad situation." Nate gestured at her drive. "How about . . . I don't know. How about you show me your place?"

"It's been a long day. Maybe some other time."

"Oh. Okay. Sure."

He seemed deflated. She didn't want to leave it like that.

"You know the place I tend bar?"

"Yea, Barry's Place."

"Well, some guys tortured him and beat him really bad."

"My god, that's terrible. Why would they do that?"

"I don't know." She waved off the question to get back on topic. "He's in the hospital and right now we don't know if he's going to make it."

"I'm so sorry to hear that. If they wanted to rob him, why didn't they just rob him? Why would they torture him?"

She couldn't tell him that he was tortured to find out where the driveway was where they were sitting at that moment.

She couldn't help feeling guilty about Barry.

"I don't know," she lied again as she ran her finger back and forth over a piece of chrome on the center console. "Listen, Barry is in bad shape. Even if he makes it, it's going to be quite a while until he is back on his feet. I don't want him to lose his bar in the meantime. Me and some of the other girls are going to open the bar tomorrow and keep it up and running for him. You know, until he gets better. We're hoping to get people to come in and support his business."

"That sounds like a great idea."

"So, I need to get some sleep—"

"Oh, sure. I understand. Maybe some other time."

She nodded without committing. "We're going in early tomorrow to see about keeping his place afloat."

"Okay. Well, I think that's a great idea. I guess I better let you get some sleep, then. It was great getting to see you again, Angela."

She popped open the door, but then paused.

"Hey, listen. I just had an idea." She hoped not to make a habit of lying to him, but it seemed the most expedient solution. "Us girls could use a guy there to kind of watch over things while we're working."

"You mean, you need a bouncer?"

"Yeah, I guess. Check IDs, that kind of thing. Make sure none of the guys get grabby with us since Barry isn't there watching over things. He used to look out for the girls that work for him." She looked up into his eyes. "It would be great if you could do that for us."

"I don't know. . . . I have my own business to run."

"You said your business is really slow right now. If you would do this, we'd pay you. I'd share my tips with you. I'm sure the other girls would appreciate having you watch over them and they'd chip in as well. I bet you'd make more money than you do teaching martial arts. And it would only be until Barry gets better, so maybe you could put a 'gone on vacation' sign on your door, or something? It might make you enough money to get ahead on your bills."

Nate tapped a thumb on the steering wheel as he considered. "Business has been pretty slow. . . ."

"I'd feel better if it was a face I knew who was watching over the girls, rather than a stranger."

"What about you?"

She flicked a hand, dismissing the thought. "Nah. Some guy taught me to take care of myself. I'm good."

He chuckled at that before turning serious again. "You really want me to do it?"

She turned back to meet his gaze. "Yes. I really would like it if you would."

He gave her a single nod. "Then I'll do it. When do we start?"

"I'm hoping we can get the place open tomorrow evening by around five. After that, afternoons until closing. All of us will be there working to start to make sure we have things running smoothly."

"Then I guess I'll see you tomorrow evening."

Angela kissed her finger and then pressed the kiss to his cheek. "Thanks, Nate. See you then."

He stayed and watched her walk up her drive until she got to the trees. She turned and waved and he finally drove off.

FORTY-FIVE

Jack parked his rental car in the crowded parking lot of the bar called Barry's Place, where he knew Angela Constantine worked as a bartender. He didn't know if she was working that night, but it was the easiest place to start looking for her.

The bar was a squat concrete block building that looked like it hadn't been painted in several decades. At night, under the light of the single streetlight, it was hard telling what the original color had been. He thought it might be a faded pink, but there was no telling for sure.

A colorful, brightly lit beer sign glowed in the only window. On the gloomy road no one would be able to miss it.

The place gave him the impression of a despairing outpost at the edge of civilization, where the great, trackless forest began, a place where people stopped for good cheer and liquid bravery before facing the dark and dangerous unknown just beyond.

That was an illusion, of course, but Jack had learned over the years to take account of such impressions, along with the vague connections he tracked. They often had meaning and purpose that could only be understood in the context of unfolding events. Those connections helped keep him alive while hunting savages that did not belong among civilized men.

Hung above the window of the bar there was a hand-painted canvas banner that said GET WELL SOON, BARRY! Jack wondered what that was about.

Another hand-painted sign said that ladies would get their first drink for free. It appeared to be working, as Jack saw three women in short dresses going into the place. They looked overdressed for the kind of dive bar it looked to be, but on the other hand dive bars seemed to be coming into vogue.

Some people were drawn to places that were fashionably dangerous. Much like a roller coaster ride, it let them have taste of peril without the high risk that peril usually entailed. Occasionally those flitting moths got burned in the flame they were drawn to.

By the kinds of lowered cars and jacked-up trucks he saw in the lot, he guessed that the free drinks that drew women had in turn drawn a lot of men as well. Which in turn drew more women.

It was a witch's brew of trouble.

Jack stood outside for a time, leaning against his car, arms folded, watching. Every time the door opened, rock music spilled out into the parking lot, seeming out of place in the surrounding forest setting.

Two men protested loudly as they were escorted out by a bouncer. When the bouncer went back in and the door closed, it muted the music to a muffled bass beat. The drunk pair got in their car and spun their tires all the way out of the parking lot. It was only luck, not skill, that kept them from hitting anything.

Jack continued to wait, watching the activity going in and out. Or maybe he was just hesitating. It was always hard for him to know how to approach someone he suspected of having the rare ability to recognize killers.

Some of those people didn't want to hear what he had to say. Some, like Kate, had been hard to convince but smart enough to listen. Those who had a trace of the ability occasionally thought of it as normal, something they thought that everyone could do. It was anything but normal, and it grew rarer all the time as super-predators killed off anyone they found with the ability.

The biggest problem was the hostility he sometimes encountered. Some people didn't like him invading their lives with what they considered crazy notions. Their ability had never manifested itself, so they thought he was a nutcase. He always did his best to convince them to at least listen to him, because the chances were that sooner or later one of those rare super-predators would come along and slaughter them. He tried to help them come to terms with their ability.

Sometimes it worked. Sometimes it didn't.

He often wished he could simply leave these people alone to live their lives. Most weren't aware of their rare vision. Others viewed it as a freak feeling they'd had once without knowing for sure if it was true or not.

Often, because it scared them, they foolishly ignored the feeling. Since it only happened to them once and there was no way to confirm their feeling, it came across to them as merely fearing a dangerous-looking person. Most of the time they wanted nothing more than to deny what they had felt so they could forget the incident.

But all Jack had to do was look into their eyes and he could see it in them. Jack couldn't see killers for who they were. His singular ability was confined to recognizing these people who had the ability to recognize killers. As far as he knew, he was the only one of his kind. Because of that, he felt an obligation to use his ability to try to save lives.

But he often wished he could just leave these people alone.

The only problem was that there were super-predators who could also recognize them for their ability. That kind liked nothing more than to eliminate those individuals, the way a wolf liked to be rid of the sheepdog.

This rare ability was genetic, so it often passed down in families. Because of that, those super-predators would sometimes kill the entire family to wipe out that trait.

Jack wished he could leave this woman, Angela, alone to live her life in this backwater town. In such a small city he expected she had never actually encountered a killer. But he was also aware that people with this ability somehow drew predators to them. He didn't know how or why, he only knew that they did.

He also knew that members of Angela Constantine's family, both in America and in Italy, had already been murdered by a super-predator named Cassiel. Since Cassiel was back in the United States, it was certainly possible that he would come after Angela or her mother. From what Jack had learned about Sally Constantine, he was far more concerned about Angela.

On top of that, there were troubling connections that he had to look into.

Jack sighed as he started across the parking lot, sorry that he was going to have to intrude in this woman's life and possibly scare the wits out of her with talk of killers. He hated it when that happened.

What weighed him down the most was that it turned out far too often that the people he found ended up murdered. After all, those super-predators were also hunting them. Cassiel already had the scent of blood from this family.

Jack often went to sleep wishing he had never found Uziel and a whole list of others like him who were now dead. He knew that by doing what he did he was able to save lives. But he often went to sleep seeing in his mind's eye the tragic, bloody end to the lives of people he had found, or found too late.

Jack pulled open the dented metal door to the bar and was immediately hit by a wall of sound from the loud music and the talking and laughter. Once inside, he stood off to the side in the back for a time, taking in the place, letting his eyes adjust to the rather dim light. There was a doorway to the side of the bar, probably going to a stockroom and office in back.

A row of neon signs for different beer brands and various kinds of hard liquor lined the back wall above shelves packed with bottles.

In the center of the ceiling a rotating ball sent little spots of light dancing around the room, playing over all the people, making them seem to melt together into a single undulating mass. Christmas lights were strung at the top of the walls all around the room. The dark-painted concrete floor was scuffed and scratched. Framed chalkboards were hung on the wall to the right. Drink specials and menus of a few light appetizers were written in chalk of various colors.

But it was the neon lights behind the bar and others around the room, most of them red, that cast their crimson spell over the place. They made the bar intimate and rather cozy, despite the place being decidedly on the sleazy side.

It was a dive, but a dive with an oddly homey appeal.

Young women in short skirts or cutoff shorts teetered on high heels as they delivered trays of drinks to tables around the room. Jack had one photo of Angela Constantine from her driver's license and another from the bond for her courier service, so he had a pretty good idea of who he was looking for.

He finally spotted her behind the bar, making drinks for the waitresses circulating around the room as well as tending to the men lined up on barstools. She didn't have blue hair like on her driver's license. It was now platinum blond tipped in red. It looked like she had dipped the ends of her hair in blood that had gradually dissipated as it soaked upward into the platinum.

With that hair she stood out from everyone else in the room. She was impossible to miss.

From a distance he couldn't really get a good look at her eyes, so he wove his way across the room full of people.

He found an empty stool down at the end of the bar, where it turned a corner to close off that end of the bar. It left just enough room for one barstool. Being where it was around the corner at the end, it afforded him a view down the length of the bar, and behind it. The seat would allow him to get a better look so he could assess Angela Constantine.

Even though he had seen a couple of photos of her, she was not at all what he expected. Not in the least. She was altogether more than he had expected.

She had on blue jean shorts with pockets hanging down below the cutoff legs. Her open-front shirt over a tube top showed her navel and a lot of territory below it before reaching the low top of the shorts. Most of all, her shorts showed off her stunning, long legs to full advantage. Her shorts didn't leave much to the imagination about what little they did cover. She had on suede boots that came up almost to her knees and only served to help draw attention to the length of her bare legs.

When she came closer to serve a guy sitting not too far away, Jack saw that she had several tattoos on her arms, but they were unlike any tattoos he had ever seen before. These were not done as art or decoration. Each was small and they clearly were not intended for others to admire. They obviously had some meaning to her, and that's all they were there for. They were personal.

On the inside of each wrist was a small tattoo of a delicate feather. Those were the only slightly decorative tattoos of the lot, and yet they were too small to be decoration. It looked more like it was meant to be a reminder to herself. He guessed it was in reference to her name, which meant "angel" in Italian.

Her fingernails weren't long, but they were painted a deep, blood red. The back of her ear was lined with rings. Above the black mascara and eyeliner was a creamy black eye shadow with little flecks of copper in it. Her lipstick was a moist, rich, luscious red. She could easily be featured in an ad for makeup—especially lipstick. She had that achingly evocative model look.

He would never have expected it from the kinds of elements she had put together, but now that he saw her up closer, he realized that her platinum hair fit perfectly with the rest of her, creating a complete, totally unique look.

She was staggeringly attractive.

But when she turned more in his direction, he almost fell off his stool when he saw her one large tattoo that was clearly meant for people to see.

At first, from the side, he had thought it was a dark-colored choker, or tall neck band of some sort, but it wasn't—it was a tattoo. Across her throat were the words "DARK ANGEL," big enough that he could clearly read them even from a distance.

This was not a shy girl. This was an intimidating woman.

When she finally came down to the end of the bar to see what she could get him, her gaze met his.

For a fraction of a second she paused as she saw his eyes.

In that instant he could tell that she recognized in his eyes that he had killed people. In his case they were predators, not innocent people. If she was aware of her ability, she would be able to grasp the distinction by what she saw in his eyes.

As stunningly beautiful as she was, her eyes were possibly the most remarkable feature about her. It was stone-cold obvious to him that she had the ability to recognize killers. But there was so much more.

She leaned over the bar to be heard over the music. "What can I get you?"

He had already decided on the straightforward approach, but he couldn't help being mesmerized by her eyes, by her very presence. He was used to seeing people who could recognize killers, but her eyes were all of that and a whole world of difference more.

"I need to talk to you about the kind of men you can recognize with those eyes of yours."

She leaned in closer on one elbow.

"Fuck off."

That had not been what he expected. "Listen to me, I need—"

"You heard the lady," a man standing just over his right shoulder said. "You need to leave."

Jack could tell that the bouncer was not someone to be taken lightly. This was not the time or place to press the issue. Starting something with a bouncer wouldn't help him talk with her. Besides, his intent was to help people, not hurt them.

He reluctantly slid off the barstool. He turned back to see Angela standing motionless, watching him.

"This is more important than you realize," he said. "Please think it over."

Before the bouncer could force him out, Jack left.

FORTY-SIX

Jack decided to sit in his car and wait for Angela Constantine to get off work. Now that he'd found her, he didn't want to lose contact and have her go to ground. He'd spooked people before and then had a hell of a time reconnecting with them. Several times he had found them again only after they had been murdered.

Although they might be able to recognize them, these people, after all, didn't know how to deal with killers.

Jack hadn't eaten since earlier in the day and his stomach was growling. He'd slept most of the time on the Israeli diplomatic jet as it flew all night from Israel to New York, but it wasn't a restful sleep. They went into JFK airport to clear customs and let off a couple of diplomatic staff personnel to go meet with Gilad Ben-Ami in New York City. That delegation was the cover story, anyway.

They could have gotten special diplomatic clearance and not have had to go into JFK, but Ehud thought it better if they didn't unduly raise the suspicion of US intel that they were conducting a mission of some kind. Ehud had said that if there really was something important going on that Jack needed to investigate, then US intel could possibly become a hindrance and/or even potentially blow Jack's cover by unmasking his identity. Such leaks and unmaskings were becoming more and more common and had already gotten several agents killed.

There were super-predators who, besides hunting people with the special ability to recognize killers, also hunted Jack. That was a big reason he stayed off the grid. If those predators could somehow find him and eliminate him, it would be far easier to kill the people he was trying to protect.

If anyone in any of the American intelligence services leaked information about Jack to the press, those predators would then have a much easier time of finding him. The press loved printing spy stories and revealing names. The consequences were unimportant to them. Some in the intel agencies wished those consequences on him and so they were only to eager to leak to the press.

There were many in the press who loved nothing more than to help get an undercover operative killed. It made them feel important. They cared more about puffing themselves up than about the lives their reckless reporting cost. On top of that, there were hundreds of thousands of people with top-secret clearances who shouldn't have them.

Jack's expertise was not politically correct, so there were those who would be only too eager to destroy his ability to find the kind of people he looked for. There were even those who would leak the story or reveal his name in the hopes of getting him killed. Political correctness didn't extend to the lives of those they didn't like.

Jack's safety—and thus the safety of those he tried to help—depended on him remaining a ghost.

After clearing customs at JFK, by midafternoon they had hopped over to the Elmira Corning Regional Airport in central New York State, where he had a car waiting for him. He knew, of course, that American intel would be tracking an Israeli plane, so Ehud managed to let it be known that it was a vacation flight to the Finger Lakes region for some of their people.

After getting his car, Jack had parked it and then walked until he found a used-car lot with an older Ford that seemed to be in good running condition. He paid cash for it and used one of his fake IDs to make the purchase. If the intel services were tracking his rental car, which he assumed they were, that would break the link with a dead end, at least for a time.

Jack had been in a hurry to get to Milford Falls and find Angela Constantine, so he had filled his new car with gas and driven the rest of the way without stopping.

All he had with him was a protein bar and a bottle of water that he'd picked up at the gas station. Now that he was waiting for Angela to come out, he didn't want to leave to go get something more to eat, so he ate the bar slowly to make it last.

He briefly considered using the time to go see Sally Constantine, but his experience told him that Angela was the one he needed to talk to, and he feared losing contact with her.

After having seen her eyes, he knew beyond a shadow of doubt that she was the one.

He didn't know if she might get off work any moment, or not until the bar closed. He had the truck she drove in sight so that he wouldn't miss her leaving. He was determined to stay there until she came out.

A little after 1:00 a.m. she finally emerged from the bar and walked toward her truck. The bar was still open and the lot had about two dozen customer cars still there. Jack got out of his car and made his way toward her pickup.

She saw him coming. She'd seen him the first moment she came out of Barry's Place, but that was okay because he wanted her to see him. He didn't want to look like some psycho trying to sneak up on her.

As she reached her truck, he walked up on the passenger side so she would feel safer with the truck between them. He knew that a woman who was this attractive, and dressed the way she did in those shorts and boots, undoubtedly had to deal with guys hitting on her all the time.

She glared at him from the other side of the truck. "I thought I told you to get lost."

Jack held up a hand in confession. "You did. Look, Miss Constantine, I've come a long way to speak with you. Just let me show you one photo—one—and then if you still want me to leave, I will. I swear."

"Not interested," she said as she unlocked her truck.

He spread his hands to show her that he wasn't holding a weapon. "Just one photo, that's all. I'll stand over here, and you can stay over there, and I'll slide it across the hood of your truck so you can look at it."

She watched him with those eyes that had him sweating. "Why? What is this photo supposed to tell me? That I should go out dancing with you?"

Jack couldn't help smiling at the way she'd put it. "No. I'm not trying to get you to go out with me. I'm not hitting on you, I swear. Just take a look at it, okay? This is really important."

Her steady gaze was still locked on him. "Important to who? To you, or to me?"

"Just look at it, would you, please?" He hated the way he sounded like he was begging. But he supposed he was.

She let out a deep breath and stepped from the driver's door to the opposite side of the hood of her truck from where Jack stood waiting.

"And once I look at this photo, then will you leave me the hell alone?"

Jack nodded his sincerity. "If you want me to, yes."

"All right. Show me this super duper special fucking photo."

Jack pulled the photo out of his shirt pocket. It had been printed on photo paper from a negative. Only a photo printed on photo paper from a negative would work for people with the ability he now knew Angela had. Any other kind of digital photo or electronic representation lost some essential quality that they would otherwise be able to see in a killer's eyes. Those other types of photos were useless for Jack's work.

For a person with Angela's ability to recognize a killer, if she couldn't see him in person, then the photo had to be a photo printed on photo paper from a real negative.

Jack set the photo down on the hood of the truck, turned it to face toward Angela, and with two fingers carefully slid it toward her across the gray-primer hood of her truck.

Angela finally took her eyes off him just long enough to lean in a little and glance down at the photo.

He didn't think she had looked at it for a full second when she twisted her arm back and in a lightning-fast move came back up with a gun. Before he knew it, she had it pointed right between his eyes. The click he had heard was the safety coming off as the weapon came out of her holster.

Jack froze.

Even more disturbing, that gun had a suppressor. By how steady the weapon was in her hands, he had no doubt that she knew how to use it. Her first finger wasn't resting along the side of the slide, which would have been somewhat less alarming, but was instead on the trigger. One twitch and he would be dead.

This stunningly gorgeous young woman was more than she at first appeared. A lot more.

Slowly, not making any fast moves, Jack put his hands up.

"Where is he," she hissed. "Tell me where I can find him."

This girl was a live hand grenade wrapped in a lollipop shell.

Without realizing it, he had just pulled the pin.

FORTY-SEVEN

Jack tried to keep his voice calm. "What do you see, Miss Constantine, when you look at this photo? When you look at his eyes?"

"Where is he!" she screamed.

"I don't know. I'm trying to find him myself. That's why I wanted you to look at the photo. I was hoping you might be able to help." Jack kept his hands up, hoping she wouldn't shoot him. He wasn't entirely confident of that. "Do you know this man?"

"No, I've never seen him before."

Jack let one hand come down just enough to gesture toward the photo lying in front of her on the hood of the truck. "Miss Constantine, can you tell me what you see when you look at this man?"

"What are you, some kind of fucking cop?"

"No. I'm not any kind of cop, or anything like that. Please, tell me what you saw when you looked at the photo of this man?"

She still had her gaze, as well as her gun, locked on him. It was pointed right between his eyes and rock-solid steady. When he shifted his weight to the other foot, the gun barrel tracked that minimal movement without the slightest deviation from its target.

"Please, Miss Constantine, what did you see when you looked at him?"

"That man is a killer."

"Are you sure?"

She glared at him a moment before speaking. "When he was still in his teens, he had a girlfriend, Zahra. She had long, straight black hair. He called her his little princess. One day she went to visit relatives. He thought she was visiting a lover. He found her cutting through an alley on her way home. He called her a whore. He hit her in the face and threw her on the ground. He straddled her and hit her with his fists as she begged him to stop. The begging excited him. He picked up a brick and used it to pound her face as hard as he could. He didn't stop until her head was smashed flat in a puddle of bone and brains and blood.

"Then he spotted an old man nearby who had been sleeping in the alley under some cardboard. The old man was horrified. Enraged that someone had seen what he had done, he found a piece of scrap metal, held the old man down with a knee on his chest, and used the piece of metal to gouge out the old man's eyes, then he strangled him to death.

"That night in the alley he learned that killing was more exciting than anything he had ever done. It made him feel powerful.

"After he was grown, and had killed several more times, he grew bored of the place where he had been born, so he traveled to Jordan. He found that he liked the nomadic lifestyle, traveling as he wished with money he took from victims. He killed an entire household in Jordan because he could see that the husband knew him for what he was. He killed them all—father, mother, grandmother, two children. He held them captive the entire night, every hour or two he started cutting on another one of them before slicing their throats. He likes bloody kills, like that first time with Zahra, who he thought was a whore and had betrayed him.

"He killed eleven members of the Maarouf family in Egypt. The mother could recognize him as a killer by looking into his eyes, just as he could look into her eyes and see her ability. He tied them up, and then bashed in their skulls with a hammer. One at a time. The children first. He likes to hear people scream in terror. They lived in an apartment over a nightclub, so that night no one heard those screams.

"He killed a woman in Germany—an immigrant. He could tell by her eyes that she could see the truth about him, just as I can. She had long black hair. She reminded him of Zahra, his first love he thought had cheated on him. Her name was Ibadah. He raped her first, stabbed out her eyes, cut out her tongue—while she was still alive.

"He made it last because it had been a while since he had killed and he was hungry to do it again. He finally cut her throat. When he was done carving on her to see what she was made of, to see if she was really Zahra, his first love, inside someone else's body come to taunt him, he threw the remains off a high bank into a river.

"It Italy, he tracked down a man he had seen. He had recognized that same, rare ability in the man's eyes. He went to the man's house in a bad neighborhood of Naples where there is a lot of crime, and played a recording of a baby crying outside the door. When a woman, Camilla, heard it, she thought it might be her granddaughter. She was frightened for the little girl's safety. When she opened the door, without knowing it, she let death itself into her house. Her daughter was in a back room with the little girl. He slaughtered the whole family."

"Do you know their last name?"

"Constantine."

The hair on the back of Jack's neck had stood up on end. The blood had drained from his face as he'd listened.

The Mossad had known some of it, but not nearly all of it. The intelligence agencies hadn't even known about some of those killings, much less suspected Cassiel. They also hadn't known, of course, what drove him to kill.

He was one of those super-predators who hunted people with the ability to recognize him as a killer.

Jack knew that the ability to recognize killers was a product of evolution, as was the ability of some killers to in turn recognize those individuals. He had theorized that the process of evolution would eventually produce people who could see into the minds of killers, see what they had done. Kate had proven his theory correct.

But Angela had taken it to an entirely new level. With Angela, he was in uncharted waters. He was looking into the eyes of a new evolutionary step.

He was looking into the eyes of a different kind of human.

He finally mustered the courage to ask. "Anyone else?"

"Lots."

"Anyone in particular stand out to you?"

The gun stayed steadily locked between his eyes as tears started running down her face. Her jaw trembled. Her voice came in a painful whisper.

"He killed my grandparents. Vito and Gabriella Constantine."

Jack ached at seeing her obvious pain. "I'm so sorry."

"Tell me where I can find him!"

He opened his hands. "I don't know. That's the truth. I'm looking for him, too."

"Why?"

"Among other reasons, to keep him from killing you."

"Who is he?"

"His name is Cassiel Aykhan Corekan. He is a very dangerous man."

"No shit."

"Miss Constantine, I came here to help you. We're on the same side. I wouldn't be here if we weren't. I'm trying to stay a step ahead of Cassiel to stop him from killing again, from killing innocent people, from killing you."

"You didn't come here just to save my ass. You came here for some other reason. What do you want from me?"

"Do you really need to keep that gun pointed at me?"

"You've killed people. A lot of people. You usually use two small knives. You have one in each back pocket. You favor cutting their carotid artery so that they lose consciousness quickly and die shortly

387

after. Simple and quick. There have been times when you've had to cut tendons to cripple them, first, and then go for another artery, like the femoral artery. Do you want me to tell you their names?"

"No," he said quietly. He swallowed back the anguish. "I don't need you to tell me their names."

"You're a lot faster at killing than most people would believe possible. That's why I have a gun pointed at you."

Jack knew this woman was not playing games. He suspected that if he lied to her, she would know that, too.

"There have been people, good people, innocent people, that I wanted to protect. People who couldn't protect themselves. People who were afraid—terrified. People like those Cassiel murdered. I killed those murderers to stop them from killing any more innocent people. If you can see in my eyes those I killed, then you must know I'm telling the truth that they needed killing. Despite what some would say, I really don't think that's wrong. Do you?"

After staring at him for a long moment, she finally clicked on the safety and raised the barrel away from him, holding the gun up against her right shoulder, pointed skyward.

"No. That's not wrong at all."

Some of the tension went out of his muscles. He sagged just a little with relief. He was relieved, too, to see her finally holster the weapon at the small of her back.

"There are a lot of things I'm unsure of, things I'm trying to find out to help me keep innocent people from being murdered," he told her. "I think you might be able to help me. In fact, you already have with part of it by recognizing what kind of man Cassiel really is just by looking at his photograph."

The fury seemed to have drained out of her voice. "I've never had that kind of reaction just from looking at a photo."

He wondered if she had ever seen real killers and had a similar reaction.

"Well, that's part of why I'm here—to help you understand all of this. I'm hoping that you in turn can help me understand some things."

She looked back over her shoulder when she heard the bouncer call her name.

He trotted across the lot and came to a stop beside her. "You?" he said, glaring at Jack. "I thought I told you to leave her alone."

Angela put her arm out to stop him from going around the front of the truck to confront Jack.

"It's all right, Nate."

"It is? Are you sure?"

"Yes, I'm sure."

He leaned closer to look at her face. "You've been crying."

"No, it's not that," she said as she pulled a tissue from her pocket and quickly wiped off the mascara running down her face. "It's the smoke in there from that jerk's cigar. It made my eyes burn and they're watering, that's all. Thanks for letting me know that it's running my mascara."

He didn't look to believe her. "Angela, I don't—"

She put a hand on his shoulder as she smiled at Jack. "He's someone I haven't seen in a very long time. It's kind of dark back in the bar, so I just didn't recognize him, especially with the smoke burning my eyes, that's all."

Nate still didn't look convinced. "Really? What's his name?"

Jack realized he hadn't told her. He immediately stretched over the hood of the truck to extend his hand. "Hi. I'm Jack Raines. I knew Angela from before. When she was younger."

Nate shook the hand. "You don't look that much older than Angela."

Jack grinned. "Why thank you. Aren't you kind."

Angela looked from Jack's eyes back to her knight in shining armor. "Thanks, Nate. But everything is fine." She put a hand against his chest. "Why don't you go back in and watch out for the other girls. I've had a long day. I just want to go home and get some sleep. I'll see you tomorrow."

Nate finally gave in. "Sure. Nice to meet you, Jack." He turned toward the bar but then turned back. "Sorry about before." He flicked a hand toward the bar. "You know, in there. Before Angela realized she knew you."

Jack flashed him a smile. "Forget about it."

"Smooth," she said to Jack once Nate had disappeared back inside.

Jack turned his attention back to Angela.

"Look, Miss Constantine, there are a number of serious things I need to talk to you about. I don't think we have a lot of time."

She continued to appraise him for a moment. "All right. Get in the truck. I can at least hear you out. But you have to promise me, first, that the minute you find out where Cassiel is, you'll tell me."

"Deal," Jack said as he opened the passenger door.

FORTY-EIGHT

Closing the doors to the truck shut out of lot of the harsh light from the streetlamp. With the sounds from outside also shut out, she didn't have to talk very loud to be heard.

"All right, this is your chance. Talk."

"Listen, Miss Constantine—"

"You said you weren't a cop."

Not knowing her point, he paused. "I'm not."

"Then stop calling me 'Miss Constantine,' would you? Only the fucking police call me 'Miss Constantine.' If you're not with the police, then who do you work for?"

"I have to admit, I like 'Angela' a lot better."

"Good. I asked who you work for."

"Actually, I work for myself."

"Doing what? And what do you want with me?"

"First of all, it's obvious that you can recognize killers by seeing their eyes."

"Obviously."

"The first thing I need to do is to help you understand why it's possible for you to do that."

"I know why I can do it. I don't need your help to understand it."

Jack hadn't expected that. He'd never met anyone before who was aware of their ability and seemed so confident in their understanding of it.

"Get on with it," she said before he could think of what to say. "I have someplace to go."

She'd just told Nate she wanted to get some sleep, not that she had somewhere to go. He turned to look out at the darkness.

"This late?"

"I asked who you work for. You weren't entirely honest in your answer. You also said that you came a long way to see me. Where did you come from?"

"Israel."

"You live there? You work there? This is not making a lot of sense."

"All right, listen, this is important so I'm going to take a chance here and be completely honest and up front with you in the hope that you will do the same with me.

"I sometimes work for the Israeli government—the Mossad, actually. I help them stop terrorists before they can kill people. I used to do the same thing for various US intelligence services, but not anymore."

"You mean you're some kind of spy?"

"Not exactly. You need to understand, there are a lot of great, dedicated people working for US intelligence services. Those services used to appreciate having my help. But their bosses didn't."

"Why not?"

"Because I help find killers by using people who can do what you can do—well, not exactly what you can do. I've seen some people who could do quite a lot, but I've never seen anyone who could do anywhere near what you can do."

"Why—"

Jack held up a hand. "Just listen for a moment. What I did fell out of favor for political reasons. There are people in those agencies now who would not just like to see me gone, but would like it just fine if I ended up dead."

She frowned. "Why, if you were helping them stop killers, why would they want you dead?"

"Probably for some of the same reasons that you don't like the police. There are good people in the intel agencies, just as there are lots of good police officers who would risk their lives to save yours."

She huffed a half laugh. "I've never met any of those."

"I understand. I have a somewhat similar problem. What I'm doing, what I'm doing here with you, is because I still believe that we can do some good in this world. I think that I have a purpose in this life, and my purpose is to find people like you. Do you have any idea what I mean? Do you understand?"

She considered his words for a long moment. "There are people among us that shouldn't be allowed to be among us."

Jack smiled. "Bingo."

"So, the spy agencies don't approve of your methods."

"No, they don't. Some people in intelligence agencies, if they could, would see to it that I was charged with murder and put away for life for stopping some of the killers I've found. Like I say, there are lots of great people in intel, but anymore I have trouble telling the good ones from the bad. So, the best thing for me to do is stay off their radar."

"I can understand that. I've had that same problem."

Jack smiled. "Then we're much the same. I'm telling you all this because I want you to understand that I have no intention of ever telling any authorities anything we discuss, or anything about you. I don't want to get you noticed by them, either. I hope you will treat me the same. People like us have to stick together."

"So what are you doing here? What is it you want from me?"

"You heard about the terrorist attacks all over the country?"

"Sure. I work all the time so I don't listen to the news much, but I heard about it. It's all the customers in the bar have been talking about. Seems like a lot of them blame Russia and want to go to war."

"People like simplistic solutions."

"You think it's more complicated?"

"Yes. One of those attacks—one of the big ones—was at the Oeste Mesa border crossing between Mexico and California."

He pulled a second photo out of his shirt pocket and handed it to her.

"That's him," she said after she looked back up. "That's Cassiel."

Jack nodded confirmation. "He was there."

She frowned back down at the photo. "Why can't I see that he's a killer from this photo, see everything about him from his eyes like I could from the other one?"

"There is an important difference between the two photos. This one was taken by one of the automatic cameras at the border crossing, just before the attack. It's a digital photo that's been digitally enhanced, enlarged, and sent over the Internet. Your ability to recognize killers only works in person, or with a photo printed from a negative onto photo paper."

"Huh. That's weird."

"Have you ever seen a photo of a killer on photo paper before, like the first one I showed you?"

"No."

He looked at her from under his brow. "So . . . then you've seen a killer before? I mean, in real life? A real killer?"

"Yes," she said, dismissing the question by not elaborating. "So Cassiel crossed during the attack?"

"Actually, we think he may have been part of the attack."

"That doesn't make a lot of sense," she said as she looked at the blowup of Cassiel's face from the camera at the crossing.

"Why do you say that?"

"Because he's a killer, a monster. He works alone. Killing is his passion. He is consumed by it, haunted by it. He can't go for long before his urge to kill overtakes everything else. It drives him to the point of taking foolish risks. It doesn't make any sense that he would be taking part in a terrorist attack."

"See, now, that's part of the puzzle I don't understand, either. All I can figure out is that it could be he just wanted to be in on the slaughter."

Angela shook her head. "No, that's not his style. He doesn't care about seeing people get killed. That's not what gets him off. It's the personal act of killing in all forms that fascinates him. He is obsessed with watching people die at his hands, whether it's cutting their throat . . . or shooting them in the back of the head."

Jack knew she was thinking about her grandparents again, so he steered her back to the puzzle pieces he was trying to fit together.

"I thought the same thing. He doesn't fit the psychological profile of a terrorist. That's why I'm at a loss as to what he was doing there, in this photo, just before the attack. The only other possibility in the back of my mind is that he might be coming back into the US to kill you, and coming in with the terrorists was the simplest way. He killed members of your family in Italy. He killed your grandparents. I think he might be coming back to kill you."

"He does like to kill entire families." She finally looked back from staring out into the dark woods across the road. "Give me that photo again—the first one."

Jack handed it over and watched as she looked into Cassiel's eyes, but this time for a long moment.

"No. That's not the reason. He was careless. He killed a woman and her family, Khorshid Hamidi. Funny." She frowned thoughtfully. "I've never heard any of these names before, but I know them now simply from looking into his eyes."

"You were saying . . . he was careless?"

"Yes. He killed that family and was captured by Iranian authorities. She was the daughter of an imam. They were going to put him to death. He was spared to be part of this mission, this terrorist attack."

Jack sat stunned by what she was able to tell from looking at his eyes.

She handed back the photo. "So what other pieces are you trying to figure out?"

"Well, I was in Israel helping them identify terrorists—killers—who were coming into Jerusalem."

She frowned. "How were you able to do that?"

He didn't think it was the right time, so he waved off the question.

"That's not important right now. The important part—one of the pieces of the puzzle that I think involves you—is that we captured a suicide bomber before he could detonate his bomb vest."

"That's fortunate."

"Yes. But the strange thing is, the guy was Mexican. He only spoke Spanish. He said he was born in Mexico."

Angela's expression darkened. "Mexican. A Mexican suicide bomber in Jerusalem. That seems pretty strange."

"They'd never had it happen before. But the key thing is, he was supposed to blow himself up in the attack. Had he succeeded we would never have known that he only speaks Spanish." He could see that behind her eyes, the wheels were turning. "One of my talents is that I find connections in things that at first don't seem like they fit together."

"You mean you work on connections like the captured Mexican suicide bomber and Cassiel crossing into the US from Mexico."

"That's part of it," he said, watching her face as she started putting pieces together in her own mind.

"Cassiel could pass for Mexican," she said as she stared off. "He speaks several languages. Spanish is one of them."

Jack smiled. "That was my thought. It's a connecting thread. But I don't know what it means."

She looked back at him. "What does this have to do with me? Why are you telling me this?"

"I found you because Cassiel killed people in Italy with the name Constantine. I read the report about your grandparents' murder. No one was ever charged with their murder. I thought it had to be Cassiel who killed them."

"It was."

"Yes, well, I know that now because you just told me he did, but before none of us knew that for sure. The thing is, one of the other pieces of the puzzle, one of the seemingly disparate facts that has me troubled, is you."

"Me? Why me?"

"I know that you were attacked by four Hispanic men. They intended to kill you and almost succeeded. I wondered why they would do that. Cassiel wants to kill you, but why did they? The only thing I could come up with was that after they raped you maybe they wanted to eliminate you as a witness. But I have this uneasy feeling that there's more to it, some other connection to all these things I'm trying to fit together."

"There is."

"Like what?"

"They weren't Hispanic," she said.

He remembered that José, the Mexican suicide bomber, only spoke Spanish, and yet he didn't know anything about Santiago de Querétaro, in Mexico, where he was supposedly born.

"What do you mean? Every report I saw said they were four Hispanic men."

She shook her head. "They weren't Hispanic. I told the police they were because that's what I thought when they first came into the bar. That's all the police needed to know."

"You're sure they weren't Hispanic?"

"Positive."

"Did they speak Spanish?"

"Yes. Spanish and English with a broken Spanish accent."

"Then what makes you think they weren't Hispanic?"

She smiled to herself just a little. "Do you think Mexicans hate America?"

"No, not really."

"Neither do I. These guys did. They despise America with every fiber of their being. That hate for America defines them."

Jack shrugged. "Okay, so then what do you think they are?"

"Middle Eastern. Muslim of some kind. My guess is Iranian."

"Iranian." Jack leaned in a little, frowning at this young woman who an hour ago he would not have believed would even know that

Iran was mostly a Muslim nation. "Okay, now you have my attention. Why do you say Iranian?"

"They called America the Great Satan. That's what I always hear Iran calling America—the Great Satan. They also called me things like 'a dirty American whore,' that kind of stuff. The kind of things the Iranians and terrorists say about us. They hold women in especially low esteem. I was no more than dirt to them so they thought they had every right, as men, to use my body."

"But if they were trying to pass as Mexican, why would they say those things in front of you?"

"Because they intended to kill me. They thought I wouldn't be alive to repeat any of it to the authorities and blow their cover, so they felt safe in being themselves in front of me."

"Wow," Jack said as he leaned back.

"But they didn't decide to kill me because they didn't want me to be able to identify them. They intended to kill me from the first because they received orders to do so."

Jack came up off the seat back. "Orders? What orders? Orders from who?"

"Orders that came in the package I delivered to them. I have a courier service. I delivered a package to them, to Hartland Irrigation, and inside there was a letter ordering them to kill the courier."

Jack stared off into the darkness as he thought about it.

"Do you know what was in the package?"

Angela shrugged. "Some kind of long tubes. They were clear. I could see wires inside the tubes."

Jack stared at her a moment. "Can you describe the wires?"

"Well . . . wait." She pulled out her phone. "Let me see if I can find a picture of what the wires looked like."

She typed something into a search engine. She clicked a lot of screens looking for one that had the right kinds of pictures. When the images came up, she started flicking her finger to scroll down through dozens of pages of photos, all the time murmuring, "No . . . no . . . no." After searching for a time, she abruptly halted. She enlarged a picture and then turned the phone toward him so he could see.

"These wires," she said. "They looked just like these. They were in tubes with red caps just like this. The wires even had the little thingamajigs on the ends like the wires in this photo."

Jack could feel the blood drain from his face.

"That's exploding bridgewire."

Angela wrinkled up her nose. "What's an exploding bridge-wire?"

"It's used to detonate a series of explosives at precisely the same time."

"Why would you need to do that?"

"To detonate an atomic bomb."

FORTY-NINE

Several of those troubling little pieces, the little worry tiles, that Jack had been turning over and over in his mind, trying to understand, were suddenly coming together to form a terrifying picture.

"An atom bomb," Angela said. "Are you fucking kidding me?"

"No, I'm dead serious. Exploding bridgewire is difficult to purchase legally, so a terrorist organization wouldn't want to try to buy it here for fear of raising a red flag with authorities. If they want to remain undetected, it would be far better for them to send it secretly.

"Terrorists operating in coordination with the Ministry of Intelligence for Iran will typically send critical items or messages through networks of agents—MOIS intelligence officers assigned to foreign missions and embassies in most countries. But that's risky in the US because any of those people very likely would be under surveillance by any number of the US intelligence services.

"With something this critical, instead of using their own agents, they sometimes use a series of couriers—innocent, unwitting mules. Only the final courier in that web of couriers is provided the final destination. That's why you were to be killed and your body disposed of where it wouldn't be found. They didn't want the final courier to be able to reveal where you took the package. At least, you were supposed to be dead."

Angela leaned in toward him. "You mean to tell me you think these people posed as Mexicans so they could smuggle in the stuff they need to make an atom bomb? Do you seriously think that's what's going on?"

"That suicide bomber we captured—the one who said he was Mexican—had a small bit of plutonium-239 stuck in his shoe. Plutonium is used to make atomic bombs. Along with a lot of other parts, you need exploding bridgewire to detonate it."

Angela held up a hand to stop him. "All right, but just because you have the plutonium, that doesn't mean you could really make an atom bomb. If it was that easy terrorists everywhere would be doing it. It can't be that easy. Lots of countries who would like a nuclear bomb aren't able to build one. So, if they can't, why do you think these terrorists can?"

"It's not really the same thing. The bombs some countries are trying to build are different and for a different purpose. Their bombs need to be much more sophisticated. They need to have precise and predictable yields. They ultimately need to be small enough to fit in a delivery system like a missile. Most importantly, they need to have safety features and fail-safe devices. None of that matters to a terrorist. Because their needs are much simpler, it's not out of the question that they might be able to build a crude device.

"It wouldn't have the precision yield of a military device, but that wouldn't be important to terrorists. What do they care if it ends up being a hundred kilotons, or two hundred kilotons? Any nuclear device in that range, pretty much regardless of size, would be devastating to America.

"They wouldn't care all that much about the risk of accidental detonation, especially if they are building the bomb here, in the US, so they wouldn't need those safeguards. A nuke going off anywhere in the US is a catastrophe.

"As for the plutonium and the necessary technical expertise, there are any number of rogue states—Iran, North Korea, Pakistan— who would be only too happy to provide expertise and materials.

Crippling the Great Satan with a nuke would suddenly make them, and those rogue nations, dominant world powers to be reckoned with."

Angela shook her head as she sat back. "I'm still not convinced I believe all this."

"Why attack a border crossing?"

"I don't—" Angela snapped her fingers with sudden realization. "Islamic terrorists know that they may not be able to blend in very well or go unnoticed, so having all their people pose as Hispanic would allow them to be practically invisible in America. They could come and go as they please. Blowing up a border crossing would destroy the detection equipment that surely must be able to detect nuclear material."

Jack was amazed at how quickly she had made the critical jump to what was going on, and why.

He turned in his seat to face her. "Angela, if you delivered the EBW here, that means they're probably building the bomb here before transporting it to a major city. If they wanted to use it in LA, they would have built it in on the West Coast. That means they likely intend to set it off in New York City."

"Milford Falls isn't that far from New York City."

"Where was the place you delivered that package?"

"I've already been there looking for those four men. They've cleared out."

"Take me there. I want to see it for myself."

She looked out the windshield, almost as if she could see the place. "I was going there now anyway. I suppose I could take you along."

"Why would you be going there now, in the middle of the night?"

"I made a promise. I intend to keep it."

Jack thought he knew what she meant. "Is it far?"

"Not too far. But I wouldn't get my hopes up if I were you. It's in a massive, deserted industrial area. It's easy to get lost in there. I suspect those men are still there, somewhere in those deserted buildings. Now I know why. I've been going there a lot, spending time learning the layout of the place."

"Looking for those men?"

"Yes," she admitted, "but so far I haven't seen any sign of them."

Jack rubbed a finger along his lower lip. Such a deserted industrial complex sounded like the perfect place to build a bomb without being disturbed or discovered.

"I need to find out if this is just a scary theory, or if we could really be on to something. There might be a clue at the place where you delivered the package."

"I'm game."

Angela turned the key, and the engine roared to life.

FIFTY

They had to drive back through town first before they could to get to the old industrial area. The main streets were mostly deserted. Jack's familiar sense of paranoia was beginning to set in. With so few cars on the streets, he felt like anyone could be watching them.

At one traffic light some guys in a car pulled up beside them on the driver's side. The driver revved the engine as some of the men opened their windows to make lewd offers to Angela.

Angela glared at them as she gave them the finger. They all laughed like it was the funniest thing in the world.

"Jerks," she muttered as she pulled away when the light turned green.

They stayed next to her. She abruptly cut around a corner to the right. She had turned too late for them to follow without stopping and backing up. By then she was gone. She took side streets for a while until returning to her course through downtown. The men were nowhere to be seen.

Jack knew that she could have ignored them. It said something about her nature that she didn't.

They wouldn't think it was so funny if they had followed her and stopped her truck only to find themselves looking down the barrel of her gun. She might not look it, but this was a woman you messed with at your own peril. The fact that she went out all alone to a deserted area late at night hoping to find the guys who had tried to kill her also said a lot.

Jack had only met this woman, and already he felt a bond with her. It was rare to encounter another person who shared an understanding of the things he dealt in, and more than rare that she was prepared to handle them alone.

As they left the lights of Milford Falls behind, they drove for a time down a lonely, winding highway. Trees in the darkness to either side of the road flashed by in a seemingly never-ending procession until the road eventually emptied them out in the middle of a vast, deserted, commercial landscape. It was an eerie scene.

Lit by moonlight, the place felt like life on earth had died out long ago and they were the last people alive in the world, wandering among the crumbling remains of civilization.

Angela drove slowly into the maze, looking left and right around every building. He could see windows broken out on most of the buildings. All of them were dark. After they made their way through the tangle of deserted buildings, stacked industrial equipment, and fenced implement yards, she turned down a road going past a long building and then parked at a door along the side. The door had a hand-painted address on it.

"This is where I delivered the package," she said as she cut the engine. "If you want to look around inside, I'll keep watch out here."

Jack thought that wasn't a bad idea, but at the same time he didn't think it was a good one, either. "All right. I'll try to be quick."

"It's pitch black in there," she said.

He pulled out his small light and clicked it on briefly to show her how powerful it was.

The door wasn't locked. It scraped on the ground as he opened it. Inside the enormous building there were walls for several rudimentary offices. Between several of the office spaces stood gray metal shelving. Some of the shelves had crumpled, dirty blankets left on them, but there was nothing underneath.

There was a filthy, greasy moving pad on the floor. He knew why Angela hadn't wanted to come inside.

Jack looked around for a good ten minutes, trying to find a clue as to what the men had been doing. He found a variety of milling machines back beyond the shelving, but they had been cleaned and the floor vacuumed. A specialized search team could probably find a speck of something, but he couldn't. Since the site had been abandoned, at this point, with the clock ticking, whatever had been there was irrelevant. They needed to find where whatever they had been making had been taken.

As he climbed back up into her truck, she said, "Told you."

Jack sighed. "They appeared to have been using milling machines for something. Like you said, they've cleared out. It was worth a look. I don't know what else we can do out here."

She started the truck but didn't answer. She pulled out and drove slowly on through the maze of crumbling buildings, chain-link fencing, and razor wire guarding piles of rusted junk. There were broad concrete areas as well and streets of sorts, even alleyways between clusters of the old buildings.

"Aren't you going to turn on your headlights?"

"No. The moon is out. The moon is enough to see by if you don't drive too fast. Your eyes will adjust."

Jack didn't object. He knew what she was doing and he couldn't say he blamed her. Besides that, those men were the only clue they had. If by some stroke of luck she was able to find them, they might be able to provide some answers.

The problem would be getting them to talk.

They drove slowly for almost an hour, weaving their way among the ruins of what used to be a thriving complex. Angela didn't say anything. She was intently focused on surveying the moonlit ghost town.

Jack hadn't had much sleep on the plane the night before and he was exhausted. The low rumble of the engine was making him even more sleepy. He slumped down in his seat. He could feel the engine's low drone through his whole body. He was having trouble keeping his eyes open as she drove slowly onward into the decaying ghost town.

"Shit," Angela said under her breath, "I don't believe it."

Jack sat up, suddenly wide awake. "What?"

She rolled to a stop and turned off the engine.

"There," she said, pointing through the windshield.

Jack squinted into the distance and finally saw a small orangish glow get brighter, then dim. It was a man smoking a cigarette. He was coming out of an alleyway and across the road they were on. Jack then spotted another man walking beside him. He was smoking, too. The two glowing dots moved along with the shadowy shapes of the two men crossing their path, their faces briefly lit whenever they took a drag.

"That's them," Angela said in a whisper.

Angela reached up and turned off the switch for interior light before carefully opening her door. Jack got out with her. They both pushed their doors closed quietly just enough to catch but not letting them latch so they wouldn't make a noise.

"Do you really think it's the men you're looking for?" he whispered.

"It's Miguel and Emilio."

"Two of the men who attacked you? Are you sure?"

"Positive."

She sounded convinced. He didn't know that he was. He thought that it might simply be two vagrants. He couldn't make out any features of the two dark shapes silhouetted against moonlit concrete and brick of abandoned factories.

Angela was convinced, though, and she was already moving out ahead of him. Jack pulled one of his knives out of a pocket and popped the blade open. She walked on the balls of her feet, making virtually no sound.

The way she moved reminded him of a large cat advancing in on prey. She would freeze in place, watching, motionless, then move again in short dashes. Jack stayed close, trying to mimic her movements. As he started to hear their voices chattering in Spanish, she moved slowly as she kept her eyes locked on the men.

When they talked and laughed and looked the other way, pointing off at something, she moved more swiftly.

Jack was surprised that she still hadn't drawn her gun as she closed the distance to the men.

He was alarmed when she suddenly broke into a run. As fast as she was moving and with her long legs, before he knew it she had opened some distance out ahead of him. He was even more alarmed that she didn't have a weapon in hand as she rapidly closed the distance to the men.

Both men halted abruptly when they saw her coming. They flicked their cigarettes off to the side and drew big knives. Jack could see the moonlight glint off the combat blades.

They started running toward her.

It seemed insane. A girl in cutoff shorts and boots with no weapon to hand, her platinum-colored hair flying out behind her, her arms pumping as she charged at a dead run toward two men with knives.

Jack didn't think this would end well, and it was too late to stop her.

FIFTY-ONE

Just before Angela reached the men, she bent down without slowing and snatched up something.

Jack thought that it looked like a metal rod of some kind—possibly a length of rebar—about three feet long. She must have seen it lying there in the moonlight when she broke into a dead run. She had been trying to get to it before the men with large knives reached her.

As the men charged toward her, she abruptly stopped. She twirled the rebar in her fingers like a high school cheerleader twirling a baton.

Just before the men reached her, she tossed it up in the air and caught it by one end. Holding it like a baseball bat, she took a mighty swing as the man out in front reached her.

Her swing connected with the man's hand as if she were knocking a ball out of the park. His knife flew away into the night. He let out a cry of pain as he crumpled to a knee. Angela used her swing to spin herself around and slam the rebar into the other man's forearm just as he tried to stab her. Jack could hear the bone break. Holding his broken arm, the man staggered back a few steps.

The first man had scrambled back to his feet and recovered his balance. He lunged at her to catch her in his arms. Gripping the rebar in both hands as he came at her, she rammed it, end-first, into his face so hard that it speared all the way through his skull and broke out the back. The man's dead weight twisted as he toppled, ripping the metal rod through his head from her grasp.

Angela ducked into a squat as the second man leaped toward her. His arm reaching out for her went over her head.

Angela pulled a large knife from her right boot. As the man was still staggering past her after missing, she pivoted and with two lightning strikes sliced through his Achilles tendons. He howled in pain and shock when the tendons snapped back up into his legs, the calf muscles pulling up into fat knots of unconnected muscle. He tried to walk on stilted legs but toppled to the ground.

He sat up, trying to reach his crippled legs with his one good hand.

Angela threw a side kick into his face, slamming him back down onto his back. Without an instant's hesitation, she landed on him, straddling his chest with her bare legs. She pressed the point of her knife to the fleshy spot just below his left eye right above the cheekbone. Blood ran from his broken nose. It was clear to Jack that if he moved, he would gouge out his own eye. The man knew that as well and froze.

"Well, well, well, if it isn't Miguel, leader of his merry little band of rapists."

"Sorry. I am truly sorry, *señorita*," he pleaded, holding his hands up to the side in surrender.

Angela smiled. "I seriously doubt that you're the least bit sorry, at least not yet, but you will be."

"Where did you take the material you made?" Jack asked from over her shoulder. "The Semtex explosive you were working on? Where did you take it?"

Jack put a hand on Angela's shoulder, not knowing for sure what she had in mind. "Angela," he cautioned in a low voice for her alone, "we need to get information from this man."

She shot a look of fury back over shoulder. "Oh, he's going to give us information. You don't need to worry about that."

She turned back to the man under her. "Isn't that right, Miguel? You're going to give us the information we want, right?"

"Please, please, *señorita*! I am so sorry!"

"Answer my friend's question. Where is the material I saw when I delivered the package to you? Where did you take it?"

"I don't know! I swear!"

At his denial, and without hesitation, Angela pushed the knife in under his eye and levered it underneath, popping the eyeball out enough for her to rip it out with her other hand. She held the mess of it in her bloody fingers up in front of his good eye as he shrieked and flopped under her.

"Stop screaming, or your tongue is next."

She didn't raise her voice. She was so calm, so dead serious, that it made her words far more frightening.

The man wept in terror but he stopped shrieking. "Please! No more!"

He suddenly reached for her hair with his good hand to try to gain control of her. Jack was just about to intervene to protect her when with two swift slashes she cut the tendons in the crook of his arm and then at his shoulder.

The nearly useless arm dropped to the concrete as he shrieked in pain. She put the point of the knife in his mouth to make him go quiet.

"I'll ask you again. Where is the material I saw when I delivered the package to you? I want you to think very carefully before you answer because if you lie to me again I'm going to start cutting things off you, things you would not like to be without." She put the point of her knife against his cheek and with a quick circular motion cored out one of his larger moles. He cried out. "I'm going to cut off something more important if you don't tell us what we want to know."

To make her point, she moved back, stabbed her knife into his leg, making him gasp, and then pulled the double-edged blade up the length of his pants. The blade was so sharp it cut through his pants, underwear, and leather belt. With the tip of the blade, she flopped the front of his pants and underwear to the side.

"There's your disgusting little balls now." She leaned closer. "Why Miguel, this little dick of yours is all shriveled up. Not so much fun like the last time you showed it to me, right Miguel?"

The man was trembling in agony and fright. Tears streamed from his good eye. Blood ran from the empty socket as well as his broken nose.

As afraid as Miguel was, in as much pain as he was, he rolled his head from side to side to let her know he wasn't going to talk. He looked prepared to let her do her worst, to die for his beliefs, but he was not going to reveal any information.

His willingness to die before revealing anything was where interrogations usually hit a wall. This was already well beyond the bounds of civilized men.

But Jack believed these terrorists were assembling a nuclear bomb. If this man didn't talk, Jack was going to have to call in help. It could easily be too late by the time they searched the entire complex. Or worse, for all Jack knew, they could have already loaded that bomb into a truck and be driving into a major city. There was simply no time to waste.

Jack would normally have stopped her long ago from what she was doing to this man, but this was that hypothetical situation come to life of what you would be willing to do to get information out of a terrorist if you knew hundreds of thousands of people would die if you didn't get him to talk.

This was no longer about what was proper or right, but about the survival of untold numbers of innocent people.

Jack contemplated having Angela move aside to let him try, but she was locked on to this man in a way that was profoundly frightening. Something told him to stay out of it.

Angela scooted back up to again sit on his abdomen to hold him down—not that he was going anywhere. She placed the tip of her knife under his right eye. "I think that by now you know I don't believe you and you also know that I'm not playing games.

"Maybe you had some grand vision of dying a glorious death striking a blow for your idiotic cause. Maybe you even thought that if you got caught, you would be put in prison and that no one would hurt you because Americans always treat terrorists with respect and they don't believe in behaving in the same barbaric way you do.

"Well, Miguel, here's your problem. If you would have been caught by the authorities it's true that they would likely take you to some nice, cozy prison cell in Guantánamo where you would be given prayer rugs and time to pray to Allah every day, food to keep away the pain of hunger, medical care, and outside playtime in the sunshine with the other killers being held there so as not to offend your dignity.

"But I'm not with any of those authorities, so you're fucked. No nice prison cell for you where you can shout your hate to the guards, spit at them, throw your shit at them, and laugh at how soft the Americans are with all their rules.

"You get none of that because this isn't about you being a terrorist. This is personal. You raped me. You hung me up by a rope around my neck. You thought I was going to die.

"But I didn't die.

"You are my captive now—not the American authorities'—and unlike them, I don't give a fuck about rules. There is no one here to keep me from doing whatever I want with you. And believe me, I have lots of things that I want to do to you—things I dreamed about when I was in the hospital.

"You long for nothing more than to be a killer of innocent women and children in the name of your cause or your god of whatever fucking lunatic gibberish you people thought up while wiping your asses with rocks. You live in filth because you are filth.

"You hunger to kill people who can't fight back because you are murderers. That's all you are, murderers. Nothing more. Nothing noble. Just common killers.

"For that, you are going to suffer at my hands. No rules. No law. No salvation. Just you and me."

"I will give you nothing," he managed to say in a pant, spittle bubbles forming at the corners of his mouth, defiance in his voice. "You are nothing but an American whore. You are dirt to me. I welcome death. I tell you nothing! I am prepared to die!"

That was it. Jack knew that whatever else she did to him, he was prepared to take it. He was prepared for the pain. Typical of terrorists, he worshipped death, so he welcomed death.

"Die? Who said anything about dying?"

"We will strike you all down. You will get nothing from me. Never! I will die—as a martyr!"

Angela looked up over her shoulder and smiled at Jack. He had absolutely no idea why.

She turned the smile back down at the man bleeding under her. "That's okay, Miguel." She patted his cheek. "That's okay. You really don't need to tell me."

"Because you will get nothing! Allah will reward me. New York City is going to vanish under a mushroom cloud far bigger than the bomb at Hiroshima!"

Angela laughed. She actually laughed.

Jack was getting worried. The clock was ticking on a nuclear weapon. He knew these kinds of terrorists. They really were happy to die for their cause. They believed they would live beyond death to look down on the destruction of their Great Satan.

"I don't think so," she said, still smiling like she thought he was a funny little man.

"Yes, you will—because I will tell you nothing."

"You don't have to, Miguel. You don't need to tell me anything." She patted his cheek again. "It's okay, Miguel."

He panted for a moment, wincing from the pain. His curiosity finally got the better of him. "What do you mean?"

Angela shrugged. "We'll simply bring in the dogs."

He stopped breathing for a second. "Dogs?"

FIFTY-TWO

Dogs? Jack didn't know what she was talking about, either.

"That's right," she told Miguel. "Didn't you ever see tracking dogs in that shithole where you lived and practiced killing innocent people?

"How long has it been since you took a bath? Huh, Miguel? A week? Two weeks? When you raped me and I had a chance to smell your filthy body up close and personal, I guessed it had been a month.

"Tracking dogs, you see, can track lost kids, lost people, abducted people, all kinds of people, and I'd bet all of those people had bathed within a day or two. So I don't imagine that tracking dogs would have the slightest trouble tracking your stink back to the place where you and your goat-fucking friends are building that bomb.

"So, you see?" She patted his cheek again. "It's okay. We don't really need you to talk. We'll just let the dogs come get a sniff of your stinking ass and they'll lead us right back to your friends.

"After that—" She cut the side of his left arm, making him flinch. "—I'm going to cut off this arm, right about here. It's useless, now, anyway. Then I'll put a tourniquet around the stump so you don't bleed to death." She grinned down at him. "Do you know what I'm going to do with you, then?"

Miguel, his one eye wide, shook his head.

"Then, I'm going to take you back over to that building where you strung me up by that rope and left me hanging by my neck to choke to death."

He let out a whine.

"Oh, don't worry, I'm not going to hang you like you hanged me." She swept a hand before him. "Put that thought right out of your mind. It seemed like an eternity to me as I was hanging there, unable to get a breath, choking to death, but I imagine that in reality it wouldn't have taken long to die that way. It would have soon been over."

"You see . . ." he said in defense, "we wanted you to die quickly. We had mercy on you to give you a quick death—so you would not suffer."

"That's nice," she said, smiling down at him again, "but you haven't earned the right to die quickly. What I'm going to do with you, my little rapist killer zealot, is strip you naked like I was, but rather than hang you by your neck, I'm going to hang you by that stump of a left arm.

"You know what I'm going to do then?" He was too transfixed by her to answer. "Then I'm going to let those dogs that tracked your scent back to your friends come in and have at you as you hang there, helpless."

"Dogs . . . ?" he whined.

"A pack of big dogs like that will go all crazy wild over fresh meat. They will strip your leg muscles right off the bone and eat it while you watch, unable to do anything to stop it.

"Since you'll be naked, the dominant dog will likely go for your genitals, first. Do you know what the English word 'genitals' means, Miguel?" When he didn't answer, she jostled them with the tip of her knife. "It means these little boys here. Dogs like these tender parts. It's a prized treat."

Her voice was so calm, so soft, so sexy, that she was even frightening Jack.

The man under her cried out in realization of his ignoble fate. She let him weep and tremble for a moment; then she leaned in again.

416

"Do you want to know what else I'm going to do to you when you're hanging there in that lonely building, much like you did to me? Hmm, Miguel?"

Terrified, he could only shake his head.

She poked his abdomen with her knife—not enough to stab him, but enough for him to feel it and flinch and for it to bleed. "I'm going to stick my knife into you, right down here, just enough for me to be able to reach in with a finger and hook your intestine, then I'll pull out a few feet of it. Kind of like I did with your eyeball, ya know?

"I'm going to let that few feet of your gut dangle out of you while you hang there, helpless. Do you know why I'm going to do that? Because dogs love entrails. They'll grab hold of that bit of your intestine and they'll pull and pull, tugging more out, fighting over it, yanking, tossing their heads from side to side to get it free, pulling more and more of it out of you while some of the other dogs start to fight over your genitals, tearing at them from either side.

"Every agonizing day you hang there, still alive, the meat hanging off your bones, every horrifying hour, every terrifying, torturous second that will seem like it lasts forever, you will wish for nothing more from your god than to die a quick death. But your god will not come to grant you that quick death. The dogs, though, when they get hungry, will wake from their nap to rip some more meat from your bones."

She grabbed his right wrist and twisted it. "And bones can hurt a lot, Miguel." Jack could hear the bone in his broken forearm crunch and grind together as she twisted his wrist back and forth.

Miguel shrieked in pain, his cries turning to sobs at what awaited him. Jack could see that the man was starting to go into shock. She didn't have much time left to get him to confess what he knew. He thought she knew it as well.

"So, Miguel, I'm going to give you this one last chance to spare yourself that very, very long, agonizing, humiliating death for nothing. One last chance to answer before we bring in the dogs. One last chance to tell me where your friends are—to tell me where they are building that bomb. One last chance to earn yourself a quick death so you can go be with Allah.

"But if you don't want to tell me," she said as she patted his cheek again, "that's all right. We will simply go get the dogs and they will track your stink back to them in no time."

She leaned in and looked into his eye. "Time's up."

Miguel shook and cried as he muttered prayers in Spanish.

Finally, he lifted his broken right arm over his chest and pointed the best he could to his left.

"I need more than that," she said, sounding totally unimpressed.

"That way," Miguel said, "the way you saw us coming from. Go that way until you get to the yard with all the train axles. Turn left. Go maybe three hundred meters until you see an alleyway to your right. If you look down that alleyway, you will see the end of a big brick building with an arched roof. You will see a rolling door on the end. That is where the others are."

Angela looked back up at Jack. He nodded that he believed the man. Thinking they had tracking dogs meant they would quickly find where he had come from anyway. Tracking dogs meant he would suffer for nothing. That ruse had taken all the fight out of him. Resistance had become pointless in his mind.

"Do you remember my promise to all of you when you were beating me nearly to death?"

"No, *señorita*," he whined.

She put the tip of her knife on his chest, just off to the left side of his breastbone. "I promised to kill all of you. Remember?"

He nodded reluctantly.

"You should have believed me. I've killed your three buddies— this one tonight and the other two when you drove up to my house. Remember? Only you are left. All your training, all that planning, and all that work you've all done is going to mean nothing now that you have betrayed all your friends."

Angela rose up enough to put both hands on the end of the knife handle as she stiffened her arms. "Oh, and Miguel? I want you to know. We don't have any dogs."

He cried out at realizing he had been tricked.

She dropped her full weight onto the knife. It sliced his heart in half and he was dead in seconds.

Jack wiped sweat from his face. That was the most brutal interrogation he had ever witnessed. And he had witnessed a number of them in other countries. It was also the most efficient and effective.

This woman was utterly ruthless.

He could have stopped it at any time, and might have, except that he was now sure that these terrorists had a nuclear weapon, it was viable, and they were on the brink of using it. If that happened, New York City would become a radioactive wasteland. The electromagnetic pulse from that bomb would likely knock out all electronic and electrical devices for a large part of the East Coast.

The consequences for the country were unimaginable. The world would be forever changed.

At that moment, in this place, in a situation this incredibly dangerous, he doubted anyone but this girl with her knife could have gotten the information any faster. He didn't really know anything about her life, but everything in her life had led her to being the right person in the right place at the right time.

In the end, it wasn't really the torture; it was the trick she had played on him, the word picture she had painted in his mind about the dogs. The things she had already done gave her the credibility to make that trick work.

She had blood on her hands and arms almost up to her elbows. Her bare legs were smeared with blood.

"I know that what you just did was far from easy or pleasant. But I hope you will take comfort in knowing that you may just have saved the lives of countless people."

"Are you kidding?" She swiped some hair off her cheek with the back of her wrist. The blood on her matched her lipstick. "I haven't felt this alive for a long time."

Jack again wondered who the hell he was dealing with.

Angela pointed off into a weedy area. "Help me drag these two over there."

Jack peered off into the moonlit weeds. "Why?"

"We can't afford to have any lookouts patrolling the area discover them and send up an alarm. There's a cistern over there. We can dump them down inside."

That actually made sense.

"How do you know there's a cistern over there?" Jack asked as they each grabbed one of Miguel's legs.

"Because," she said as they dragged him close and dropped his legs, "I met a man once who dumped the body of a girl with red hair down there. I recognize the place from seeing it in his mind."

Jack slid the heavy lid aside as he shot her a suspicious look. "What happened to him?"

"He went down a different hole."

Jack was having a hard time keeping up with everything he was learning about her. It was obvious that her "interrogation" technique wasn't something she'd thought up on the spot. Not many people would have had the stomach to do that to another human being, regardless of what they were guilty of.

She seemed to relish it. Of course, after what they had done to her, he supposed he couldn't blame her.

Once they had dumped both men down into the cistern, Angela went back for the eyeball she had cut out and tossed it in. Jack slid the lid back on.

They needed to hurry and find the place where the men were building an atom bomb.

Jack hoped they weren't already on the road with it.

"We had better get going," he said. "We may not have much time to stop them."

FIFTY-THREE

"**W**ait back here," Jack whispered.

He was thankful that Angela didn't argue. He left her in the alleyway behind a partially crumbled brick wall and then moved on alone into the moon's shadow cast by the large building with the arched roof.

As far as he could see, the only windows in the long building were up high, mainly for ventilation and to let daylight in. He moved quietly along the entire length of the building, looking for a way to see inside. The building was brick, and had stood the test of time. Around the back there were steel doors, but they were all locked. He might have been able to break into them, but not without making enough noise to send up an alarm. For all he knew, they could even be booby-trapped. There was a rolling door at the back of the building, but it, too, was locked.

When he reached the far side of the building, he found a shed of some sort. It had been built right up next to the main building. He climbed on a heap of discarded diesel engine blocks and gears stacked beside the shed and then used the gutter to help him climb up onto the roof. Standing on the roof of the shed, he found a place where the brick was broken up around a jagged vertical crack in the outer wall of the main building.

Jack pushed on the bricks around the broken area, looking for any that were loose. He found several. After jiggling them a little to see how easily he would be able to pull them out, he found one that was looser than the others. He carefully wiggled it out, inch by inch, being careful to make sure none of the other bricks would come tumbling down.

He was armed only with a couple of small knives. He knew how to use them, and they were often better in close quarters, but they were no match for guns at a distance. He had learned that lesson the last time he had brought a knife to a gunfight. It did not end well. He had spent months in a coma and then recovering in the hospital. If that experience taught him anything, it was that he didn't want to get shot again.

It had also lost him Kate. She believed he was dead and so she had gone off the grid to keep any super-predators from finding her. Unfortunately, Jack couldn't find her, either. It was discouraging to try so hard and not even be able to get any leads on her whereabouts. At the same time, he was in a way happy about it because she was keeping herself safe from any killers who might also be trying to find her.

After he had finally managed to wiggle the brick out of its place in the wall, he carefully set it down against a ledge so it wouldn't fall off the roof and possibly alert the men inside.

He leaned down and squinted through the hole to see what he could of what was inside.

The first thing he saw almost made him fall off the roof.

There, in the middle of the room, was a spherical device about three feet in diameter. Several men were holding half of a metal outer shell up to it as another group of men were feeding a mass of wires through an opening in the shell.

A cargo van sat not far away, both of its back doors wide open. A bundle of electrical cables hung out the back.

The bomb didn't look like some of the more sophisticated devices he'd seen, but with all the clues finally making sense, he didn't doubt that at a minimum he was looking at a crude nuclear weapon. Except it wasn't nearly as crude as he would have hoped. This was a relatively sophisticated device, and he would bet that its yield was enough to take out much of a big city like New York.

He could see machined brass sleeves for the exploding bridge-wire already placed in the Semtex. The way the explosive was precisely shaped into geometric pieces that were being assembled into a sphere looked to have been done with care and precision.

The plutonium-239 the Mossad had found in the tread of José's boot was bomb-grade plutonium, which told him that it surely had a plutonium pit. He could see the lead shielding of the tamper beneath where the Semtex was still being placed.

For the moment, where the plutonium for the bomb had come from was irrelevant. The only thing that mattered was that it was here, now.

Jack was sure, now, that this was undoubtedly the reason they had blown up the Oeste Mesa border crossing. They used the diversion of all the other terrorist attacks to dilute the importance of that one. Different terrorist organizations claiming credit for various attacks created confusion among the intel agencies as to what was going on. That confusion had helped them to get the plutonium pit and associated material needed for the bomb across the border and into the United States.

Everyone thought all those attacks were the big event. The other terrorists might not have realized they were pawns being used as a diversion, but they had served the desired purpose anyway, and while all that was going on this group had gotten the most crucial material for their bomb into the country. Everyone was searching the country for Muslim extremists, raiding mosques, making arrests, pulling in and questioning known radicalized people on watch lists, and poring over Islamic chatter.

No one was looking for Mexicans.

Jack estimated that the bomb was possibly only hours but no more than a day away from being fully assembled and ready. He was sure that by morning it would be loaded into the van and on its way. From what Miguel had confessed, the target was New York City. There was no reason to doubt that.

With no time to waste, Jack slid back down the roof and jumped to the ground. He moved quickly but as quietly as possible as he made his way back from the building with the bomb to where he had left Angela.

When he got to where she was supposed to be he didn't see her. He looked around when he heard dripping water and finally spotted her, bathed in moonlight, just climbing up out of a large metal tank that had been cut in half and was lying on its side. It was partially filled with rainwater. Dripping wet, Angela climbed out over the side.

Jack was incredulous. "What the hell are you doing?"

She frowned at him like it was the stupidest question she'd ever heard. "Washing off all the blood." She shook water off her hands. "I don't want to get blood all over the interior of my truck."

In an odd, crazy way, he had to admit that it made sense.

He ushered her a safe distance away from the building with the nuke. He had seen at least a couple of dozen men inside working to assemble the bomb. There could easily have been more that he couldn't see through the small hole. He had seen a lot of AK-47s leaning against posts and tables.

He didn't know if there were men other than the two Angela had killed who might also be walking around, taking a cigarette break, or even walking guard duty. If there were, he didn't want to run into them.

He scanned the area one last time, then pulled his phone out and pressed one of the numbers he had programmed in.

When a woman answered, Jack gave her the code in. She checked briefly, then asked what she could do for him.

"Give me Dvora. It's an emergency."

It was the middle of the day in Israel, so he expected she would be available. As Jack waited he continued to watch for trouble. Angela was doing the same.

Dvora quickly picked up. "Jack—what's the emergency?"

"I'm in Milford Falls—"

"Did you find Angela Constantine, then?"

"Yes. Listen to me. You need to tell the Americans to activate NEST. They're going to need to get people in here."

There was a brief moment of stunned silence before she came back. "The Nuclear Emergency Support Team? Has there been a radiological accident?"

The purpose of NEST was to be ready to send teams to recover any kind of nuclear material or devices like dirty bombs. He wasn't sure they were prepared for a fully functional, live nuclear bomb, but if anyone was prepared to deal with it, it was the NEST team.

"No. Listen to me. We've got a live atomic bomb."

Again, there was a moment of silence. "All right, we're contacting them right now. Is the site secure?"

"Hell no it's not secure. The device is shortly going to be on its way to New York City."

"They monitor for radiation levels all over the place around the East Coast."

"This is a plutonium bomb. Plutonium is hard to detect in the first place and this one has a lead tamper around the pit. From the looks of the sophistication of it, they will probably use other shields to protect it on their way to New York City. These people know what they're doing. I expect their truck is shielded. Any radiation will likely be tightly contained. It's highly unlikely it would be detected.

"But even if some new, supersecret detection equipment did pick it up before it got into the city proper, that will be little consolation if they set it off when they're intercepted. The blast radius, the firestorm, and the radiation would devastate a vast area. They don't need to have a direct hit. With a nuke, close will do."

"I've got red lights going up across the board with our contacts," Dvora said. "Do you have coordinates?"

"I took the coordinates right at the site of the building they're in. Sending them now."

"Okay, got them."

Jack knew that once the authorities secured the weapon they would need to get the NEST team in to disarm it.

"Let the Americans know that it's not likely to have any fail-safe systems. But I would bet they have contingency plans for an attack."

"I've got other operators notifying the DHS, NSA, and the FBI as well as the Pentagon as we speak. I don't know what kind of tactical team they are going to want to deploy."

"I suspect that whoever is closest will go in."

"All right, Jack, we're on it. We've got our entire center activated. We're lighting up the Americans."

Jack let out a sigh of relief. "Thanks, Dvora. I'll stay on site until they get here just to make sure the terrorists don't leave with the bomb. If they do we'll follow them and I'll update you with any information. Call me if you need anything more."

"Stay well back from the area in case they can't get boots on location fast enough. They may decide to send in a drone or jet to put ordnance on the site."

"For god's sake, I really don't think they ought to be using explosives around a nuclear bomb."

Explosives wouldn't set off a nuke—it needed an electrical charge to detonate it—but there was always the risk of radioactive contamination from debris. They could inadvertently turn it into a dirty bomb.

"Given the situation, and the potential risk, that may be what they need to do. It's their call," Dvora said.

Jack knew what she meant. If an atom bomb was going to go off, better it go off in central New York State than in a major population center.

"Please tell them I advise against any heavy ordnance."

"Do you think they will listen to what we tell them?"

"No, I suppose not. By the way, don't let them know who is providing this intelligence. I'm not exactly welcome on the inside anymore."

"Already anticipated that, Jack. We're only saying that we have eyes-on intelligence. Since it's us calling they will assume that it's one of our agents."

"Thanks, Dvora. I'll call you if anything changes on the ground."

After he hung up, he turned to Angela. She was watching him.

"I think it would be safer if we got some distance away from here. There's liable to be lots of gunfire. I wouldn't want either one of us getting hit with a stray round. Is there somewhere with some elevation where we can watch and see what happens?"

Angela nodded. "I know a place."

They rushed to the truck but drove slowly out of the industrial complex. If the terrorists had lookouts, Jack didn't want to alert them to the sound of a truck racing away. That would surely get them riddled with bullets.

Once they were on the road leaving the complex, Angela took the first turnoff onto a dirt road. It took them up through heavy woods to the crest of a hill, where she parked the truck at a gravel area at the end of the road. She grabbed a pair of binoculars from behind the passenger seat before they got out. They walked a short distance through maple and oak trees to a spot where they could overlook the entire area.

Angela handed him the binoculars. Jack surveyed the sprawling complex. The moonlight was enough to allow him to see all the buildings and vast stretches of concrete. He located the building where the terrorists had the bomb. If their truck left, he would be able to spot it.

If their cargo van left, and no one showed up in time, Jack knew he would have to try to stop it. If necessary, they would have to ram it to disable it so it couldn't get to New York City.

Angela and Jack sat down on a rock ledge and waited, watching to make sure the men down in that building didn't leave with the bomb. The minutes felt like hours as they waited for someone to show up. Jack didn't know if it would be police cars, a drone that would fire a missile, or something in between. The problem with getting a team like SEALs or Delta Force in here was that they were likely not close by. But then again, Jack didn't know anything about what American forces were available, where they were deployed, or what kind of aircraft they had at their disposal. He did know that they were effective and always ready.

He hoped they were close enough.

FIFTY-FOUR

A little over half an hour later Jack thought he heard something. He stood and took a few steps farther out from under the trees. He could feel a rapid thump, thump, thumping in his chest more than he could hear it. For all he knew there could have been more than one running in total blackout mode. He caught a glimpse of a blurred black shape as it passed across the nearly full moon high overhead.

"That sounds a little like helicopters," Angela said.

"It's a military stealth helicopter. Whoever is on board a ship like that is going to be the best of the best."

Jack was relieved it was that kind of team that would be handling the situation.

The sound of the stealth helicopter died out in the distance. The dark scene below them was silent again. Jack watched but couldn't hear anything or see anything. He figured they would have landed some distance away and would be approaching the building on foot.

As they waited, listening to the night birds singing up in the trees and the monotonous chirp of insects, the night suddenly erupted in the crackle of gunfire. The birds broke out of the trees overhead, squawking in fright as they fled. Jack put the binoculars to his eyes and saw a crisscross of tracer rounds going in every direction. The sound of the gunfire was probably the outgoing fire from the building. That type of assault group would likely have suppressors.

He handed the binoculars to Angela so she could see, too. As he did so, a massive explosion suddenly lit up the night. The building with the bomb vanished under an expanding, bright yellow-orange ball of fire. Jack could see the shock wave racing across the industrial site.

He put an arm around Angel's shoulders and took her to the ground with him, holding her down protectively as the shock wave and the sound of the blast slammed into the trees all around.

As soon as it was past, Jack jumped to his feet and looked through the binoculars. The building was virtually gone. Only a small portion of the rear wall was still there. Bricks from the walls had been thrown out in every direction.

He doubted the US forces would have set off an explosion like that with a nuke inside. It had to be that the terrorists inside the building had wired the place with explosives beforehand. Lots of explosives. By the size of the blast they obviously wanted to die as martyrs and make sure there were no survivors who could be taken prisoner and questioned. Clearly, they also wanted to take as many people with them as possible.

With an explosive kill zone that large, whatever force had gone in there would have lost a lot of men.

Angela took the binoculars so she could have a look. After a moment she said, "I can see people moving around. There are men going into what's left of the building. That, and no more gunfire, is a good sign, right?"

"Right." He put a hand on Angela's shoulder. "You did a good thing, Angela. It looks like we were in time. The bomb was close to being assembled and then on its way to New York City. You saved the lives of a great many people."

She didn't show any emotion, but she said, "Thanks, Jack."

After a short time, Jack's phone vibrated. It was Dvora.

"They recovered the nuke and have it secured," she said. "It's still mostly in one piece. My god, Jack, that was close."

"Too close," he said. "Did the team report anything else?"

"They lost men. I don't know any numbers. There are a lot wounded. But they have the scene secured. They haven't found any terrorists alive. They don't know yet if there might have been look-outs who survived, but they're searching now."

"Okay," Jack said. "Now that they have everything under control, I think we'd better get out of here."

"I'll let you know if we get any other information. Just so you know, we kept your name out of it."

After he hung up, he and Angela made their way back through the trees to the truck. Quiet had returned to the night. With the danger ended and the bomb secured, he suddenly felt drained.

"How about running me by the bar so I can get my car. I'm exhausted. I could use a good night's sleep."

"I think we both could," she said. "I'm glad I was able to help."

"Help? If not for you getting the information out of Miguel, an atom bomb would be on its way to New York City within a day or two. The world owes you a lot."

"I'd rather be left out of it, if it's okay with you," she said as they reached the truck.

Jack chuckled his understanding of her rationale. They drove back out onto the highway and turned toward the city.

"You and I are a lot alike," he told her. "I don't want them to know I'm involved, either."

Her face was lit in the glow of the dash lights as she looked over. "Why not?"

He sighed. "They don't like that I work with people like you who can recognize killers. It's not politically correct. They canceled the contract I had with them over it. The Israelis are thankful for my help, though."

She looked skeptical. "You mean, there are other people like me?"

"Well," he said, "I know a great deal about people who can rec-ognize killers, but I've never met anyone like you."

As she was thinking it over while negotiating the curving mountain road, a car closed rapidly from behind. Its high beams lit up the cab of the truck. When it cut into the oncoming lane and charged up beside the truck, Jack could see that it was a beige Toyota.

Angela glanced briefly out her window and saw the car.

"Hell no," she muttered, "this isn't happening."

The car cut over toward them, trying to slam into her truck to drive her off the road and into the trees. Angela anticipated what they were about to do and floored the gas. The truck accelerated so hard it laid Jack back in his seat. The car cut over, but as the truck had already shot ahead they completely missed her.

Jack looked out the back window and saw what he thought were the silhouettes of AK-47s sticking out the passenger windows.

"I think you had better give me your gun."

"You won't need it," she said, completely composed as she kept the gas pedal floored. "These guys don't know what they're doing."

The truck flew into the night, the tires at the edge of adhesion as they arced around curves at speeds he would have thought impossible. He knew this was no ordinary truck and Angela was proving to be no ordinary driver. On top of that, she knew the road well. Jack had to brace himself between the door and the center console.

She led the car following them on a wild chase along the mountain road, sometimes only feeding in half throttle on the straights so that the Toyota could catch up, then accelerating to stay just far enough ahead to goad their predatory chase instinct.

As she reached a particularly twisty section of road that in places revealed steep drop-offs, she backed off just enough for the car to begin to catch up again, to let them feel confident they had her. Jack realized she was giving them slack and then reeling them in, playing them along, until she could get them where she wanted them.

As they came around a bend onto a straight section, she again accelerated at full power. Jack glanced to the speedometer and saw that they were surging past a hundred miles an hour. He looked up and in the headlights saw a road sign with an arrow curving to the right.

Angela backed off the gas as she approached the curve enough to allow the car to inch up beside them in the oncoming lane. Just as it did, she suddenly slammed on the brakes. As the car shot past, she cut the wheel to the left and caught the rear right quarter of the Toyota with her bumper. At that speed, they had no chance to regain control as momentum turned their car. It slid sideways into a sharp, right-handed curve around the side of the mountain. In a high-speed sideways slide, the Toyota flew off the road as Angela shot past them. The out-of-control, sideways Toyota hit a small ditch and flipped. It barrel-rolled down the embankment at tremendous speed, throwing chrome moldings, glass, and dirt flying everywhere.

Angela braked hard to a stop, then backed up and pulled off to the left side of the road just in time to see the car tumbling down below them abruptly slam roof-first into a tree. With a resounding boom it instantly came to a dead stop.

The world suddenly went dead quiet. Steam and wisps of smoke rose from the crumpled remains.

Angela, cool as could be, opened her door and calmly got out. "Let's go have a look."

She pulled her gun from the holster at the small of her back and started down the embankment. Jack pulled out his knife. In this circumstance he would rather have had a gun as well.

After making their way down a rocky, forested hillside, they came to the site of the wreck. It amazed him that the car had managed to barrel-roll over and over down the steep hillside, shearing off a series of saplings, without hitting any of the mature trees until it finally encountered a big one just before a drop-off over a sheer cliff. Had it missed the tree, it would have sailed out into thin air and landed far below on a boulder field. As it was, encountering the tree was no salvation. It was lethal.

The car had hit roof-first and wrapped itself backward around the tree. No one had been thrown from the car as it tumbled down the hillside. Everyone had somehow remained inside until the impact.

As Angela, in her cutoffs and suede boots, stood guard with her gun, Jack climbed up on the car to look down through the narrow openings that were all that was left when the roof hit the tree trunk and crushed the windows. The bodies inside were ripped and crumpled into a gory mess. There was no one remotely in one piece. There was nothing alive to be rescued.

Angela had efficiently killed them all without having to fire a shot. He doubted that anyone looking at her would realize how deadly this woman truly was. He couldn't begin to imagine what her life had been like up to this point, but he hoped to find out.

The sky was just beginning to get a blush of color. It wouldn't be long until dawn.

"Let's get back to town," he said.

The remainder of the drive back was uneventful. He had a lot of questions, but right then wasn't the time. No one followed, so Angela drove, if not at the speed limit, at what was probably a reasonable speed for her. When they arrived back at his car, parked at Barry's Place, the sun wasn't yet up, but the sky was already turning a golden blue. The bar was long closed. A few pieces of what looked like hamburger wrappers danced with each other across the empty lot in the predawn glow.

"I have to work tomorrow," she said. "This is going to be a busy Friday night, so the other girls will need me to help out. I need to get home, shower, and get some sleep. You look like you need some sleep, too."

He would be able to get the sleep he needed, but it wouldn't be long until the bar opened again. By the time she got home and to bed, she wouldn't have the chance to get much sleep.

Jack nodded as he opened his door. "You're right. You did something incredible tonight, Angela. There are a lot of things we need to talk about. But for now, get some rest. I'll let you work and then come by later tonight, close to closing time."

FIFTY-FIVE

When Jack arrived at Barry's Place that night it was still a little while before their 2:00 a.m. closing time. He knew Angela would be busy helping to keep the bar up and running for Barry, so after everything that had happened the previous night he had wanted to let her do what she needed to do. The parking lot was still half full, so the bar appeared to be doing well.

Now that the people with the bomb had been stopped, he and Angela could take a breather. But Jack still had a lot he needed to talk to her about. He really needed to learn more about her ability to have visions from killers. That was well beyond anything he had ever seen in anyone else.

He didn't really know yet exactly what he was dealing with. To be honest, it chilled him to the bone.

Jack had checked in with Dvora so she could fill him in with what information she had. She said the incident had been kept well above top secret, which he already knew because the news hadn't said a word about it. If it had been merely top secret, it would have been leaked by now.

Apparently, after the recent terrorist attacks that had the whole country up in arms and demanding retaliation, the US government didn't want people to know how vulnerable they were to being nuked.

The incident had probably been kept confined to as few people as possible. Even most people in the intel community wouldn't know about it.

Dvora gave him a report on the killed and injured. She said the nuclear device itself had been blown several hundred feet, but because the bomb required such a heavy steel case for the initial implosion, it hadn't ruptured. It was secure and NEST was already going about rendering it safe.

The explosives the terrorists had rigged were massive to insure no one at the site survived. None had. He knew that the few lookouts who had chased them were dead as well. Jack was hoping that Cassiel was among the dead. It would take some time, but the authorities investigating the site should eventually be able to confirm his identity from remains found at the site. Once they knew, the Mossad should be able to find out and then let Jack know.

Dvora told him that, from the chatter, it sounded like they had a terrorist in custody. Jack found that surprising. She said they were keeping the captured terrorist under tight wraps and they weren't saying anything. Jack assumed they must have captured another lookout.

After getting a fitful sleep in a motel room where the curtains let in too much light, he had spent the rest of the day and evening, in the room, doing research over a pizza. He had a lot of information that he had collected over the years about different types of people with the ability to recognize killers. All of those people could do it to a greater or lesser extent. Most to a lesser extent.

Then there was Kate. She had abilities to know things from looking into the eyes of killers that he had previously reasoned would at some point come about because of evolution.

But he couldn't begin to explain Angela's abilities. They went far above and beyond any of his own theories. Some very rare individuals, Kate especially, could get shadowy hints of things from looking at killers or their photos.

Angela saw more than shadows. She could name names.

As Jack walked across the parking lot half full of cars, it seemed that a lot of people weren't leaving, yet. Everyone was probably staying for last call. He wanted to let Angela do her job, but he was eager to talk to her.

The primal woods across the street stood a silent watch. The bar, as he had first thought, looked to be a last outpost before the great, trackless forests. Such things always left him wondering at his place—at mankind's place—in the greater cosmos. Sometimes he just wanted to vanish into one of those ancient forests and live out the rest of his life alone and at peace without having to deal with killers and their prey.

A wall of pounding rock music hit him when he opened the door on the dark den. Inside was a totally different world than the quiet, surrounding forest just outside.

The people inside were varying degrees of drunk, loud, and seemed to be having a great time. The place was filled with cigarette smoke. Colorful lights played over everyone, making them look almost like they were being sprinkled with pixie dust. Some people danced to the music among the tables. Some women in low-cut tops and short skirts danced on guys' laps.

Jack saw the girls who worked in the bar having a last drink with their customers. It was a party atmosphere, but he knew that Angela wouldn't be taking part in the drinking. One of the things he had learned about her was that, like most people with the ability to spot killers, she had an aversion to mind-altering substances of any type.

As Jack made his way across the room among animated people hanging all over each other, drinking, talking, laughing, and dancing, Nate spotted him and rushed over to take him by the arm and drag him around the side of the bar and then to a doorway into a back room where it was a little quieter, but not much.

"Where's Angela?"

"Please!" Nate said, sounding rather desperate. "Come back here where we can talk."

Nate dragged him into the back stockroom, where it wasn't quite so noisy.

"Where's Angela?" Jack asked again.

"They took her!" Nate said, still gripping Jack's arm. "Those fucking bastards came and—"

"Wait a minute," Jack said holding up a hand. "Slow down. Tell me what happened."

"I wanted to call you—I tried—but I didn't know how to reach you. I called every motel in Milford Falls and no one had a Jack Raines registered there."

Jack didn't use his real name at motels. He had fake IDs he always used so that people couldn't find him.

"All right. I'm here now. What happened?" Jack's level of alarm was growing by the second, but he tried not to let it show. "Where's Angela?"

Nate pressed his fingertips to each side of his head as he took a calming breath.

"When we opened early today in the late morning I had just arrived and was waiting because I don't have a key. Angela showed up about that time to open the place. None of the other girls had arrived, yet.

"As she was unlocking the door all hell broke loose. Men in black tactical gear from head to foot, with only their eyes showing, pointed machine guns at Angela. They shoved me to the side. They were all screaming orders at once. It was insane."

Jack leaned in, his jaw hanging open. "What?"

"Yeah, there were dozens of them. They rushed in and slammed her up against the wall. Like fifteen guys all had their hands on her, pressing her up against the wall so she couldn't move. Everyone was pointing guns at her. I was yelling and screaming at them to leave her alone and not to hurt her.

"Then, as they were holding her against the wall, a whole bunch of black SUVs came roaring into the parking lot, completely surrounding us. About half a dozen of these guys in black with machine guns dragged me back and frisked me. They told me to keep my fucking mouth shut."

"What about Angela?" Jack asked.

"They had her pressed flat against the wall. A few guys searched her while some others were putting handcuffs and leg irons on her. They took a gun out of a holster in her waistband in back. Another guy pulled a knife out of her right boot."

"What was she doing? Did she say anything? I hope to god she didn't resist."

"No, she didn't try to fight them. She looked like a rag doll in their hands. I felt terrible for not helping her, but I had half a dozen guns in my face. These fuckers weren't fooling around. They told me that if I didn't stay back and keep my mouth shut they would shoot me. I don't think they were bluffing."

"They weren't," Jack told him.

"Then four or five of them picked Angela up—picked her right up off the ground like a rolled-up carpet—and carried her to the back of one of those big black SUVs. Just before they got her there and stuffed her inside, she turned her head back and yelled for me to keep the bar open.

"I knew what she meant. Lots of the girls need the work and Barry is going to need to make a living—if he lives. But at that moment that was the last thing in the world I cared about. I was afraid for Angela. I have no idea who these men were. They didn't have any markings and I sure as hell wasn't about to ask to see their ID.

"As soon as she said that, they stuffed a gag in her mouth as they were putting her in the SUV. Then the whole lot of them piled into their vehicles and blew out of here."

Jack stared off in fury. "Damn."

"Do you know who they were, or what they wanted with Angela? Did it have something to do with that big explosion I heard about over in the old industrial area? I heard they have the entire area closed off and there are troops all over the place. They said a military plane had crashed.

"Do you know why they came in here and took her like that? I mean, putting her in handcuffs and leg-irons and all? These weren't police. I've seen SWAT. This wasn't SWAT. This was something else, some kind of armed-forces people."

"I don't know what's going on, Nate."

Jack really didn't. His mind was racing, trying to think what to do.

"We've got to help her!" Nate sounded desperate.

"What time did this happen?"

Nate threw up his hands. "I don't know. Right before we opened. Just before noon. Something like that."

"That means they've had her for over fourteen hours."

"I didn't know what to do. The other girls started arriving, and customers were showing up, so I let the girls open the place up. I told them what happened to Angela—well, I only told them that she had been arrested—and that Angela told me to open the bar."

Jack's mind was racing, trying to decide on what to do next.

"Is there a federal building in Milford Falls?"

"Yeah, sure," Nate said. "A small one. It has Social Security Administration offices there, things like that."

Jack didn't know why in the world they would have taken Angela prisoner, but since it had to be about the bomb, it would be some kind of high-level federal force.

That kind would probably want to question her on the spot before any more time elapsed or anyone else horned in on what they had claimed as their territory. Those kinds of men wouldn't want to wait until they got her back to Washington. They would want to be in an obscure location, since their agency was being watched all the time by reporters looking for news or leaks about the mass terrorist attacks.

"Where's this federal building?"

Nate gave him directions. Jack raced out to his car and took off. If they did take her to the federal building for the initial questioning, they might still be there.

FIFTY-SIX

Jack parked almost a block away in a spot at the end of a side street where he would be able to keep an eye on the small, local federal building. There were a half dozen black SUVs parked on the street. Since there was underground parking, there were likely more he didn't see. They all had government tags but no agency identification. He hoped those vehicles meant that Angela was still in there.

He hoped, too, that he could find a way to get her out. They would never in a million years understand her and what she had done for the country. That was irrelevant to them. Otherwise they wouldn't have picked her up and treated her like they had just captured Osama Bin Laden. They had their own agenda.

They'd had her in there for fifteen hours. He knew she wouldn't be sleeping in a cell. These people had no intention of letting her sleep. They would be hammering away at her in a relentless interrogation. He didn't know for certain why they had her, but he had his suspicions.

If they got her back to Washington she would vanish in a maze of bureaucratic organizations and secret locations. She would be at the mercy of elements of intel agencies and a justice department that were above the law or accountability. Because he had worked with some of those people he knew that this was his best chance to intercede before they took her to Washington.

There weren't many cars parked on the street at the late hour. That made Jack uncomfortable, because he stood out like a sore thumb.

He knew that if he was going to accomplish anything, he was going to have to come out of the shadows. He had stayed off the grid for years. Now, if he was going to help Angela, he had no choice but to surface.

Jack checked his watch. It was 3:00 a.m., so that made it 10:00 a.m. in Israel. He pressed the speed dial.

Once he had coded in, Dvora immediately picked up.

"Dvora, I've got a problem."

"What is it?"

"Federal agents snatched Angela. I don't know who or why."

"I can at least help with the 'why,'" Dvora said. "We've been monitoring some of the deep chatter. We believe they think she was involved with the terrorists."

"What? That's bullshit. She's the one who stopped them!"

"What do you want me to do?"

Jack's grip on the steering wheel tightened. "I'm going to have to contact some people who think I'm dead. They may decide to make sure I stay dead this time. I need you to initiate our fail-safe protocol should anything happen to me."

"Are you sure it's that serious?"

"I have at least a half dozen snipers on rooftops zeroed in on me as we speak."

Dvora paused for a moment. "All right, I'm patching it in now." There was another pause. "Okay, it's set. If you fail to check in every twenty-four hours, the packet will be released to all the places listed. Let's hope it doesn't come to that. When do you want the clock to start ticking?"

Jack checked his watch again. "I don't know if I'm going to be able to get the person I need to speak with to answer his phone in the middle of the night. Let's make it eight a.m."

"You got it. At eight a.m. where you are, three p.m. here, the clock starts. You will need to call in by eight a.m. every day until you abort, or the packet will automatically go out."

"Understood. Thank you, Dvora."

She paused a moment. "Is this subject worth the risk, Jack?"

"I couldn't even begin to explain to you how important she is, except to say that because of her alone, New York City won't vanish under a mushroom cloud."

Dvora let out a low whistle. "Wow. Okay, Jack, we have your back. Do what you need to do to get her out of there."

When she hung up, Jack dialed another number. There was no answer. He hadn't expected there would be. He dialed the number every fifteen minutes throughout the night.

It was seven thirty in the morning before a man answered. "This had better be important." He sounded more than a little grumpy.

"It is, Angus," Jack said.

"Who is this?"

"Jack Raines."

There was a long pause. "Jack Raines is dead."

"I regret to inform you I'm still alive and kicking."

"How the hell do I know this is really Jack Raines?"

"Because I called you on this number."

"That doesn't prove anything. You could have stolen it or taken it off a dead man—a dead Jack Raines."

"You mean like you took that dead man's little black book in Cincinnati? I was there, remember? I watched you take it out of his breast pocket after your man, Sam, if memory serves, garroted the guy."

"Jack . . . good god . . . it really is you?"

"Afraid so, Angus."

"We thought you were dead. Everyone thought you were dead."

"I know. I wanted to be dead. Now, I need to be alive."

"What's this about?"

"This is about something I need you to do."

"Well, I'm not sure I would still be able to—"

"Or else, among other things, I expose your agency's existence and where it is in the black budget."

"That could get you killed."

"Maybe. I need something and you are going to help me."

"I don't think I can, Jack. We don't have a working agreement with you anymore."

"That's a really shitty attitude, Angus, considering everything I've done for you."

"And we appreciate it. You saved our asses any number of times. But I must advise you not to start getting troublesome. You could find yourself dead again, only this time it would be permanent. Then what you know gets buried with you."

"That's where you're wrong, Angus. You see, if I don't report in on a regular basis, everything I know about the entire alphabet soup of agencies, including yours, along with various operations that would cause an uproar if it were to be divulged, is going to be revealed in detail to Congress, the Senate, the Justice Department, the media, and posted online for everyone to see in black and white."

There was a long silence.

"I think you should be careful making threats, Jack."

"Here's the deal, Angus. I'm not fucking around. Either you help me and do what I need done, or a whole lot of people are going to find a noose around their necks. Yours may be one of those necks."

His resistance finally broke down a little. "All right, Jack, I'll hear you out. I owe you that much. You've done a lot of good things for us. Maybe I can help. What do you need?"

Jack decided to let him pretend he was doing the right thing for the right reasons.

"I'm in a city called Milford Falls, New York. I'm parked outside the federal building there. The first thing I want is for the snipers on rooftops to point their weapons elsewhere."

"Okay. I don't know why they would be doing such a thing, but I'll put an end to it. No problem. Is that it?"

"You heard about the atom bomb that was assembled here and just about to head into New York City?"

"Jesus Christ, Jack, that's classified at the highest level. How the hell did you find out about that?"

"I'm the one who called it in. I'm the one who provided the coordinates so a team could get in there and stop it."

"That was you?"

"That was me."

Angus let out an audible sigh. "Okay, you have my attention. What's your problem?"

"Black ops of some kind swooped in here and took my asset."

There was a long pause before the man finally spoke. "Your asset? All I'm at liberty to say is that our people followed some terrorists in a sedan and a pickup on satellite imagery as they were speeding away from the scene. Before the team could stop them, the sedan crashed and four men were killed. They traced the pickup to a bar and picked a woman up later."

Jack took a breath to calm himself. "Angus, my asset and I went in there and found the bomb. I provided the coordinates. As we were getting out of there four terrorist lookouts chased us. That's why we were going fast. They crashed. We didn't."

"The car crashed, she didn't. That doesn't prove she isn't one of the terrorists."

"There is a cistern out there. You will find the bodies of two men down inside. One has a piece of rebar through his skull. The other one is missing his left eye. My asset did that to them to find out where the bomb was. She is the one who got that information and saved your ass, along with the lives of hundreds of thousands of people."

"We don't approve of torture."

"Ah, okay, thanks for letting me know. The next time I'll just let the nuke go off. Is that the way you want it, Angus?"

"Look Jack, this is a messy situation. Politicians are involved now."

"I don't see it as messy at all. My asset stopped a nuclear attack. She is on our side. I want her back. What's messy about that?"

Angus let out a deep breath into the receiver. "Can I be completely honest with you?"

"I wish you would."

"Those terrorist attacks all over the country have everyone screaming for blood. The Russian hack has us on the brink of war."

"It wasn't a Russian hack. It was the terrorists making everyone think it was the Russians as a diversion. Are all your people stupid enough to fall for that remote-server trick? Do I need to explain to you how it works?"

"No, of course not. But that's what was leaked to the press. Perception is reality. It doesn't matter if it's true or not. Everyone wants blood. The government has to be seen as delivering it. With such fragmented attacks involving so many groups, no one knows where to strike back, so the Russians have become the target of everyone's anger. We have our nukes on alert."

"What the hell does that have to do with you people snatching my asset?"

"Those attacks caught every agency with their pants down. Most of those terrorists were on watch lists. You and I both know that watch lists are largely propaganda to satisfy the public. The lists don't mean squat if the people on them weren't stopped before they launch attacks. They weren't. Everyone from the FBI to the NSA to Justice dropped the ball."

"That's because they're all too busy spying on Americans instead of doing their job," Jack said. "There are a lot of dedicated people there—or at least there used to be—"

"You're right, Jack, but look, the agencies need to shift public anger from them by putting the blame on something other than radical Islamic terrorism. They needed a sacrificial lamb.

"That girl is a nobody. She's just a bartender who grew up in a trailer park. It's easy for them to paint her as a right-wing terrorist. That fits the narrative they want to push—a white female terrorist who isn't Muslim. That fits their political agenda perfectly, so they've latched on to her with their claws and they aren't going to let go.

"They caught her with a knife, an unregistered gun, no permit to carry it, and an unlicensed suppressor. That's a federal offense in and of itself. That fits the picture they intend to paint. Once they get a confession out of her, that will redirect everyone's anger to her, rather than Islam. If they hang her as a traitor and terrorist that will cement public opinion that it's right-wing terrorism, and not Islamic radicalism that's to blame. That's what they want to push to the public.

"You know as well as I do, Jack, that sometimes sacrifices have to be made to keep the public happy. She's the sacrifice. You need to let it go. The public perception is more important."

Jack was so angry he could hardly speak. "So you want to fry the very person who saved the country from a nuclear attack? Are you fucking kidding me!"

"Calm down, Jack. It's necessary for the good of—"

"That girl is my asset," Jack said in a menacing voice. "Not yours, mine. What would your life be like right now had the nuke gone off in New York City?"

"Well, I—"

"I'm done fucking around, here, Angus. Here is what you're going to do. You're going to get the people who have her to release her. I don't give a fuck which agency has her. You are going to get them to let her go. At the same time, you are going to bless her so that she is never touched again. Do you hear me?"

"You expect her to be blessed? I don't know that I can—"

"You can and you will. You're also going to have the feds issue her a license to carry any goddamn weapon she wants to. Got that? She uses those weapons to fight for us."

"All I can do, Jack, is see if—"

"I don't think you understand, Angus. I'm not asking, I'm telling. Your ass, and the asses of a lot of people above your pay grade, are on the line right here, right now, and my finger is on the trigger.

"There are a lot of brave, unsung heroes working in those agencies. You used to be one of them. But there are also a lot of fucking assholes shifting the priorities of those intel agencies to their political schemes. Those rotten apples don't give a goddamn about the country, they only care about political ends. If I pull the trigger a lot of those agencies are going to come crashing down. Including yours. Maybe it's time that happens—"

"All right, Jack, calm down, calm down. There is no reason to get crazy. I'll see what I can do."

"You're not going to 'see what you can do,' Angus, you're going to fucking do it, period. I'm not playing games here.

"I want Angela Constantine released. I want her name cleared. I want her blessed. I want her licensed to carry anything, including a goddamn rocket launcher if she wants one so that no one can pull this crap again. And I want everyone—everyone—to leave her the hell alone from now on. Make one misstep here, Angus, and it's all over for you and a lot of other people. Is that clear?"

"Yes, all right, that's clear. Let me go and get to work on this. But Jack, my people aren't the ones who have her. I'm not running this show. I'll need to drill down and find out exactly who is involved, what their game is, and then pull rank where I can and where I can't, I'll have to make some serious threats to get everyone marching to the same drum."

Jack switched to a calm, quiet tone. "All right, Angus. You do that. I'm going to sit right here with eyes on that building. If one of those snipers pulls a trigger on me, or if anyone lays a finger on my asset, or they try to run to ground with her, or you don't get her out of this exactly as I say—and right bloody now—you are going down, your agency is going down, and a whole lot of other people and agencies are going to find themselves in the middle of a wildfire they can't control.

"I came back from the dead to save Angela Constantine. That should tell you how serious I am. I've never threatened you before, Angus—you know that—but I'm threatening you now. I think you know I'm not bluffing."

"No, Jack, if there's the one thing I know about you it's that you don't bluff. But please, this is going to take me some time to unwind."

"Do you have the number of this phone?"

"Yes."

"You go unwind it and then call me. I'm not going anywhere until this is resolved. And Angus, the longer I sit here, the itchier my trigger finger is going to get."

He hung up without waiting for a response.

As Jack sat in his car, watching the federal building, he fumed as he thought about what they were putting Angela through. It was Saturday, so no one went into the federal building, but there were other businesses open. All day long people came and went. The snipers on top of the federal building had vanished shortly after Jack's call with Angus ended.

But still, Angela didn't come out. He knew how terrifying those people could be in an interrogation. He had to smile to himself. He guessed they couldn't hold a candle to how terrifying Angela was at running an interrogation.

Angus called every few hours to assure Jack that he was working on it. Gradually, over the course of those calls, the man warmed up to Jack and little by little came to realize he wanted to be working on the same side as Jack—the right side. Jack thought it sounded like Angus gradually came to remember the kind of man he used to be, and why he had wanted his job.

Politics were a plague to dedicated agents like Angus, but he had to play the game. Over time it was corrosive. What was going on with Angela Constantine for political reasons was more than wrong and had nothing to do with legitimate national security. Throughout the day, Angus became ever more intolerant of it. Jack assumed that part of the reason was that Angus was encountering resistance, and Angus didn't appreciate resistance. He expected his calls to be taken and his orders to be followed.

In early evening, Angus called again.

"I'm still working on it, Jack. Sit tight. I'm going to get this straightened out, I swear. I'm on your side, here."

"Right now, I'm on Angela's side. I want this ended."

"I know, I know. Please understand, it's more complicated than you realize. I'm dealing with a lot of hotheads who think that executing her as a traitor will make their careers. They're still interrogating her. They want a quick conviction and execution."

"She's innocent. What could they possibly get out of her?"

"Honestly? They are pushing her to sign a confession. So far, they haven't let her rest or have any water. So far, though, they've only gotten three words out of her."

"What three words?"

"The only thing she's said to them—the only thing—is 'Go fuck yourself.' That is one tough girl."

Jack had to smile. "I know. Get her out of there, Angus."

"I'll call back as soon as I've cracked this nut and gotten everyone down on the carpet at my feet."

After he hung up, Jack rubbed his eyes as he slid down in his seat a little and then folded his arms. He was tired, worried, angry, and frustrated. He knew that he had to rely on Angus's sense of self-preservation.

Sometime in the late evening, Dvora called. She told him that they were picking up a lot of internal friction between agencies. She said that whatever was going on behind the scenes, it was big.

"They want a scapegoat," he told her. "Now that they have a rope around her neck they don't want to let go."

"Let me know as soon as you get her out."

Jack promised he would, and then went back to waiting.

A little after midnight, his phone rang again.

He answered it immediately.

FIFTY-SEVEN

Agent Lumley placed the knuckles of his fists on the far side of the table and leaned in, his face hovering in close to hers. Angela was handcuffed to the chair she was in, so there wasn't much she could do about it.

"I've about had it with you, Constantine."

Angela didn't say anything.

He slapped her hard enough that she thought it might have loosened some teeth. "You're a worthless human being."

She wiped the blood running from the corner of her mouth on her shoulder.

He straightened and took a long swig of water from a half-full bottle. He slammed the bottle down on the table in front of her.

"Thirsty?"

Angela stared off at nothing. She didn't answer. With her wrists handcuffed behind her back she wouldn't have been able to take the water bottle even if he had allowed it.

She was so thirsty that that was about all she could think about. Her tongue felt like it was turning to paste. She tried not to think about it. When she'd been in the hospital they hadn't let her drink anything for a time. They had given her ice chips. She would love to have some ice chips.

She was dead tired, but her anger, at a continual slow simmer, kept her awake. That, and the way they yelled at her nonstop, asking, demanding that she admit her part in the terror group. The agents had waved a confession in front of her face countless times, promising her that if she would sign it, then she could have all the water she wanted and they would let her lie down on a bed and get some sleep.

Angela didn't believe there was any bed to sleep on. She'd often been in the federal building delivering and picking up courier packages for lawyers. She had been in most of the rooms, or at least walked by them and seen inside.

These men were holding her down in the basement. She'd never been in the basement before. It looked like nothing more than a utility room of some sort. The walls and concrete floor were painted gray. Folding chairs and tables were stacked against the wall behind her. The lighting was two humming fluorescent fixtures.

They had opened one of those tables and sat her down on one side of it. They handcuffed her arms behind her back and her legs to the chair. Agents Goddard, Holgado, and Lumley usually faced her from the other side of the long table. Sometimes, though, one of them would circle around behind her and grab her by her hair to tip her face up to look at the one yelling at her nonstop.

They all had long since shed their coats and ties and opened the collars of their white shirts. They all had sidearms but no badges on their belts. They had never said what agency they were with and she never asked, because, as far as Angela was concerned, they were all basically the same people. She had always known it was best to avoid any kind of authority, like the police, but she had no way to avoid these men.

Angela had, at one point, figured them out, and figured out what they were doing. They had come in here first in response to the bomb she and Jack had found. Since they were here first, they wanted to be the ones to break her and then take her back, like a pig tied to a pole.

They wanted to be the heroes bringing her in. If they took her back to Washington before they got what they wanted out of her, then someone else would snatch her away and get to be the hero. Someone else would have a chance to get the credit for getting her to confess to being a terrorist.

She knew from the outset that it was pointless to answer their questions or talk to them. This whole thing was absurd. These men didn't care about the truth. They only cared about getting a confession out of her so they could play the hero and advance their own stock within their agency.

Angela was, for the most part, no longer listening to them. They had nothing important or truthful to say. She had dealt with abusive men before who only wanted what they wanted from a woman who was weaker than they were. She did what she had learned to do when she was little. She let her mind go to another place. Her body was there in that basement room while the three men questioned her, accused her, yelled at her, threatened her, smacked her. It didn't matter. She was gone.

She might as well have been on the moon.

Every once in a while, one of them, or occasionally two of them, would leave the room to take a phone call. She could hear their voices out in the stairwell, but she couldn't tell what they were saying.

Agent Lumley returned to the other side of the table and slammed the confession down in front of her again.

"What do you say, Constantine? If you sign this confession, you can have a nice drink of water and finally get some rest. Most of all, you'll be doing the right thing for a change."

Angela came back from that faraway place to look up at him.

"Go fuck yourself."

He straightened, his jaw clenching.

"How many people would have died, Constantine?" Agent Goddard asked for about the thousandth time.

She wanted to say that she was the one who had prevented those deaths, but she didn't. They didn't want to hear it. They had their own plan. That plan was to get her to confess to being a terrorist so they could be heroes.

"You should be thankful we stopped you when we did," Agent Goddard said. "You would have been a murderer. What does that say about you? You should be grateful we stopped you from becoming that kind of person."

"If you sign the confession," Agent Holgado said, somewhat more gently, "it's kind of like going to confession at the church and confessing your sins to the priest, who then asks God to absolve you of those sins. It cleanses your soul. That's what we're doing here. We're like priests, helping you to cleanse your soul.

"Are you Catholic, Constantine? Your name is Italian, so I think maybe you are, so you know what we're talking about. You know we're only trying to help you. Confessing your sins is your only way to salvation."

Angela was already back in her distant place. These men were nothing but meaningless voices mumbling in the distance.

Agent Lumley's phone rang. He pulled it off the clip on his belt and glanced at the caller ID.

"I gotta take this," he told the other two.

He went out of the room, but had been gone for only a short time when he stuck his head back in the door.

"Both of you, get out here."

Angela was suddenly alone for the first time since they'd thrown her in the back of that black SUV. It was the first time that at least one of them wasn't in the room hammering away at her. Sometimes one or two of them left for quite a while. She figured that they had gone out to snatch a little sleep while one of the others took a shift working on her, keeping her awake. But they never left her completely alone.

They were gone for so long that Angela's eyes closed and she nodded off. Because they had her handcuffed to the chair she couldn't fall, so when her eyes closed her head sagged forward as she dozed off.

She didn't know how long she had been asleep when they came back in, but it seemed like it was at least a couple of hours—not nearly as much sleep as she needed, but welcomed, nonetheless.

When Agent Holgado unlocked her handcuffs and leg-irons, she didn't know what was going on. She wouldn't put it past them to beat her to death down in that basement and say she tried to escape.

Agent Lumley put a full bottle of water down in front of her. Angela rubbed her wrists as she looked up at him. She suspected the water was a trick, or more likely drugged.

He opened it and gulped down nearly half of it, then set it down in front of her again. "There. It's not poisoned. Go ahead and have a drink."

His voice sounded different. He sounded defeated. The other two looked rather sheepish as well.

Angela didn't trust any of them, and she was not about to take the water no matter how thirsty she was.

"Some new information has come to light." Agent Goddard ran his hand back over his buzz-cut hair. "We've just learned that you had absolutely nothing to do with those terrorists. This was all a big mistake due to . . . an abundance of caution."

Angela was still rubbing her bruised wrists. She didn't say anything.

Four more men in dark suits and ties came into the room and approached the other side of the table to face Angela.

"You're free to go," one of them said in an official tone. "You have been cleared of any wrongdoing."

"It seems that you have friends in very high places," Agent Goddard said. "A guardian angel."

Angela didn't trust any of them. She didn't get up. She didn't say anything.

One of the four new men pulled something from the breast pocket of his dark suit coat. It was about the size of a credit card. When he set it down it sounded like plastic, too. He slid it across the table to her.

She glanced down just long enough to see her photo on it. Holographic seals partially covered her face and signatures she couldn't read. She saw the word "Federal" but couldn't read the rest of it.

Another of the four men in suits, a big black guy with a shaved head, laid her Walther P22 down on the table beside the card with her photo. Her gun still had the suppressor on it.

"Here is your weapon back, Ms. Constantine," he said. "Nice choice, by the way. You don't have to worry about overpenetration, yet lethal if you know what you're doing, and with the subsonic rounds it's loaded with, I would guess you do."

She didn't say anything. She didn't want to take the weapon and give them an excuse to shoot her. She stayed in the chair.

He gestured to the card and went on. "That's a special federal weapons permit. It authorizes you to carry any gun you choose. That includes things like suppressors and fully automatic weapons. Anything. And of course, your knife. Another smart choice."

He was sounding more like a weapons instructor than anything else.

One of the other men, another big black guy in a dark suit that fit him well, handed over her knife, handle-first. She stared at it in his hand for a moment, then took it and slid it down into the sheath in her boot.

Agent Lumley, looking beat, gestured to her gun and the permit card. "It's not a trick. You can have your weapon back. You've been completely cleared of all charges. We'll escort you safely out of the building. I would assume that it's your guardian angel who is waiting outside for you."

Angela finally stood. Keeping her eyes on Lumley, she picked up the gun and slid it back into her grandfather's holster at the small of her back. She could tell by the weight that it was loaded.

She held her hand out, palm up.

"Oh," one of the other men said. He reached in the side pocket of his suit jacket and brought out three loaded magazines. He placed them in her palm. Angela slid them into a pocket.

She picked up the federal weapons permit, glanced at it briefly, and then slipped it into her back, left pocket.

With the four new men in front and the three agents who had been interrogating her following behind, they led her up the stairs and out of the building. It was somewhere in the middle of the night. She'd lost track of time.

At the top of the stairs, Agent Lumley grabbed her wrist to stop her.

In a heartbeat she reversed the grip, levered his hand over, and twisted it to the side, stopping just before it broke the bones. He went to one knee, contorting his body sideways to try to take the pressure off his wrist. If he tried anything she could break it.

"Jesus, Constantine, I was only going to say 'no hard feelings.' "

Still holding his hand twisted within a hairsbreadth of breaking bones, she leaned down toward him. "Use some mouthwash, would you, Lumley? Your breath smells like dick."

A couple of the men in dark suits chuckled.

"Angela." It was a voice behind her that she recognized. "Leave him be and let's go."

Angela released Agent Lumley and after giving him a dark look turned to see a welcome face. It was Jack.

He smiled, and everything suddenly seemed all right.

The dread of what was to become of her suddenly lifted. He was the friend in high places, her guardian angel.

FIFTY-EIGHT

As Jack led her down the steps, they left the agents standing up at the top of the stairs in front of the dark federal building lit by streetlights. The three who had been interrogating her looked like schoolboys who had been reprimanded by nuns and sent to Mother Superior's office.

They walked calmly to Jack's car, parked on a side street. He held the door for her and shut it after she sat down. She wasn't used to men with manners. Jack had manners.

"What time is it?" she asked as she looked around the dark streets.

"It's about one thirty," he said as he pulled away from the curb. "I'm sorry it took so long. I was trying my best to get you out of there sooner."

"It's okay," she said. "I'm used to getting slapped around by guys."

"I'm glad they didn't do worse. I'm especially relieved they didn't take you to Washington. It would have greatly complicated matters if you'd have gone down that rabbit hole."

Angela rode in silence for moment.

"They said that I have a friend in high places. They said that friend vouched for me."

Jack smiled along with a one-shoulder shrug. "I talked to some people and convinced them to do the right thing and release you."

"You told me that you were off the grid and everyone thought you were dead. You would have had to come out of the shadows to get me out of there. That's bound to cause you problems."

He glanced over at her. "Getting you released was more important to me than staying dead. They would have fed you to the wolves. I'm guessing they wanted you to sign a confession?"

"Yeah, they did. I could tell they thought this would make them big shots. But I wouldn't do it."

"In the end, they would have simply signed your name and in short order you would have been tried, convicted, and executed.

"They would have given a big press announcement that they had captured the right-wing terrorist mastermind behind the recent attacks. The case would be sealed a few tiers above top secret. No one would know the truth.

"They would not have mentioned a word about any atomic bomb. With you dead and buried, and that confession sealed, no one would ever see it or dispute it, that would have been the end of the story, the end of Angela Constantine."

"Except those assholes who got my 'confession' would end up heroes."

He smiled again. "That's the game they were playing. None of the intel agencies knew squat about the nuke until we told them about it, so to redeem themselves they needed a scapegoat."

Angela frowned over at Jack as he drove through the dark, deserted streets. "What did you have to do to get me away from them?"

"I vouched for you—let them know you were the one who actually stopped the terrorist."

Angela looked out at the dark, empty streets. "I think you must have done something more than that."

"Hey, let me see the card they gave you," he said, changing the subject.

Angela pulled it out of her back pocket and handed it over. "What, exactly, is this, anyway?"

He looked at it a moment and then handed it back. "It's a very special federal permit. Think of it as a double-oh-seven kind of thing. It means you can legally carry any weapon you want. Your suppressor is now legal. You can carry a machine gun if you want. With that permit you could get on an airplane with a gun."

"Wow," she said in a whisper as she studied the card.

"Keep the phone number on the back in a safe place. Commit the number of the card on the front to memory. If you ever lose the card you can call, give them that number, and get a replacement. It's good for life, too. Did they also tell you that you've been blessed?"

Angela scrunched up her nose. "Blessed? No, they didn't mention that. What does that mean?"

"It means you've been vetted and given clearance at the highest levels. If there is ever an investigation of something, you will be left out of it. You're already blessed. It will keep anyone from going after you again."

She looked at his face lit by the instrument panel.

"Why would you do all this for me, Jack?"

"Because you're a very special person, Angela. You can recognize killers, and you stopped an atomic bomb from going off in America. My ability is to see in people's eyes that they can recognize killers. That's what I do. That's all I can do.

"But you are a whole order of magnitude more than any other person I've found with that ability. I know because I've worked with people like that for a very long time. Like I say, you're a very special person, Angela."

She looked down at her hands in her lap for a long moment.

"Not so special. I was born broken."

He frowned over at her. "What are you talking about?"

"My mother used all kinds of drugs when she was pregnant with me. Whoever my father was would have been a drug addict as well. All those drugs in her system when she was pregnant with me messed me up. I'm not like normal people. I'm a freak."

Jack was silent, thinking about it as they drove through the city toward the bar.

Finally he said, "I don't know if that's true, Angela. Your natural genetic ability may simply be more advanced than it is in other people—like people who are born smarter, with a higher IQ than anyone else. You may be the first of a better kind of human—better than those of us who can't do what you can. You're special, Angela. Don't you ever forget that, and don't you ever doubt it. You're not a freak. The world needs you."

"You mean you want to use me for what you do, like you do in Israel. Use me like the other people you find who can recognize killers?"

"None of them ever knew what killers had done, or what they were thinking. Only you, Angela, can see into their minds. That's incredibly special."

"Not so special," she said as she looked out her window again. "Seeing into the minds of killers is like being part of their world of madness. Seeing the things they've done and how it makes them feel is not special. It's a curse. I have to live with the things I've seen.

"I see those things when I try to go to sleep. I see them in my sleep.

"It's a lonely kind of insanity."

"I can only imagine," he said in soft consolation.

When they got to the bar where her truck was parked, the bar was just closing.

"Nate was the one who told me what happened to you. He will want to know that you've been released and that you're safe."

"Would you mind going in and telling him? I'm really tired." She hesitated. "Besides, I'm kind of embarrassed that he saw me being handcuffed and carried away like that."

"Sure," Jack said. "Wait while I run in and tell him so I can follow you to make sure you make it home safely. But you shouldn't be embarrassed. You did nothing wrong. They did."

Sitting in her truck waiting, Angela saw Nate pop his head out of the door with Jack and wave. She waved back.

She rolled down the window when Jack reached the side of her truck.

"He was pretty relieved," Jack told her. "He was really worried for you."

She glanced back at the bar. "He's a nice guy."

"Maybe the guy for you?" Jack asked.

"I'm not a nice girl," she said as she started the truck.

She was still wired from her anger over those men snatching her, so at least that kept her awake on the ride home. At her road off the highway, after she'd driven her truck in, Jack helped her put the cable back up across her drive. She didn't think she had the strength to do it by herself. Now that she was home and safe, her eyes kept closing.

"Your second wind is running out," he told her. "Get some rest."

"What's this?" she asked as he handed her a phone.

"It's a disposable phone no agency knows about, so they won't be listening in on it. It has my number programmed in. Just hit the first speed dial if you need me."

Angela nodded. "I'll call you tomorrow."

"Have a good sleep, Angela. We'll talk then."

He waited until he saw her truck go up the road through a meadow and then vanish into the trees. Twin mountains, lit by the moonlight, looked to be welcoming her home.

FIFTY-NINE

Angela was in the sleep of the dead when her eyes suddenly popped open and she sat bolt upright in bed.

She didn't know why, but her heart was hammering.

The room was pitch black. She couldn't have been asleep for more than an hour or two. It was still somewhere in the middle of the night.

She had been so tired she hadn't bothered to shower or take off her makeup. She simply took off everything but her panties and fell into bed. She had been asleep before she'd had a chance to savor the feel of being all alone in her own bed in her own house.

Even though she was suddenly awake, her brain was still having trouble emerging from a mental fog of sleep deprivation. She couldn't quite figure out what had made her wake up so suddenly. For a fraction of a second, she thought that maybe she was dreaming. But as soon as she'd had the thought, she already knew she wasn't dreaming.

Something was wrong.

In her dead-tired state, her normal thought process wasn't up to speed and she just couldn't figure out what was out of place.

She carefully put her bare feet on the floor and stood in one fluid, quiet motion. She waited for a second, listening, thinking that maybe it had been a deer coming close to the house. Still in somewhat of a mental haze, she took the three silent, familiar steps to the light switch at the right side of the doorway.

Wiping her face with her left hand, trying to banish the sleep from her eyes, she turned on the light with her other hand.

There was a man standing in the doorway.

A big man.

Angela froze, standing naked except for her panties right in front of him. A slow smile contorted his cruel features as he looked down the length of her.

He had on a baggy, collarless, V-neck, long-sleeved linen shirt. His loose-fitting pants seemed to be made of the same light linen material. His hair and beard were both black and short, framing his compacted, square features and the deep lines of his face. Even though he had on a shirt, she could tell by his bull neck and the width of him that he was big-boned and heavily muscled.

She had seen his photo. Two of them, in fact. She knew without a doubt that this was the international serial killer, Cassiel Aykhan Corekan.

Angela had seen plenty of scary guys. Cassiel was the king of scary.

She wasn't sure what other people saw when they looked at this man, but what she saw was a deadly predator, a killer without a shred of remorse or mercy. This was death itself in the form of a living man.

Standing close in front of this powerful figure, looking into his dark eyes, she was overwhelmed with images flooding through her mind. Scene after scene of him murdering people flashed past her mind's eye at lightning speed, each one gruesome, each person she saw in the grip of horror under this ruthless monster.

And then those scenes rushing past started to slow. They came to a stop on her grandparents.

Angela stood frozen, her eyes wide, as she stared up into this man's eyes, stared into the vision of him with Vito and Gabriella on their knees, facing away from him. Angela saw Cassiel step forward and shoot her grandfather in the back of the head. As simple as that, the man that had meant so much to her was dead. He collapsed into the tall, dusty weeds beside the road.

Her grandmother was on her knees beside him. She was weeping silently. Her head was bowed and her hands were together in prayer. Cassiel put the barrel of his gun to the base of her skull and pulled the trigger. There was a bang and a flash. She fell beside her beloved husband.

Cassiel had been in a hurry. For that reason only he hadn't made their death as grisly as most of the others. He had simply wanted to dispatch family members of people with the vision to recognize killers. It was not mercy. He was in a hurry to go rape a young woman he had tied up in a basement in a nearby town. It was all he could think about. He kept getting an erection every time he thought about her and what he was going to do to her. But first, he wanted to eliminate these two members of the Constantine family.

In that instant, Angela's grandparents had ceased to exist. Their light went out of her world. Her whole life had been cast into darkness.

Angela could feel tears running down her face.

" 'Dark Angel,' " Cassiel said in a mean, gravelly voice as he read the tattoo across her throat. He reached out and gently took hold of her left nipple between a thumb and finger. He could see in her eyes that she recognized him as a killer. "I knew that those four fools wouldn't be able to kill a woman like you. It takes a man like me to do that. And I knew that a woman like you would be living in this remote place your grandparents built."

Terror shredded her ability to think. She couldn't make herself move as he stood towering over her, rolling her nipple in his fingers, smiling, imagining all the things he would do with her before he killed her.

"I have at last come back for you, my little angel."

Angela finally began to form thoughts. She realized that she had to do something or she was going to die a long and agonizing death.

Her boots with her knife were on the other side of him, at the foot of the bed, so she abruptly turned to dive for the gun she kept on her nightstand. The gun wasn't there. He must have taken it.

He slammed into her from behind. His big arms wrapped her in a bear hug. He lifted her from her feet.

As panic brought her fully awake, she remembered Nate's lessons. She knew she had three seconds to live.

The bear of a man bent her forward, his feet spread as he walked her toward the bed, toward her death.

Bent forward, Angela shifted her hips to the left, reached back with her right hand, and forcefully grabbed his genitals. She gritted her teeth and abruptly twisted them with every fiber of her strength.

He might have been big and strong, but he was no less vulnerable down there.

Cassiel let out a surprised cry as he reflexively released the bear hug to break away from the source of sudden pain. As soon as he did, Angela spun around and with a backhanded swing hit him on the side of his bull neck as hard as she could, shocking his carotid artery.

It stunned him momentarily. He staggered back, drunkenly, his knees nearly buckling. It gave her just enough time and space to dart past him and out through the bedroom doorway before he fully recovered.

She had plenty more guns in the basement, but she kept the basement door locked. But even if she did manage to unlock the door in time, those guns were all new and none of them were loaded. There was no way to load one of them before he would be on her.

She briefly considered running into the kitchen to grab a knife. But if Cassiel had her gun from the nightstand he would simply shoot her. He was an expert shot. He would undoubtedly shoot to cripple so she couldn't get away. Then he could start in on her with his sick desires.

Even if he didn't have a gun, he was experienced at knife fights. Using a knife was his preferred way to murder people, so he was deadly with an edged weapon. So was Angela, but it would be a risky gamble to grab a knife from the kitchen and get into a knife fight with someone that big, powerful, and experienced. If he got the knife away from her she would be dead, but not quickly.

The keys to her truck were back in the bedroom. Even if she had them, she didn't think there would be any way to unlock it, get in, and get it started before Cassiel was able to stop her.

Angela rejected all those options in a fraction of a second and instead bolted out the back door. She snatched a quick look over her shoulder as she leaped down onto the hard ground and saw him coming out of the house right behind her. In the light of the full moon she could see that he had a knife in his fist. His jaw was clenched in rage. She told herself that at least it wasn't a gun.

Angela only had on panties. Her feet were bare. Running outside barefooted was risky.

She didn't have a choice. She was committed.

SIXTY

Angela knew that her only chance was to somehow even the odds. As she ran, she glanced up at the twin mountains rising up in the moonlight. Before the trail split, she quickly made her choice and raced up the trail to the right, up Grandfather Mountain.

She'd climbed that trail so often she could probably do it in the dark. The moonlight certainly helped. But running was different. She had to make split-second decisions as she raced into the night. Being barefoot made each of those split-second decisions potentially fatal.

As she plunged into the woods, Cassiel was right behind her. He wasn't quite close enough to grab her, but he was right there if she faltered for even a second. He yelled at her to stop, promising to slice to her throat for a quick end rather than a night of the worst he could do.

She knew from the visions when she had looked into his eyes what kinds of things he liked to do. That made her run faster.

She used outcroppings that she knew rose from the forest floor, jumping from one to the next, avoiding as much as possible running across ground littered with everything from pine needles to sticks to pinecones. She put her thoughts about the man chasing her out of her mind and focused on the task at hand. She had climbed this trail more times than she could remember. She knew every rock, every tree so well she would have been able to run it through her mind without forgetting an inch of the trail.

She let her conscious thoughts go and instead let her inner mind take over. The trail had long ago been indelibly imprinted there. She tried not to think of where she had to step. Instead, she raced along the trail, putting every foot in the exact right place without being aware she was doing it. As the trail began to climb, she knew ahead of time which foot she needed to use in each spot so as not to get crossed up.

Cassiel didn't know the trail, and since he was running he couldn't see where he was going very well. He stumbled a few times, but recovered quickly. As Angela ran past a balsam fir, she grabbed a bough that hung across the path. She pulled it with her, then let it go to spring back and smack him in the face. He growled in rage as he slashed his arms to get past it.

She had to run up a stream for a brief distance to get to the trail on the opposite side. Ordinarily she would have danced across the dry rocks sticking up out of the water, jumping from one to another, but with a killer right behind her there was no time to pick those places to step.

The water was only six to eight inches deep, but it was freezing cold, and in places smooth rock ledge under the water was slimy and slippery. She lost her footing and went to one knee on one of those smooth, slippery spots, but kept her balance and immediately got up and kept going. Cassiel slipped and fell on his ass. That gained her a few precious seconds.

When she reached the trail on the far side of the stream, she jumped up out of the water onto the mossy bank and ran into the forest on a trail that was mostly a cushion of pine needles. The trail was also littered with small bits of branches and sticks. They hurt when her feet landed on them. She had no choice but to ignore the pain.

She knew where there were tree roots across the path. She had to be careful lest she trip over one and fall. When she reached a wet, low-lying area where there were too many roots to miss, she danced over the tops of fatter roots worn smooth from the countless times she had done the same thing while wearing boots.

Her grandfather had first taken her on this trail when she had been a little girl. She'd often climbed one of the two mountains with her grandmother to have a picnic at the top while enjoying a view out on the world. The man chasing her had murdered them both.

In the moonlight Angela saw familiar landmarks of rock formations and the curving limb of an oak that let her know which way the trail was going to turn before she even got there. That helped her stay ahead of the big man in boots pursuing her. They might as well have been the only two people in the world. There was no one anywhere near enough to hear her call for help. If he caught her and started cutting on her with that knife, only Grandfather Mountain would hear her screams.

When she reached the maple with a low limb that dipped down and stuck out over the trail, she knew she had to make a sharp left up the trail as it climbed more sharply over rock formations. Her grandfather had been the one who had scouted and built the trail, long before she had even been born. Now she was using his trail up the mountain to try to escape a killer.

She knew that the rock configuration of broken granite close to the left side of the trail meant she was rapidly approaching a fork. The fork to the left continued to the top. The one to the right was a gentler trail that circled both mountains down lower, going past small ponds.

She took the one to the left. It was a hard climb. She hoped that her experience could outpace his easier time with boots. Since he was somewhat older, possibly in his late forties, she was also hoping to get him winded with the climb. If she could lose him, she could go down the back side of the mountain and then take a smaller side trail that led back to the house, where she could get a gun.

In the dark, he might not be able to follow that trail. Although, there was a full moon high overhead. Even with the full moon, though, the woods occasionally fell darker in denser areas.

Angela scrambled along a narrow ledge, staying close to the wall that rose vertically on her left. To her right the tops of trees rose from far below. It was a dangerous place to be careless. When she reached the far side of the wall of rock, the trail made a sharp left, following the granite formations.

When she rounded the corner, she spotted a length of dead limb. It was a little bigger around than her wrist and maybe five feet long. Cassiel was only seconds behind her. Angela knew it might be her only chance. She snatched up the deadwood, turned, and cocked her arm back.

As Cassiel rushed around the corner into view, Angela took a mighty swing. He hadn't expected her to be standing right there in front of him. Angela grunted as she put all her power behind the swing. The dead limb caught him square across the face. The wood was partially rotten, so it splintered and broke in half across his face.

Even so, it was still strong enough to break his nose and crush the bone around his left eye socket. A four-inch splinter speared into his right eye. He put his hands up to his face as he screamed in pain and rage.

Even as she was still in the follow-through of her swing, he had come to a dead stop as his hands went to his injured face. Angela didn't waste the opportunity. As she came around she side-kicked him in the knee of one leg. The kick wasn't powerful enough or at the right angle to break his knee, but it was enough to knock that leg out from under him.

Cassiel slipped, did an ungainly pirouette on his other leg, and toppled over the side of the rock face.

Angela stepped carefully forward to peer over the edge to see him drop maybe thirty feet and then tumble down a broken boulder field from granite that had sheared off the cliff over the millennia. The rocks of that boulder field were sharp.

It was hard to tell for sure because all the trees were shading the moonlight, but she thought she saw him sprawled near the lower trail that went around the mountain. He was moving, but he didn't seem able to get up.

Angela knew she could probably make it back to the cabin well ahead of him if he did manage to get up. But it was possible that he could still see and that he might get up and cut her off. This might be her one and only chance.

In that moment of hesitation, she again saw in her mind's eye her grandparents kneeling in the dusty weeds at the side of the road as he shot them both in the back of the head.

Her rage overtook everything else and made up her mind for her. She raced back down the trail to the fork and then took the lower trail. All she could think about was that she finally had the man who had killed them.

When she made it down the trail and found Cassiel, he had obviously broken both legs, and by the way he twisted his upper body, possibly his spine. One leg was broken below the knee. A splintered tibia jutted through his bloody pant leg. His other foot was bent back at an impossible angle. He was on his back, writhing in pain, his face covered in blood. Once she saw him she realized he couldn't see anything.

Angela picked up a jagged, heavy chunk of granite and leaped onto him, straddling his chest. He let out a grunt as she landed. He waved his arms, blindly trying to protect himself from what he couldn't see.

When his waving arms swung wide open, Angela saw her opening and struck. She slammed the heavy rock down into his face. The chunk of granite was big enough that the weight and her strength behind the blow caved in the center of his face. Blood shot out to either side. A groan of pain gurgled out as his arms dropped wide apart and he went still.

Angela had always wanted to have the man who had killed her grandparents down in the basement for days and days while she extracted vengeance.

But now that she had downed him, her blind rage took over. She couldn't think of anything else but how much she hated this man, how he had come into her life to destroy the only two people she had ever truly loved.

She used both hands to lift the rock and smash it down on his head. The rock was heavy, but she was glad to have the weight to help her smash his big, solid head.

After the third hit, his jawbone skewed off to one side. She could see his teeth sticking up amid a mass of bloody pulp. She brought the rock down again, breaking those teeth from his jaw, breaking the jaw.

She cried in fury as she lifted the rock over and over, crashing it down on him. Tears streamed down her face as she used that rock to crush the head of the monster who had killed her grandparents and so many other innocent people.

She didn't know how long she straddled the man who had haunted her for years, the man she had fantasized about killing for years. She wept as vengeance carried her away and she pounded away at his skull.

Eventually, sobbing with emotion, she stopped.

This man, of all men, belonged down the hell hole her grandfather had found and built his cabin over, the cabin that he and Angela's grandmother had left to her. The place they wanted her to have.

She stared down at what was left of Cassiel's misshapen head. His face was unrecognizable. The rock had split his skull open. Jagged white bone stuck out through the scalp in places. Through those gaps, she could see his brain.

Angela pushed her fingers down into the hot mess to grip the bone. She cried out with the effort of pulling his skull the rest of the way open. The bone made cracking noises as it came apart. She reached in and pushed the brain to one side, and then with her other hand she gripped the spinal cord to help rip the brain from it so she could lift it out.

Angela sat there, straddling his still, barrel chest, holding up the brain, the nerve center, of the monster she had bested. Cranial fluid and coagulating blood dripped in warm globs off her hands. Some of it ran down her arms to hang off her elbows in long strings.

As she sat there, holding his brain in her hands, staring at it, an unexpected flow of visions, his visions, raced through that connection with her hands and into her own mind.

Angela sat, unblinking, as images flooded through her consciousness. They were unlike the visions she got from looking into a killer's eyes, those visions of savage acts of murder.

A person's eyes, she had heard it said, were a window into their soul. That was what it felt like when she looked into their eyes—like looking into their dark souls and seeing the black marks that killing had left on those souls.

This was completely different. These were not conscious thoughts of conscious acts. She sat transfixed at these images. It was unlike anything she had experienced before.

In her own mind she was witnessing a stream of subconscious impressions. She knew she was not seeing visions, but memories.

The strongest of those images were the most recent memories. They flooded through her mind, unending, disjointed, unbidden, desperate. They were jammed together, memory on top of memory, image on top of image, sensation on top of sensation. She was seeing the final dying thoughts of a human brain as it grasped the inevitable and tried to claw back memories, as if gathering them up to try to save itself from the approaching black abyss.

She was experiencing a mind dying. She could sense the profound desperation. The wish to live. The anger. The fear.

The memories dimmed, held together by connecting threads of thought that started coming apart like wet tissue.

The last visions—leaving a stolen car over a mile away and walking through fields and woods to reach her house, coming inside, seeing her asleep by the light of a small flashlight, and finally the sensation of falling from the cliff—faded away until they were unrecognizable snatches of thoughts.

It all finally ended with a dull pulse of white light, and then there was nothing. Everything was gone.

Angela knew that she had just been inside a human mind as its thoughts died away, as the spark of life left the cells and synapses, as brain tissue transformed into dead, meaningless matter.

She had just felt a soul pass out of existence.

She was amazed at how long those threads of thought and memory had persisted after the body was clearly dead.

Angela sat there in the moonlight for a long time, the dead brain in her hands, reliving over and over those frantic streams of visions. They were not visions of him killing anyone. These visions were completely different. It was like seeing the world through his eyes, through his thoughts, in little snippets of fading memories of recent events.

It left her stunned and wondering at what kind of freak of nature she must be to be able to do such a thing.

It was the craziest, creepiest thing she had ever experienced. And, it was positively exhilarating. She reveled in having killed this man with her bare hands and of the experience of seeing his last, desperate, dying thoughts, knowing she was the one who had brought them to an end.

The monster was dead. She was alive.

After sitting on his dead body for a time, savoring the realization that she had carried out her promise to herself to kill the man who had murdered her grandparents, after she had cried for a time in grief, rage, and relief, her chest no longer heaving with the emotion of it, she finally got up. She was drenched in blood. The blood of the man who had killed Vito and Gabriella.

She was drenched in victory, in glory.

Angela opened her arms, blood dripping from her fingers, as she leaned back to look up at the full moon and howl in triumph.

Angela finally hiked back home and got dressed in some old clothes even though she was still covered in blood.

Then, she put on the boots her grandfather had bought her that day in the thrift store. They were too tight to wear comfortably, but she could wear them. For this, she could wear them.

She retrieved her knife from her boot in the bedroom and collected a bunch of heavy-duty black plastic garbage bags from the kitchen. She picked up a small hatchet her grandfather had used to split kindling. With everything she needed in hand, she went back to the site where Cassiel lay dead.

The monster was far too big and heavy for her to carry him back to the hell hole. So, Angela worked to cut off his arms and legs by disjointing them at his shoulders and hips with her knife. She used the hatchet to chop through tough sinew. She cut the legs into two sections to make them short enough to fit in a plastic bag.

She carried the limbs inside black plastic bags back to her house. The arms were surprisingly heavy, but she found she could carry both in one bag. She unceremoniously tossed it down through the open hatch into the hell hole.

The legs were heavier. She had to take the legs one at a time, each in two pieces to fit in a plastic bag, and threw them down the abyss. The bags contained the blood and kept it from dripping all over her house until she could throw them down the hell hole.

The torso was too heavy to carry, so she gutted it like a deer. Once she had scooped out his intestines and dumped them to the side, she reached in and tore all the organs out of his chest cavity. The guts and organs would be gone within a day, carried away in the stomachs of coyotes and scavenger birds. Bugs would consume any scraps.

She cut off what was left of his head and put it in one black plastic bag, then put the torso in another. She found that she could sling the bag with the torso over her shoulder. It wasn't easy, but it was satisfying work carrying it back.

The most satisfying part, though, was looking at his crushed face as she stood over the hell hole. The jaw was only attached at one side. Everything was largely unrecognizable, except to her, of course, because she knew what she was looking at.

She gripped the remainder of the head by the hair. She held it out over the hell hole for a long, satisfying moment and then let it drop. The black plastic bag she'd carried it in had a couple of large fragments of the skull and various other unrecognizable, gooey bits. She tossed the whole thing down the hole.

After she was finished, she threw every stitch of her clothes down the hole.

It felt like closure to toss in the beloved boots her grandparents had bought her. It seemed only fitting. She had used them to avenge their murder. They were covered in Cassiel's blood.

Once finished, she hosed down the basement and herself, then went upstairs and took a shower.

When she had finished, she got dressed, then called Jack.

Then she sat down on the living room floor to wait.

SIXTY-ONE

The cable was still hooked across the driveway up to Angela's house. Jack had helped her put it up only a few hours earlier. Since it was locked on, he simply parked by the side of the road and got out to walk.

He didn't know why she had called him. All she'd said was "Can you come over to my place?" He had only been asleep himself for a few hours. "Now?" he'd asked. She said, "Yes." Something in her voice made the hairs on his arms stand on end.

While he didn't know what was going on, he realized that there had to be some kind of trouble. The trouble should be over. They had found the nuke, called in help, and prevented the terrorists from detonating it. Angela had been taken into custody by people wanting to use her for their own political ends, but he had put a stop to that.

Everything seemed to be in order. Now, for some reason, it wasn't.

The walk up the road to her house crossed a beautiful meadow. Up ahead, lit by the light of the full moon high overhead, he could see twin mountains. He hadn't seen it before, but he knew that Angela's house was somewhere in the woods at the base of those mountains. They weren't enormous mountains, like out West. Rather, they were the typical, smaller, rounded mountains of the Northeast.

As he left the meadow, he entered a forest of virgin wood. The pine, spruce, and balsams smelled wonderful. He could also see the leaves of maples and an enormous oak gently moving in the light breeze as if welcoming him into an inner sanctum. Those leaves would soon be turning color. He imagined fall would be beautiful in these mountains.

Jack found Angela's house nestled among towering fir trees, right at the base of those twin mountains. It was as idyllic a setting as he could imagine.

He stepped up on the porch of the brick home and knocked on the door. Angela called out for him to come in.

The living room wasn't big, but it looked cozy and inviting. One light in the hall to the left was on but the living room was mostly lit by scented candles.

Despite the comfortable-looking couch and chairs, Angela was sitting cross-legged in the middle of the floor. She had on shorts and was barefooted. Her nails and makeup were freshly done. Her hair was perfect. Her lipstick looked like she was ready for a night on the town.

Jack didn't know what was going on, but she looked to be in an eerie mood. Rather than question, he simply sat on the floor in front of her and crossed his legs.

After a moment of staring into her own thoughts, she finally looked him in the eye, as if finally noting his arrival.

"Cassiel Aykhan Corekan came here a while ago—while I was asleep."

Jack was instantly on high alert. He wanted to pull out a knife, but she didn't act like there was any imminent danger.

"My god, Angela, what happened?"

"I killed him."

Jack blinked at her. "You killed him?"

She nodded. "He was standing in my bedroom while I was asleep. He was watching me. I woke up. My gun was gone off the nightstand, so I ran."

"Ran where?"

She flicked a hand back over her left shoulder. "Up Grandfather Mountain."

Jack instinctively glanced in that direction even though there were no windows to see the mountain.

"And he followed you?"

"Yes. So I killed him."

"Are you sure he's dead? I mean, are you positive?"

She turned around, leaned back, lifted one of those disposable, milky, semitransparent plastic bowls that were used for leftover casseroles and such, and set it down between them.

"This is his brain."

Jack was momentarily stupefied. The smell told him why she had lit scented candles. The brain was lopsided, as if it had been partially crushed.

"Why in the world do you have his brain?"

She looked genuinely puzzled by the question. "I thought that maybe you would want to run DNA tests or something. He's an international serial killer. I thought that a lot of people in other countries would want confirmation that it was him and that he was dead. I thought relatives would want the closure of knowing that the man who killed their family members was dead. I figured that if I only saved some blood, people could worry that he was still alive. So, I saved his brain for you, for proof."

Jack's jaw was hanging. Her cold, calm logic left him stunned. He stared down at the bloody brain in the plastic bowl. He finally found his voice.

"What happened? How did he die?"

"I bashed in his skull with a rock."

"Oh. Well, that would do it."

All kinds of questions were flying around in his head. But in the uncomfortable silence he wanted most to comfort her after such a violent ordeal. "I suppose you know that Angela means 'angel' in

Italian." She nodded. "Well, 'angel' means 'messenger from God.' So, I guess you were God's messenger with Cassiel."

"Not exactly. It may mean 'messenger of God' ordinarily, but it means something different in my case."

Jack squinted a bit. "What does it mean in your case?"

" 'Wrath of God.' "

He could only stare at her. From everything he knew about her, and the things he suspected, he thought that maybe she had it right.

"If you don't want his brain," she said, "I'd be happy to get rid of it."

Jack was dying of curiosity as to where the rest of him was, and how she had come to have only his brain, but he could tell that she had not called him to discuss the disposal of bodies.

"Did something else happen, Angela?"

She nodded. "Something really creepy."

"Really creepy." He tried to imagine something more creepy than having the man's brain in a plastic bowl, but couldn't, so he asked. "Like what?"

"Well, you know the way I could tell you all sorts of things about Cassiel when you showed me that photo?"

"Yes. I believe it's because of your genetic makeup. Because of that, you somehow had visions of the things he did."

"That happens with any killer," she said. "You think it's genetic, but I know I'm not normal. I know I'm a freak. But now I think that I may be an even bigger freak than I ever thought."

"You're not a freak, Angela," he insisted, softly.

"I think maybe I have those visions because I'm meant to be here for something bigger than me. You know? I think that, in a way, I'm here to be the wrath of God."

Jack didn't want her to think of herself as a freak. He knew she wasn't. She was something quite extraordinary.

"If it's any comfort, I know other people with some of your ability, and I know of another woman, Kate, who could do things similar to what you can do. She can tell things from looking into a killer's eyes, too."

"Really?" She sounded hopeful.

"Yes, but nothing like you can," he admitted.

"Oh." She sounded disappointed. "Well, anyway, after I split Cassiel's skull open with a rock, I tore his brain away from the spinal cord and held it in my hands."

Jack wondered why on earth she would do that, but he didn't ask. "Go on."

"As I was holding his brain in my hands, his memories were still firing. There was still some kind of electrical activity, or something, still functioning. I saw all kinds of things in my own mind that he'd seen recently. They were his memories."

"Angela, I don't think that's possible. I mean, he was dead. You just said you'd split his skull open with a rock."

"That's just what I thought. But when I was holding his brain, still warm in my hands, I could see his thoughts. I don't know how I could, but I could. Without a blood supply, his brain was rapidly dying—I could feel it happening—but it was still viable enough to have some rudimentary, primitive function.

"His brain was racing through recent memories. I could see them."

Jack decided that rather than express doubt or offer alternate explanations he would keep it simple and let her explain her experience. He thought that after she had killed the man in such a horrific fashion it would be cathartic for her if he just listened and let her talk.

"Like what? What did you see?"

"I saw where he parked the car he stole to get here. It's about a mile away. I could take you to it. It's blue. I could see his memories of walking through the fields and then the woods to get to my house. I saw the memory of him using his knife to get in the back door. I saw his memory of using a little flashlight to look down at me in bed while I was asleep. I only had on panties. I saw his memory of getting an erection as he considered the things he was going to do to me."

"How long did this go on—these memories?"

"Not long at all. They were going past a mile a minute—thousands upon thousands of them in little snippets. In my mind I could see them all, as if they were my own memories, my own thoughts, the way you can remember an entire event—sights, sounds, smells, people, conversations—all together in an instant. That's what this was like. They were also fading away.

"I saw his brain die and his soul wink out of existence."

"Okay," Jack said as he let out a deep breath, "that is pretty creepy."

Jack still didn't know if what she described had really happened, or if it was merely her own mind dealing with the disorienting mix of rage, grief, and the enormity of killing a man with her bare hands. He also didn't know why she needed to tell him this at five in the morning, before the sun was up.

"Angela, is there something about those memories that was particularly disturbing? Something you needed to tell me?"

A sudden tear ran down her cheek. She wiped it away.

"Yes. Later today—this afternoon—a lot of people are going to die. A lot of awful people."

"What are you talking about? What people?"

Angela stared down at the brain.

"That growing nest of people in the powerful and corrupt ruling class. The arrogant people in the ivory towers who think they're better than all the rest of us." Her voice sounded bitter. "The people who make the laws to rule over everyone else, to control everyone else, but don't have to follow those laws themselves because they're above the law.

"I think the world would be better off without them.

"For a time, I thought about how fitting that would be—letting all those greedy, corrupt, lying, cruel, crooked, evil people wink out of existence. I thought it would be so good to let that happen."

She looked up at him, her eyes beginning to well up. Tears overflowed to run down her cheeks. He didn't know what she was talking about, but decided to let her explain it her way.

"I can imagine it happening, kind of like I can see killers murdering people. I can see the totality of it. It's spellbinding, like watching a car sliding into a train, and knowing that the people you can see in that car are about to die. . . . and not caring.

"But then, as I got past the satisfaction over the thought of that overbearing elite class being gone, I started thinking about all the others.

"There are so many people who aren't like that. You know? People who work hard to provide for their family. Despite all the bad people and all the evil that goes on day in and day out, there are those other people who aren't part of that. Simple people. Innocent people. People who only want to live their lives and enjoy those they love."

Jack leaned in. "Angela, what are you talking about? Who is it that you think is going to die?"

"Lots of terrible people the world would be better off without, but also lots of innocent people who don't deserve to die. People who fight every day to keep us all safe. People who work every day to keep their own families safe.

"Those people deserve to live their lives, kind of like the way innocent people get to live now that I killed Cassiel. He won't be able to go on to slaughter any more innocent people. Those people will never ever know that they will get to live their lives because tonight I killed the monster who otherwise would have murdered them.

"But they don't need to know that what I did saved them. I know. That's all that matters."

Jack listened to the candles sputtering for a moment. "I understand how lonely that can be, Angela. I work to eliminate that kind of person, too."

"I know. I can see the things you've done in your eyes, the people you've killed, and why you do it. I can see you saving a woman named Kate. A woman you love."

Jack swallowed. He tried to push those painful memories aside and instead focus on the problem at hand.

"So, as I thought about it," she said, "even though it was momentarily satisfying to think of the justice of those people dying, I realized I couldn't do it. There are far too many innocent lives at stake. I'm not a monster like the monsters you and I hunt. I'm not a murderer like the ones I kill."

"That's why I do what I can to help people like you, Angela."

"Well, I could use your help, now."

Jack shrugged. "Okay. What's up?"

"There's a second nuke."

SIXTY-TWO

The hair on the back of Jack's neck lifted and stood stiffly on end.

"What?"

"The bomb we stopped before was supposed to go off in New York City later this afternoon—at four o'clock, when the city is full of people working as well as tourists and rush hour traffic that would have the streets clogged. The more people outside, the more radiation and burn deaths there would be."

"Angela, we stopped that from happening."

"Yes, but there's a second bomb. This one is going to go off in Washington, DC, later today at the same time—four p.m. The terrorists wanted two bombs to strike at the heart of the Great Satan—New York and Washington. We stopped that first bomb, but there's a second one. It's completely assembled, it's in place in Washington, it's live, and it's ready to detonate."

Jack almost felt as if he were having an out-of-body experience, as if he were looking down on himself having this conversation.

"Angela, how do you know this?"

"I saw it all in Cassiel's memories as I held his dying brain in my hands."

Jack took a breath to compose himself. He told himself that it wasn't possible, that she was simply imagining the worst. And yet, he had already seen this young woman do the impossible.

"What did you see in these visions, or memories? Can you tell me exactly what you saw that makes you believe this?"

"I saw the leader of the terrorist group responsible for the entire mission, for both bombs. His name is Rafael. Rafael always had Cassiel stay close by him.

"Rafael and his team are Iranian, but they grew up speaking Spanish, eating Mexican food, and dressing as Mexicans so that they would be able to easily infiltrate the US. Mexicans can go virtually unnoticed here in the US. That was their plan: blend in as Mexicans.

"But make no mistake. They are Iranian, steeped in the Iranian goal of world dominance. They believe that the ISIS caliphate is illegitimate. They intend to bring about the *real* caliphate.

"They've spent their entire lives training for this mission. They've studied with not only Iranian nuclear scientists, but nuclear scientists from North Korea and Pakistan. Rafael knows enough to be a physicist, but this mission is his purpose in life, his only purpose. They want to die with the bombs they have built, the culmination of their life's work.

"The first time I saw those four, I thought they were Mexican. The entire team snuck into the US illegally posing as Mexicans. Out of all of them, only three were caught. American lawyers helped get them out of detention and got them a court hearing six months from now. They vanished into America as the lawyer knew they would. The authorities didn't stop any of the others, and some sanctuary cities and states even protected them, like my own state did, and like California did.

"Cassiel wasn't raised with Rafael and his team. An Iranian commander named Hasan saved Cassiel from execution for murder and assigned him to go with Rafael. Rafael didn't like it. Neither did Cassiel.

"Rafael left half of his team to complete the assembly of one of the two bombs. That was the bomb we found. That team was supposed to take that bomb to New York City when it was finished, but they all died in the explosion when they were attacked.

"When Rafael could no longer get in touch with any of that team, he rightly assumed that they had been discovered and were dead. He knew they would blow up the place and themselves with it to prevent any chance of discovery of their larger plan. They wanted Rafael's part of the mission to go on to succeed. When they detonated those explosives, it left it all up to Rafael to complete the mission he and his team members were raised to do.

"That was why Rafael had split his group—to increase the odds that one of them would succeed. Once split, the two teams had minimal contact.

"Rafael built the second bomb at another location—on a long, backwoods loop off the main road not far from here. That loop, Duffey Road, only goes past a scattering of houses and camps. Most of the houses belonged to factory workers and have been long abandoned. Rafael's team finished the construction of the second bomb in a barn on one of those properties. Anyone who saw them thought they were Mexicans who didn't speak English.

"When it was finished, Cassiel rode in the cargo van with Rafael as he took the bomb to Washington, DC. The other members of his team went in separate cars so they wouldn't all be together if anything went wrong.

"Yesterday they set up the bomb on the top floor of a tall building owned by a shell company owned by a series of shell companies owned by their Iranian-backed terrorist group. The building was selected to get the bomb as high in the air as they could to create the maximum destruction and death possible. Everything has been in the planning stages for decades.

"Cassiel was the one part of the mission that had not been part of the plan. Cassiel didn't want to die a martyr with the rest of them.

"Once they got the bomb in Washington, Cassiel had time to kill, literally. So, he snuck away when they weren't paying attention to him, stole a car, and came here to kill me."

Jack pressed his hands to his head. "Where is this bomb? We need to call people who can stop it."

Angela was shaking her head. "I can't tell you where it is."

"What? Why not?"

"I only know where they built the bomb, here, in Milford Falls, in a place on Duffey Road, because I recognized that road in Cassiel's memories. But I've never been to Washington, so those snippets of his memories don't tell me the location of where it is now."

Jack gestured down at the brain in the bowl between them. "Can you touch it or something and get more information?"

Angela made a face. "It's dead, Jack. It's just gray mush, now."

Jack stood, pressing his hands to his head again as he paced. "We have to stop it. We can't let it go off."

"That's why I could use your help."

He turned back. "What do you mean?"

"I need you to drive me. I don't think I could stay awake the whole way if I drove myself. I'm totally exhausted. If you drive, I can nap a bit on the way."

"Drive you? What the hell are you talking about? Are you out of your mind? How is that going to locate the bomb?"

"Don't you see? If we go on the roads Cassiel took going to Washington from here in that van, and then back the same route from Washington in the car he stole, back here to kill me, I will see things I recognize from his memories.

"I will be able to use those memories I saw from his mind like a trail of bread crumbs to find my way back to the bomb. That's how we find it."

Jack was near to sputtering in frustration. "And then what?"

"And then I'm going to kill them."

Jack gaped at her. "As simple as that. You're going to kill them."

"Yes."

"You held a brain in your hands, and you saw a second atomic bomb that's now in a building somewhere in Washington, DC."

"That's right. Are you going to help me or not?"

The whole thing was so crazy he could hardly keep his composure.

"Better yet, I'll call in help and have a tactical force go with us. They will be able to handle the situation once we get there and find the place."

"No."

"What do you mean, 'no'?"

"You think I'm going to trust the same kind of people who had me in chains and wanted me to confess to being one of these terrorists? Fuck them. Fuck them all."

"Angela, for god's sake, this is different! We're going to need a tactical team. They're the only ones who can handle a situation like this."

"Listen to me, Jack. I saw everything Cassiel saw. The bomb is ready. They have the electrical equipment attached to fire the exploding bridgewire to detonate the bomb. It's ready now.

"They have observation points from windows. They have lookouts on the street. If they so much as see a SWAT team doing a drug raid down the street, they will blow the bomb. They will not risk failure. They will not delay. If they get so much as a whiff of something wrong, they will detonate the bomb."

"But if the team—"

"They have a dead man's switch—a man sitting on a metal chair that's wired to the electrical supply. If an assault team rushes the place and he moves it will detonate the nuke.

"It's all wired up and ready to go. They're only waiting until the scheduled time of four p.m. to set it off because they want darkness settling over the scene in the aftermath to add to the terror, but if they need to, they will go earlier.

"If you call in anyone, they will fuck it up and that bomb will turn Washington, DC, to glass."

"But the military can strike from a distance. They can send in rockets or if they have to, take down the whole building."

"Rafael explained to Cassiel how even if the enemy sent in a rocket, the speed of that explosion is not as fast as the detonation of the exploding bridgewire. He said that in a race of microseconds, the nuke will win."

"But—"

"Look, Jack, this group has been planning for this mission their entire lives. These are the point men. They plan to die in the glorious explosion against the Great Satan. This is the culmination of their life's work.

"Their commanders have consulted with experts from North Korea to Pakistan on the construction of the bomb to make it as big as possible and they've gamed out every conceivable possibility of attack or countermeasure. They have it all thought out and every base covered.

"Those terrorist attacks all across the country were meant to cover what they were doing at the border crossing. They took out that border crossing with ease despite the power of the government arrayed to stop nuclear material coming in over the border. They made it look easy. No one, none of these experts you talk about, even realized that in that attack this group drove two nuclear bombs right across the border, did they?

"The only thing any 'experts' or tactical team or whatever you get to go in there are going to accomplish is to detonate that nuke a few hours ahead of schedule. They will get Washington, DC, wiped off the face of the earth.

"You're thinking exactly like they expect you to think. You're playing their game, just the way they want you to play it. You can't win playing by their rules."

"Jesus Christ, Angela, we have to get experts in there!"

"No, we don't. I'm telling you that won't work. I'll handle the situation myself once we get there."

Jack took a step back to stare at her. "How the hell do you think you're going to do that?"

"I've already seen everything." She tapped her temple with a finger. "It's all in here. I know what the building looks like, inside and out. I know all the people with Rafael. I know Rafael. I will stop them.

"I'm the only contingency they haven't modeled. I'm the only thing they haven't planned for. Just like all the killers I find, I'm the wild card they hadn't expected."

"Angela, you have to listen to reason—"

"I'm telling you for the last time. I'm not going to cooperate with your fucking experts. They'll get everyone killed. That's not speculation, it's a fact. I'm not going to allow that to happen.

"I'm not offering you a choice, Jack.

"It takes about six hours to drive from here to DC, maybe a little less. That will get us there late morning. We'll have plenty of time—at least four hours. If something goes wrong, like I get killed, then you can still call in your government people. But I'm telling you, that will be the end of Washington, DC, and a lot of innocent people."

Jack was shaking his head. "This is nuts."

But at the same time he could see that what she was saying actually made sense—in a weird, crazy, psycho way. To Angela it made perfect sense. To her way of thinking, Rafael would be expecting the possibility of an attack by a tactical team.

What they would not be expecting, was . . . Angela.

SIXTY-THREE

"We're wasting time," Angela said. "Are you going to drive me, or do I drive myself?"

"No, no," Jack said, waving off that idea. "With as little sleep as you've had since those federal goons picked you up, and then running around in the dark bashing in Cassiel's skull, you have no business driving right now. We can't have a nuclear bomb going off because you fell asleep at the wheel. We'll be better off with me driving. Maybe that way you can get some sleep along the way."

"That's my thought," she said.

Jack ran his fingers back through his hair. "I may be as crazy as you are for going along with this, but since you insist on doing this your way and you don't have an actual location I could call in, I think it would be better if I was there to help you."

"That's why I called you," she said with a smile.

"We can go in my car. It has a backseat, so you should be able to get some sleep."

"All right, then, let's get what we'll need." After blowing out the candles, she picked up the plastic casserole bowl with Cassiel's brain. It was beginning to smell. Red fluid in the bottom sloshed around as she turned toward him. "Do you want this or not?"

He cleared his throat. "I don't think I need it."

She shrugged and took it with her.

Jack didn't know what she meant about getting what they would need, but he followed her as she carried the brain in the plastic bowl to a door in the hall. She reached up on her tiptoes and retrieved a key from on top of the molding, then unlocked the door. When she flicked on the light, he saw that it was a basement.

At the bottom of the stairs he looked around as she set the brain down on a counter to the left. The floor was made up of strips of wood that looked to be teak. There were small gaps between each row. Oddly enough, there was a garden hose coiled up on a holder on the wall.

Angela opened doors on the lower cabinet and pulled out a pair of suede boots like the ones he usually saw her wearing. After putting them on, she opened a box from that same cabinet and took out a new knife, in a sheath. She checked the sharpness of the blade by shaving off some hairs on her arm, then slid the sheath with the knife into her boot.

When she opened the upper cabinet doors, he saw stacks of boxes, most of them brand-new boxes of Walther P22s. There were some Glock 19 cases as well. Next to the boxes was a row of suppressors standing on end.

She took a Walther out of one of the boxes and locked back the slide. With a little wrench from the counter she removed the ring that protected the threads at the end of the barrel. Once that was removed, she screwed a suppressor onto the end of the barrel. She laid the weapon on the counter.

"I have Walther P22s and nine-millimeter Glocks," she said. "The Glocks have better stopping power, but I only have suppressors for the Walthers. Since the object is stealth and surprise, I think we should both use Walthers with suppressors. Suppressors keep the sound down, which makes it less nerve-racking shooting indoors, and you can hear someone coming for you. They also keep people from hearing us so easily. Also, if something goes wrong, if we both carry a Walther our magazines will be interchangeable."

He was a little surprised at how tactically levelheaded she was. "I'd have to agree with you. Walthers it is."

She took three new guns out of boxes, prepared two with suppressors, and handed them both to Jack. She added a suppressor to a second one for herself.

"If anything goes wrong with one of our guns, a backup gun could save our lives."

"You'll get no argument from me," he said. He still had trouble believing that he was going along with this whole plan. "Besides that, we both have knives. They may come in handy."

Eliminating people with knives was good in that if you did it right it could be silent. That provided a stealth approach. But it took precious seconds. If there were multiple targets and little time, a small-caliber gun with a suppressor was a good choice—as long as you were a damn good shot. With a .22, shot placement was critical. If you missed even a little, you would only piss off the enemy and they could be all over you in no time at all, to say nothing of them shooting back.

Angela took magazines out of the boxes and pulled out more from the cabinet.

"They hold ten rounds, but don't load ten rounds," she said. "I've found that they don't always feed reliably if they have ten rounds in the magazine."

Jack was a little surprised that she knew enough to be aware of that. But he was beginning not to be surprised by anything she said.

They loaded several dozen magazines with nine subsonic rounds each, then a full ten rounds into magazines they loaded into their guns. Chambering a round left nine in those magazines. That would give them ten rounds in the gun the first time around, but nine thereafter.

She even had a couple of holsters Jack could use. The bottoms were cut out so the suppressor would fit through. She set out a couple of extra boxes of ammo to take along.

He had trouble imagining why she had all these things, but then again, she could recognize killers, and some of those killers would be able to recognize her.

When you hunted killers, killers hunted back.

He was beginning to see how she had survived. He wished more of the people he found had Angela's sense of self-preservation.

Besides the holster at the small of her back, she clipped another just behind her hip to give her two guns, the same as he was carrying. She pulled her top over the one on her hip to conceal it. With her shape and size, it didn't conceal very well.

After the magazines were all loaded, she picked up the bowl with the brain, then went to the far end of the basement and opened a hatch. Without ceremony, she tossed Cassiel's brain, plastic bowl and all, down into the black opening.

Jack came up behind her and looked down. "What is this?"

"It's where bad people go," she said in a quiet voice. "It's called the hell hole."

He stared down into the darkness for a moment, his head spinning with everything he was learning. He usually had to work hard and long to try to convince people with the ability to recognize killers that they needed to take it seriously and learn to protect themselves.

Angela was in a different league. She was from a different planet.

"Most of the time I feel like life has no meaning," she said as she gazed down into the darkness. "Sometimes this place feels like it's drawing me. Ya know? I think that one day I may end up down there."

"What makes you think that?"

"Just . . . everything," she said in a faraway voice, still staring down into the darkness.

The pain and emptiness in her voice was heartbreaking.

"Angela," he said, gently taking her arm and pulling her back from the abyss, "a person who is determined to go off to stop terrorists from detonating an atomic bomb, and may very well end up getting herself killed in the process, certainly has meaning in her life

496

and does not belong in a hole that leads down to hell. Only killers—predators who prey on innocent people—belong in a place like that. People like Cassiel, not you, belong in such a place."

She turned back to look at him with a sudden, wicked grin. "Good, because he's already down there."

Once they were back upstairs, Angela locked the basement door and replaced the key. He could see, now, why she didn't want anyone wandering down there.

Ready to leave, he took a critical look at her. "Are you going to change? You aren't really going to wear those same cutoff shorts to a gunfight that you wear to tend bar, are you?"

"Yes."

Jack was at a loss. "Why?"

"Because none of the terrorists we're going to kill are women."

"So?"

"Women wouldn't be distracted by my legs."

It suddenly made sense. Crazy Angela sense. She was on her way to kill terrorists. Those terrorists were men.

In a fight to the death, any distraction, even if it was only for a fraction of a second, was a precious advantage.

Four of these terrorists had interrupted their mission to rape her. Clearly they were vulnerable to leggy female distraction.

And if anyone's legs were distracting, it was Angela's.

In that light, Angela wasn't crazy at all.

She was deadly.

SIXTY-FOUR

Angela slitted her eyes. The light was too bright for her to open them all the way. She had to squint to see. She yawned and stretched in the backseat as she sat up a little to take in the view out the windows.

She peered all around at the sights going by just off the interstate. They drove past a sign on the right saying they were on Interstate 270. In a moment more, she hunched down to be able to look out the windshield as they drove under an overhead sign for the Interstate 495 East exit in two miles.

She thrust her arm forward, pointing over Jack's shoulder. "There. You need to take that exit."

"I know, I know. You already told me that you knew this much about the roads we needed to take."

Most of the visions from Cassiel were of places where he looked—memories of what he saw. He had looked at that interstate exit because it was so prominent. It was frustrating not to know most of the other roads they needed to take.

Cassiel had looked at buildings, places to eat, stores and businesses that interested him for one reason or another, and in particular, women on the street. A good percentage of his recent memories now residing in her head seemed to be of women's asses. His vision had been like a heat-seeking missile for ass. Those women were of course long gone, leaving blanks along the route they needed to follow. Those memories explained some of the perverted things he had liked to do to the women he murdered.

She often wished she didn't have to live as the curator of the terrible visions and memories from killers' minds. Being in their heads, seeing the things they did, and how much they liked doing them, made her sick and angry. When she killed one of those savages, like when she had killed Cassiel, she at last had the chance to unleash vengeance on them.

She was the wrath of God.

Angela bent forward between the front bucket seats, over the center console, and squeezed herself through to get up front with Jack, her legs finally making it up and over with the rest of her.

Once they had taken the exit and were on Interstate 495 going east, Angela got serious about looking out the windows, scanning from side to side, trying to overlay the scenery with memories, looking for matches for everything she saw, hoping that would help lead them to the place where Rafael had the second bomb. She knew some of the things—besides women—that seemed to have drawn Cassiel's attention, so she looked for those things. If she saw a shopping center, or an ethnic food store, or a smoke shop, she tried to fit a memory to it.

Hard as she tried, nothing seemed to match.

She didn't say anything to Jack, but inside she was beginning to feel panicky that her plan was not working. Everything depended on her being able to follow the bread crumbs of his memories to lead them to the nest of terrorists. So far, she wasn't finding any bread crumbs other than that one sign.

Scanning everything she could out the windows while running memories through her mind didn't seem to be working. She began to seriously worry that maybe it would never work. She worried that if they couldn't find the building with the bomb, then Jack might have to call the shadowy intel people he knew.

But how could they ever find it, especially in time? There were only a few hours left before Rafael would detonate the bomb. Even if by some miracle those government forces did manage to find the building, Rafael was prepared for every eventuality. She knew there was no chance they would be able to stop the bomb from going off. They would be the cause of it going off.

If Angela's plan didn't work, Washington had only a few hours of existence left, and then the world would change forever. None of the people going about their lives there had any idea they were about to die.

She kept coming back to the same problem. Finding it and stopping it were two different things. Everything she had told Jack about the terrorists' plans was true. They had contingencies for any kind of attack to stop them.

Being eager to die removed the self-preservation factor. Being eager to die added a level of certainty for success.

Rafael knew they couldn't win a gun battle or survive a heavy assault, but he didn't need to win because he didn't plan to survive, so they didn't make any plans for it. Their endgame was to detonate the bomb, not win a gunfight with a SWAT team. The bomb was ready to go. If anything happened to interrupt or threaten their schedule they were prepared to simply set it off ahead of time. Either way worked for them.

"There," Angela said when she saw a store that struck a chord with the memories. "Turn right just before that store on the corner. The one with Uncle Sam posters in the window."

Jack turned down the street without comment or objection.

Angela sat back, relieved that she had at last recognized something significant. It was proof that she was on the right track.

She let herself sink into a kind of trance as she scanned everything as they drove along. As she watched, the buildings grew gradually more run-down. As she let herself become immersed in Cassiel's memories, letting them run nonstop through her mind, fragments of images were beginning to make her feel that they were going the right way. She saw a Laundromat she recognized from Cassiel's memory, and a corner market with hand-painted advertisements for a sale on hamburger. Both the Laundromat and the market were busy.

Cassiel had memories of fat-assed women in stretch pants carrying black plastic bags full of laundry into the Laundromat. Angela had to smile at her own memory of carrying pieces of Cassiel in black plastic bags back to the hell hole.

"Up there, on the right a block ahead, there's an old abandoned theater. See it? Turn left just past it."

The vertical theater sign was coming detached at the top, so that it leaned out, attached only by a bottom bracket. Because it was leaning out, it had caught Cassiel's attention.

As they drove past it, Angela saw plywood nailed up across the doors and windows of the building to keep people out. Cassiel had looked at the graffiti on that building. The meaning of it all had puzzled him. He had considered how universal graffiti was, how the ghettos in all the countries he'd been to had the same multicolored mess of graffiti.

They turned onto a street lined with older cars and pickups parked along a curb. Homes occupied long buildings, each home painted a different color to make it look like they were individual row houses. Each house had steps and a small porch. Some people sat on the steps, others sat on the porches on rusty benches or overstuffed chairs with padding hanging out of torn seams. Little kids ran up and down the steps, and in and out of the houses.

"Here, take a right at this street, go down one block, then hook a left."

They drove past empty lots with chain-link fences that had strained newspapers, pizza boxes, burger wrappers, and all kinds of other debris out of the gusty breezes the way a colander strained pasta out of water.

"Go a little slower, please," she said to Jack from inside her trance of a killer's memories.

The farther they went, making turns where she instructed, the more unsavory the areas became.

"Are you sure they went on such a random route?" Jack asked.

"It's not random. They studied the city. They've been sending advance people in for years to scout the whole city for locations and routes that would be least likely to encounter scrutiny and searches. They took thousands of photos. They knew that if they drove close to the Capitol Building or the White House there would be a lot of security. They wanted to use poor areas because they would fit in with people in those places. Their cargo van was old and has primer spots so that it wouldn't raise eyebrows on any of these streets. In wealthier areas they were more likely to look out of place or suspicious."

"It's frightening the way they thought everything through."

"From what Cassiel learned, Rafael, his advisors, and his team have had years—decades—to make sure they eliminated variables, dangers, or problems. They bought an abandoned building eleven years ago. They occasionally ran a small distribution business out of it to look legit and so they could be sure it was kept up just enough. They've planned for every contingency."

"Except for you," he said.

Angela smiled to herself as she gazed out the windows at a crumbling landscape. In ways, it reminded her of the buildings her grandfather had built. Some of these buildings were painted, but under the layers of peeling, faded paint they were brick. Some of them were long abandoned, now only forlorn shells. Walls here and there had collapsed, leaving piles of rubble, mostly bricks, scattered out onto empty lots beside them. Shopping carts lay capsized among the rubble like ships that had run aground on shoals.

The memories were fitting the scenery more closely the farther they moved into the deteriorated areas.

"These are the kind of dangerous shithole places Cassiel liked to haunt in third-world countries," she told Jack. "Lots of crime so that the things he did would stand out less, or not at all. He felt comfortable in places like this, so his memories are more vivid along here. He viewed this area through the eyes of a predator. This is a hunting ground."

"Believe it or not," Jack said, "we're not many miles from the center of US government—Capitol Hill and the White House."

"Expensive homes. Zillions of tourists. Massive security presence protecting it all. Not at all easy to attack directly," she said. "But easy enough to take out from a distance with an atomic bomb."

Jack rested his wrist on the top of the steering wheel as they drove slowly past a whitewashed brick building with plywood over the windows. "You're right. It's a terrifyingly brilliant plan. Most terrorists just want to kill people at familiar places and take out landmarks. These guys want to take out an entire city."

Angela gazed out at places that looked like they had already been bombed. A lot of people had long ago fled the area, leaving haunted shells of buildings. But there were still lots of dangerous-looking thugs hanging out on the street corners, on steps, and in alleyways. She saw drug deals going down. She had seen so many of those growing up she could spot them in her sleep.

As she glanced down a narrow alley with overflowing Dumpsters, she saw people sitting on the landings of iron fire escapes. All up the five flights, laundry hung on the iron railings and in the narrow spaces between buildings like colorful flags. Lots of innocent people lived in these areas as well. They didn't dare to come out much, and when they did, they were often prey.

She saw no-trespassing signs nailed up on dirty white doors in a row of abandoned homes beside railroad tracks. Homeless people were sleeping on the porches of those derelict homes, their collections of blankets and cardboard piled up protectively around them. Many had their belongings piled high in shopping carts parked nearby, like cars parked in front of homes.

"Any idea if we're close?" Jack asked.

She could understand his impatience. He was risking everything on her word.

"Sorry," she said. "I recognize places, not distances."

"We have to be close. We're going to be at the Capitol Building soon."

Angela pointed. "Turn right down here."

One of the abandoned brick buildings had a big white skull painted on the side of it. Her memory—Cassiel's memory—fit it perfectly. Cassiel had looked at that crudely painted skull.

The area around various buildings looked like garbage dumps. Angela saw a small plastic pedal car as well as other broken toys sticking out of the rubble. It reminded her of the way she had played outside her mother's trailer when she had been little, making mud pies, picking weeds and putting them in empty beer cans like flowers in a vase, completely oblivious to the poverty, drugs, and crime going on around her. To her, it was simply home and completely normal to walk around winos who tried to entice her from their lawn chairs in front of their trailers, or to hide from scary men under blue tarps covering cars that didn't run and never would again.

The children who pedaled around on those toys were the innocents who would be vaporized under a mushroom cloud if she didn't stop that bomb from going off.

As they drove down the street, they began to encounter buildings that looked like giant, stacked building blocks. The blocky structures formed a variety of shapes. It was once a bustling business area.

"Stop the car!" she yelled.

Jack flinched from her scream but put on the brakes, slowing rapidly without squealing the tires.

He looked over at her. "What?"

"Pull over and then slowly back up along the curb."

He did what she wanted without knowing why.

"Okay stop. Now, roll down your window."

Jack gave her a questioning look as he held down the window button. "What—"

"Lean back," she told him, her focus elsewhere.

Angela pulled out her gun, holding it in both hands across in front of him as she aimed out the open window.

It made a soft, muffled pop when she pulled the trigger, along with the metallic sound of the slide cycling to eject the shell and chamber the next round. The small ejected brass casing hit the windshield and bounced along the top of the dash.

Across the street, a man, looking like a puppet whose strings had been cut, dropped straight down. Some of the other people standing down the street didn't even notice.

"Drive," she told him as she pulled her gun back.

SIXTY-FIVE

"What the hell?" Jack said.

She looked out the back window to see three men approach the man on the ground. They looked all around, then bent down to go through the dead man's pockets.

"It was a lookout," Angela told him. "We're close."

"Are you sure?"

"Yeah, his name was Jesus, one of the lookouts they have posted at street level." Angela pointed. "Up there. See that building with the dark, octagonal, three-story tower at the corner? Turn left there."

Jack turned the corner. The street became more than a street. It had been used by commercial trucks to load and unload at the buildings rising up at the edge of narrow sidewalks. Some of the buildings had roll-up metal doors with small loading docks. Rusted metal railings kept people from falling in the loading pits. Wooden pallets lay on some of the docks. In other places pallets were leaned up against corners of buildings.

Chain-link fences with barbed wire on top spanned the gaps between some of the buildings. Those canyons between vertical walls were filled with years of accumulated trash.

All the buildings, docks, railings, roll-up doors—everything—had been hit by scribble monkeys. Buildings seemed to melt together in endless gang graffiti, all the tags proclaiming affiliation and territory, or boasting threats.

The tall building on the left at the far corner of the block was different from the others all around it. It was made up of a gridwork of cement columns and beams, with brick filling in the centers and forming the main part of the walls. The brick squares had windows in long rows up high that looked to be for light and ventilation, not for a view. Higher up, the building's walls were set back, and were all brick as it rose a number of stories more.

A vertical sign attached at the corner of the building said STILTON. The letters had once been filled with rows of lightbulbs, now all missing. She didn't see that sign in Cassiel's memories, but she saw the rest of the building. He had gone in and out from a loading dock in an alley of sorts.

"Go left at the end of the block," she said.

Jack took the left at the corner with the Stilton sign and then took the next one when she told him to.

"What are we doing?" he asked. "We're starting to drive around in circles."

"The bomb is in the Stilton Building," she said.

Jack craned his neck to look back over his left shoulder. "Damn."

She had him turn the car around and drive around the block again, checking for lookouts and to be on the same side of the street for a better view of the building and for her to get a better shot if she needed one.

"Did you notice where the lookouts are?" she asked.

"Yes, at that blind alley with a loading dock at the back end."

"Right." Angela let out a deep breath. "Well, this is it."

He shot her a sidelong glance. "This had damn well better work," he muttered. "From here a nuke would take out the government."

She nodded absently, thinking instead about the enormity of what was about to happen, the magnitude of everything resting on her shoulders. It seemed insane, but at the same time she knew she was right that this was the only sane course of action that could stop it from happening.

As they went around the building again, a DC police car drove slowly past, both black cops looking everything over for any sign of trouble. They had no idea that the Stilton Building they were passing was filled with trouble. The cop car drove on down the street and eventually turned a corner in the distance.

Just before they came around the corner again, before the street that would take them past that blind alley with the loading bay, Angela gestured to the side. "Okay, park back here. Back before the corner. I don't want them to see us drive by again or it will alert them."

"Are those two men standing beside the alley men you recognize from Cassiel's memory?" he asked as he pulled to the curb and leaned forward to try to look out past her.

"Yes," she said as she pushed him back in his seat before she popped open her door. "Silvino and Ronaldo. Back up a little so they can't see your car." When he did, she said, "Okay, wait here."

"What do you think you're doing?" Jack asked.

"I need to take out the lookouts. When I come back out of that loading alley, I'll signal, so be looking for me, then you can come in the back entrance with me. Do you have all your magazines on you?"

"Yes. What do you mean you're going to take out the lookouts?"

Angela didn't answer as she got out and shut the car door.

All four of her pockets were loaded with five or six magazines each. That was far more than she expected to need, but as her grandfather always told her, you can never have too much ammo. At times it felt like he was with her, reminding her of a hundred little details.

Leaving the car waiting back around the corner, she strutted down the street to where the two men were leaning against a wall beside what at first glance looked like an alley. Rather than an alley, though, it was a short dead end, deep enough for a large truck to park and unload at an elevated dock at the rear. The dock had wooden stairs to the left.

She recognized the two men standing watch beside the alley—Silvino and Ronaldo—because Cassiel had spent a good deal of time with Rafael and all his men. She recognized them the same as he would have. None of the men really liked Cassiel—he was an outsider.

For his part, Cassiel didn't respect or care about any of them, either. He had only been with them until a time came when he could make an escape and again be on his own.

Once the bomb went off and the entire team was dead, their minders back in Iran would think he had died along with them. Having escaped death twice, he would then be free to hunt again. But the third time had been the charm. He died hunting Angela.

When she walked past the pair, they grinned, then pursed their lips to make kissing sounds as they grabbed their crotches. Angela stopped and smiled at them.

"You called?"

"Maybe," Silvino said.

"Well, do you want something or not? I ain't got all day, ya know."

"Maybe you could suck my cock?" Silvino asked with a grin.

She stepped close and ran a finger along his collar.

"Maybe."

"How much?"

"Ten. With a condom. Twenty without."

"Is good for me. Twenty dollars." He pointed a thumb back over his shoulder. "We go back there."

Ronaldo leered down at her legs, his gaze coming to a stop on her crotch. "How much for fuck?"

"Forty. But I'm running a special today. Two for sixty."

Silvino whispered something to his buddy.

Ronaldo looked somewhat annoyed. "This is my last chance for *coño*," he answered back. "If you don't want, you can wait here."

"No, I will have *coño* too," Silvino said, finally giving in. "We both will have this American *puta*."

Angela smiled and sauntered into the blind canyon of brick. The wall at the back was whitewashed halfway up. Windows to the side were boarded over from the inside. The short, blind alley was filled with garbage and trash of every sort. She saw the desiccated carcasses of rats among the rubble. A truck tire without a rim sat to the side.

The men pointed at the dock.

"Disgusting," she said. "I'm not going to lay down in this trash. You got someplace a little nicer and more private for a lady?"

"Yes," Ronaldo said, nodding eagerly as he started up the wooden stairs at the side of the dock. He pointed at the metal door. "In there."

Angela let them both usher her up the steps onto the dock and then through a dented metal door. Inside was an empty space with iron posts. Scraps of stained, ripply cardboard lay scattered about among bits of junk. She looked around in the dim light of a few high windows to make sure there weren't men inside. She saw a stairwell far back in the right corner.

Satisfied that they were alone, she turned around. Both men were staring at her legs as they were unbuckling their belts. One of them had laid down a bed of cardboard scraps for her to lie on.

Angela pulled out her gun as they were staring at her legs.

"Up here, boys."

When they looked up, she shot both men between the eyes— two quick pops. The bullets ricocheted around inside their skulls, scrambling their brains in a lethal instant. With no motor function, they dropped straight down. With everything from their motor cortex to the brain stem scrambled, their eyes remained open in death. They hadn't even had time to close them.

Gun in one hand, Angela used her other hand to pick up the scraps of cardboard to cover the bodies in case anyone came down to check on them. She went back out the door and out the alcove to peek around the edge of the building. She saw Jack taking a stealthy look around the corner. Angela waved for him. He came at a trot.

"That was quick," he said.

She gave him a look. "Did you expect me to fuck them first before I shot them?"

Angela hadn't meant to snap at him, but she was already sinking down into a familiar, merciless mood she knew all too well. He seemed to recognize it, so he let it pass.

She pressed the lever at the bottom of the trigger surround to release the magazine. She'd already used three bullets. She put in a fresh magazine and put the partially empty one in her back right pocket where she wouldn't use it unless needed. She wanted a full ten rounds when it started.

Jack followed her into the blind alley. "Tell me about the building, and where the men will likely be located."

SIXTY-SIX

Angela and Jack stood quietly inside near the cardboard-covered corpses of Silvino and Ronaldo. There were bales of scrap paper piled nearby, along with stacks of beat-up cardboard boxes.

In the dead silence she spoke in a low voice, briefing Jack on what she knew from Cassiel's memory about the interior layout and where Cassiel had last seen the men.

"Keep in mind that what I know could miss a lot of important stuff and the men could easily not be in the same places as before. From this point on, they could be anywhere. Cassiel wasn't at all interested in dying for Allah. He wanted to be out of here before the bomb went off. He was only watching for a chance to slip away so he could come and kill me. I was on his Constantine kill list. That's what he was thinking about."

"I understand," Jack said. "Whatever information you have from his memory is better than nothing, but we shouldn't rely on it."

"Right. Once it starts," she said, "it's going to take on a life of its own."

"If I didn't know better, I'd say you've done this before."

In a way, she had. "We both know what we need to do, so we just have to go in and do it."

Jack nodded as he looked around, watching for any sign of trouble. "Agreed."

"I'm going to go first," she told him.

"I don't think—"

"If they see you, they'll shoot first and ask questions later. If they see me, they'll ask questions first."

Jack made a face as he glanced around again. "I hate to admit it, but you've got a point. Do you know how many of them are armed?'

"All of them carry AK-47s. They trained with them and know how to use them, but shooting was never part of their plan. They rarely spent time target practicing or in firearms training. Their training was focused on physics and machining skills. These are sophisticated bomb makers, not soldiers.

"They consider other terrorists who use guns little more than unskilled amateurs. These men think they're smarter than that, deadlier than that. And they're right. They have guns more for the testosterone factor than anything else."

With Angela in the lead they both moved up the broad, concrete stairs as quietly as possible. The sliding metal door at the top stood half open. They both slipped through, guns at the ready.

The room they emerged into was filled with a forest of rusting iron posts holding up iron beams. The ceiling was a mass of pipes covered in disintegrating asbestos. A few sections of pipe lay on the floor along with crumbled masonry and other unrecognizable detritus that had drifted into ankle-deep piles here and there. The place had an echo, so they walked slowly and carefully near the wall and used hand signals.

They both tiptoed on the larger chunks of broken concrete to make as little noise as possible. It reminded her of crossing the stream on Grandfather Mountain by dancing from one dry rock to another.

Angela heard a sound, like water running. She held an arm out to stop Jack. He froze in place.

The far side of the room had a row of short concrete block walls jutting out from the rear wall to make a series of cubicles. A man turned from the corner of one of those cubicles, zipping up his pants after having urinated. He had an AK slung over his shoulder.

His hand on his zipper froze as he looked up. His eyes were opened wide.

Angela put a bullet between them.

He collapsed, his head banging the floor hard. It made an echoing thud. The ejected shell from her gun pinged with a metallic ring as it bounced against a pipe lying on the floor.

They both stood still for a moment to see if anyone had heard either the man's dead weight landing in the rubble or the soft pop of the suppressed shot.

When Angela started heading for the back corner to her left, Jack pointed at a stairwell to the right, letting her know they should go that way.

Angela shook her head. She pointed to a dark corridor in the distance to the left side. When he came close to question why, she leaned in and whispered in his ear.

"This leads to a back stairwell. They don't realize it's here."

"How the hell do you know that?"

"The main stairs had lookouts. Cassiel found this back way out and used it to sneak away without being seen."

Jack didn't look convinced. "It could be a dead end," he warned. "We could get trapped in a tight place like that and be sitting ducks. Are you sure?"

She started toward the narrow passage in wordless answer. She knew that surprise was invaluable. The main stairs had lookouts. They were the only stairs the men knew about, so they had them covered. Jack followed without further complaint.

The spooky-looking passage had a small window at the far end, so at least it wasn't completely dark, but the bright light coming into the dark space made for high-contrast shadows that were difficult to see into. It smelled musty. Deeper in, she could see that it appeared to be a utility service passageway of some sort.

Big pipes running along the ceiling with faded white paint had peeled for years, leaving chips and crumbles of plaster all over the floor to crunch underfoot. She pointed for Jack to big footprints in those curled paint chips.

"Cassiel," she whispered.

There were vertical pipes as well as exposed wiring. In one spot a beam crossed at chest height. They ducked under it and kept moving.

A brick wall they came to on the left had partially collapsed, spilling bricks out across the floor of the narrow corridor. Since there was no going around it, they had to step carefully over it to get past. Angela pointed out Cassiel's footprints again on the dusty floor. Jack nodded that he knew what they were, finally conceding that she was right.

Broken stubs of pipes sticking out low on the right threatened to catch their ankles. To the left was a room left exposed by the collapsed brick wall. Rusty tanks stood against a wall. They looked like they might be some sort of old, industrial water heaters. Everything was covered with a heavy layer of greasy dust. Ductwork and pipes coming out of the water heaters went in all directions back into the darkness, while some came out of the room to run overhead along the ceiling of the corridor.

Jack grabbed her sleeve between a finger and thumb to urgently stop her. He pointed ahead to a place in the floor that was hard to see in the flare of light coming in from the window directly ahead.

"There's a hole in the floor," he whispered. "Be careful."

Angela nodded and moved on, hugging the wall to shuffle past the rectangular hole. It was probably a utility pass-through. She looked down as she went by. It would have been a long fall two stories into a dark basement.

When they reached the window, the passage turned to the right and terminated at a flight of open, iron-tread stairs. The wall studs were exposed. Dusty insulation and thick veils of filthy cobwebs hung down in places. Fallen plaster lay on some of the iron treads.

They started up, both pointing their guns up at any threat that might be above them. Plaster crunched softly underfoot.

On the next floor, Angela gently pushed open a door. It squeaked. A man standing guard at the main stairwell not too far away immediately turned and saw them. He turned back to shout an alarm up the stairs. That denied her the preferred target of the triangle between his eyes at the tip of his nose. She admonished herself for not taking the shot immediately. She knew better.

Before he had a chance to make a sound, Angela put a round through his windpipe, immediately followed by a second one through the center of his left ear. By the way he dropped, the round through his ear had penetrated his skull just fine.

The guards at each flight of stairs were the reason Cassiel had avoided the main stairwell and instead snuck away down the utility stairs at the back. Now that they knew where the guards were posted, Angela took them out at each level on their way up. She didn't want men left down below rushing up the stairs behind them once the fight started.

After they had made their way up the lower floors, which looked to be more for manufacturing type of work, they reached the smaller upper floors. The stairs there had proper railings that looked more ornamental. She also saw iron radiators and more windows. Some floors had dust-covered desks and chairs.

At each level she took out the guard.

Before going through the final doorway at the top floor, she stopped and put in a full magazine.

She held her weapon in both hands, pointed up, adjusting her grip, taking a couple of deep breaths, preparing to go through the final door.

This was where the bomb was. She could see it in her mind, in the memories from Cassiel. This was where Rafael and the rest of his team were gathered for their final religious act.

She could feel her heart pounding. She repeated the mantra to herself: *Speed and violence of action.*

Angela remembered her grandfather snapping his fingers as fast as he could, teaching her to pull off shots that fast as she fired at the target.

Angela looked back at Jack. "It's been nice knowing you."

SIXTY-SEVEN

"**R**emember, we have to stop them from detonating that bomb," Jack whispered with earnest concern. "Nothing else matters. We need to stop the guy sitting on that dead man's switch from getting up. If he gets up from that chair, it's over."

Angela nodded. "I know what he looks like. I'll find him." She gave him a long, last look. "I've got this, Jack. Stay behind me and take care of anyone who tries to sneak up on me from behind."

Jack answered with a single nod.

Angela took a last deep breath and then shoved the utility door open with her shoulder.

She burst into a semidark room. In the span of a heartbeat she took in the entire room, matching it to the memory in her head. Iron posts held up a network of overhead trusses. The ceiling above naked girders was broken open in places, letting insulation and corrugated tin panels hang down. The windows ringing the room were covered with cardboard. Two big skylights let in light.

The place was a tangle of dusty, broken, water-stained desks and chairs. Junk lay scattered across the floor among the desks. Nails, screws, iron fittings, torn metal scraps, soggy cardboard boxes, and lengths of pipe of every size lay toppled over one another, some with one end resting on desks.

She made note of it all, but mostly she took note of the men. She knew she would have to be careful not to trip over things as she focused on the men.

It felt like she was watching herself move in slow motion.

Broken glass lay scattered everywhere, reflecting flashes of light as she charged into the room. A counter to her left with a tile front looked like a truck had fallen on it and splintered it apart. Boards leaned against filthy walls to the right. Metal doors of gutted utility boxes stood open with wires hanging out.

Angela spotted the spherical bomb sitting on a square stack of cement blocks. Wires attached to brass studs stuck out from the metal casing here and there around the bomb. A narrow metal cabinet of some sort stood close to the bomb. Clusters of wires, reminding her of umbilical cords, sagged between the metal gray cabinet and the bomb. Rows of amber lights on the front of the cabinet flickered on and off.

In this filthy, abandoned ruin of a building, the bomb and the cabinet with flickering lights looked like nothing so much as an alien spacecraft.

There were men scattered throughout the room—some bent in prayer, some sitting in groups talking, some with their arms crossed as they leaned back in chairs against walls or posts. Some were gathered around desks or stools playing card games, some were on the far side of the room peeking out a window past a curtain of cardboard, while others paced in nervous boredom, anticipating their imminent martyrdom.

At the crash of sound Angela made plunging in through the metal door, faces everywhere turned toward her and froze in surprise.

As her heart beat a second time, her gun came up, slowly, slowly, yet as fast as she could possibly raise it. Angela felt as if she were mired in the agonizing slow motion of a deep dream.

Her boots crunched on debris. She heard glass snap as it broke. A board behind the door she'd burst through toppled. It didn't matter anymore. Nothing else mattered anymore. The rest of her life up to that moment didn't matter anymore.

Her heart's second beat ended.

The closest man turned as he heard the glass break under her boot. Without conscious thought, he made the fatal mistake of reflexively looking down at her legs.

With his face frozen in time beyond the front sight of her gun, Angela pulled the trigger.

With that pop and metallic clack of the slide cycling in another round, it started.

As he dropped straight down, others in the dim room saw the flash from her gun and the man falling to the ground. They realized the sounds they heard hadn't been one of their brothers knocking something over.

She saw men everywhere in the room going for AKs leaning against desks, chairs, iron columns, and construction debris.

Suddenly the whole room was moving with men, like when she used to flip on the light switch in the kitchen of the trailer where she'd grown up and cockroaches scattered.

Angela was already firing at targets.

Speed and violence of action.

This was what she had practiced for her whole life.

Now, she had a roomful of living triangles before her. They all bobbed and swayed beyond her front sight.

In her head, her grandfather's fingers snapped as fast as he could snap them, a human metronome setting the beat for her as she fired her gun.

Angela was in the slow-motion trance of the zone. Any man who went for a weapon was a primary target. Men who were close and pulled knives were next.

She fired without pause. Men collapsed, their guns dropped to bounce on the floor as bullets ricocheted around inside craniums. As dead men fell, they flipped over chairs and stools being used as game tables. Playing cards flew up as tables broke.

Angela planted her boot on a chair as a man fell and boosted herself up and over him, into the heart of the storm.

She counted rounds. The instant the slide locked back she was ready and pressed her thumb down on the lever, dropping the magazine. Another was immediately slammed home. She racked the slide to load a round and she was already shooting again at the closest men rushing toward her.

Automatic fire suddenly broke out, filling the room with deafening noise and the raging scream of the man firing the weapon. She saw flashes from the gun rattling off rounds to her right. She could hear the bullets zipping past her head, flicking her hair as they passed close but just missed killing her.

Jack rolled through the debris on the floor and between desks, using them for cover. With a well-placed shot he took out the man firing the automatic weapon before he could take aim for another burst at Angela.

She hardly noticed. It was irrelevant. She was in her own world of converging chaos, firing into faces as fast as she could lock her sights onto them. When a man turned to reach for a gun on a desk, she put a round in the back of his head, right at the base of his skull.

She spotted the man she needed beyond the gray cabinet with the flickering amber lights. His eyes were still wide in shock.

The air was filled with the smell of gunpowder and blood.

It was intoxicating.

Angela had always thought there was a rhythm to shooting—a kind of metallic music. *Bang, bang, bang.* Pause. *Bang.* Bullets splashed into the center of those triangles, and men spiraled down toward the floor, dancing with her to that beat. *Bang, bang, bang.* Pause. *Bang.* Every bullet found its target. Men tumbled. Reload. *Pop, pop, pop.* Pause. *Pop.*

It was the rhythm of life. It was the rhythm of death.

Angela was firing in every direction to that beat. Men fell all around her as the unforeseen specter of death itself swept through the room.

Dust billowed up as men crashed down among debris. To her left, when a dead man landed on one end, a board flipped into the air, throwing up a cloud of dust. To the right pipes stacked against an iron post clattered down as a dead man fell into them. The room was pandemonium. Men everywhere were yelling.

Lost in her own world, Angela hardly heard them.

She didn't need to watch men fall to know she had killed them. She could sense the bullet hitting home. She was focused only on taking out targets as fast as possible to get where she was going.

She didn't need to look into the eyes of any of these men. They were all cold-blooded killers who had worked their entire lives toward their goal of mass murder. They didn't belong among the living. Her only purpose was to exterminate them.

It was an orgy of annihilation.

Angela had already emptied three magazines in a handful of heartbeats as she charged through the terrorists, cutting a bloody swath, the dead falling all around her.

With a gun in her hand, Angela felt like she imagined knights must have felt with a sword in their hands as they scythed down an onrushing enemy. It felt intimately familiar, brutally liberating. It was positively exhilarating.

With a gun in her hands, these men weren't bigger than her, stronger than her. With a gun in her hands she became more than their equal.

Terrorists liked to tout themselves as superhuman, as welcoming death. Despite their claims, they responded to shock, surprise, fear of death, and pain virtually the same as anyone would. She used that to her advantage.

Angela shot men as they were coming up out of chairs, killing some before they had the presence of mind to stand, as they went for guns, or pulled knives. Many were so surprised they froze as they stared at her in confused shock, at a woman with platinum hair suddenly there in their midst. It made no sense to them. Some saw her legs and were distracted for a fraction of a second—just long enough for her to make that the last thing they ever saw.

Automatic gunfire erupted from other parts of the room. Bullets splattered against iron posts. She felt the hot sting of one just clipping her left arm at the shoulder. She paused momentarily to put a bullet between the eyes of the guy firing at her. Jack took out others.

As a man fell in front of her she jumped on him to boost herself up onto and over a desk toward the man she was after—the man sitting on the dead man's switch.

If he came up off his chair, the bomb would go off.

Suddenly no one else existed but her and that man in the chair. He was momentarily frozen, wide-eyed, in shock. His hands gripped the chair seat. Some of the wires from the metal cabinet ran to the bottom of his chair.

He was a deer in the headlights, wanting to run, wanting to detonate the bomb, waiting for a command from his leader. He was so confused and panicked by the ferocity of what was happening all around him, from seeing his friends falling dead everywhere, that for a fleeting moment he was paralyzed.

Angela didn't pay any attention to anything else happening around her. If she died going after this target, then so be it.

Before the man could regain his wits and jump up off that dead man's switch, Angela fired as she leaped over the desk. When she landed with her feet spread in front of him, she emptied a nearly full magazine into his face.

The bullets shut down his motor function so fast he hadn't been able to move a muscle. Because the bullets didn't have enough energy to physically knock him off the chair, he simply slumped in place.

Jack was already in midair, flying over men ducking aside.

He landed on the net of wires between the bomb and the electrical panel. Sparks showered through the room as the weight of his body ripped out that electrical umbilical cord.

When he hit the floor, he went still. Angela didn't know if he'd been shot, stabbed, or electrocuted.

Her being distracted by Jack enabled a man to rush up in her blind spot, swinging a board. The stunning blow caught her on the side of the head.

The world went black.

The next thing she knew she was rolling through the debris on the floor. She lost her gun. A screaming man with a handgun fired wildly at her. Bullets shattered pieces of glass right beside her head as she tumbled across the floor.

As she rolled to a stop on her back, she saw her gun. She stretched and snatched it up, then ducked to the side. The man standing over her was trying to aim at a moving target. She fired first. It was the last bullet. The slide locked back. He dropped on top of her right leg. She kicked him over with her left foot and scrambled back to her feet.

As she dropped the empty magazine, she saw that the man who had been sitting on the dead man's switch was slumped in the chair, feet straight out, his arms hanging at his sides, blood running down both sides of his mutilated face. He'd never had a chance to stand, leaving his dead weight slumped on the switch.

Now, thanks to Jack, even if someone else got to him and knocked him off the chair, it wouldn't do any good.

Angela slammed home a new magazine just in time to fire into the face of a man with a knife charging up right in front of her and then another just behind him. Both men fell at her feet, one to either side.

She was disoriented from the blow to her head and didn't know how many more men there were. She decided there was no point in trying to count them, she just needed to focus on the task at hand and shoot any of them still alive.

The shock of seeing so many of their companions falling dead so unexpectedly and so swiftly had more than a few of the men frozen stock-still, paralyzed by the fear. This wasn't glorious martyrdom for Allah, this was simply being shot and killed for nothing. Focused as she was on shooting moving targets, she temporarily ignored the panic-stricken men to take out ones going for guns or racing toward her with knives.

During the rolling drumbeat of the rhythm in her head as she fired, she used some of those stock-still human targets for punctuations in the beat.

As three men charged her all at once from different directions, she took out two and then the slide locked back as her gun went empty.

As she was dropping the magazine the third man dove in to grab her free arm. She dropped the gun and used both hands to reverse his hold on her forearm. She bent his wrist to the side until she felt bones snap.

As Angela held his wrist bent over in an impossible position, he cried out, crouching down under the pressure, leaning over to the side to try to relieve the strain she was holding on his broken wrist.

When he grimaced up at her in agony, she recognized him from Cassiel's memories. It was Rafael.

Keeping the tension on his wrist with her left hand, Angela pulled her second gun from the holster on her hip. She pointed the weapon down at his face.

"Shoot me! Go ahead! Shoot me!" he yelled. "Allah will welcome me! I will be a martyr! A hero!"

Angela smiled. "Okay, but don't say you didn't ask for it."

She shot him in both knees. She released his hand to let him fall to the floor, thrashing and screaming in pain.

"What? Not so fun to be in pain?" she asked him. "You expected to be vaporized in a glorious, pain-free instant in the blinding light of a nuclear explosion? I guess things aren't turning out so well for you, are they, Rafael?"

He reached for her with his free hand as he called her names in Farsi. She shot the hand stretching for her.

He flinched back with a shriek. "American whore!"

She grinned down at him. "Just think, Rafael, you've been beaten by a woman. Twice—with both bombs. Your whole plan, your life's work, has been defeated by an American woman who has just proven she is better than you and all your men."

A breathless Jack ran up beside her. "Sorry, that jolt knocked me for a loop. I think I must have been out for a few seconds."

He looked around, gun in hand and ready. He couldn't find a target. He looked down at the man groaning on the ground.

"This is Rafael," Angela told him as she pointed with her gun.

"Well don't shoot him," Jack said. "He's valuable alive for intelligence."

"Fuck intelligence. If he's dead that's all they need to know."

Jack pushed her hand aside. "No, really, Angela. We need to turn him over alive. US intelligence will need to know how they were able to pull all of this off."

Angela looked around to see if anyone else was moving. She saw a man, covered in dusty debris, who had been pretending to be dead, trying not to be noticed as he slowly crawled away. Angela walked over and pointed her gun down at him as she told him to stay where he was. He looked back over his shoulder at her gun and did as he was told.

"This one looks like he wants to live," she told Jack. "Let them have him, too. He'll talk. Isn't that right, Lobo?"

Jack yanked some wires out of the electrical panel and used them to tie up both Rafael and Lobo.

Angela looked around at all the dead lying everywhere.

It had only lasted seconds. It had lasted forever.

She wondered if her mother ever felt this high when she did a line.

SIXTY-EIGHT

Jack heard men on the floors below yelling "Clear!" as they went through everything along the way. He didn't hear any gunshots. Angela had already cleared the floors below, as well as the lookouts, on their way up.

He leaned toward her. "Let me do the talking. Okay? Even though I'm the one who called this in, these men aren't going to assume anything. With something of this nature they have to consider everything as a potential threat. They're not going to take chances. It's nothing personal."

Jack could tell by the way her eyes flicked over everything, looking for any sign of trouble, any target, that she was still wired and in kill mode. Her carotid artery was pulsing a mile a minute. Things were about to get a different kind of dangerous. He didn't want any accidents.

"Angela, listen to me. It's over. Take a deep breath. Keep your mouth closed, and let me take it from here. Don't freak out about anything I tell them. It will be what I need to say to keep you safe."

Angela let out a deep breath. "Okay. I understand."

Jack was relieved she was listening to him, but then, she was smart and he would have expected nothing less.

Dozens of men in black tactical gear poured up the stairwell and fanned out into the room like a black flood oozing up from below. It was a fearsome sight, and meant to be. Under their helmets, everything but their eyes was covered. They all moved quickly, weapons up and ready for anything. Many of those weapons were quickly pointed toward Angela and Jack.

"Hands! Hands!" several of them yelled at the same time, as if they'd just cornered the Devil himself.

Jack was relieved to see Angela lift her hands with him.

They were both quickly surrounded by guns pointed at them from every direction.

"Hands behind your heads! Now! Do it now! Lace your fingers together!" one of them yelled as others pulled out handcuffs.

Angela and Jack both did as instructed.

"Where's Angus?" Jack asked as a man pulled one of his arms down around behind his back.

"Here," a familiar voice called out from beyond the wall of men in tactical gear. He was huffing as he hurried up the steps.

As he got closer, he urged the men to let him through. They had already handcuffed Angela and Jack.

"Take it easy," Angus told them. "These two are friendlies. They're the ones who called us in. Take off the cuffs, please."

One of the men took the cuffs back off. He gave Jack a nod and moved back. Some of the big men kept an eye on them while others moved away to help check all the bodies as they went about clearing the room.

Angus was a big man himself, standing six-six. He weighed at least 250 and very little of it was muscle. His tailored suit did a fair job of disguising his prominent pear shape. He had several fat chins but a nice head of brownish-blond hair combed straight back. Surprisingly, it wasn't going gray. Angus gave others gray hair.

"My god, Jack, I could hardly believe your call."

"I'm glad you made it here before we were handcuffed, hog-tied, and carted off."

"Me too," the big man said as he took in Angela.

"Angus, I'd like you to meet Angela Constantine. Angela, this is Angus, the man who got you released before from those overly enthusiastic intel agents."

Angela reached out and shook the man's hand. "Thank you for helping me, sir."

Jack almost did a double take at how polite she was. He realized, then, that she was doing her part to help him with a tense situation. He knew that what she really wanted to do was give him an earful about the injustice of those men taking her prisoner when she had been the one who had discovered the bomb for them—done their job for them.

Jack silently let out a sigh of relief that she didn't.

The sight of this woman in cutoff shorts, boots, platinum-blond hair tipped in red, piercings down her ears, a big DARK ANGEL tattoo across her throat, there in the room with Angus and all his men in tactical black, was quite the contrast.

Angus quickly returned to business. "I can't believe this place is only minutes from my office." He looked a little sick as he gazed at the bomb. "I simply can't believe it. Had that thing gone off . . ."

"You would have been vaporized, along with most of the government and a large part of DC," Jack said.

Angus nodded, still looking queasy as he stared at the bomb. "I still can't catch my breath over how close this was to being a catastrophe for our country."

"Is the NEST team on its way?" Jack asked. "That bomb is still live."

"Yes," Angus said, returning his attention to Jack. "They should be here any minute. The sooner that thing is made safe, the sooner I'll be able to breathe." He looked at Angela again, then back to Jack as he cleared his throat. "What's she doing here? Was it really necessary to bring her along?"

"I didn't bring her," Jack said. "She brought me."

Angus frowned. "What are you talking about?"

"You owe her for stopping that other nuke from going to New York City."

Angus smiled politely. "Yes, we do. That's why we released her after things were cleared up. And we gave her that special weapons permit as a token of our deep appreciation."

"You should be thanking your lucky stars that you did."

Angus clasped his hands behind his back. "Why's that?"

"Because after you had her released, she found out about this second bomb." Jack pointed a thumb back at the device. "Had you not released her—had those rogue agents had their way with her—Washington would be under a mushroom cloud at four p.m. today."

"Well I don't know that I can entirely believe—"

"Angus, you need to listen carefully to me so that you can comprehend the seriousness of this situation. None of your people knew there was a second bomb, did they? Any evidence about the second bomb was destroyed in the explosion when you went in after the first one. Even if they would have gotten any intel, you would still never have found this one, but even if you had, it would have been disastrous."

"Why do you say that?"

Jack gestured off behind the electrical equipment to the dead man in the chair, his legs straight out in front of him, his arms hanging, his face a bloody mess. "That guy there is sitting on a dead man's switch. If by some miracle you would have found out about this bomb in time, your men would have blown him off that chair and that would have detonated the device."

Angus wiped his forehead. He was looking a little green.

"Goddamn, Jack. You're scaring the crap out of me."

"Angela found out about this device, not unlike she found the other one. She was able to track it to this place. Angela, no one else, was able to find it in time and deal with it without letting that guy on the dead man's switch move a muscle."

Angus looked at the man in the chair, then around at all the bodies. "So then you shot all of them when you got here?"

"No, she did. I was just her backup."

The men in the tactical gear, their eyes the only thing visible in their black masks, exchanged looks. They were probably all just as good shots, but they found it hard to believe.

Angus frowned. "Are you serious?"

"I am," Jack said. "She a better shot with that twenty-two than anyone I've ever seen. No shots to center mass. Every one a head shot. Every bullet she fired today killed a terrorist. One bullet, one man."

"Well, it took two for that guy down on the second-floor stairs," Angela corrected. "I screwed up and waited a fraction of a second too long, so it took two bullets."

"Yeah," Jack argued to her in defense, "but you put that second round through his ear—from across the room—after you put the first one through his throat so he couldn't call out an alarm."

The men in black exchanged looks again. They had probably found the guy below with the bullet hole in through his ear.

Angus gaped at her a moment and then shook his head. "Hundreds of billions of dollars' worth of national security, and stopping this threat came down to you two—down to her with a twenty-two." He turned back to Jack. "We're going to need to debrief her about all of this, of course."

"I'm afraid I can't allow you to do that, Angus. Angela is my asset. Not yours."

He looked shocked. "But this concerns national security."

"That's not my job, and it's not hers."

Angus's eyes narrowed. "Is this about the program that was canceled?"

"My contract that was canceled, yes. I'm happy that we were able to stop these two bombs from destroying New York City and Washington, DC, but I don't work for you anymore. I don't provide intel for you any longer—by your choice."

"Well, I'm sorry about the way all of that went down, Jack, but the political people in charge don't approve of profiling."

"I understand," Jack said. "I'm not complaining. I was able to find work."

"With the Mossad."

Jack knew it was an educated guess. He simply shrugged.

"The Israelis aren't perfect, either," Angus said.

"No they aren't, but they don't put political correctness ahead of stopping terrorists. They can't afford to.

"So, since I don't have a contract with you any longer, I'm afraid that the assets I've developed are my assets alone. I need them in my work for those who employ me. Since your agency isn't interested in the work I do, or employing me, I'm afraid that Angela can't discuss anything about what she was able to do in stopping this terrorist event."

Angus chewed his lower lip for a moment. "Jack, it's critical that we find out what went wrong that allowed it to get this close to disaster."

"As a professional courtesy," Jack said, "after I get Angela safely home, I'll fill you in on what I found out. I won't discuss what Angela was able to do, but I will let you know what we learned so that you can understand how everything went so wrong."

"Well," Angus said with a sigh, "that would be helpful."

Angela pointed at the two prisoners. Medics were tending to Rafael. "We saved you two prisoners. I didn't shoot them so that you can interrogate them all you want. Jack's idea."

"What happened to that one?" Angus asked.

"He asked me to shoot him," Angela said. "So I did. Just not where he wanted me to shoot him. His name is Rafael. He is the leader of this entire mission. The other one is Lobo. He's a coward. I expect he will talk."

Jack smiled. Angus stared at her in astonishment for a moment.

"Anyway," Jack said, "Rafael, there, brought the material for the two bombs in through the Oeste Mesa border crossing during the big attack. All the rest of it, all the other attacks, all of it, was merely meant to obscure the fact that the border crossing was the one that mattered. That's how they got the critical bomb material in."

Angus could only stare in disbelief.

"Like I say, if you want to continue to enjoy my cooperation as your unpaid personal advisor, she is to be left out of it. If you should get any unpleasant ideas, please keep in mind my previous warning about the consequences of what I know getting out."

Angus cast a suspicious look at Jack, then at Angela. "And what does she want out of this?"

"Nothing," Jack said. "She doesn't want recognition or any reward. She did this to save innocent lives. She just wants to be left alone to live her life. I think you owe her that much.

"But a great many people owe her a great deal. They owe her their lives, even if they don't know it and never will. This government owes it to her to let her live hers."

Angus lifted an eyebrow, then stuck a finger in his thick hair and scratched his scalp as he thought it over for a moment. Finally, he looked Angela in the eye.

"In light of the fact that you saved untold lives today, young lady, to say nothing of the damage it would have done to the government, the infrastructure, the electromagnetic pulse that would have taken out a large part of the East Coast, and the possibility this could have cascaded into global nuclear war, I want you to know that you have your government's deepest gratitude, even if that gratitude can't be expressed publicly—for obvious reasons. I'm afraid that in the national interest, this entire matter must be kept several levels above even top secret. Top-secret things are routinely leaked. This must never be. Ever."

"I understand, sir, and I'll keep it that way," Angela said. "You have my word."

Angus nodded his relief. He even added a grateful smile.

Jack doubted that Angus could ever comprehend her reasons for doing what she had done. It was not for recognition.

It was because she was a stone-cold killer of killers.

The United States had just been saved by a serial killer.

Angus smiled with an idea. "Well, there is one thing I am able to do for you. You have that weapons permit we gave you?"

Angela nodded. "Yes, sir, thank you."

Angus's smile widened. "I'll tell you what. We're going to upgrade it for you."

Angela frowned. "How can you upgrade it? I was told it already allows me to carry whatever I want wherever I want."

"Yes, that's true enough. But now it's going to give you access to our special armory and gunsmiths. Anything you want will be yours."

"You mean you have a catalog of guns for spies?"

Angus laughed. "Not quite, but almost. You'll have a personal contact who will be able to advise you and make suggestions. I realize that you know what you're doing, but these people know a great deal about weapons. They will see to it that you get whatever you want—things you likely don't even know exist—the best of the best."

Angela gestured around at all the dead. "Do you think I'm lacking? I think my twenty-two worked just fine."

"Yes, it did." Angus arched an eyebrow. "But I think our armory can get you a twenty-two, or anything you might want, that you will find special, and just for you. It's a small token of appreciation from a grateful government, a government with a lot of good people, despite the fools you encountered before.

"Really, Angela, considering what you went on to do here today for everyone, despite how you were treated before, that shows what a special person you really are. We have hundreds of billions of dollars invested in making sure this never happens. Yet it almost did. Only your initiative stopped it. You deserve a small token of our appreciation. I hope you will accept it."

Angela bowed her head. "Thank you, sir, I would be glad to."

"Now," Angus said. "Our NEST team is right behind me. They need to get in here and dismantle this thing and make sure the plutonium is safe."

SIXTY-NINE

Angela was glad that she had stopped to see Barry. He'd already had one operation on his face, and he would need several more, but he was in good spirits to have survived.

He was glad that those four men hadn't managed to find Angela and harm her. He felt tremendously ashamed for telling them where she lived. Angela convinced Barry that it was all right, that no one could have stood up to what they were doing to him without talking. She told him that she was far more worried about him and wished that he had told them what they wanted to know before it had gone as far as it did.

He asked what had happened to the men. She told him that they'd gotten into a fight with someone and they had been shot and killed. He was surprised to hear it. She smiled and told Barry that karma was a bitch. He laughed a little, and said not to make him laugh because it hurt.

He knew about Angela and the rest of the girls keeping the bar open for him. They had all been visiting him. He thanked her over and over for that. She'd told him that she only did it because she needed the money, not because she was keeping it open for him. He'd laughed again, and winced in pain again.

He hadn't been too keen on the ladies' night thing, but after Tiffany had let him know how much money it had brought in for the bar, he was warming up to the idea, especially since Nate was there to keep things under control.

Angela turned in to the trailer park just before the MILFORD FALLS KOZY KOURT sign. The road in had once been blacktop, but very little of that paving still showed through the dirt and gravel.

A man named Al, in a dirty white T-shirt, sitting in a rusty blue metal chair in front of his trailer, watched her drive by. Angela remembered Al sitting in that chair watching the world go by back when she had lived with her mother. She'd heard that he was on disability of some sort. He had seemed harmless enough but never spoke to her as she had walked past him on her way home from school.

Nearby, a heavyset woman in a flowered dress stretched up to hang laundry on a line. At another trailer, an old couple sat together on their small porch. Angela drove past a man in shorts and flip-flops leaning in under the hood of a beat-up car.

Behind a group of mobile homes she saw thick brush where she used to hide at night rather than go home. At least until Boska had put an end to that. Seeing the all too familiar place where she had grown up gave Angela a sick feeling in the pit of her stomach.

A lot of bad things in her life had happened in this place.

Ages ago, in the beginning, it had probably been a nice place to live. But in Angela's lifetime it had always been an overgrown, run-down, squalid area on the wrong side of the tracks infested with meth and all the criminal activity that went with it. A lot of people who lived here were nice enough, but they had nowhere else to go, so they had no choice but to put up with all the trouble.

Angela had been one of those who'd had nowhere to go and who had to put up with a lot of bad things.

She drove past mobile homes all parked at the same angle to an ancient master plan. Some had no skirting, so the wheels were exposed. All of them were up on blocks of some sort to make them level. Most had broken lattice panels covering the space under them. Others had corrugated metal skirting.

A lot of places had dogs on chains. The dogs tended to live in the dirt under the mobile homes to stay out of the sun, or the rain, or the snow. Cats roamed freely. When she'd been little, Angela used to feed scraps of food to some of the cats to get the opportunity to pet them.

Because most of the mobile homes were up off the ground on blocks, they all had elevated porches with steps up to them. Some of those steps were wooden, with rickety railings, while others were made of concrete blocks. Most of the elevated porches had corrugated metal awnings overhead, some held aloft with wrought iron, some with a couple of two-by-fours.

Most of the mobile homes were a rust-stained off-white, but there were some that were weather-worn turquoise, mint green, and sky blue. Those with color also had areas of white for contrast.

Mature trees stood among the homes, providing shade. Uncut, dusty weeds grew everywhere. Derelict vehicles sat up on blocks as they were slowly cannibalized, or used for junk storage. Old barbecues and lawn chairs sat around outside many of the homes.

Angela turned down a street with water-filled potholes that looked like bomb craters. Her truck bounced through the unavoidable potholes until she reached her mother's faded pink and white trailer. The white door and trim were streaked with decades of water and rust stains. A corroded brown air conditioner jutting out a front window was propped up with a scavenged board.

Sally's faded, maroon Pontiac GTO sat at a crooked angle beside the trailer, one of its back tires long flat. A newer economy car was parked there, too.

After parking, Angela sat for a long moment before she tapped her horn.

Her stomach roiled as she climbed the sagging, gray, wooden steps to the porch. A pair of little, dirty white dogs next door yapped at her. She knocked on the bent aluminum screen door and stood to the side, waiting.

When the door opened, an older, short, round woman peered out. She had on a clean, neat, pale blue dress.

"Hi, I'm Angela."

The woman immediately broke into a warm smile as she held the door open with one arm and motioned Angela in with her other, as if they were old friends.

"Angela—I'm so happy to meet you at last! I'm Betty. We spoke on the phone. My, but aren't you a pretty thing, and so tall." Her face suddenly creased with concern. "How are you, dear? Are you okay?"

This was a woman who was sincerely concerned for the well-being of others. She had a warm heart. Angela found it refreshing, but also troubling. She was the kind of person who often ended up, because of their kind nature, being victimized by evil people.

"I'm feeling a lot better," Angela said as she stepped through the doorway.

She had used the excuse of her hospital stay as the reason for not being able to come by sooner. It was more believable than saying she had been away gunning down terrorists.

Seeing the inside of the trailer made her insides feel like they were twisting into a knot.

The far wall still had the same wrinkled wallpaper with pink flowers lifting at the seams. It was coming up in more places, now. In one corner a triangle of wallpaper hung down. The wall to the left still had the multilayered brown stain down the middle from years of a leaky roof. The beige linoleum flooring had a missing section in the kitchen corner, leaving the subfloor exposed, the same as when Angela had lived there.

She had forgotten about the off-putting smell of mold. It made her want to hold her breath or at least cover her mouth.

The kitchen table with the tubular chrome legs was still there, but the sagging, blue velour couch was gone, as was the brown vinyl and plaid cloth reclining chair, its bursting seams held together with duct tape. There had always been baskets of dirty clothes lying around, and a lot of clothes that had missed the baskets. Those were all gone, now.

The place seemed so much smaller, so much less threatening, than Angela remembered.

The room had obviously been cleared out to make space for the hospital bed provided by Hospice. There was a heart monitor over the bed as well as a stand with an IV drip.

Hospice provided all the pain medication Sally needed or wanted on the condition that if her heart stopped, there would be no resuscitation. With cancer that had spread through her internal organs there was nothing that could be done for her, and resuscitation would be a pointless exercise of merely gaining a few more pain-filled, delirious, semiconscious hours of life. Hospice meant to make the end of life as dignified and pain free as possible in the comfort of home. In return, the family had to accept it when the patient's time had come.

Betty hurried over to the bed. "Sally." She shook the skeleton's arm. "Sally, your daughter is here. Angela came to see you."

Angela's mother rolled her head from side to side, mumbling something as she worked at opening her eyes.

"That's right, your daughter Angela is here."

"The girl in the moon?" her mother said in a thin, moaning voice. "Is it really the girl in the moon?"

Betty beamed a smile back over her shoulder at Angela as she motioned for her to come stand next to her mother.

Angela did as instructed. Betty put a comforting hand on Angela's back, urging her a little closer.

"Hi, Ma."

Her mother was so thin Angela could make out all the bones in her hands and arms. A nightdress—one of her mother's favorites, the one with the leopard print—covered her sunken chest. Her face was hardly more than a skull covered with waxy, blotchy skin. Her eyes were set deep into their nearly hollow sockets. She had only a few white wisps of hair over a scalp covered with irregular, dark spots.

She had lost a few of her remaining teeth since Angela had seen her last. Now there was only one yellow, rotted tooth on the top, and three on the bottom.

She had the smell of death about her.

When Sally held her arm out a little, opening and closing her fingers, Betty knew what she wanted. She put a plastic glass of water in Sally's hand, helped guide it closer, and put the straw between Sally's cracked lips so she could take a sip.

A towel lay beside her shoulder. It was obvious that she used the towel to spit up blood. Betty snatched it away and replaced it with a clean one.

"It's time for her pain medication," Betty said in a low voice.

"No!" Sally said, her eyes opening, suddenly more alert. "Not yet."

She reached out for Angela's hand. When Angela offered it, she grasped it in frail, cold fingers. Wrinkled, paperlike flesh clung to bone.

Betty leaned to the side so she could speak to Angela confidentially. "She's a little more lucid when it's time for her pain medication, which is good, but it also means she's starting to have a lot of pain. Even on the medication, she's still in pain, but for the most part she's not conscious enough to feel it. We give her the medication every four hours, but if she is feeling pain she can have more as often as she wants."

"That's good," Angela whispered back.

"It's powerful narcotics. Very addicting," Betty confided. She cast a sidelong glance at Sally. "But that's not something to worry about at this point. I thought you should know."

"Sure, thanks." Angela didn't think there was any point in saying anything about addictive drugs and her mother.

Angela thought it was ironic that Sally would die as she had lived—doped up and stoned out of her mind.

"I'm going to go in the kitchen and get your next round of pain medication ready," Betty told Sally in a rather loud voice as she patted her frail arm. "You have a nice visit with your daughter."

Angela's mother nodded.

SEVENTY

Watching the ever-cheerful Betty shuffle toward the kitchen, Angela thought the woman seemed downright out of place in the dreary trailer. She was a lone streetlight happily illuminating the gloom in a storm. The world needed more people like Betty, instead of people like Rafael. Or Cassiel. The thought of Cassiel lusting to kill people like the innocent, ever-agreeable Betty made Angela's anger boil up.

She reminded herself that she had stopped those men from harming innocent people. And Cassiel was no more.

Angela finally looked up at the hallway leading to her old bedroom. The dirty, beige shag carpeting had been worn through to the jute backing in places. The hallway looked narrower than she remembered.

She had told herself that she would visit her mother, but she was not going to go back to look at her old room.

"Betty is going to get your pain medication, Ma," Angela said, turning her attention back to her mother.

"I don't want it yet," her mother said, her head rolling from side to side to emphasize the point. "I want to be awake to see you, first."

Angela had never known her mother to turn down narcotics in favor of remaining aware of anyone.

Sally grasped Angela's hand in both of hers. "Do you think God will take me in when I come to call on him?"

"If anyone could use his compassion, it would be you, Ma."

Her mother smiled. The smile twisted as the pain started to bear down. She grabbed the towel by her shoulder to cough into it for a moment.

"I'm sorry it hurts, Ma," Angela said, feeling a pang for her mother. "I wish I could make the pain go away."

Her mother put the towel down as she gasped to catch her breath. She lifted a hand partway both in frustration and to dismiss the concern.

"The pain will end soon enough." She finally looked up at Angela as tears welled up in her eyes. "All the pain will end soon enough."

Angela didn't know if her mother meant the pain would end when Betty brought another dose of drugs, or if she meant when she died. Either way, Angela didn't ask.

"Can you tell me something, Ma?"

Her mother's brow drew down as she focused on Angela's face. "What?"

"Why have you always called me the girl in the moon?"

"Ah," her mother said with a nod as she sank back a little.

"Why have you always called me that?"

"Because that's who you are," her mother said.

"I don't understand."

"That's who you are. You're the girl in the moon. Cold. Distant. Hauntingly beautiful. Untouchable. That's you—the girl in the moon—that's who you are.

"You rise above us all, silently looking down on us, watching us, seeing what we can't see.

"You're not like any of us. We are all lost souls. You watch over us all. That's what you do. You are our light in the darkness, our guardian angel. My little angel.

"You are apart, up there all alone." Her mother shook her head. "None of us are worthy of loving you. We are all lost souls, that's what we are. Lost souls who have lost our way. We can only look up to you, up there in the sky so very far away."

Angela swallowed back a lump in her throat. She felt a tear run down her cheek.

She had never thought of it that way, but her mother was right. That was exactly what she was.

She was the girl in the moon.

Her mother was right, too, in that Angela felt no normal human connections. She felt no emotion at all most of the time.

The only time she felt a rush of emotion was when she came down to earth to kill men who needed killing.

She had been born broken because of all the drugs her mother took. Her mother's habit left Angela something less than normal.

And something more.

Angela had always wanted to confront her mother about all the things that she had done, and not done.

But she realized now it would be pointless.

What was the use of confronting a hollow shell of a woman lying there at the end of her life. A life wasted. A life she herself never valued.

"I've got your pain medication," Betty said as she returned and saw Sally grimace and roll her head.

Sally nodded. "Yes, please. God yes, give me that hit."

Betty stuck the needle into the IV port and started pushing the plunger. "Your drugs are coming now, Sally. This will take away your pain."

Sally smiled up at Angela. "Karma is a bitch."

Angela couldn't help smiling back through the tears as she watched Betty push a syringe full of narcotics into Sally's IV. Her mother smiled peacefully when she felt the rush of it coming over her. Her eyes rolled up in her head.

Her hand slipped off Angela's.

The only thing her mother had ever valued was being loaded. She had lived her life the way she wanted, and now she would die with drugs taking away her pain, her regrets, and any last thoughts.

"The drugs will have her incoherent for the next three or four hours," Betty confided.

"How long?" Angela swallowed. "How much longer does she have?"

Betty hesitated. "To tell you the truth, we're all surprised she has lasted this long. My own personal feeling is that she lasted until she could see you again. I think that's what kept her alive this long. It meant that much to her to see you.

"Now that you've come to see her, I kind of doubt she will live until the next dose. I'm glad you could be here to speak with your mother. That's a comforting thing—for both of you. I suspect that was the last coherent thing she will ever say. I'm glad you could hear it."

And it was the last hit of narcotics she would ever feel.

This time, with this hit, she would live forever.

Angela thought it was profoundly sad to see a life never lived slipping away.

Within ten minutes after receiving the syringe full of drugs, her mother's last breath rattled out of her.

Angela was in a daze as she left the trailer park after her mother had died. She had trouble feeling anything. She felt like she was looking down on it all from very far away.

She had talked to Betty about the arrangements.

A funeral home was coming to collect the body of a woman who had been able to see the moon looking down on her, and know that it meant something.

SEVENTY-ONE

Angela was tired when she left work after Barry's Place had closed. She felt good, though, because Barry had stopped in for a short time. Everyone had been happy to see him and toasted drinks to his health. His doctors wanted him at home, resting. Barry thought that going in to see how the bar was doing would be the best medicine.

He had been shocked to see how busy they were, as well as how good the new decorations looked. He had never liked the idea of a ladies' night because of potential problems. But when he saw how much business they were doing, how well Nate had things under control, and especially the WELCOME BACK, BARRY sign hanging out front, it put him in a good mood.

At one point he had pulled Angela aside and asked her if she remembered the first time they met, when she had delivered a package for him. He had offered her a job when she turned twenty-one and promised that she would make more money than she ever had before. She remembered, of course. He said that he hadn't known that day that it would turn out that he would also make more money than he had before.

As she drove through the darkness after the bar had closed, Angela thought about her mother's life and her funeral. Betty had come. A few people from the trailer court had come. That was about it. Her mother had never really lived, so there was not much of a life to mourn.

Angela supposed that at least her mother had given her life. But she hadn't cherished that life growing in her and had continued to do all kinds of drugs while she was pregnant.

Jack had helped put it into perspective for her, though. He had explained how her ability to recognize killers was merely a genetic trait, like big muscles, or long legs, or brown eyes. He believed, though, that the gene responsible for her ability had mutated, as genes occasionally did when living things reproduced, and that mutation was likely what gave her an enhanced version of that genetic ability to recognize killers. Any prey animal that evolved new ways of evading predators had a survival advantage. He said it was the same with humans.

Jack allowed that Angela might be right, that all those drugs had done something to her in the womb and maybe altered that gene, enabling her to have those visions, but he thought it was more likely a natural mutation of the gene—an enhancement that nature conferred on random offspring. That was how life advanced.

He said that since the ability was genetic and passed on in family lines, it was highly likely that either her grandmother or grandfather, or even both, had that ability to recognize killers.

That clicked in Angela's mind. That was why her grandfather had built their house over the hell hole. That was why her grandmother had told her that they thought little clues they had seen in her meant she was destined for something more than other people. It was why they wanted to leave the place to her rather than Sally. Because her grandparents had recognized that special trait in her, they had trained her with firearms, as well as the virtue of life.

For the first time in her life she thought that maybe it all made sense.

Jack told her that the base ability was in her genes, so if she had kids, that gene would very possibly pass on to them. It was why super-predators killed entire families.

As far as Angela was concerned, that was a good reason not to have kids. She didn't think she would wish her ability on anyone. At the same time, she wouldn't give it up for anything.

That ability that ran in the Constantine family had also gotten her grandparents killed, along with relatives in Italy. She wouldn't want to have kids only to have them hunted down and butchered by some super-predator like Cassiel.

She wasn't sure which explanation of her ability was correct, but she liked Jack's theory. She had always thought of herself as a freak. She would rather be what Jack thought she was—an advancement of the species.

A different kind of human.

Angela drove deep in thought for a time, mulling it all over. She trusted Jack. He was doing something important. He was using people with the ability to recognize killers to try to save lives. She grasped the importance of that.

Besides, since she had first recognized a killer, she thought that was what she was meant to do. She saw eliminating murderers as her mission in life. Whatever else she might do in life, that was her thing.

Angela Constantine, slayer of monsters.

Jack was, in a way, doing the same as Angela: going after murderers, eliminating people who should not be allowed to live among innocent people. He also tried very hard to protect those with the ability from the predators hunting them.

She reached over and touched one of the tattoos of the moon she had gotten on her shoulders—crescent of a new moon on her left shoulder, full moon on her right. She'd had them done by the same guy who did the tattoo on her throat, the same guy she had bought her truck from. He'd done a great job. It felt good having those there now, in addition to DARK ANGEL across her throat.

She would see Jack again, and she found herself looking forward to it. They shared something that other people couldn't understand. That was a good feeling. She knew that she and Jack would work together in the future. She looked forward to that, to going after killers.

She was already feeling that itch that needed to be scratched.

Jack also protected her from bureaucracies that didn't like what she could do—that dark swamp of the nameless, faceless intelligence complex and authoritarians who would use her as a scapegoat, twist her life for their own agenda, or, more likely, eliminate her because they didn't like what she was able to do.

Jack had worked it out with Angus so that she would not be touched by any of those government agencies ever again—as long as she kept the whole atomic bomb thing a secret. Jack had something that he held over their heads to make sure they kept their end of the agreement. Jack told her, though, that if she talked to anyone about the atomic bombs that had gotten into America, if she let that secret get out, he wouldn't be able to protect her. She had absolutely no intention of ever telling anyone that the United States had almost been nuked.

Angela was very, very good at keeping secrets.

Just then, blue lights suddenly illuminated the cab of her truck and strobed in the mirror. A police siren flicked on for a moment, commanding her to pull over. Angela had been so deep in thought she didn't even know if she had been speeding, but she usually did, so it wouldn't surprise her to get a ticket.

She pulled over to the side of the road and rolled to a stop. They were at the edge of Milford Falls, so she could see the city lights, but the highway out of town was deserted at that time of night.

Angela rolled her window down and gripped the top of the steering wheel as she waited, so the cop could see her hands and wouldn't get nervous. In her mirror she saw the door of the police car open and the cop get out with a flashlight.

When the cop reached the side of her truck, the flashlight shined in, blinding her. She squinted, trying to see.

"Well, well, well, look who we have here. Ms. Constantine."

It was a woman's voice. Angela shielded her eyes with a hand, trying to see who it was.

SEVENTY-TWO

"That's right," Angela said. "I'm Angela Constantine. Do I know you?"

"I'm Officer Denton. We met at the hospital. You were carrying a concealed weapon. I let you off with a warning."

"Well I told you at the time—"

"Step out of the vehicle. Hands where I can see them."

Angela groaned inwardly. She just wanted to go home and go to sleep, but she did as she was told, hoping the officer would simply write her a ticket for speeding and then let her go.

"Hands behind your head. Lace your fingers together."

When she did, Officer Denton bent Angela's hands down behind her back, one at a time, and put on handcuffs.

"Is that necessary?" Angela asked. "I didn't do anything."

"Walk to my car."

Angela let out a heavy sigh as she walked toward the headlights. Officer Denton stopped her in front of the car, in view of the police car's camera, and started patting her down.

She immediately found the gun in the holster at the small of Angela's back. She pulled it out, holding it between a finger and thumb. She whistled as she held it up.

"Would you lookee here at the fancy weapon the trailer park tramp got for herself."

"Is it against the law to live in a trailer park?"

"Keep your fucking mouth shut unless I tell you to talk."

Still holding the weapon with a finger and thumb, she inspected it in the headlights. "I've never seen a weapon anything like this, or this kind of red dot scope. Looks a little like a Vortex Razor, but it's not. It's different. And this gun is some kind of high-end shit, here."

"It's just a twenty-two."

"Yeah? Well I wish I could afford something like this."

After looking over the weapon, she removed the magazine, emptied the chamber, and then set the gun on the hood of her car. "And with a matching suppressor, no less. What are you—an assassin for a drug lord?"

"I don't have anything to do with drugs," Angela said.

"Yeah, sure."

The woman leaned down. "Seems I remember you also carry a knife in your boot. Why, here it is, and after I told you that it was illegal to carry it. Illegal gun, suppressor, and knife. You are in a whole hell of a lot of trouble, young lady."

Angela didn't say anything.

"Anything dangerous in your pockets that's going to hurt me? Needles? Rocket launchers?"

"No, nothing."

The woman gave Angela a little slap on the tattoo on her shoulder. "Looks like you got yourself a new tattoo of the moon since the last time I saw you. What are you now? The girl in the moon? Is that it?"

Angela smiled. "That's right."

Officer Denton wormed a hand down into the small right front pocket of Angela's shorts, where she kept her tips. She pulled out fat wad of bills and put them on the hood of the car.

"Lots of small bills. Looks like you've been selling drugs at that trailer park. That means we can confiscate your truck."

Angela rolled her eyes. "I don't live there anymore, and I don't sell drugs."

"Uh-huh. Then why would you be carrying a gun illegally?"

"It's not illegal. I have a permit. It's in my back left pocket."

"Yeah, sure. I haven't seen a dealer yet who had a gun that wasn't stolen or being carried illegally."

Angela knew that it was useless to argue, so she kept her mouth shut.

"What the fuck is this?" Officer Denton asked as she frowned at the weapons permit, turning it to look at the back.

"It's a federal weapons permit," Angela said as patiently as possible.

The woman snorted a laugh. "Yeah, right. A federal permit." She shook her head. "Fucking drug dealers," she muttered to herself.

"That's my photo, isn't it? There's a number on the back to call if you have any questions."

"You can call it from jail," she said as she slammed Angela face-down on the hood of the cop car. "I gave you a warning before. This time you're going to be charged with carrying a concealed weapon—and not just a knife. Carrying gun with a suppressor is a felony weapons charge."

"Just call the number on the back, would you? It will save you a lot of embarrassment later when you find out it's legal."

Officer Denton stood over her, looking at the card, considering. "Never heard of a fucking federal permit."

"Just call the number? Please?"

"All right. You stay right there where I can see you. If you run I'll break those long legs of yours. Got it?"

Angela nodded as she straightened. She watched Officer Denton in the front seat talking on the radio.

"Call the number, would you?" Angela yelled.

Officer Denton looked up, not at all pleased. She finally ended the radio conversation and pulled out her phone.

Angela watched as she held the card out, dialing the number. When there was an answer, she told them who she was. Angela couldn't hear much of anything other than a brief account of the stop and the weapons she found.

Angela didn't know what was being said—she'd never called the number and didn't really know what would happen if she did. She had only been told to call the number if there was ever any problem. She hoped it would get her out of trouble.

After a few minutes of listening to someone on the other end of the line, a nodding Officer Denton ended the call. She sat in her car for a moment, then put on her hat and got out. She rushed around to the front of the car.

"I'm so very sorry, Miss Constantine. This has been a terrible mistake."

The woman fumbled at unlocking the handcuffs but finally got them off. Angela rubbed her wrists once they were off.

Officer Denton bent down with the knife and returned it to Angela's boot. When she stood, she picked up the gun, loaded in the magazine, and held the gun out in both hands.

"Here you go. Again, I'm so sorry. This was a big mistake. I don't know what got into me. I hope you can forgive me."

Angela replaced the gun in the holster at the small of her back. "Of course."

Officer Denton reached into a shirt pocket, pulled out a card, and handed it to Angela along with her federal weapons permit. "Here is your permit back, and my personal business card. If you ever need anything—anything at all—or have any kind of problem, you call me and I would be more than happy to help in any way I can."

Angela slipped them into the back pocket of her cutoffs, but she didn't say anything. She didn't know what to say.

Officer Denton tipped her hat. "Again, sorry to have bothered you, ma'am. It won't happen again."

Angela stood beside her truck and watched as the cop car spun its wheels, throwing gravel as it roared away.

Angela took out her federal permit and looked at it a moment. "Huh. I guess it works."

She put it back in her pocket along with Officer Denton's business card and got back in her truck, no longer feeling quite so tired.

She knew now that she wasn't a freak or born broken.

She was the girl in the moon.

AVAILABLE NOW FROM TERRY GOODKIND AND SKYHORSE PUBLISHING

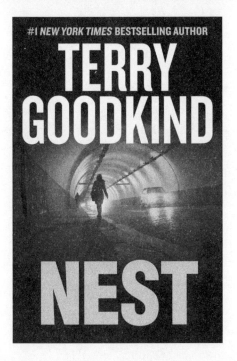

#1 *New York Times* bestselling author Terry Goodkind reinvents the thriller with a provocative, page-turning walk among evil.

Kate Bishop thought she was an ordinary woman living and working in Chicago. But when she unexpectedly finds herself in the middle of a police investigation into a brutal murder, Kate makes a shocking discovery: she has the ability to identify killers just by looking into their eyes.

An explosive mix of action and suspense, *Nest* is a landmark new novel from worldwide bestselling author Terry Goodkind, and a complete reinvention of the contemporary thriller. Travel with Goodkind on a dangerous journey to the back alleys of the darknet, to the darkest corners of our minds, and to the very origins of what it is to be human.

$24.99 hardcover • 978-1-5107-2287-3
$15.99 paperback • 978-1-5107-3640-5

AVAILABLE NOW FROM TERRY GOODKIND

Follow Angela Constantine in this thrilling novella of revenge and justice, as she goes down the rabbit hole after a serial killer in the making.

Trouble always finds Angela Constantine. And Angela's impulsive, hot-tempered colleague Wanda is about to cause more trouble than anyone could know. Except Angela. She's not like the rest of us. She sees things we don't—she can recognize a killer just by looking in their eyes. And Angela knows that sooner or later, one way or another, everyone pays for their sins. She'll make certain of it.

Angela Constantine is . . . **The Girl in the Moon**

$5.99 paperback • 978-0-985020-55-2